LE PÈRE GORIOT

LE PÈRE GORIOT

HONORÉ DE BALZAC

Disclaimer
Throughout the text readers may find that some of the language used
and sentiments expressed are offensive and unacceptable by today's standards.
These reflect the attitudes and usage common at the time the book was written.
In no way do they reflect the attitude of the publishers.

This edition published in 2025 by Arcturus Publishing Limited
26/27 Bickels Yard, 151–153 Bermondsey Street,
London SE1 3HA

Copyright © Arcturus Holdings Limited

All rights reserved. No part of this publication may be reproduced, stored in a
retrieval system, or transmitted, in any form or by any means, electronic, mechanical,
photocopying, recording or otherwise, without prior written permission in
accordance with the provisions of the Copyright Act 1956 (as amended). Any
person or persons who do any unauthorised act in relation to this publication may be
liable to criminal prosecution and civil claims for damages.

Cover design: Peter Ridley
Cover illustration: Victor McLindon

AD012319UK

Printed in China

Introduction

Honoré de Balzac was born in 1799 to Bernard François and Anne Charlotte Balzac. He was the eldest of four children, though his mother – 32 years younger than her husband – saw childrearing simply as a tedious requirement of marriage. As an infant, Balzac was sent away to a wet nurse and then spent most of his childhood in boarding school, leading to further detachment from his parents. For six years, he studied at the Collège des Oratoriens at Vendôme and spent much of his time rebelling through misbehaviour. As a result, he was often forced into seclusion by his teachers as punishment which led him to seek solace in books. Balzac read voraciously to escape his unfortunate situation at school, leading to what he called 'intellectual congestion' [and perhaps physical collapse] and causing him to be sent home in 1813. Shortly after, his family moved from Tours to Paris where he continued his education for two more years.

Balzac spent the next three years working as a law clerk and writing in his spare time. First, he wrote plays which were considered tragic and unsuccessful. Then he wrote novels in different genres and using pseudonyms – his early works ranged from mystic, philosophical stories to gothic potboilers. While this made him a decent living, he decided to pursue several business ventures which quickly fell apart and left him with a debt of sixty thousand francs.

After these financial struggles, Balzac committed to writing full time and found success with his historical novel, *Les Chouans*, and his satirical essay, *La Physiologie du mariagein*, in 1829.

His short story collection in 1830, *Scènes de la vie privée*, solidified his place as a rising literary force, and his growing success allowed him to stay in Paris where he started to move in circles of high society.

While Balzac had brief affairs, his relationship with Éveline Hańska, a Polish heiress, was his one serious romance. Their relationship started in 1832 when Hańska wrote to him in admiration, as many young women did. However, at the time, she was married to an elderly landowner. Balzac and Hańska continued to write and see each other when possible with the promise to wed after her husband's death.

In 1834, driven by the desire to clear himself of his debts and marry Hańska, he wrote *Le Père Goriot* which was published the following year. Set in 1819, the novel follows the young and ambitious Eugène de Rastignac and the elderly Goriot who sacrificed everything for the happiness of his children only to be abandoned by them. While the novel was met with mixed reviews at the time, it is now regarded as an insightful commentary on obsession with wealth and status. These themes are present in most of Balzac's work, and he became well-known for his depictions of daily life, customs, social relations and love.

Despite her husband's death in 1841, Hańska only agreed to marry Balzac in 1850. At this point, his health was declining rapidly and their eventual marriage in March would be short-lived. The two were wed at her home in Poland, after which they travelled back to France. Balzac died shortly after in August of that year. He was 51 years old.

I

Madame Vauquer, *née* de Conflans, is an old lady who for forty years has kept a second-class boarding-house in Paris – a *pension bourgeoise* – in the Rue Neuve Sainte-Geneviève, between the Latin quarter and the faubourg Saint-Marceau. This *pension*, known as the Maison Vauquer, is for both sexes and all ages; and up to the time of which we write, scandal had found nothing to say against the manners or the morals of so respectable an establishment. It must be admitted, however, that for more than thirty years no young woman had ever lived in the house, and it is certain that any young man who may have done so received but a slender allowance from his family. Nevertheless, in 1819, the date of the opening of this drama, we shall find a poor young girl living there.

Though the word *drama* has been recklessly ill-used and misapplied in our degenerate modern literature, it is necessary to employ it here; not that this story is dramatic in the true sense of the word, but that when it ends some reader may perchance have dropped a tear *intra muros et extra*. Will it be comprehended beyond the walls of Paris? I doubt it. Its minute points of personal observation and local colour can be caught only by the inhabitants of that valley which lies between the hills of Montmartre and the higher elevations of Montrouge – a valley full of plastered architecture crumbling to swift decay, its gutters black with foulest mud; a valley teeming with sufferings cruelly real, and with joys often as cruelly false; a place so full of terrible agitation that only some abnormal event occurring there can give rise to more than a passing sensation. And yet, here and there, even in Paris, we encounter griefs to which attendant circumstances of vice or virtue lend a solemn dignity. In their presence self and self-interest pause, checked by a momentary pity. But the impression made is like that of a toothsome fruit, forgotten as soon as eaten. The car of civilization, like that of Juggernaut, is hardly stayed a moment by the resistance of some heart less easily ground to atoms than its fellows: the wheels roll on, the heart is crushed, the car advances on its glorious way. You will do the same – you my reader, now holding this book in your white hand, and saying to yourself in the depths of your easy-chair: 'I wonder if it will amuse me!' When you have read the sorrows of Père Goriot you will lay the book aside and eat your dinner with an appetite, and excuse your own callousness by taxing the author with exaggeration and poetic licence. Ah! believe me, this drama is no fiction, no romance. *All is true* – so true that you may recognize its elements in your experience, and even find its seeds within your own soul.

The house in which the *pension* is carried on belongs to Madame Vauquer. It is situated at the lower end of the Rue Neuve Sainte-Geneviève, where the ground slopes toward the Rue Arbalête so steeply and abruptly that horses rarely come up or down. This contributes to the silence which reigns in the nest of little streets crowded together between the dome of the Val-de-Grâce and that of the Panthéon – two buildings which change the very colour of the atmosphere in their neighbourhood, throwing into it a yellow tone, and darkening all by the shadows flung from their cupolas. The pavements of these streets are dry, unless it rains; the gutters are free from mud and water; grass grows in tufts along the walls. The most light-hearted of men catches something as he passes of the common sadness of a place where the houses resemble prisons, and the roll of a carriage is an event. A Parisian, wandering into it by chance, will find there only these grey *pensions* and charitable institutions, sombre with the gloom of poverty and *ennui* – the gloom of old age slowly passing through the shadow of death; of youth, whose youthfulness is crushed out of it by the necessities of toil.

No part of Paris is so depressing, nor, we may add, so little known. The Rue Neuve Sainte-Geneviève, above all, may be likened to an iron frame – the only frame fit to hold the coming narrative, to which the reader's mind must be led by sombre colours and solemn thoughts; just as, step by step, when the traveller descends into the catacombs, the light fades and the song of the guide is hushed. An apt comparison! Who shall say which is the more awful – to watch the withering of a living heart, or to gaze upon the mouldering of skulls and bones?

The front of Madame Vauquer's house looks out upon a tiny garden, so that the building runs at right angles from the Rue Neuve Sainte-Geneviève at its steepest part. Along this front, between the house and garden, is a gutter-like piece of paved work six feet wide; in front of this runs a gravel walk bordered by geraniums, lauristinus and pomegranates growing in large vases of blue and white pottery. The street gate opens on this path, and is surmounted by the inscription, 'Maison Vauquer', in large letters: underneath appears, 'Pension Bourgeoise for both sexes, and others'. During the day this gate, with an open iron lattice, fitted also with a shrill bell, permits those who pass the house to look into the garden. There, at the end of the pavement and opposite to the street, the wall has been painted by some artist of the neighbourhood to resemble an alcove of green marble. Before this fictitious depression of the wall is a statue of Cupid; a half-effaced inscription on the pedestal indicating that the age of this ornament is coeval with the popular enthusiasm for Voltaire on his return to Paris in 1778:

> Whoe'er thou art, thy master see!
> He is, he was or he will be.[1]

At dusk this gate with its barred openings gives place to a stout wooden door. The garden, wide as the *façade* of the house, is enclosed by the street wall and by the wall which divides it from the garden of the next house. From these fall a drapery of ivy which conceals them, and which attracts attention by a picturesque effect not common in a city. On both walls fruit-trees have been trained and grapevines, whose sickly, dusty products are every year the objects of Madame Vauquer's solicitude, and afford a topic of conversation between herself and her guests. Under each wall runs a narrow path leading to a spot shaded by lindens – *tilleuls.* The word *tilleuls* Madame Vauquer, though presumably of good family, being *née* de Conflans, persists in pronouncing *tieuilles,* although she has often been corrected for it by her more grammatical Parisians. Between these paths is a bed of artichokes, flanked by a row of fruit-trees trained as standards; and the whole is bordered by potherbs, sorrel, lettuce and parsley. Under the lindens stands a round table, painted green and surrounded by benches. Here, during the dog days, those guests who can afford to take coffee come forth to enjoy it in heat sufficient to hatch out a brood of chickens.

The house is of three storeys, with attic chambers. It is built of rough blocks of stone, plastered with the yellow wash that gives so contemptible a character to half the houses of Paris. The five windows of each storey of the *façade* have small panes and are provided with green blinds, none of which correspond in height, giving to the outside of the house an aspect of uncomfortable irregularity. At the narrow or street end, the house has two windows on each storey; those on the ground-floor have no blinds and are protected by iron gratings. Behind the house

---

[1] *Qui que tu sois, void ton maitre!*
   Il l'est, le fut, ou le doit être.

is a courtyard twenty feet square, where dwells a 'happy family' of pigs, rabbits and fowls. At the far end is a woodshed. Between this shed and the kitchen window the meat-safe is hung up directly over the spot where the greasy water from the sink runs into the ground. The court has a small door opening on the Rue Neuve Sainte-Geneviève, through which the cook sweeps the garbage of the house into the street gutters when she washes out the drain with great sluicings of water, a needful precaution against pestilence.

The ground-floor, necessarily the part of the house where the affairs of such an establishment are carried on, consists, first, of a parlour lighted by two windows looking upon the street, which is entered through a glass door. This, the common sitting-room, leads into the dining-room, which is separated from the kitchen by the well of the staircase, the steps of which are of wood, laid in squares and polished. Nothing can be more dismal than this sitting-room, furnished with chairs and armchairs covered with a species of striped horsehair. In the centre stands a round table with a marble top, and upon it one of those white porcelain tea-sets with gilt edges half effaced, which now-a-days may be seen everywhere. The room has a shabby ceiling, and is wainscoted a third of the way up; the rest of the wall being covered by varnished paper representing the adventures of Telemachus, the principal classic personages being clad in colour. The space between the barred windows offers to the guests at Madame Vauquer's table a view of the feast prepared by Calypso for the son of Ulysses. For forty years this feast has served the younger members of the household with a theme for jests, and enables them to feel superior to their position by making fun of the wretched fare to which for lack of means they are condemned. The mantel is of marble, and the hearth, always clean, gives evidence that a fire is never kindled there except on great occasions. The mantel-shelf is adorned by two vases, filled with old and faded artificial flowers under glass cases, which flank a clock of blueish marble of the worst taste. This room is pervaded by a smell for which there is no name in any language. We must call it an *odeur de pension, l'odeur du renfermé* – the odour of the shut-in. It suggests used air, rancid grease and mildew. It strikes a chill as of malaria to the bones; it penetrates the clothes with fetid moisture; it tastes in the mouth like the stale fumes of a dinner; it fills the nostrils with the mingled odours of a scullery and a hospital. Possibly it might be described if we could invent a process for analysing the nauseous catarrhal elements thrown off by the physical conditions and idiosyncrasies of a long procession of inmates, young and old. And yet, in spite of these horrors, compare the *salon* with the dining-room, and you will end by thinking it as elegant and as fragrant as a lady's boudoir.

The dining-room, with panelled walls, was once painted of a colour no longer discernible, which now forms a background on which layers of dirt, more or less thick, have made a variety of curious patterns. The room is surrounded by shelves serving as sideboards, upon which stand chipped water-bottles, cloudy and dim, round mats of zinc metal and piles of plates made of thick stoneware with blue edges, from the manufactory at Tournai. In one corner is a box with pigeon-holes, in which are placed, according to number, the wine-stained and greasy napkins of the various guests. The whole room is a depository of worthless furniture, rejected elsewhere and gathered here, as the battered relics of humanity are gathered in hospitals for the incurable. Here may be seen a barometer with a hooded monk, who steps out when it rains; execrable engravings that turn the stomach, framed in varnished black wood with a thread of gilding; a clock-case of tortoise-shell inlaid with copper; a green porcelain stove; lamps with dust floating on the oil; a long table covered with oilcloth, so greasy that a facetious guest has been seen to scratch his name upon it with his finger-nail; wretched little mats made of broom-straw, slipping from the feet yet always in the way; dilapidated foot-warmers, with their internal arrangements so worn out that the wood is beginning to be charred. To describe how old, how ragged, rotten, rusty, moth-eaten, maimed, shabby and infirm these remnants are would delay too long the current of this story, and readers in haste to follow it might complain. The red-tiled floor is uneven, worn in places either by hard rubbing or by the crumbling action of the colour. In a word, here is poverty without relieving sentiment; hard, bitter, rasping poverty. If filth is not yet seen, foul stains are there; rags and tatters may not appear, but rottenness has eaten into warp and woof with a sure decay.

The room appears in full perfection when at seven o'clock in the morning Madame Vauquer's tom-cat walks in, preceding the arrival of his mistress. He jumps upon the sideboard, sniffs at the bowls of milk, each covered by a plate, and purrs his matinal contentment. The widow follows in a tulle cap and front of false hair set on awry, her slippers flapping as she walks slip-shod across the room. Her faded and flabby cheeks, from which projects a nose like the beak of a parrot, her fat hands and plump person, with its bust too plump and undulating visibly, are all in keeping with that room, where misfortune oozes from the very walls, and greed crouches in the corners, and whose fetid air its owner breathes without sickening. Her face, chilling as the first frosts of autumn, her eyes and wrinkled brows changing in expression from the hollow smile of an actress to the grasping frown of a moneylender – all express the character of her *pension*, just as the *pension* itself implies its mistress. The pasty plumpness of this woman is the unwholesome outcome of her life, as pyæmia is the product of the exhalations of a hospital. Her knitted worsted skirt drops below a petticoat made out of an old gown, of which the wadding shows through gaps in the worn covering: it sums up to the eye the *salon*, the dining-room and the tiny garden, and gives an inkling of the cookery and the character of the guests.

About fifty years of age at the time of which we write, Madame Vauquer looked as women commonly look who tell you they have seen better days. Her eyes were light and glassy, and could take on the innocent expression of one who would serve an evil purpose and make her innocence raise the price of it; a woman who, to better her own condition, would betray Georges or Pichegru, if Georges and Pichegru still had a market value. And yet – 'after all, she is a good creature' is the set phrase with which her lodgers speak of her; for, as she goes moaning and coughing about the house, they take her to be as poor as they are themselves. But how about Monsieur Vauquer? Madame has never given any information concerning her late husband. How did he lose his fortune? By reverses, she implies. He had not been a good husband; he had left her nothing but her eyes to weep with and this house to live in, and the privilege of having no pity to give to others, because, so she said, she had already suffered as much as it was possible for her to bear.

When Sylvie, the fat cook, hears her mistress in the dining room, she knows that it is time to serve up breakfast to those lodgers who are inmates of the house. The table guests usually come only for dinner, which costs them thirty francs a month. When this story opens, there are but seven lodgers. The first floor – that is, the floor up one flight of stairs – contained the two best suites of rooms. Madame Vauquer lived in the smaller of these; the other was occupied by Madame Couture, widow of a paymaster in the army under the French Republic. Living with her was a young girl named Victorine Taillefer, whom she treated as a daughter: the board of these ladies amounted to eighteen hundred francs a year. The two suites on the second floor were taken, one by an old gentleman named Poiret; the other by a man of forty, who wore a black wig, dyed his whiskers, said he was in business, and called himself Monsieur Vautrin. The third storey was divided into four single rooms, of which one was occupied by an old maid named Mademoiselle Michonneau; and another by an aged manufacturer of vermicelli and other Italian pastes, who allowed himself to be called Père Goriot[2]. The two remaining chambers were kept for birds of passage, who, like Père Goriot and Mademoiselle Michonneau, could only afford to pay forty-five francs a month for board and lodging. But Madame Vauquer was not desirous of such guests, and only took them when she could do no better; for, to tell the truth, their appetites made them unprofitable. At this time one of these rooms was occupied by a young man who had come to Paris to study law from the neighbourhood of Angoulême, where his family were practising the strictest economy to provide him with the twelve hundred francs a year which enabled him to live.

Eugène de Rastignac – such was his name – was one of that large class of young men taught to work by sheer necessity; men who understand from infancy the hopes their parents place upon them, and who prepare for success in life by directing all their studies to fit them to take advantage of the future set of the current, and thus be among the first to profit by any onward movement of society. Unless we were aided by this young man's powers of observation, and by the address which enabled him to make his way in the great world, this story could not have been coloured to the life, as we now hope it may be, owing to his sagacity and his perseverance in penetrating the mysteries of a terrible situation – mysteries carefully concealed both by those who created them, and by him who was their victim.

---

[2] *Père (pronounced like the fruit, pear; Pear Gorio, the t not sounded), used in this manner, implies 'Old Goriot', rather than its exact meaning, 'father'.*

Above the third storey was a loft where clothes were dried, and two attic rooms, in one of which slept a man of all work named Christophe, and in the other Sylvie, the fat cook. Besides her regular house-lodgers, Madame Vauquer usually had, one year with another, about eight students of law and medicine, and two or three *habitués* of the neighbourhood, all of whom came to dinner only. The dining room could seat eighteen persons comfortably, and squeeze in twenty. In the mornings, however, there were but seven to breakfast – a circumstance which made that meal seem a family affair. Everyone came down in slippers, confidential observations were exchanged concerning the dress and manners of the dinner guests, and comments were made on the events of the previous evening with all the freedom of intimacy. The seven lodgers were supposed to be in especial favour with Madame Vauquer, who meted out to them with the precision of an astronomer their just dues of care and consideration, based on the arithmetic of their board-bills. The same standard governed the intercourse of the guests with each other, although mere chance, poor waifs, had thrown them here together.

The two lodgers on the second floor paid seventy-two francs a month. This extremely cheap board, which could have been found only in the Faubourg Saint-Marcel, between La Bourbe and the Salpêtrière, and to which Madame Couture made the sole exception, gave sufficient proof that every inhabitant of that house was weighted with the cares of poverty. In fact, the wretchedness of the whole place was reflected in the shabby dress of its inmates. All the men wore frock-coats of an uncertain colour, frayed linen, threadbare trousers and boots or shoes which would have been flung away in the more prosperous parts of the city. The gowns of the women were shabby, dyed and faded, their lace darned, their gloves shiny from long service, their collars soiled, and their *fichus* frayed at the edges. Such were the clothes they wore, and yet the wearers themselves looked sound; their constitutions appeared to have resisted the storms of life; their cold, hard, washed-out countenances resembled the effigy on a well-worn silver coin; their withered lips covered teeth still keen. They gave the impression of having had, or having still, a share in some life-drama; not a drama acted before the foot-lights amid painted scenery, but a drama of life itself, dumb, icy, yet living, and acted with throbbing hearts – a drama going on, and on, without conclusion.

Mademoiselle Michonneau was in the habit of wearing a dingy green-silk shade over her weak eyes, a shade stiffened by a wire rim, which must have scared the very Angel of Pity. Her shawl, with its melancholy mangy fringes, seemed wrapped about a skeleton. What drop of acid in her cup of life had deprived this forlorn creature of all feminine lines of grace? She must have had them once. Had she lost them through her faults, her sorrows, her cupidity? Had she once loved, not wisely? Was she expiating the insolent triumphs of her youth by a despised old age? Her blank gaze chilled you; her sapless features made you shudder; her voice was like that of a cricket in the bushes, lamenting shrilly the approach of winter. She said that she had once taken care of an old gentleman afflicted with an incurable disease, who had been cast off by his children under the belief that he had no property. The old man, however, had saved money, and left her an annuity of a thousand francs, which his heirs-at-law disputed at every payment, reviving scandals of which she was the object. Though the play of passions had seared her face, she retained some slight traces of past beauty, and also a certain delicacy of complexion which allowed it to be supposed that her form still kept a fragment of its charm.

Monsieur Poiret was a species of automaton. Had you seen him flitting like a grey ghost through the alleys of the Jardin des Plantes, a shapeless cap on his head, his cane with its discoloured ivory knob dangling from his limp hand, his faded coat flying loose, disclosing to view breeches which seemed well-nigh empty, lank legs in blue stockings which quavered like those of a drunkard, a dirty white waistcoat, and a crumpled shirt-front of coarse cotton which barely met the old cravat twisted about a neck as long and wrinkled as a turkey's – you might indeed have asked if this spectral figure could belong to the gay race of those sons of Japhet who sunned themselves like butterflies on the Boulevard des Italiens. What occupation in life could have shrunk the makings of a man to this? What passions had blotched that bulbous face which caricature itself could not exaggerate? What had he been? Well, possibly a clerk of the Department of Justice – in that office where they keep the record of moneys spent on the black veils of parricides, or bran for the baskets of the guillotine, and count the cost of pack-thread to hold the blades in place. Could he have been the receiver of beasts at a slaughterhouse; or a sub-inspector of public health and sewers? Whatever his occupation, he was surely one of the asses which are used to turn the mill of our system of civilization; a pivot round which had once revolved the misfortunes and impurities of society; a being of whom we say, in vulgar formula, 'It takes all sorts to make a world.' Gay Paris has no eye for faces pale through physical or moral wretchedness. But Paris is an ocean; heave your lead, and you will never find the bottom. Fathom it, describe it – yet however carefully you search, however minutely you describe, however numerous may be your explorations, there will remain some virgin region, some unsuspected cavern in the depths, where flowers or pearls or hideous sea-monsters still lie safe, undiscovered by the divers of literature. The Maison Vauquer is one of these hidden monsters.

Two figures stand out in striking contrast to the rest of the household. Though Mademoiselle Victorine Taillefer was of a sickly paleness like a girl in feeble health, and though this paleness, joined to a habitual expression of sadness and self-restraint, linked her with the general misery which formed the background of the life about her, yet her face was not an old face, and her movements and her voice were young and sprightly. She seemed like a sickly shrub transplanted into uncongenial soil. Her fair complexion, her auburn hair, her too-slender figure, gave her the grace which modern critics find in the art of the Middle Ages. Her eyes, which were grey with a radiation of dark streaks, expressed the sweetness and resignation of a Christian. Her dress was simple and cheap, but it revealed a youthful shape. She was pretty by juxtaposition. Had she been happy she might have been lovely; for happiness lends poetic charm to women, and dress adorns them like a delicate tinge of rouge. If the pleasures of a ball had called out the rose-tints on her pallid face; if the comforts and elegancies of life had filled out and remodelled her cheeks, already, alas! too hollow; if love had ever brightened her sad eyes – then Victorine might have held her own among the fairest of her sex and age. She needed two things – two things which are the second birth of women – the pretty trifles of her sex, and the shy delight of love letters. The poor girl's story told at length would fill a volume. Her father believed that he had reasons for not acknowledging her; he refused to let her live with him, and only gave her six hundred francs a year for her support; moreover he had arranged to leave his fortune wholly to his son. Madame Couture was a distant relative of Victorine's mother, who had died of sorrow in her arms; and she had brought up the little orphan as her own. Unfortunately, the widow of a paymaster in the army of the French Republic had nothing but her dower and her pension. The time might come when she would have to leave the poor girl, without money or experience, to the tender mercies of a cruel world. The good woman took Victorine to mass every Sunday, and to confession twice a month, hoping to prepare her for the chances of her fate by making her a pious woman. She was right; this cast-off daughter might come to find in her religion a refuge and a home. Meantime poor Victorine loved her father, and once a year she went to his house to assure him of the dying forgiveness of her mother. In vain she knocked at that closed door; it was inexorably shut. Her brother, who alone could have interceded in her behalf, neglected her, and gave her neither sympathy nor succour. She prayed to God to enlighten the eyes of her father and to soften the heart of her brother; but her prayers conveyed no reproach. When Madame Couture and Madame Vauquer strove for words to characterize this barbarous conduct, and loaded the millionaire with abuse, Victorine interposed her gentle remonstrance like the cry of the wounded wood-pigeon, whose note of suffering is still the note of love.

Eugène de Rastignac had a face altogether of the sunny south – a pure skin, black hair and blue eyes. His bearing, his manners, his habitual attitudes, marked him as belonging to a good family, where his earliest training must have been in accordance with the traditions of high birth. If ordinarily he was careful of his clothes, wearing on working-days coats of a past fashion, he always dressed with care and elegance when he went into the world. At other times he appeared in an old frock-coat, an old waistcoat, a shabby black cravat tied in a wisp after the manner of students, trousers out of shape and boots resoled.

Between these two young people and the rest of the household Vautrin – the man of forty, with dyed whiskers – formed a connecting link. He was one of those whom people choose to call 'a jolly fellow!' He had broad shoulders, a deep chest, muscles well developed and strong square hands, the knuckles marked by tufts of red hair. His face, prematurely furrowed, showed signs of a hard nature not in keeping with his compliant and cordial manners; but his strong baritone voice, which harmonized with his boisterous gayety, was not unpleasing. He was obliging and always cheerful. If a lock were out of order he would unscrew it, mend it, oil it, file it and put it on again, saying, 'Oh, I know how!' In fact he knew something about many things; about ships, the sea, France, foreign countries, business, public events, men, laws, hotels, prisons. If anyone complained of hard luck, Vautrin offered his services. Several times he had lent money to Madame Vauquer, and even to her guests; and these creditors would have died sooner than not repay him, for in spite of his apparent good temper there was a keen and resolute expression in his eye which inspired them with fear. His very method of spitting marked his imperturbable *sang-froid*, the *sang-froid* which shrinks from no crime to escape personal difficulty or danger. A stern judge, his keen eye pierced to the core of all questions, into all consciences, and even into the depths of all feelings. His custom was to go out after breakfast, to come home to dinner, to be off again for the whole evening and to get in late at night with a latch-key which Madame Vauquer entrusted to him alone. He was on the best terms with his landlady, calling her 'Mamma Vauquer', and catching her affectionately round the waist – a flattery not understood on its real merits, for the widow believed it an easy feat, whereas Vautrin was the only man in the house whose arms were long enough to encircle that solid circumference. One trait of his character was to pay lavishly fifteen francs a month for the *gloria* (coffee with brandy in it) which he took at dessert. People less superficial than those about him, who were chiefly young men carried away by the whirl of life in the great city, or old men indifferent to all that did not touch them personally, would have examined into the doubts with which Vautrin inspired them. He knew, or guessed, the private affairs of everyone about him; yet no one knew anything of his, nor of his thoughts and occupations. He set up his good humour, his obligingness and his unfailing gayety as a barrier between himself and others; but through it gleamed from time to time alarming flashes of his hidden nature. Sometimes a saying worthy of Juvenal escaped his lips, as if it gave him pleasure to scout at law, to lash society or drag to light its inconsistencies; as if he cherished some grudge against the cause of order, or hid some mystery in the dark recesses of his life.

Attracted, unconsciously, by the strength of one man and the beauty of the other, Mademoiselle Taillefer divided her shy glances and her secret thoughts between the man of forty and the law student. Neither of them appeared to take notice of her, although her position might at any time undergo a change which would make her a match worth looking after. None of Madame Vauquer's guests were at much pains to enquire into the misfortunes which their co-inmates claimed to have suffered. Profound indifference, mingled with distrust, was the upshot of their relations to each other. They knew they had no help to offer: each had heard the tale of sorrows till their cup of consolation held nothing but the dregs. Like old married couples, they had nothing more to say to one another; their daily intercourse was now mechanical; the friction of machinery unoiled. All could pass a blind man in the street without looking at him, or listen, untouched, to a tale of woe; death was for them the solution of the problem of poverty, and they stood coldly beside its bitterest agony. The happiest among these hapless beings was Madame Vauquer herself, the ruler of this asylum for broken lives. To her the little garden, arid as a *steppe*, chill, silent, dusty, humid, was a smiling pleasure-ground. To her the dismal yellow house, which smelt of the corrosions of life, had its delights. Its dungeon cells belonged to her. She fed the prisoners who lived in them – prisoners sentenced to hard labour for life – and she knew how to make her authority respected. Indeed, as she said to herself, where could these people find elsewhere in Paris, at so low a price, food that was as wholesome and as plentiful as that which she gave them? Each had his own room which he was free to keep sweet and clean, if he could not make it elegant or comfortable. They knew this well themselves, and had she been guilty of even crying injustice her victims would have borne it without complaint.

Such a household might be expected to offer, and did offer, in miniature, the elements of a complete society. Among the eighteen inmates, there was, as maybe seen in schools or in the great world, one repulsed and rejected creature – a *souffre-douleur*, the butt of jests and ridicule. At the beginning of his second year, this figure became to Eugène de Rastignac the most prominent of those among whom necessity compelled him to live. This pariah of the household was the old paste-maker, Père Goriot, upon whose head a painter would have cast, as the historian casts, all the light of the picture. How came this scorn dashed with a tinge of hate, this persecution mixed with a passing pity, this insolence towards misfortune, to fall upon the oldest member of the *pension*? Had he provoked such treatment by oddities and absurdities less easily forgiven by his fellows than actual vice? These are questions which bear closely on many an instance of social injustice. Human nature is hard on those who suffer humbly from a consciousness that they are too feeble to resist, or wearily indifferent to their fate. Do we not all like to test our power by working our will on something or on somebody? The weakest of beings, the ragged street-boy, rings our doorbell and runs away, or climbs some monument to scratch his name upon the unsullied marble.

II

In 1813, Père Goriot, then about sixty-two years of age, came to live at Madame Vauquer's, having, as he said, given up business. He took the apartment afterwards occupied by Madame Couture, paying twelve hundred francs a year, like a man to whom five louis more or less was of little consequence. Madame Vauquer fitted up at his expense the three rooms of this suite for a sum which just repaid her, she said, for the outlay. They were miserably furnished with yellow cotton curtains, chairs of painted pine covered with worsted velvet and a few worthless coloured prints upon the walls, which were hung with papers rejected, one might suppose, by the wineshops of the suburbs. Perhaps the careless liberality shown in this transaction by Père Goriot, who at that period was respectfully called Monsieur Goriot, caused his landlady to consider him as a simpleton who knew little of business.

Goriot brought with him a well-furnished wardrobe, suitable for a rich tradesman who on retiring from business could afford to make himself comfortable. Madame Vauquer especially admired eighteen linen shirts of the best quality, to which attention was attracted by two pins worn on his shirt-frill and united by a chain, in each of which shone a large diamond. The old man usually wore a light-blue coat, and he put on a clean white waistcoat every day, beneath which rose and fell his portly stomach, upheaving as he breathed a thick gold chain adorned with seals and charms. His snuffbox was of gold, with a medallion on the cover containing hair, which created a suspicion of *bonnes fortunes*; and when Madame Vauquer accused him of gallantry, the complacent smile of a man whose vanity is tickled flickered on his lips. His closets, *ses armoires* (he pronounced the word *ormoires* after the manner of common people), were full of silver plate, the relics of his housekeeping. The widow's eyes sparkled when she helped him to unpack and arrange these treasures – ladles, forks and spoons; castors, sauce-boats, dishes and a breakfast service in silver gilt, the various pieces weighing many ounces, all of which he had been unwilling to part with on breaking up his home, many of them recalling events which were sacred in his family history. 'This,' he said to Madame Vauquer as he put away a dish and porringer, on the cover of which were two turtle doves fondling each other with their beaks, 'was the first gift my wife made me. She gave it to me on the anniversary of our wedding day. Poor dear! it cost her all the little money she had saved up before our marriage. Ah! Madame, I would rather scratch a living with my nails out of the ground than part with that porringer; but, thank God! I can drink my coffee out of it as long as I live. I am not badly off: I have plenty of bread baked, as they say, for some time to come.'

In addition to this, Madame Vauquer's prying eyes had seen a certain entry in what is called the great book, *le grand livre* – that is, the list of those who have money in the state funds – from which, roughly calculated, it was evident that the worthy Goriot had an income of eight to ten thousand francs. From that moment Madame Vauquer, *née* de Conflans, who was then forty-eight years old, and owned to thirty-nine, nourished a dream of ambition. Though Monsieur Goriot's eyelids were swollen, and an obstruction of the tear-passage caused him to wipe his eyes frequently, she thought his person agreeable and his manners *comme-il-faut*. Moreover, the stout calves of his legs, and even his long square nose, seemed to her to denote points of character which suited her intentions; and this opinion was confirmed by the roundness of his face and the *naïf* silliness of its expression. She put him down for a sturdy fool, whose mind ran to sentiment, and who could be led by his feelings in any direction. His hair, which he wore in 'pigeon-wings', *ailes de pigeon* – that is to say, drawn low over the ears and tied behind in a queue – was dressed and powdered daily by the hairdresser of the École Polytechnique, who arranged five points on his low forehead, which she thought very becoming. Though somewhat uncouth in manner, he was always spick and span in his dress, and took snuff with so opulent an air, scattering it liberally as if confident the box would be always full of the very best, that the night after his arrival Madame Vauquer went to bed turning over in her mind a project for shuffling off the shroud of Vauquer and coming to life again as Madame Goriot. To be married; to get rid of her *pension*; to have the arm of this high flower of *bourgeoisie*; to become a notability in her own quarter; to *quêter* (collect money) for the poor; to make up little parties for Sunday jaunts to Choisy, Soissy or Gentilly; to go to the play when she liked, and sit in a box she should pay for, instead of waiting for free passes given to her occasionally and only in July, in short, all the Eldorado of Parisian lower-class middle-life seemed possible for her if she married Monsieur Goriot. She had never told anyone that she had forty thousand francs laid by, scraped together *sou* by *sou*. Thus she was an equal match for the worthy man in point of fortune; and 'as to everything else, I am quite as good as he', she reflected, turning over in her bed, where the fat Sylvie found every morning the impress of her fair form.

From that day, and for about three months, Madame Vauquer employed the hairdresser of Monsieur Goriot and made some improvements in her toilette, which she explained by the necessity of keeping the decorum of her house on a level with the distinguished people who frequented it. She did her best to make the *pension* select, by giving out that henceforth she would admit no one who had not some special pretentions to gentility. If a stranger came to inspect the rooms, he was made aware of the preference which Monsieur Goriot – 'one of the most distinguished and respectable men of business in Paris' – had given to the establishment. She sent out a prospectus headed MAISON VAUQUER. 'It was,' she stated, 'one of the oldest and best patronised *pensions bourgeoises* in the Latin quarter. It commanded a fine view of the valley of the Gobelins (seen from one window in the third storey), and had a lovely garden, at the end of which stretched an Avenue of Lindens.' She concluded by extolling its pure air and the quiet of its retired situation. This prospectus brought her Madame la Comtesse de l'Ambermesnil, a woman thirty-six years of age, who was expecting the final settlement of the affairs of her late husband and the payments due to her as the widow of a general officer who had died, as she phrased it, upon *fields* of battle. Madame Vauquer now took pains with her table, made fires in the *salon* and the dining room and justified her prospectus so well that she was actually out of pocket by her liberality. The countess was so pleased that she promised Madame Vauquer, whom she called her 'dearest friend', to bring to the house the Baronne de Vaumerland and the widow of Colonel Piqueoiseau, two of her acquaintances then living at a *pension* in the Marais, an establishment more expensive than the Maison Vauquer. All these ladies expected to be in easy circumstances when the War Office made up its accounts. 'But,' as they said, 'government offices keep you waiting so long!'

Madame de l'Ambermesnil used to join Madame Vauquer in her private room after dinner, where they gossiped over small glasses of ratifia and tit-bits from the table, set aside for the mistress of the house. The countess much approved the views of her hostess as to the alliance with Monsieur Goriot. The idea, she said, was excellent; she had planned it from the moment of her arrival.

'Ah! my dear lady, he is all a man ought to be,' said the widow; 'a man thoroughly well preserved. He might make a woman very happy for several years to come.'

The countess was not chary of her criticisms on Madame Vauquer's dress, which harmonised ill with her intentions. 'You must put yourself on a war footing,' she said.

After much consultation the two widows repaired to the Palais Royal, where, in the Galeries de Bois, they bought a hat, and a bonnet with many feathers. Then the countess enticed her friend to the famous shop called La Petite Jeannette, where they chose a dress and mantle. When these preparations were made, and the widow was fairly under arms, she looked a good deal like the figure on a signboard of the Bœuf à la Mode. However, she thought herself so changed for the better, and so much indebted to her friend, that, though naturally stingy, she begged her acceptance of a hat costing twenty francs. It is true she expected in return her good offices with Monsieur Goriot, and asked her to sound him as to his views. Madame de l'Ambermesnil was quite ready to undertake the negotiation, and got round the old gentleman so far as to bring him to a conference; from which, however, finding him shy – not to say refractory – when she made advances to him (on her own account), she came away disgusted, and pronounced him a mere boor.

'My angel,' she said to her dear friend, 'you will never make anything of that man. He is a miser, a fool, a perfect wretch, who will give you nothing but annoyance.'

Whatever may have taken place between Madame de l'Ambermesnil and Monsieur Goriot, the result of the interview was that the former declared she would not remain in the house with him. The next morning she went off, forgetting to pay her bill, and leaving nothing behind her but a parcel of old clothes to the value of five francs; and although Madame Vauquer did her best to get upon her traces, she could never discover in all Paris the smallest sign of Madame la Comtesse de l'Ambermesnil.

She often alluded to this trying affair, and invariably blamed herself for her rash confidence in human nature, though she was in reality more distrustful than a cat in her dealings with her fellow men. But like many other people, while suspecting those about her, she fell an easy prey to persons she did not know – a curious and contradictory fact; but the root of its paradox will be found in the human heart. There are people who come at last to perceive that they have nothing more to gain from those who know them well. To such they have shown the hollowness of their natures; they know themselves judged and severely judged; yet so insatiable is their craving for flattery, so devouring their desire to assume in the eyes of others the virtues which they have not got, that they court the esteem and affection of strangers who do not know them and therefore cannot judge them, taking the risk of losing all such credit eventually. There is also another class of minds born selfish, who will not do good to friends or neighbours because it is their duty to do it, while by paying attention to strangers they secure a return of thanks and praise which feeds their self-love. The nearer people stand to them the less they will do for them; widen the circle, and they are more ready to lend a helping hand. Madame Vauquer's nature was allied to both classes; it was essentially mean, false and sordid.

'If I had been here,' Vautrin used to say to her, 'this would never have happened. I'd have unmasked the woman fast enough. I know their tricks.'

Like all narrow-minded people, Madame Vauquer never looked beyond the limits of the events around her, nor troubled herself about their hidden causes. She liked to blame others for her own mistakes. When this disaster happened, she chose to consider the old vermicelli maker as the author of her woe, and began from that time to get sober, as she phrased it – to *se dégriser* about him. No sooner did she recognize the inutility of her advances and of her outlay upon allurements, than she set up a theory to account for it. The old man must, she said, have *liaisons* elsewhere. She admitted that the hopes she had nursed were built upon imaginary foundations; that the countess, who appeared to know what she was talking about, was right in saying that nothing could be made of such a man. Of course she went further in hate than she had gone in friendship, her hatred not being the child of love, but of hopes disappointed. If the human heart pauses to rest by the wayside, as it mounts to the summits of affection, it finds no stopping-place when it starts on the down-incline.

Monsieur Goriot, however, was her lodger, and the widow was obliged to repress all outward expression of her wounded feelings, to smother the sighs caused by her self-deception, and to choke down her desires for vengeance, like a monk taunted by his superior. Little minds vent their feelings, bad or good, in little ways. The widow used her woman's wit to invent subtle persecutions for her victim. She began by cutting off the superfluities of her housekeeping. 'No more pickles, no more anchovies,' she said to Sylvie the morning she went back to the old programme; 'pickles and anchovies are delusions.' Monsieur Goriot, however, was a frugal man, habitually parsimonious, as most men are who have saved up their fortunes: soup, *bouilli* and one dish of vegetables was, and always had been, the dinner he liked best; so that it was difficult for Madame Vauquer to annoy him by offending his tastes in this line. Disheartened by her failure, she now began to treat him with contempt, and to snub him before the other guests, who, chiefly for amusement, joined in the persecution, and thus assisted her revenge. At the end of a year she had pushed her ill opinion of him so far as to ask herself why a man with eight to ten thousand francs a year, and superb plate and jewellery, should live in her house and pay a price so small in proportion to his fortune?

During the greater part of his first year Goriot had dined out once or twice a week; then by degrees, only once in two weeks. His absence had suited Madame Vauquer so well that she was displeased at the regularity with which he now came to his meals. This change she attributed to a falling off in his means; also to a wish to disoblige her. One of the despicable traits in lilliputian natures is their habit of attributing their own meannesses to others. Unfortunately, at the end of his second year Monsieur Goriot confirmed some of the gossip in circulation by asking Madame Vauquer if he could take rooms on the second storey and pay only nine hundred francs a year; and he became so economical that he went without a fire in his room all winter. The widow, under this new arrangement, demanded payment in advance, to which Monsieur Goriot consented; and from that day forth she called him Père Goriot. It now became a question with the whole household, why was he going down in the world? Difficult to answer. As the false countess had said, Père Goriot was reticent and sly. According to the logic of empty heads who tattle because they have brains for nothing else, people who keep their own counsel must have something suspicious to conceal. The late distinguished man of business now sank into a cheat; the elderly gallant became a dissipated rogue. Some, following Vautrin (who by this time was living at Madame Vauquer's), thought he dabbled at the Bourse, where, having ruined himself by speculations, he now picked up a few francs by fleecing others. Some said he was a petty gambler playing for ten francs a night; others that he was a spy of the police, though Vautrin declared him 'not deep enough for *that*'. Then he became a usurer, lending money by the week in small sums at extortionate interest; finally a speculator in lotteries. In turn, they guessed him to be all that vice, impotence and trickery made most shameful and mysterious. Yet, however low his conduct or his vices, the aversion he inspired never went so far as to propose that he should leave the house. He paid his board regularly. Besides, in a way they found him useful. On him they could vent their good and evil humours by jests or stinging sarcasms. The opinion generally adopted among them was Madame Vauquer's. According to her, the man she had lately pronounced 'all that he ought to be; a man who might make a woman happy for years to come', was a libertine with extraordinary tastes.

Here are the facts on which the widow based her calumnies. Some months after the departure of the disastrous countess who had lived six months at her expense, she was awakened early one morning by the rustle of a silk dress and the light footfall of a young woman going up to Goriot's apartment, the outer door of which was left conveniently ajar. A few moments later, Sylvie came to tell her that a 'creature much too pretty to be what she ought to be', dressed *like a goddess*, wearing prunella slippers 'not even dusty', had glided like an eel from the street to the kitchen, and had asked her the way to Monsieur Goriot's apartment. Mistress and maid listened, and caught several words pronounced in tender tones. The visit lasted some time. When Monsieur Goriot conducted *his lady* downstairs, Sylvie picked up her basket and pretended to be going to market as an excuse for following them.

'Madame,' she said to her mistress when she returned, 'Monsieur Goriot must be deucedly rich to carry matters in that way. Would you believe it? at the corner of the Estrapade there was a splendid carriage waiting, and he put her into it!'

That day at dinner Madame Vauquer drew down a curtain to shade the old man's eyes into which the sun was shining.

'I see that you know how to attract pretty women, Monsieur Goriot,' she said as she did so; 'the sun follows you,' alluding by means of the proverb to his visitor. 'Well, you have good taste; she is very pretty.'

'That was my daughter,' he said, with a gleam of pride, which those present mistook for the conceit of an old man pretending to save appearances.

A month after this visit Monsieur Goriot received another. His daughter, who came the first time in morning dress, now came after dinner in full evening toilette. The company, who were all sitting in the *salon*, saw, as she passed, that she was a lovely blonde, slender, graceful and far too distinguished looking to be the daughter of a Père Goriot.

'Why, he's got two!' cried Sylvie, who did not recognize her. A few days later another daughter came, tall, dark, with black hair and brilliant eyes; she too asked for Monsieur Goriot.

'Three!' said Sylvie.

This lady, who came early in the morning at her first visit, came again a few days later in a carriage and dressed for a ball.

'That makes four!' exclaimed Madame Vauquer and Sylvie, who did not recognize in the fine lady of the evening the simply dressed young woman who paid her first visit on foot at an early hour.

Goriot was still paying twelve hundred francs a year when this took place; and Madame Vauquer was indulgent, nay, even amused at what she thought his adroitness in passing these ladies off as his daughters. Still, as the visits explained his indifference to her own attractions, she permitted herself to call him an old scamp; and when, soon after, he suddenly fell to paying nine hundred francs a year, she fiercely asked what business he had to receive people of *that kind* in her house. Père Goriot answered that the lady she alluded to was his eldest daughter.

'I suppose you will tell me next that you have thirty-six daughters,' she said sharply.

'I have only two,' he replied, with the gentleness of a broken spirit beaten down to the docility of misery.

Towards the end of the third year, Père Goriot reduced his expenses still further, by going up to the third storey and paying only forty-five francs a month. He gave up snuff, dismissed his barber and ceased to wear powder. When he appeared for the first time without it, his landlady uttered an exclamation of surprise on seeing the colour of his hair. It was a dirty, greenish grey. His face, which had grown sadder day by day under the influence of some secret sorrow, was now the most desolate of all those that met around that dismal dinner-table. The widow had no longer any doubt. Here was a miserable wretch who had worn himself out by his excesses.

When his stock of linen was exhausted, he replaced it by cotton at fourteen *sous* a yard. His diamonds, his gold snuff-box, his chain, his jewels, disappeared one after the other. The light-blue coat was given up with the rest of his comfortable clothing, and he now wore, summer and winter, a frock-coat of coarse brown cloth, a waistcoat of cheap cotton and woollen stuff and trousers of grey twill. He grew thinner and thinner; the calves of his legs shrank; his face, which once had the beaming roundness of a well-to-do *bourgeois*, was now furrowed with wrinkles, the lines on his forehead deepened and his jaws grew gaunt and sharp. At the end of his fourth year in the Rue Neuve Sainte-Geneviève he bore no likeness to his former self. The sound old paste-maker of sixty-two, who might have passed for forty; the jolly, fat *bourgeois*, foolish and simple-minded, whose jaunty bearing amused even those who passed him on the street, and whose smile had something of the gayety of youth – seemed now a worn-out septuagenarian, stupid, vacillating, wan. His lively blue eyes had tarnished into a dull steel-grey. They never watered now; but the red rims still encircled them, and seemed to weep tears of blood. Some people regarded him with horror, others pitied him. The young medical students, who observed the drop of his under lip and took note of his facial angle, said to each other, after teasing and tormenting him and getting no reply, that he was falling into imbecility.

One day, after dinner, Madame Vauquer said to him, 'So your daughters don't come to see you anymore?' in a tone as though she doubted the relationship. He started as if she had pricked him with a dagger.

'They *do* come – sometimes,' he said sadly.

'Ah, ah! so you still see them sometimes – *sometimes*?' cried the students. 'Bravo, Père Goriot!'

But the old man did not hear the jests that followed his simple answer. He had fallen back into that passive state which those who observed him superficially took for senile indifference. If they had really known what was passing before their eyes, they might have felt an interest in his state as a moral and physical problem. But they did not know, nor would it have been easy to know, the old man's real life. The elderly people of the *pension*, who alone felt any interest in it, never went out of the neighbourhood – they lived like oysters in a bed; and as for the young men, the excitements of their Parisian life put the poor old man at whom they gibed out of their heads as soon as they turned the corner of the Rue Neuve Sainte-Geneviève. To narrow minds, like those of these thoughtless students, the blank misery of Père Goriot and his dull stupidity were incompatible with the possession of any means or indeed of any capacity whatever. As to the women whom he called his daughters, every one shared the opinion of Madame Vauquer, who argued – with that severity of logic which the habit of attributing low motives cultivates in old women given over to gossiping – that 'if Père Goriot had daughters as rich as these women seemed to be, he would not be living in my house, paying forty-five francs a month and dressing like a beggar'. These inductions could not be gainsaid; so that by the end of the month of November, 1819, the time of the opening of this drama, everyone in the house had made up his or her mind concerning the unhappy old man. He had never had, they declared, either wife or daughter; he was a snail, a mollusc, 'to be classed with the shellfish', said one of them, an employee at a neighbouring museum. Poiret was an eagle, a gentleman of fashion, beside Goriot. Poiret could talk, argue and answer. To be sure he *said* nothing, for his talking, arguing and reasoning were only the repetition in his own words of the last thing said by other people. But at least he took a share in the common talk, he was alive, he seemed to have his faculties; while Père Goriot, as another employee at the museum remarked, was 'always below zero'.

III

Eugène de Rastignac had returned from his vacation in a state of mind not uncommon in young men of talent, or in those to whom circumstances of difficulty impart for a time the qualities of picked men. During his first year in Paris the slight application required to pass through the first stages of his profession had left him free to enjoy the external charms of the capital. A student finds his time well filled up if he wishes to study the windings of the Parisian labyrinth, to see all that is worth seeing at the theatres, to know the customs, to learn the language, to get used to the special pleasures of the great capital, to ransack all its corners good and bad, to attend those lectures that may amuse him, and make a mental catalogue of the treasures collected in the museums. He begins by an enthusiasm for some foolery that he thinks grandiose. He chooses a hero – possibly a professor who is paid to keep himself above the level of his audience; or he pulls up his cravat and assumes an attitude at the Opera-Comique, glancing at some lady in the first tier of boxes. But after these initiations he usually peels off his husk, enlarges the horizon of his life and ends by getting an idea of the various human strata which make society. If he begins by admiring the carnages on a fine day in the Champs-Elysées, he ends by envying those who own them.

Eugène had unconsciously gone through much of all this before his vacation, when he went back to his father's house with his bachelor's degree in Law and Letters. The faith of his childhood, his *idées de province* – his country ideas – had left him. His enlarged intelligence, his excited ambition, made him now see the true condition of things in his old home. His father, mother, two brothers, two sisters and an aunt who had only a life income, lived on the little estate of Rastignac. This property at no time brought in more than three thousand francs a year, which was subject to the uncertainties attendant upon grape culture; and yet out of that limited revenue twelve hundred francs were subtracted for Eugène's expenses. The sight of their perpetual pinching, which they tried generously to conceal from him; the comparison he was forced to make between his sisters, whom he once thought pretty girls, and the Parisian women who realized the loveliness of his boyish dreams; the uncertain prospects of the large family dependent on his success; the frugality with which everything was cared for; the wine squeezed for family use out of the last strainings of the press; together with innumerable shifts that need not be told here – increased ten-fold his desires for success, and made him thirst for the distinctions of the world. At first he felt, as high-strung spirits do feel, that he would owe nothing except to his own merits. But his nature was eminently southern; when the time for action came, he was liable to be assailed by hesitations such as seize men in mid-ocean when they have lost their reckoning and know not how to lay their course, nor at what angle to set their sails. At first he had been eager to fling himself body and soul into the work of his profession; then he was led away by the importance of forming social ties. He observed the influence which women exert upon society; and he suddenly resolved to try for success in the great world, and to win the help and protection of women of social standing. Surely, they might be won by a young man, ardent and intelligent, whose mental gifts were aided by the personal charm of elegance, and who possessed the beauty which eminently attracts women – the beauty of strength.

These ideas worked within him as he walked about the fields listening to the merry chatter of his sisters, who thought him greatly changed. His aunt, Madame de Marcillac, had been at court in the days before the French Revolution, and her associates were among the greatest people of that time. All at once it occurred to him, as he pondered his ambitious designs, that among the recollections of her past life, with which she had amused his boyhood, were the elements of a social success more brilliant than any he could hope to attain by the study of law. He questioned her as to family ties, which she might renew on his behalf. After shaking the branches of her genealogical tree, the old lady came to the conclusion, that, of all the persons who might be useful to him among the careless multitude of her great relatives, Madame la Vicomtesse de Beauséant was likely to prove the most available. She therefore wrote to this young woman an old-fashioned letter of introduction, and told Eugène that if he pleased Madame de Beauséant she would undoubtedly present him to the rest of his relatives. A few days after his return to Paris, Rastignac sent his aunt's letter to the viscountess, who replied by an invitation to a ball for the next evening.

Such, then, was the general situation of affairs in the Maison Vauquer at the end of November, 1819. Two days later, Eugène, having been to Madame de Beauséant's ball, came home about two o'clock in the morning. That he might redeem the time lost in gayety, he had made a vow, in the middle of a dance, to sit up and read law till daylight. It was the first time he had stayed awake in that still and silent quarter of Paris, but he was prepared for it by the strong excitement of his introduction to the splendours of the great world. Eugène had not dined that day at the Maison Vauquer, and the household were left to suppose that he would not return before daylight, as had sometimes happened after a fête at the Prado, or a ball at the Odeon, to the detriment of his silk-stockings and the stretching of his dancing-shoes. Before slipping the bolts of the front door for the night, Christophe had opened it and stood looking down the street. At that moment

Rastignac came in and went up to his room without making any noise, followed by Christophe who made a great deal. Eugène took off his evening coat, put on his slippers and an old dressing-gown, lit his fire of *mottes* – little blocks of refuse bark prepared as a cheap fuel – and sat down so quickly to his work that the noise of Christophe's heavy footsteps drowned the lesser sound of his own movements. He sat thinking a few moments before he opened his books.

He had found Madame de Beauséant one of the queens of Parisian society, and her house considered the most agreeable in the Faubourg Saint-Germain. She was by birth and fortune an acknowledged leader in the fashionable world. Thanks to his aunt de Marcillac, the poor student had been welcomed in this brilliant house; though as yet he did not realize the extent of the favour. To be admitted into those gilded *salons* was equivalent to a patent of nobility. Once launched in the society he met there, the most exclusive of all societies, he had obtained the right to go everywhere. Dazzled by the brilliancy that surrounded him, Eugène, after exchanging a few words with his hostess, had given all his attention to one lady in that circle of Parisian goddesses – a lady whose beauty was of a type that attracts at first sight the admiration of young men. Countess Anastasie de Restaud, tall and well-made, was thought to have one of the finest figures in Paris. With large dark eyes, beautiful hands, a well-turned foot, vivacity and grace in all her movements, she was a woman whom such an authority as the Marquis de Ronquerolles declared to be 'thoroughbred'. Her high-strung, nervous temperament had not impaired her beauty. The lines of her figure were full and rounded, though not at all inclining to *embonpoint*. 'Thoroughbred', 'pure-blooded', – these expressions were beginning to take the place of the old forms of approval – 'angels of heaven', hyperboles from Ossian and all the mythological vocabulary rejected by modern dandyism. To Rastignac, Madame de Restaud seemed the woman who might serve his purpose. He secured two dances in the list written upon her fan, and talked to her during the pauses of a quadrille.

'Where may I hope to meet you again, Madame?' he said, with that insistent admiration which has so much charm for women.

'Oh,' she said, 'in the Bois, at the opera, at home – everywhere.'

And this bold son of the south pressed his way with the charming countess as far as a man could go in the intervals of a waltz and a quadrille. When he told her that he was cousin to Madame de Beauséant, the countess, whom he took for a great lady, invited him to visit her. From the smile she gave him at parting, Rastignac judged that the invitation was one he might accept immediately. He had the good fortune, in the course of the evening, to make the acquaintance of a man too noble to ridicule his ignorance – a vice in the eyes of the impertinent young dandies of the period, gifted themselves with the vice of superciliousness. They were all there in full force: the Maulincourts, the Ronquerolles, the Maxime de Trailles, the De Marsays, the Adjuda-Pintos, in the glory of their self-conceit, and dancing attendance on the most elegant women of Paris – Lady Brandon, the Duchesse de Langeais, the Comtesse de Kergarouet, Madame de Serizy, the Duchesse de Carigliano, Comtesse Ferraud, Madame de Lanty, the Marquise d'Aiglemont, Madame Firmiani, the Marquise de Listomere and the Marquise d'Espard, the Duchesse de Maufrigneuse and the de Grandlieus.[3] Happily, therefore, for the inexperienced student, he stumbled upon the Marquis de Montriveau, who was present in attendance on the Duchesse de Langeais – a general, a brave soldier and

---

[3] *These were all living people to de Balzac, and their histories can be found in his other books.*

simple-hearted as a child. From him Eugène learned that Madame de Restaud lived in the Rue du Helder.

To be young, to thirst for distinction, to hunger for the smiles of a woman, to see unclosing before him the doors of these great mansions, to plant his foot in the Faubourg at Madame de Beauséant's, to bend the knee in the Chaussee d'Antin at Madame de Restaud's, to glance through the long vista of Parisian *salons* and know himself attractive and fit to win help and protection from a woman, to feel that he could tread firmly the social tightrope, where safety depends upon nerve and self-confidence, and to have found already in one of these rare women the balance-pole of his ambition – with such thoughts, with visions of this woman rising in the smoke of his bark fire, Law on the one hand, Poverty on the other, what wonder that Eugène pierced the future in a waking dream, and attained in fancy to his goal – success? His vagrant thoughts were in full career, and he was picturing himself by the side of Madame de Restaud, when a sigh broke the silence of the night – a sigh so deep and piteous that it echoed in the heart of the young man as though it had been a death-rattle.

He opened his door softly, and slipping into the corridor, saw a line of light along Père Goriot's threshold. Fearing that his neighbour was ill, he stooped and looked through the key-hole. The old man was at work in a way so apparently criminal that Rastignac thought the interests of society required him to watch and see what came of it. Père Goriot had fastened two pieces of plate, a bowl of some kind with the dish belonging to it, to the leg of his table. He had twisted a piece of rope round these objects, which were richly embossed, and was pulling upon it with all his strength, evidently trying to reduce them to a mere lump of silver.

'The devil! What a fellow!' cried Rastignac to himself, as he saw the strong arms of the old man kneading up the silver as if it had been dough. 'Can he be a robber; or a receiver of stolen goods? Does he make believe to be a fool, that he may carry on his iniquities in secret? Is this what makes him live here like a beggar?' added Eugène, taking his eye from the key-hole.

He looked again. Père Goriot had unwound his rope. He took the lump of silver and laid it on the table, where he had spread a cloth, and rolled it into a bar – an operation he performed with the utmost ease.

'Why, he must have arms like Augustus the Strong, King of Poland!' cried Eugène, when the bar was nearly fashioned.

Père Goriot looked sadly at his work, and his tears fell fast upon the silver. He then blew out the rushlight by whose glimmer he had done the deed, and Eugène heard him lie down upon his bed with a heavy sigh.

'He must be mad!' thought the student.

'Poor child!' groaned Père Goriot.

On hearing these words Rastignac suddenly resolved to say nothing about what he had seen, and not to condemn his neighbour too hastily. He was about to return to his room when he became aware of another noise, and one difficult to define, as if men in felt shoes were treading softly on the stairs. Eugène listened, and was sure that he heard the breathing of two men. No door creaked, and no distinct steps were heard, but he caught a sudden gleam of light on the second storey shining through the chinks of Vautrin's door.

'Mysteries enough for one night in a *pension bourgeoise*,' he said to himself. He went down a few stairs and listened intently. The chink of gold coin struck his ear. In a few moments the light was extinguished, the breathing of two men was again heard, but again no door creaked. The men were going softly down the stairs, and the slight noise of their steps died away.

'Who is there?' cried Madame Vauquer, opening a window in her apartment which looked on the stairs.

'I have just come in, Mamma Vauquer,' replied the strong voice of Vautrin.

'That's odd,' said Eugène returning to his chamber, 'for I am certain I saw Christophe slip the bolts! They say you must sit up all night in Paris if you want to know what your neighbours do.'

His dreams of amorous ambition being dispelled by these interruptions, Eugène now began to study; but with little profit. His mind wandered to the suspicions roused by Père Goriot, then to the face of Madame de Restaud rising before him as the pharos of a brilliant destiny; and before long he went to bed and to sleep with his hands clinched. Out of every ten nights which young people vow to study seven are spent in sleep. Ah! we must be more than twenty to stay awake all night.

IV

The next morning Paris was enveloped in a dense fog; one of those fogs that wrap themselves about the city and make the atmosphere so dark that even punctual people lose note of time. Business engagements are not kept, and many think it eight o'clock when it is nearly midday. It was half-past nine, and Madame Vauquer was not out of bed. Christophe and Sylvie, who were both behindhand, were taking their coffee – made with the top skimmings of the milk, the rest of which Sylvie boiled a long time to thicken it, so that Madame Vauquer might not discover the tithe thus illegally levied.

'Sylvie,' said Christophe, soaking his first bit of toast, 'Monsieur Vautrin – a good fellow all the same – had two more men to see him last night. If Madame asks about it, you needn't say much.'

'Did he give you anything?'

'Paid me five francs for his month; that's as much as to say, "Hold your tongue."'

'He and Madame Couture,' said Sylvie, 'are not mean; all the rest would like to take back with their left hands what their right hands give us on New Year's Day.'

'And what's *that*, anyhow?' cried Christophe. 'A miserable five-franc piece – that's all! There's Père Goriot, who has blacked his own boots these two months. That old miser, Poiret, won't use blacking; he'd drink it sooner than put it on his broken old shoes. As to that slip of a student, he only gives me forty *sous* a month. Forty *sous* doesn't pay for my brushes; and he sells his old clothes into the bargain. What a hovel, to be sure!'

'Bah!' said Sylvie, slowly sipping her coffee, 'our places are the best in the quarter. We do very well. But as to that big Vautrin – Christophe, did anybody ever ask you about him?'

'Yes, I met a gentleman a few days ago in the street, and said he, "Haven't you got at your house a stout gentleman who dyes his whiskers?" I said, "No; our stout gentleman's whiskers are not dyed; a man who goes the pace he does hasn't the time to dye his whiskers." I told Monsieur Vautrin about it, and he said, "Quite right, my boy; always answer such questions like that. There's nothing more disagreeable than to have people finding out your little infirmities. Marriages can be balked that way."'

'Well, in the market the other day,' said Sylvie, 'they tried to lime me too. A man asked if I had ever seen him putting on his shirt. Think of that, now! – Goodness!' she cried, interrupting herself, 'there's a quarter to ten striking on the Val de Grace; and everybody in bed!'

'Pooh! they are all out. Madame Couture and her young person went to mass at Saint-Etienne's at eight o'clock. Père Goriot was off early with a bundle; the student won't be back till after lecture. I saw them all go out as I was cleaning my stairs. Père Goriot knocked me as he passed with the thing he was carrying; it was as hard as iron. What on earth is he about, that old fellow? All the rest of them spin him round like a top. But he's a good man, I can tell you; worth more than the whole of them put together. He does not give me a great deal, but the ladies where he sends me give famously. They are finely dressed out, I can tell you.'

'Them that he calls his daughters – *hein*? Why, there's a dozen of them!'

'I only go to two – the two that came here.'

'There! I hear Madame getting up. She'll make an uproar about it's being late. I must go. Look after the milk, Christophe, and see that the cat doesn't get it.'

So saying, Sylvie went upstairs to Madame Vauquer.

'Why, Sylvie, how is this? A quarter to ten, and you have let me sleep so late. I have slept like a dormouse. Such a thing never happened to me before.'

'It's the fog; you could cut it with a knife.'

'But about breakfast—'

'Bah! the devil got into the lodgers, and they turned out *dès le patron-jaquet*' (at daybreak).

'Sylvie, do speak properly, and say *le patron-minet*.'

'Well, Madame, any way you like. But you'll all breakfast to-day at ten o'clock. Old Michonneau and Poiret are not out of their beds. There's no one else in the house, and those two sleep like logs – as they are.'

'But, Sylvie, why do you always mention them together, as if—'

'As if what?' said Sylvie, with her horse-laugh, 'why not? Two make a pair.'

'Something happened – very odd – last night, Sylvie. How did Monsieur Vautrin get in after Christophe had bolted the front door?'

'Oh! it was this way, Madame. Christophe heard Monsieur Vautrin, and he came down and unfastened the door. That's why you thought—'

'Give me my wrapper, and go and see about breakfast. You can hash up the remains of that mutton with potatoes; and give us some baked pears – those that cost three *sous* a dozen.'

A few minutes later, Madame Vauquer came into the dining-room just as her cat had knocked off a plate which covered a bowl of milk, and was lapping the contents.

'Mistigris!' she cried. The cat scampered off, but soon returned and rubbed up against her legs. 'Yes, yes, you old hypocrite! you can coax when you've been stealing. Sylvie! Sylvie!'

'Yes, what is it, Madame?'

'Just see how much the cat has stolen!'

'That animal of a Christophe! it's his fault. I told him to watch the cat, and set the table. Where has he gone to, I wonder? Never mind, Madame, I'll keep that milk for Père Goriot. I'll put some water to it, and he'll never know. He takes no notice of what he puts in his mouth.'

'What took him out early this morning, the old heathen?' said Madame Vauquer, as she put the plates round the table.

'Who knows? He trades with all the five hundred devils.'

'I believe I slept too long,' said Madame Vauquer.

'But the sleep has made Madame as fresh as a rose.'

At this moment the door-bell rang, and Vautrin came into the *salon*, singing in his strong voice—

"'Long have I wandered here and there,
And wherever by chance
I cast my glance—"

'Oh! Oh! good morning, Mamma Vauquer,' he cried, as soon as he perceived his landlady, gallantly catching her round the waist.

'Come, come – don't!' she said.

'Say, "Don't, you impertinent rascal!" Ah! do as I tell you; say so! Now I'll help you to set the table. I'm a pretty good fellow, am I not?

"'I courted the brown, and I courted the fair—"

'I saw something odd just now—

"'When I happened by chance
To cast my glance—"'

'What was it?' exclaimed the widow.

'Père Goriot, at half-past eight o'clock, in the goldsmith's shop in the Rue Dauphine – the fellow, you know, who buys old spoons and gold lace. Père Goriot sold him, for a good round sum, some sort of utensil in silver-gilt quite skilfully twisted out of shape – considering he has never followed the profession.'

'Bah! really?'

'Yes, truly. I was coming back that way after seeing off a friend by the Messageries Royales. I followed Goriot to see what he would do next – just for fun. He turned into the Rue des Gres, where he went to the house of an old usurer whom everybody knows, named Gobseck – a thorough rascal, capable of turning his father's bones into dominos; a Jew, an Arab, a Greek, a Bohemian, a fellow confoundedly hard for a man to rob; puts all his money into the bank.'

'But what does this old Goriot really do?'

'He does nothing,' said Vautrin; 'he undoes. He is fool enough to ruin himself for worthless women, who—'

'He's coming in,' said Sylvie.

'Christophe!' called Père Goriot from without, 'come up to my room.'

Christophe did as he was bid, and came back for his hat in a few moments.

'Where are you going?' said Madame Vauquer.

'On a message for Monsieur Goriot.'

'What have you got there?' cried Vautrin, snatching a letter out of Christophe's hand and reading the address – *To Madame la Comtesse Anastasie de Restaud.*

'Where are you going to take it?' he continued, giving the letter back to Christophe.

'Rue du Helder. I was told to give it into the hands of Madame la comtesse herself.'

'I wonder what's inside of it?' said Vautrin, taking it back again, and holding it up to the light; 'a bank-note? No—' he peeped into the envelope – 'it's a cancelled note!' he cried.

'What a gallant old rascal! Be off, my boy!' he added, putting the palm of his big hand on Christophe's head, and spinning him round like a thimble. 'You ought to get a good *pour-boire*.'

The table being set, Sylvie proceeded to boil the milk; Madame Vauquer lit the dining-room stove, and Vautrin helped her, still humming—

'Long have I wandered here and there.'

By the time all was ready, Madame Couture and Mademoiselle Taillefer came in.

'Where have you been so early, my dear lady?' said Madame Vauquer to Madame Couture.

'We have been to pray at Saint-Etienne du Mont. This is the day, you know, we are to go to Monsieur Taillefer. Victorine, poor little thing, is trembling like a leaf,' said Madame Couture, sitting down before the stove, and putting up her damp feet, which began to smoke.

'Pray, warm yourself, Victorine,' said Madame Vauquer.

'It is all very right, Mademoiselle, to pray to the good God to soften your father's heart,' said Vautrin to the young lady; 'but that's not enough. You need a friend who will speak his mind to the fierce old fellow – a savage, they say, who has three millions of francs, and won't give you a *dot* [a dowry]. Every pretty girl needs a *dot* in times like these.'

'Poor darling!' said Madame Vauquer, 'your monster of a father will bring punishment on his own head.'

At these words tears started in the eyes of the poor girl, and Madame Vauquer stopped, restrained by a sign from Madame Couture.

'If we could only see him – if I might speak to him and give him the last letter of his poor wife,' said the paymaster's widow. 'I have never dared to send it to him by post; he knows my writing.'

'"O woman! innocent, unhappy, persecuted," as the poet says,' cried Vautrin, 'see what you have come to! In a few days I shall interfere in your affairs, and then things will go better.'

'Ah, Monsieur!' said Victorine, casting a look at once tearful and eager upon Vautrin, who seemed quite immoved by it; 'if you know any way of communicating with my father, tell him that his love and the honour of my mother are dearer to me than all the riches of the world. If you could succeed in making him less harsh to me, I would pray God for you. Be sure that my gratitude—'

'Long have I wandered here and there,'

sang Vautrin, in a tone of irony.

At that moment Goriot, Mademoiselle Michonneau and Poiret came down, attracted probably by the savoury smell of Sylvie's mutton. Just as the seven sat down to table and exchanged good mornings, half-past ten struck, and the step of the student was heard on the gravel.

'Well, Monsieur Eugène,' said Sylvie,' to-day you will get your breakfast with the others.'

The young man bowed to the company, and took his seat by Père Goriot.

'I have just had a strange adventure,' he said, helping himself liberally to the mutton, and cutting a slice of bread which Madame Vauquer measured with her eye.

'An adventure!' repeated Poiret.

'Well, old fellow, why should that astonish you?' said Vautrin. 'Monsieur looks as if he were made for adventures.'

Mademoiselle Taillefer glanced timidly at the young man.

'Come, tell us!' said Madame Vauquer.

'Last night I was at a ball at the house of my cousin, Madame la Vicomtesse de Beauséant. She has a splendid house – rooms hung with silk; in short, she gave us a magnificent fête, where I amused myself as much as a king—'

'Fisher,' interpolated Vautrin.

'Monsieur,' said Eugène angrily, 'what do you mean?'

'I said *fisher*, because kingfishers amuse themselves a great deal better than kings.'

'Yes, indeed; I'd rather be a little bird that has no cares, than a king; because – because—' said Poiret, man of echoes.

'Well, anyway,' continued the student, 'I danced with one of the loveliest women at the ball – a charming countess, the most delightful creature I have ever seen. She wore peach-blossoms in her hair, and flowers at her waist – natural flowers of delicious fragrance. Pshaw! you ought to have seen her; it is impossible to describe a lovely woman animated by dancing. Well, this morning I met this same divine countess about nine o'clock, on foot, in the Rue des Gres. Oh! my heart jumped! I fancied for a moment—'

'That she was coming here,' said Vautrin, looking the young man through and through. 'She was probably going to look up Papa Gobseck, the money-lender. Young man, if you ever get an insight into the hearts of Parisian women, you will find money more potent there than love. Your countess's name was Anastasie de Restaud, and she lives in the Rue du Helder.'

At this the student turned and stared at Vautrin. Père Goriot raised his head quickly and shot at the two speakers a glance so keen and anxious that he astonished the other guests who noticed him. 'Christophe will get there too late; she will have gone,' he murmured sadly.

'I guessed right, you see,' said Vautrin, leaning over and whispering to Madame Vauquer.

Goriot went on eating his breakfast without knowing what he was doing; he sank back into himself, and never looked more stupid and self-absorbed than at this moment.

'Who the devil, Monsieur Vautrin,' cried Eugène de Rastignac, 'could have told you that lady's name?'

'Ha, ha!' laughed Vautrin. 'Père Goriot knew it – why shouldn't I?'

'Monsieur Goriot!' cried the student.

'What did you say?' asked the poor old man.

'Was she very beautiful last night!'

'Who?'

'Madame de Restaud.'

'Look at the old wretch; how his eyes sparkle!' whispered Madame Vauquer to her neighbour.

'Yes, she was marvellously beautiful,' replied Eugène, at whom Père Goriot was now looking eagerly. 'If Madame de Beauséant had been absent, my divine countess would have been queen of the ball. The young men had no eyes but for her. I was the twelfth written on her list; she danced all the evening. The other women were jealous of her. If any creature was happy last night, it was she. The old saying is true – the three most beautiful things in motion are a frigate under sail, a horse at full speed, and a woman dancing.'

'Last night at the top of the wheel, at the ball of a duchess; this morning down in the mud in the shop of a money-lender,' said Vautrin. 'If their husbands cannot pay for their unbridled extravagance, they will get the money in other ways. They would rip open their mother's breasts to get the means of outshining their rivals at a ball.'

Père Goriot's face, which at the praise of Madame de Restaud had lighted up like a landscape when the sun falls upon it, clouded over as he listened to these words.

'Well,' said Madame Vauquer, 'how about your adventure, Monsieur Eugène? Did you speak to her? Did you ask her if she was coming into this neighbourhood to study law?'

'She did not see me,' said Eugène; 'but to meet such a lady

in the Rue des Gres at nine o'clock in the morning – a woman who could not have got home from the ball for some hours after midnight – does seem to me very singular. Paris is the only place for such strange things.'

'Bah! there are many far more strange,' said Vautrin.

Mademoiselle Taillefer had scarcely listened, so preoccupied was she by the fresh effort she was about to make to see her father. Madame Couture made her a sign that it was time to dress; and when the two ladies rose and left the room Père Goriot left also.

'Did you notice him?' said Madame Vauquer to Vautrin and the rest. 'I am convinced those women are his ruin.'

'You will never make me believe,' cried the student, 'that the beautiful Comtesse de Restaud has anything to do with Père Goriot—'

'Who wants you to believe it?' said Vautrin, interrupting him. 'You don't know Paris yet – you are too young. You'll find out later that there are men absorbed by passions – a passion.' At these words, Mademoiselle Michonneau raised her head and looked at him, like a war horse that hears the sound of a trumpet. 'Ah!' said Vautrin, interrupting himself to send her a piercing glance; 'we know, do we, all about that? Yes,' he resumed, 'such men pursue one idea, one passion, and never relinquish it. They thirst for one water, from one fountain – often stagnant. To gain it they will sell wife and children – they will sell their own souls. For some this fountain is play, or stocks, collections of pictures – even insects, music. For others it is a woman who ministers to some taste; to these you may offer every other woman upon earth – they will not look at them. They will have the woman who satisfies their want, whatever it is. Often this woman does not love them – nay, will ill-treat them, and despoil them, and make them pay dearly for small shreds of satisfaction. No matter – the fools will not let go; they will pawn their last blanket for her sake, and bring her their last *sou*. Père Goriot is one of these men. Your countess gets all she can out of him – he is safe and silent. The poor fellow has no thought except for her. Watch him: outside of this passion he is little more than a dumb animal; rouse him about her, and his eyes sparkle like diamonds. It is easy enough to guess his secret. He carried his bit of plate this morning to be melted; I saw him afterwards going into Gobseck's, in the Rue des Gres. Now, mark! as soon as he got home he sent that simpleton Christophe to Madame de Restaud with a letter containing a cancelled note. Christophe showed us the address. It is clear that the matter was pressing, for the countess went herself to the old money-lender. Père Goriot has been raising money for her. It doesn't take much cleverness to put two and two together here. And this shows you, my young student, that last night, when your countess was laughing and dancing and playing her tricks, and fluttering her peach-blossoms, and shaking out her gown, her heart was down in the soles of her little satin slippers, thinking of some note of hers that was going to protest – or, of her lover's.'

'You make me savage to know the truth,' cried Eugène; 'I will go to-morrow and call on Madame de Restaud.'

'Yes, to-morrow,' said Poiret; 'better call to-morrow on Madame de Restaud.'

'But, Paris!' said Eugène, in a tone of disgust, 'what a sink of iniquity your Paris must be.'

'Yes,' replied Vautrin, 'and a queer sink, too. Those who get muddy in their carriages are virtuous; those who get muddy afoot are knaves. Hook a trifle that is not your own, and they show you up on the Place du Palais de Justice as a public curiosity; steal a million, and you are received in good society and called "a clever fellow". And you pay thirty millions annually to the law courts and the police to keep up that sort of morality! Pah!'

'Do you mean to say,' said Madame Vauquer, 'that Père Goriot has melted up his silver-gilt porringer?'

'Were there two turtle-doves on the cover?' asked Eugène.

'Yes, there were.'

'He must have cared for it. He wept when he broke it up. I happened to see him – by chance,' said Eugène.

'He did care for it, as for his life,' answered Madame Vauquer.

'Now see the force of passion!' said Vautrin. 'That woman can wring his very soul.'

Eugène went up to his own chamber. Vautrin went out. A few minutes later Madame Couture and Victorine got into a hackney coach which Sylvie had called. Poiret gave his arm to Mademoiselle Michonneau, and they walked off together to wander in the Jardin des Plantes during the fine part of the day.

'Don't they look almost married?' said Sylvie. 'They are so dried up that if they knock together, they'll make sparks like flint and steel.'

'Look out, then, for Mademoiselle Michonneau's shawl – it will catch like tinder,' observed Madame Vauquer.

V

At four o'clock, when Père Goriot returned, he saw by the dim light of two smoky lamps Victorine Taillefer sitting silent with red eyes, while Madame Couture was volubly relating the result of the visit made to the father. Tired of refusing to see his daughter and her old friend, Taillefer had granted them an interview.

'My dear lady,' Madame Couture was saying to Madame Vauquer, 'would you believe me, he did not so much as ask Victorine to sit down; she stood all the time that we were there. He told me, without any anger, but sternly, that we might for the future spare ourselves the trouble of coming; that mademoiselle (he did not say daughter) only injured herself by persisting in coming after him – once a year! the monster! He said that as Victorine's mother had brought him no fortune, her daughter was not entitled to expect any; in short, he said all kinds of cruel things which made the poor dear cry. She flung herself at her father's feet, and found courage to tell him that she only pressed her case for her mother's sake; that she would obey him without a murmur if he would only read the last words of his wife. She offered him the letter, saying the most touching things you ever heard. I don't know where she got them; God must have inspired them, for the poor child was so carried away that I, as I listened to her, wept like a fool. What do you suppose that brutal man did while she was speaking? He pared his nails! He took the letter which his poor wife had written with so many tears, and flung it into the fire, saying, "That's enough." He tried to make his daughter get up from her knees: she wanted to kiss his hand, but he would not let her. Wasn't it atrocious? His great booby of a son came in while we were there, but he would not take any notice of his sister.'

'Can such monsters be?' said Père Goriot.

'And then,' continued Madame Couture, paying no attention to this interruption, 'father and son walked off together, begging me to excuse them, and saying they had pressing business. So ended our visit. Well! at any rate he has seen his daughter. I don't know how he can refuse to acknowledge her, for they are as like as two raindrops.'

All the guests now came in, one after another, wishing each other good day, and interchanging a style of jest by which certain classes of the Parisian world keep up a spirit of drollery of which sheer nonsense is the principal ingredient, the fun being chiefly confined to gesture and pronunciation. This sort of *argot* varies continually. The best joke never lasts over a month. An event in politics, a trial in the criminal courts, a street ballad or an actor's jest, sets the fun afloat and keeps it going; the amusement consisting, above all, in treating ideas and words like shuttlecocks, and bandying them to and fro with the utmost rapidity.

Just at this time the invention of the diorama, an exhibition which carried optical illusion beyond that of the panorama, had set the artists in their studios to ending all their words in 'rama'. The fashion had been introduced into the Maison Vauquer by a young painter, one of the dinner guests.

'Well, Monsieur-re Poiret,' said the employee at the Museum, 'how goes your *healthorama*?' Then not waiting for a reply, 'Ladies,' he said to Madame Couture and Victorine, 'I regret to see that something has gone wrong with you to-day.'

'Are we going to *diniare*?' cried Horace Bianchon, a medical student and a friend of Rastignac; 'my little stomach has gone down *usque ad talones.*'

'It is a regular *frostinorama*,' said Vautrin. 'Draw back a little,

Père Goriot; your foot takes up the whole front of the stove.'

'Illustrious Vautrin,' cried Bianchon, 'why do you say *frostinorama*? That's wrong; you should say *frostorama*.'

'No!' cried the employee at the Museum, 'it is *frostinorama*. I have frost in my toes.'

'Ha! Ha!'

'Here comes his excellency the Marquis de Rastignac, Doctor of Laws,' cried Bianchon, catching Eugène round the neck and hugging him till he was nearly strangled.

'Oh! oh! Help, all of you! Help! Oh!'

Mademoiselle Michonneau here entered stealthily, bowed silently to the guests, and took her place among the ladies.

'That old bat of a woman makes me shiver,' whispered Bianchon to Vautrin. 'I am studying phrenology, and I tell you she has the bumps of Judas.'

'Do you know anything about her?' asked Vautrin.

'Nothing but what I see. I give you my word of honour that her lanky whiteness puts me in mind of those long worms that eat their way through beams.'

'I'll tell you what she is, young man,' said the man of forty, pulling his whiskers—

> '"Rose, she has lived the life of a rose –
> The space of a summer's day."'

'Here comes a famous *souporama*,' cried Poiret, as Christophe entered respectfully bearing the tureen.

'Pardon me, Monsieur,' said Madame Vauquer; 'it is *soupe aux choux* [cabbage soup].'

All the young men burst out laughing.

'Beaten, Poiret!'

'Poir-r-r-rette is done for!'

'Score two for Mamma Vauquer,' cried Vautrin.

'Did anyone notice the fog this morning?' asked the employee.

'It was a fog out of all reason,' cried Bianchon; 'a fog without a parallel; a dismal, melancholy, green, stupid kind of a fog – a fog Goriot.'

'*Goriorama*,' cried the painter; 'because it is no go when you want to see through it.'

'Ha! my lord Goriot; they are talking of you.'

Sitting at the lower end of the table, near the door opening on the pantry, Père Goriot looked up at this, smelling, as he did so, at the piece of bread placed under his napkin – according to an old habit in sampling flour, which mechanically reappeared when he forgot himself at table.

'Well!' cried Madame Vauquer sharply, in a voice that rose above the general clatter; 'don't you find the bread good enough for you?'

'It is very good, Madame,' he replied; 'it is made of Étampes flour, first quality.'

'How do you know that?' asked Eugène.

'By its taste; by its colour.'

'By the taste of the nose, you mean; for you have done nothing but smell it,' said Madame Vauquer. 'You are getting so economical that by and by you will be trying to get your meals by sniffing the smells of the kitchen.'

'Take out a patent for the process,' cried the employee; 'you will make your fortune.'

'Let him alone; he does it to make us believe he really has been engaged in selling flour,' said the painter.

'Is your nose a corn-chandler?' asked the young man from the Museum.

'Corn-what?' said Bianchon.

'Corn-market.'

'Corn-stalk.'

'Corn-starch.'

'Corn-et.'
'Corn-er.'
'Corn-elian.'
'Corn-ucopia.'
'Corn-orama.'

These eight answers rattled from all parts of the table like a volley of musketry, and made everybody laugh – all the more when poor Père Goriot looked round with an air of utter bewilderment, like a man trying to make out some meaning in a foreign tongue.

'Cor?' he said to Vautrin, who sat next to him.

'Corn – corns on your toes, old gentleman,' said Vautrin. patting him on the head in such a way as to drive his hat down over his eyes.

The poor old man, stupefied by this brusque attack, remained motionless for a moment, during which Christophe carried away his soup; so that when Père Goriot, having taken off his hat, picked up his spoon to begin his dinner, it tapped upon the table instead of a plate. All present burst out laughing.

'Monsieur,' said the old man, 'that was a poor joke; and if you give me any more such—'

'Well, what then, papa?' said Vautrin, interrupting him.

'Well, you shall pay dearly for it some day—'

'Ah! in the infernal regions – that's it,' said the painter; 'in the little black hole where they put naughty children.'

'Well, Mademoiselle!' said Vautrin, addressing Victorine; 'you seem to eat nothing. Was your papa refractory to-day?'

'He was horrible!' said Madame Couture.

'Ah!' cried Vautrin; 'we must bring him to reason.'

Rastignac, who was sitting next to Bianchon, said to him—

'Mademoiselle can't bring an action for alimony, for she eats nothing. Eh! eh! just see how Père Goriot is looking at her.'

The old man had stopped eating to gaze at the young girl,

whose face was convulsed with grief – the grief of a child repulsed by the father she loves.

'My dear fellow,' said Rastignac in a whisper, 'we are all astray about Père Goriot. He is neither weak nor imbecile. Just turn a phrenological eye on him, and tell me how he strikes you. I saw him last night twist up a silver dish as if it had been wax; and at this very moment his face shows that his mind is full of strange emotions. His life seems to me so mysterious that it might be worth some pains to study him. Oh, very well, Bianchon; you may laugh, but I'm not joking.'

'I grant you the man has a medical interest; he is a case,' said Bianchon. 'If he'll let me, I'll dissect him.'

'No – just feel his head.'

'I don't know about that; his stupidity might be catching.'

VI

The next day Rastignac, elegantly dressed, started about three o'clock in the afternoon to call upon Madame de Restaud, indulging as he went along in those adventurous hopes which fill the lives of young men with varying emotions. In moods like these they take no account of obstacles or dangers; success is their only vista; life is made poetic by the play of imagination, and they are saddened or unhappy by the overthrow of projects that exist only in their unbridled fancy. If they were not handicapped by their ignorance and their timidity this social world of ours would be an impossibility. Eugène went along the muddy streets, taking every precaution to keep his boots clean; and as he walked he turned over in his mind what he should say to Madame de Restaud – providing himself with the repartees and witty sayings of an imaginary conversation, rehearsing phrases à la Talleyrand, and inventing tender scenes favourable to his project of pushing his future in society. He did get his boots muddy, however, and had to have them blacked and his trousers brushed in the Palais-Royal. 'If I were rich,' he said to himself as he changed a five-franc piece which he had put into his pocket ('in case of accident'), 'I should have driven in a carriage to make my call, and could have thought things over at my ease.'

At last he reached the Rue du Helder, and asked for Madame de Restaud. With the silent wrath of a man certain of future triumph, he noticed the impertinent looks of the lacqueys, who saw him crossing the courtyard on foot heralded by no sound of carriage wheels at the gate. Those looks were the more galling because already he had been smitten by a sense of social inferiority on seeing, as he entered the courtyard, a fine horse in glittering harness attached to one of those exquisite cabriolets, which evince the luxury of extravagant existence and the habit of taking part in the pleasures of Parisian life. Eugène grew out of temper with himself. His brains, which he had stored with clever sayings, refused to work; he became stupid. While waiting to know if the countess would receive him, he stood by a window in the antechamber, leaning his arm on the knob of its fastening and looking down mechanically into the courtyard. He thought he was kept waiting a long time, and would have gone away in displeasure had he not been gifted with that southern tenacity which works wonders if kept to a straight line.

'Monsieur,' said the footman, 'Madame is in her boudoir, and is very much occupied; she did not answer me. But if Monsieur will go into the *salon*, he will find someone there who is also waiting.'

Wondering within himself at the power possessed by servants to judge and to betray their masters by a word, Rastignac deliberately opened the door through which the man had just passed, wishing, perhaps, to prove to the lacqueys in attendance that he knew the ways of the house. But he brought up like a fool in a press-room, full of lamps and wardrobes, and an apparatus for warming bath-towels, which led to a dark passage and some back stairs. Smothered sounds of laughter in the antechamber behind him put the finishing stroke to his confusion.

'Monsieur, the *salon* is this way,' said the footman, with that false respect which is the last touch of impertinence.

Eugène stepped back with such precipitation that he knocked against a bath-tub, but happily held fast to his hat so that it did not fall into the water. At this moment a door opened at the end of the dark passage (which was lighted by a lamp), and Rastignac heard Madame de Restaud's voice, Père Goriot's voice, and the sound of kisses. He went back into the antechamber, crossed it, followed the servant, and entered the first *salon*, where he took his station at a window which he saw at once must command the courtyard. He wanted to see if Père Goriot could really be Père Goriot. His heart beat violently as he remembered the horrible insinuations of Vautrin. The footman stood waiting to usher him through the door of an inner drawing-room, when out of it came an elegant young man, who said to the servant, crossly—

'I am going, Maurice; you can tell Madame la comtesse that I waited for her more than half an hour.'

This gay young man of fashion, who evidently had the right of entrance, walked on, humming an Italian melody, until he came near the window at which Eugène was standing. He tried to see the face of the student, and he also wished to get a glimpse into the courtyard.

'Monsieur le comte had better stay a moment longer; Madame is now at liberty,' said Maurice, going back into the antechamber.

At this moment Père Goriot came out of the house near the *porte-cochère*, through a door that opened from the back staircase. The old man raised his umbrella, and was about to open it without noticing that the gates had been thrown back to admit a young man wearing the ribbon of the Legion of Honour, who was driving himself in a tilbury. Père Goriot had only time to step backward; a moment more and he would have been run over. The opening of the umbrella had frightened the horse, which shied, and then dashed forward to the steps of the portico. The young man looked round angrily, saw Père Goriot, and bowed to him with the constrained civility often bestowed upon a money-lender whom it is advisable to propitiate, or vouchsafed to some smirched man reluctantly, and with an after sense of shame. Père Goriot returned it with a little friendly nod, full of kindness. These things passed like a flash. Too absorbed to notice that he was not alone, Eugène suddenly heard the voice of Madame de Restaud.

'Maxime, are you going?' she cried in a tone of reproach, not unmingled with vexation.

The countess had not noticed the arrival of the tilbury. Rastignac turned and saw her, dressed coquettishly in a breakfast gown of white cashmere with pink ribbons, her hair put up with the simplicity which is the morning fashion of Parisian women. A fragrance diffused about her seemed to suggest that she had just taken her bath; her eyes were limpid, and her beauty was softened by an air of indolence and languor. Young men have the eyes to see these things; their minds open to all the rays of a woman's charm as plants assimilate from the air they breathe the substances which give them life. Eugène felt the soft freshness of her hands without touching them; he saw through the folds of her cashmere the lines of her beautiful figure. She needed no steels or lacings – a belt alone held in her flexible and rounded waist; her feet were pretty even in their slippers.

When Maxime raised her beautiful hand to his lips Eugène for the first time perceived Maxime, and Madame de Restaud perceived Eugène.

'Ah! is that you, Monsieur de Rastignac? I am very glad to see you,' she said in a tone which a man of the world would have accepted as a dismissal.

Maxime looked first at Eugène and then at the countess with an expression which might well have expelled the intruder. 'What impertinence!' it seemed to say; 'my dear, I hope you are going to show that puppy the door.'

Rastignac took a violent aversion to this man. In the first place, the blond and well-trimmed head of Maxime made him ashamed of his own hair; then Maxime's boots were elegant and spotless, while on his, in spite of all his care, there were spots of mud. Maxime wore a frock-coat, which fitted him round the waist like the corset of a pretty woman; Eugène, on the contrary, was wearing a black coat in the middle of the afternoon. The clever son of the

Charente felt the advantages dress gave to this supercilious dandy with his tall slender figure, light eyes, and pale skin – a man, he thought to himself capable of bringing ruin on the fatherless.

Meantime Madame de Restaud, without waiting for any reply, flitted back into the great *salon*, the lappets of her dress floating backward as she went, in a way that gave her the appearance of a butterfly on the wing. Maxime followed her; Eugène, in a savage mood, followed Maxime; and all three stood before the fireplace in the great *salon*. The student knew well enough that he was in the way of that odious Maxime; but even at the risk of displeasing Madame de Restaud, he was determined to annoy him. Suddenly he remembered seeing the young man at Madame de Beauséant's ball, and guessed what might be his relations to Madame de Restaud; but with that youthful audacity which makes a man commit great follies or secures him great successes, he said to himself, 'That man is my rival. I will put him out of my way.' Imprudent youth! He did not know that Count Maxime de Trailles was a dead shot, always ready to take up an insult and kill his man. Eugène was a good sportsman, but he could not hit the mark nineteen times out of twenty in a shooting-gallery. The young count threw himself into an easy chair by the fire, picked up the tongs, and tossed the wood about in so violent and savage a manner that the fair face of Anastasie clouded over with distress. She turned to Eugène and gave him one of those chill interrogative looks which plainly say, 'Why don't you go away?' to which well-bred people at once reply by what we may call the phrases of leave-taking.

Eugène, however, put on an agreeable manner, and said, 'Madame, I was in haste to see you, because—'

He stopped short, for a door opened, and the gentleman who had driven into the courtyard entered the room. He was without a hat, and did not bow to the countess, but looked attentively at Rastignac, and held out his hand to Maxime saying, 'Good morning,' with an air of intimacy which greatly surprised Eugène.

'Monsieur de Restaud,' said the countess to the student, motioning towards her husband. 'Monsieur,' she said, presenting Eugène to the Comte de Restaud, 'is Monsieur de Rastignac, a relative of Madame de Beauséant, through the Marcillacs. I had the pleasure of meeting him at her ball.'

'*A relative of Madame de Beauséant, through the Marcillacs*' – these words, uttered by the countess with a certain emphasis (for a lady likes to make known that she receives only those who are people of distinction), had an almost magical effect. The count lost his coldly ceremonious air, and bowed to the student.

'Delighted, Monsieur, to be able to make your acquaintance,' he said courteously.

Even Count Maxime de Trailles, casting an uneasy look at de Rastignac, abandoned his impertinent manner. This touch of a fairy wand, the magic of an aristocratic name, let a flood of light into the brain of the young southerner and gave him back his premeditated cleverness. He suddenly caught a glimpse into the great world of Paris, hitherto only cloud-land for him, and the Maison Vauquer and Père Goriot vanished from his thoughts.

'I thought the Marcillacs were extinct?' said Monsieur de Restaud to Eugène.

'You are right, Monsieur,' he replied; 'my great-uncle, the Chevalier de Rastignac, married the heiress of the house of Marcillac. They had only one daughter, who married the Maréchal de Clarimbault, Madame de Beauséant's grandfather on the mother's side. We are the younger branch; all the poorer for the fact that my great uncle, the Vice-Admiral, lost his fortune in the service of the King. The Revolutionary government would not admit our claims when it wound up the affairs of the India Company.'

'Did not Monsieur, your great-uncle, command the "Vengeur" previous to 1789?'

'Precisely.'

'Then he must have known my grandfather, at that time commanding the "Warwick".'

Here Maxime shrugged his shoulders slightly with a glance at Madame de Restaud, which meant, 'If they begin to talk of naval affairs we shall not get a word with each other.'

Anastasie understood the look, and with the ease of a practised woman she smiled and said, 'Come this way, Maxime; I will show you what I want you to do for me. Gentlemen, we will leave you to sail in company with the "Warwick" and the "Vengeur".'

She rose as she spoke, making a treacherous little sign to Maxime, and the two turned to leave the room. As this morganatic couple (morganatic is a pretty and expressive German word, which as yet has no equivalent in the French language) were leaving the room, the count stopped short in his conversation with Eugène.

'Anastasie,' he said sharply, 'don't go, my dear; you know very well—'

'I shall be back in a moment,' she said, interrupting what he was about to say. 'It will only take me a second to tell Maxime what I want him to do.'

And she did come back. Like all women who study the character of their husbands that they may be able themselves to live as they please, she knew just how far she could go without straining his forbearance, and was careful not to offend him in the lesser things of daily life. She was now aware from the tone of his voice that it would not be safe to prolong her absence. These *contretemps* were due to Eugène. The countess expressed this by a glance and a gesture of vexation directed to Maxime, who said pointedly to the count, his wife, and de Rastignac, 'I see you are all engaged. I do not wish to be in your way. Adieu,' and he left the *salon*.

'Don't go, Maxime,' cried the count.

'Come to dinner,' said the countess, leaving Eugène and the count together for the second time, and following Maxime into the outer salon, where they remained long enough, as they thought, for Monsieur de Restaud to get rid of his visitor.

Eugène heard them laughing together, talking and pausing at intervals; but the perverse youth continued his conversation with Monsieur de Restaud, flattering him and drawing him into discussions solely that he might see the countess again and find out the secret of her relations to Père Goriot. That this woman, evidently in love with Maxime, yet all-powerful with her husband, should be secretly connected in any way with the old paste-maker, seemed to him a singular mystery. He was resolved to penetrate it. It might give him, he thought, some power over a woman so eminently Parisian, that might serve the ends of his ambition.

'Anastasie,' said the count, again calling her.

'Well, Maxime,' she said to the young man, 'we must put up with it. This evening—'

'I do hope, Nasie,' he whispered, 'that you will give orders never to admit that young fool, whose eyes sparkle like live coals when he looks at you. He will make love to you and compromise you, and I shall have to kill him.'

'Don't be absurd, Maxime,' she said; 'these little students are, on the contrary, very useful – as lightning-rods. Restaud shall be the man to deal with him!'

Maxime laughed, and left the countess standing at the window to see him get into his cabriolet and flourish his whip over the champing steed. She did not come back till the outer gates were closed.

'Just think, my dear,' said the count, as she entered; 'the country-seat of Monsieur's family is not far from Vertueil on the Charente. His great-uncle and my grandfather used to know each other.'

'Charmed to be so nearly connected,' said the countess, with an absent manner.

'Nearer, perhaps, than you think for,' said Eugène in a low voice.

'In what way?' she said quickly.

'Why,' said the student, 'I have just seen leaving your house someone whose room is next to mine in our *pension* – Père Goriot.'

At the jovial word 'Père', so disrespectfully applied, the count, who was mending the fire, flung down the tongs as if they burned his fingers, and started from his chair.

'Monsieur, you might at least say Monsieur Goriot,' he cried.

The countess turned pale when she saw her husband's displeasure; then she blushed, and was evidently embarrassed. She replied in a voice which she strove to render natural, and with an air of assumed ease: 'It is impossible to know anyone whom we love more.' Here she stopped; and looking at her piano as if struck by a sudden thought, she said—

'Do you like music, Monsieur?'

'Very much,' said Eugène, flushing, and stupefied by a confused sense that he must have committed some enormous blunder.

'Do you sing?' she said, going to the piano and running a brilliant scale, from C in the bass to F in the treble – r-r-r-rah!

'No, Madame.'

Monsieur de Restaud was walking up and down the room.

'That's a pity; you are cut off from one great means of social success. *Ca-ro, ca-a-ro, ca-a-a-ro, non dubitare!*' sang the countess.

By pronouncing the name of Père Goriot, Eugène had for the second time waved a magic wand; but its effect was the opposite of that produced by the words, 'a relation of Madame de Beauséant'. He was like a man introduced by favour into the cabinet of a collector of curios, who touching thoughtlessly a case full of sculptured figures, knocks off by accident three or four heads which have been ill glued on. He felt like jumping into an abyss. The face of Madame de Restaud wore an expression of cold and hard indifference, and her eyes pointedly avoided his.

'Madame,' said he, 'I leave you to converse with Monsieur de Restaud. Be pleased to accept my homage, and permit me—'

'Whenever you come to see us,' said the countess quickly, cutting him short by a gesture, 'you will be sure of giving Monsieur de Restaud and myself the greatest pleasure.'

Eugène bowed low to husband and wife, and went out, followed, in spite of his remonstrances, by Monsieur de Restaud, who accompanied him through the antechamber.

'Whenever that gentleman calls again,' said the count to Maurice, 'remember that Madame and I are not at home.'

When Eugène came out on the portico he found that it was raining.

'Well,' he said to himself, 'I have made some horrible blunder – I don't know what it is, nor what it may lead to; and now I am going to spoil my hat and clothes! I'd better have stayed at home grubbing at law, and contented myself with being a country magistrate. How am I to go into the world, when to get along with decency one must have lots of things – cabriolets, dress-boots, riggings that are absolutely indispensable, gold chains, buckskin gloves for the morning that cost six francs, and kid gloves for the evening? Old rogue of a Père Goriot – *va!*'

When he found himself in the street the driver of a glass coach, who had probably just disposed of a bridal party and was ready to pick up a fare on his own account before returning to his stable, made a sign to Eugène, seeing him without an umbrella, in a black coat, white waistcoat, yellow gloves, and varnished boots. Eugène was in one of those blind rages which prompt young men to plunge deeper into the gulf they have fallen into, under the idea of finding some lucky way of getting out. He signed to the coachman, and got into the carriage, where a few orange blossoms and scraps of silver ribbon attested the recent presence of a bridal party.

'Where to, Monsieur?' said the man, who had taken off his white gloves.

'Hang it!' thought Eugène, 'since I am in for it I may as well get something out of it. To the Hôtel Beauséant,' he said aloud.

'Which one?' asked the coachman.

This question wholly confounded our embryo man of fashion, who was not aware that there were two Hôtels Beauséants, and did not know how rich he was in grand relations to whom he was equally unknown.

'Vicomte de Beauséant, Rue—'

'De Grenelle,' said the driver, nodding and interrupting the direction. 'You see there's the hôtel of the Comte and the Marquis de Beauséant, Rue Saint-Dominique,' he added, putting up the steps.

'I am aware of it,' said Eugène dryly. 'Is everybody laughing at me to-day?' he said to himself, angrily flinging his hat upon the seat before him. 'I'm launched on a prank which is going to cost me a king's ransom. But at least I'll pay a visit to my so-called cousin in a style that is solidly aristocratic. Père Goriot has cost me not less than ten francs – the old scoundrel! Confound it! I'll tell the whole story to Madame de Beauséant; perhaps it will make her laugh. She may know what bond of iniquity unites that old rat without a tail to his beautiful countess. I had better on the whole stick to my cousin, and not run after that shameless woman; besides, I foresee it would be horribly expensive. If the very name of the Vicomtesse de Beauséant is so powerful, what immense weight her personal influence must have! Aim high, and put your trust in the Lord!'

These words contain the substance of the thousand and one thoughts which floated through his mind. He recovered some calmness and self-possession as he saw the rain falling, for he said to himself that if he was forced to part with two of his precious five-franc pieces they were well spent in saving his best coat and hat and boots. He heard, with a touch of hilarity, the coachman call 'Gate, if you please!' A *Suisse*, in red livery and gold lace, made it swing on its hinges, and Rastignac, with much complacency, saw his carriage pass in under the archway, turn round in the courtyard, and draw up under the roof of the portico. The coachman, in a big great-coat of blue with red facings, let down the steps. As he got out of the carriage Eugène heard sounds of stifled laughter proceeding from the men-servants, three or four of whom were watching the bridal coach from the colonnade. Their mirth enlightened the student, who now compared his vulgar equipage with one of the most elegant coupés in Paris, drawn by a pair of bay horses with roses in their headstalls, that were champing their bits under the charge of a powdered coachman who kept a tight hand on his reins. In the Chaussée d'Antin the stylish cabriolet of a dandy of twenty-six stood in the courtyard of Madame de Restaud, while in the Faubourg Saint-Germain waited, in all the pomp of a grand-seigneur, an equipage that thirty thousand francs would scarcely have paid for.

'Who can that be?' thought Eugène, beginning to be conscious that in Paris all women of fashion have their private engagements; and that the conquest of one of these queens of society might cost more money than blood.

'The deuce! my cousin too may have her Maxime.' He went up the broad front steps with a sinking heart. A glass door opened before him, and he found the footmen within looking, by this time, as solemn as donkeys under the curry-comb. The ball had been given in the state apartments which were on the ground-floor of the hôtel. Having had no time to call upon his cousin between the invitation and the ball, he had not yet penetrated to her private apartments, and he was now to see for the first time those marvels of personal elegance which indicate the habits and the tastes of a woman of distinction – a study all the more interesting because the *salon* of Madame de Restaud had given him a standard of comparison. At half-past four the viscountess was visible; five minutes earlier he would not have been admitted. Eugène, who knew nothing of these various shades of Parisian etiquette, was shown up the grand staircase, which was banked with flowers and was white in tone, with gilt balusters and a red carpet, to the rooms of Madame de Beauséant. Although she was his cousin he knew nothing of her biography, and was not aware that her affairs were at this time passing from ear to ear in the *salons* of Paris.

VII

For three years the Vicomtesse de Beauséant had been on terms of great intimacy with a wealthy and celebrated Portuguese nobleman, the Marquis d'Adjuda-Pinto. It was one of those innocent friendships which have so great a charm for those who are thus allied that they cannot endure to share the companionship with others. The Vicomte de Beauséant himself set the example of respecting, willingly or unwillingly, this Platonic intimacy. Visitors who in the early days of the alliance came to call upon the viscountess at two o'clock always found the Marquis d'Adjuda-Pinto in her *salon*. Madame de Beauséant was not a woman to close her doors to society; but she received her visitors so coldly, and her manner was so preoccupied, that they soon found out they were in her way at that hour. When it was understood in Paris that Madame de Beauséant preferred not to receive visitors between two and four o'clock, she was left in peace at those hours. She went to the Bouffons or the opera accompanied by Monsieur de Beauséant and Monsieur d'Adjuda-Pinto; but Monsieur de Beauséant had the tact to leave his wife with her friend the Portuguese after he had established her for the evening. Monsieur d'Adjuda was now about to be married. He was engaged to a Mademoiselle de Rochefide; and in all society there was but one person who knew nothing of this engagement. That one was Madame de Beauséant. Some of her friends had indeed vaguely alluded to the event as possible; but she had laughed, believing that they wished to trouble a happiness of which they were jealous. The banns, however, were on the eve of being published; and the handsome Portuguese had come to tell the viscountess on the day of which we write, but had not yet dared to put his treachery into words. There is nothing a man dreads more than to break to a woman the inevitable end of their relations. He would rather defend himself against another man's rapier pointed at his throat than meet the reproaches of a woman, who, after bewailing her wrongs for hours, faints at his feet, and asks for salts. At this moment Monsieur d'Ajuda-Pinto sat on thorns and was thinking of taking leave, saying to himself that Madame de Beauséant would surely hear the news from others; that he would write to her; and that it would be easier to administer the fatal stab by letter. When, therefore, the footman announced Monsieur de Rastignac, Monsieur d'Ajuda-Pinto made a slight gesture of relief. Alas! a loving woman is more ingenious in perceiving her wrongs than in varying pleasures for the man she loves. When about to be forsaken, her instinct divines the meaning of a gesture as unerringly as Virgil's courser divined in distant pastures the presence of his mares. Therefore we may be sure that Madame de Beauséant saw and understood that slight yet significant movement of relief.

Eugène had not yet learned that before entering society in Paris a man should inform himself, through some friend of each family, about the history of husband, wife, and children, lest he commit any of those gross blunders which require him, as they say in Poland, to 'harness oxen to his carriage' – meaning, doubtless, that the force of an ox team alone can drag the blunderer out of the mud-hole into which he has plunged. If as yet there is no term in the French language for such conversational mistakes, it is because they are practically impossible for Parisians by reason of the publicity which all kinds of scandal instantly obtain. After having gone heels over head into the mire at Madame de Restaud's, where he had no chance to harness his oxen, it seemed likely that our provincial might yet need the services of a teamster by presenting himself at an equally inopportune moment at Madame de Beauséant's. However, if his visit had been horribly annoying to Madame de Restaud and Monsieur de Trailles, he was now, on the contrary, most welcome to Monsieur d'Adjuda.

'Adieu,' said this gentleman, making for the door as Eugène was shown into the charming inner drawing-room, all rose and grey, combining luxury with elegance.

'But this evening?' said Madame de Beauséant, turning from Eugène and looking after Adjuda; 'are we not going to the Bouffons?'

'I cannot,' he said, laying his hand on the doorknob.

Madame de Beauséant rose and called him back, without paying the least attention to Eugène, who was left standing, bewildered by the sparkle of great wealth – the reality, to his mind, of the 'Arabian Nights' – and much embarrassed to know what to do with himself in the presence of a woman who took no notice of him. Madame de Beauséant lifted her right forefinger, and by a graceful gesture signed to the marquis to come back to her. There was something so passionately imperative in her air that he let go the handle of the door and came back into the *salon*. Eugène looked at him with eyes of envy.

'That's the man who owns the coupé,' he said to himself. 'Must one have blood horses, and liveries all covered with gold lace, to make one's way in Paris with a fashionable woman?'

The devil Belial bit into his mind; the fever of money-getting was in his veins; the thirst for gold parched his heart. He had one hundred and thirty francs left, to last him three months. His father, mother, brothers, sisters and aunt had but two hundred francs a month among them all. This rapid comparison of the realities of his position with the end that he was planning to attain, staggered him.

'Why cannot you go to the theatre?' said the viscountess, smiling.

'I have business. I dine with the English ambassador.'

'But you can come away early.'

When a man deceives, he is forced to prop one falsehood by another. Monsieur d'Adjuda answered, smiling—

'You insist, then?'

'Of course I do.'

'Ah! that was just what I wanted to make you say!' he replied, giving her a look sufficient to reassure any other woman. He took her hand, kissed it, and went out.

Eugène passed his fingers through his hair and turned toward Madame de Beauséant to make his bow, thinking she would now give her attention to him. To his surprise, she sprang from her chair, ran into the gallery, and looked out at Monsieur d'Adjuda as he got into his carriage. She listened for his orders, and heard the chasseur repeating to the coachman, 'To Monsieur de Rochefide's.'

These words, and the way d'Adjuda plunged into his coupé, were like a flash of lightning and a thunderclap to the poor woman. She drew back sick with dread. The worst catastrophes in the great world take place thus quietly and suddenly. The viscountess turned aside into her bed-room, took a dainty sheet of note-paper, and wrote as follows: 'When you have dined at the Rochefides' (and not at the English ambassador's), you owe me an explanation. I shall expect you.' After straightening a few letters made illegible by the trembling of her hand, she added a C, which meant 'Claire de Bourgogne', and rang the bell.

'Jacques,' she said to her footman, 'at half-past seven take this note to Monsieur de Rochefide's, and ask for the Marquis d'Adjuda. If he is there, have the note taken to him at once. There is no answer. If he is not there, bring it back to me.'

'Madame la vicomtesse has a visitor in the *salon*.'

'Yes, true,' she said, closing the door.

Eugène began to feel very ill at ease; but Madame de Beauséant at last came in and said in a voice whose emotion thrilled him to the heart, 'I beg your pardon, Monsieur; I had to write a few words. Now I am quite at your service.'

She did not know what she was saying. She was thinking, 'Ah! he must be going to marry Mademoiselle de Rochefide. But will he? Can he? Tonight this marriage shall be broken off, or I – But, no! it *shall be!*'

'Cousin,' said Eugène.

'*Hein?*' said the viscountess, giving him a look whose cold displeasure froze his very blood. He understood her exclamation, for he had learned much during the last few hours, and his mind was on the alert.

'Madame,' he resumed, colouring; he stopped short, and then continued, 'forgive me; I need help so much – and this little shred of relationship would be everything to me.'

Madame de Beauséant smiled, but the smile was sad. 'If you knew the situation of my family,' he continued, 'I think you would find pleasure in playing the part of a fairy godmother who removes all difficulties out of the way of her godchild.'

'Well, cousin,' she said laughing, 'what can I do for you?'

'How can I tell you? To be acknowledged as your relative, though the link is so far back as to be scarcely visible, is in itself a fortune. I am confused – I don't know what I had to say to you. You are the only person whom I know in Paris. Ah! I ask your advice; look on me as you might on some poor child clinging to your dress – as one who would die for you.'

'Would you kill a man for my sake?'

'I would kill two!' exclaimed Eugène.

'Foolish boy! – for boy you are,' she said, repressing her tears. 'You could love truly, faithfully?'

'Ah!' he replied, throwing back his head.

The viscountess felt a sudden interest in the youth, and smiled at his answer. This son of the south was at the dawn of his ambition. As he passed from the blue boudoir of Madame de Restaud to the rose-coloured drawing-room of Madame de Beauséant he had taken a three-years' course in the social code of Paris – a code never formulated in words, but constituting a high social jurisprudence, which, if well studied and well applied, leads to fortune.

'Already,' said Eugène, 'I was attracted at your ball by Madame de Restaud, and this morning I went to call upon her.'

'You must have been very much in her way,' remarked Madame de Beauséant.

'Indeed I was. I am an ignoramus who will set everybody against him if you refuse to help me. I think it must be difficult in Paris to find a young, beautiful, rich and elegant woman who is not already occupied by the attachment of some man. I need one who will teach me what you women know far better than we do – *life*. Unless you guide me I shall be forever stumbling on some Maxime de Trailles. I have come to ask you in the first place to solve a riddle and explain to me the nature of a blunder I have committed at Madame de Restaud's. I mentioned a Père—'

'Madame la Duchesse de Langeais,' said Jacques, cutting short Eugène's words. He made a gesture as if greatly annoyed by the interruption.

'If you wish to succeed in society,' said Madame de Beauséant, in a low voice, 'you must begin by being less demonstrative. – Ah, good morning, dear,' she cried, rising and going to meet the duchess, whose hands she pressed tenderly, while the duchess responded by fond little caresses.

'They are dear friends,' thought Rastignac; 'heart answers to heart. I shall have two protectoresses, both taking interest in my future.'

'To what happy thought do I owe the pleasure of seeing you to-day, dear Antoinette?' said Madame de Beauséant.

'I saw Monsieur d'Adjuda-Pinto going into Monsieur de Rochetide's, and I knew that I should find you alone.'

Madame de Beauséant did not bite her lips, nor blush, nor did the expression of her face change; on the contrary her brow seemed to clear as Madame de Langeais uttered the fatal words.

'If I had known you were engaged—' added the duchess, glancing at Eugène.

'Monsieur is Monsieur Eugène de Rastignac, one of my cousins,' said Madame de Beauséant. 'Have you heard,' she continued, 'of General Montriveau lately? Serizy told me yesterday that no one sees him now. Has he been with you to-day?'

People said that the Marquis de Montriveau had broken with Madame de Langeais, who was deeply in love with him. She felt the intended stab, and blushed as she answered, 'He was at the Elysée yesterday.'

'On duty?' asked Madame de Beauséant.

'Clara, of course you know,' said the duchess, spite gleaming in her eyes, 'that to-morrow the banns are to be published between Monsieur d'Adjuda-Pinto and Mademoiselle de Rochefide.'

This blow struck home. The viscountess grew pale, but she answered, laughing—

'That is merely a piece of gossip set afloat by people who know nothing. Why should Monsieur d'Adjuda-Pinto ally one of the noblest names in Portugal with that of the Rochefides? Their title dates from yesterday.'

'They say Berthe will have two hundred thousand francs a year.'

'Monsieur d'Adjuda is too rich to marry for money.'

'But, my dear Clara, Mademoiselle de Rochefide is charming.'

'Ah!'

'He dines there to-day; the settlements are drawn; I am astonished that no one has told you.'

'What was that blunder you were telling me about, Monsieur?'

said Madame de Beauséant, turning to Eugène. 'Poor Monsieur de Rastignac has so recently entered the gay world, dear Antoinette,' she continued, 'that he cannot understand our conversation. Be good to him, and put off all you have to say about this news until to-morrow. To-morrow we shall know it officially, and you can be just as officious then, you know.'

The duchess gave Eugène one of those ineffable looks which envelop a man from head to foot, strike him flat, and let him drop to zero.

'Madame,' he said, 'without knowing what I was about, I seem to have plunged a dagger into the heart of Madame de Restaud. Had I done this on purpose I might not have been in disgrace; my fault lay in not knowing what I was doing.' Eugène's natural cleverness made him conscious of the bitterness underlying the affectionate words of the two ladies. 'People,' he added, 'do not break with the friend who intentionally wounds them, though they may fear him for the future. But he who wounds unconsciously is a poor fool – a man of too little tact to turn anything to profit, and every one despises him.'

Madame de Beauséant gave the student a look that expressed her gratitude, and yet was full of dignity. This glance was balm to the wound inflicted by the duchess when she looked him over and over with the eye of a detective.

'About my blunder – you must know,' resumed Eugène, 'that I had succeeded in securing the goodwill of Monsieur de Restaud, for—' turning to the duchess with a manner partly humble, partly mischievous, 'I ought to inform you, Madame, that I am as yet only a poor devil of a law-student, very lonely, very poor—'

'Never say so, Monsieur de Rastignac; we women do not value that which is not valued by others.'

'But,' said Eugène, 'I am only twenty-two, and I must learn to put up with the natural misfortunes of my age. Besides, I am making my confession: could I kneel in a more charming confessional? Here we commit the sins for which we receive penance in the other.'

The duchess listened to these irreligious remarks with studied coldness, and marked her sense of their bad taste by saying to the viscountess: 'Monsieur has just arrived?'

Madame de Beauséant laughed heartily both at her cousin and at the duchess. 'Yes,' she said, 'he has just arrived in Paris, my dear, in search of a preceptress to teach him taste and manners.'

'Madame la duchesse,' said Eugène, 'is it not permissible to try to possess ourselves of the secrets of those who charm us? – There!' he said to himself; 'now I am talking just like a hairdresser—'

'But I have heard that Madame de Restaud is a pupil of Monsieur de Trailles,' said the duchess.

'I did not know it, Madame,' resumed the student; 'and like a fool I broke in upon them. However, I was getting on very well with the husband, and the wife had apparently made up her mind to put up with me, when I must needs tell them that I recognized a man whom I had just seen leave their house by a back door, and who kissed the countess at the end of the passage—'

'Who was it?' exclaimed both ladies at once.

'An old man, who lives for two louis a month in the Faubourg Saint-Marçeau, where I, a poor student, live myself; a forlorn old man, whom we all ridicule and call Père Goriot.'

'Oh, child that you are!' exclaimed the viscountess; 'Madame de Restaud was a Mademoiselle Goriot.'

'Daughter of a man who makes vermicelli,' said the duchess; 'a person who was presented at court on the same day as a pastrycook's daughter. Don't you remember, Clara? The king laughed, and said a good thing in Latin about flour – people – how was it? People—'

'*Ejusdem farinæ,*' suggested Eugène.

'That was it!' said the duchess.

'And so he is really her father?' exclaimed the student, with a gesture of disgust.

'Just so; the man had two daughters, and was quite foolish about them. Both of them have since cast him off.'

'The youngest,' said Madame de Beauséant, addressing Madame de Langeais, 'is married, is she not, to a banker with a German name – a Baron de Nucingen? Is not her name Delphine – a fair woman, who has a side box at the opera, and who comes to the Bouffons, and laughs a great deal to attract attention?'

The duchess smiled as she answered, 'My dear, you astonish me. Why do you care to know about such people? A man must be madly in love, as they say Restaud was with Mademoiselle Anastasie, to powder himself with flour. Ah! but he made a poor bargain! She has fallen into Monsieur de Trailles' hands, and he will ruin her.'

'Did you say that they have cast off their father?' asked Eugène.

'Yes, indeed; their father, the father, a father,' cried the viscountess; 'a good father, who gave these daughters all he had – to each of them seven or eight hundred thousand francs – that he might secure their happiness by great marriages, and kept for himself only eight or ten thousand francs a year; thinking that his daughters would remain his daughters – that he would have two homes in his old age, two families where he would be adored and taken care of. Before three years were over, both sons-in-law cast him out as if he had been the veriest wretch living—'

Tears gathered in the eyes of Eugène de Rastignac, who had recently renewed the pure and sacred ties of home, and still clung to the beliefs of his boyhood. He was making his first encounter with the world on the battle-field of Parisian civilization. Real feeling is contagious; and for a moment all three looked at each other in silence.

'Good heavens!' said Madame de Langeais; 'it seems horrible;

and yet we see the same thing every day. And why? My dear Clara, have you never thought what it would be to have a son-in-law? A son-in-law is a man for whom we may bring up – you or I – a dear little creature to whom we should be bound by a thousand tender ties; who for seventeen years would be the darling of the family – "the white soul of her home", as Lamartine says – and who might end by becoming its curse. When the man for whom we brought her up takes her away, he will use her love for him as an axe to cut her free from every tie that binds her to her family. Yesterday our little daughter was our own, and we were all in all to her; to-morrow she will seem to be our enemy. Don't we see such tragedies around us every day? The daughter-in-law coolly impertinent to the father who has sacrificed everything for her husband, the son-in-law thrusting his wife's mother out of doors? I hear people say that there is nothing dramatic now-a-days in society. Why, this drama of the son-in-law is horrible – not to speak of our marriages, which have become sad follies, to say the least. I perfectly recollect the history of that vermicelli man, Foriot—'

'Goriot, Madame.'

'Yes, true; Moriot was president of his section during the Revolution. He was behind the scenes, and when the great scarcity was at hand he made his fortune by selling flour for ten times what it cost him. My grandmother's bailiff sold him wheat to an immense amount. Goriot no doubt divided his profits – as all those people did – with the Committee of Public Safety. I recollect the bailiff saying to my grandmother that she might feel quite safe at Grandvilliers, because her crops were an excellent certificate of citizenship. Well! this Loriot, who sold flour to the men who cut our heads off, had but one passion – he adored his daughters. He contrived to perch the eldest in the Restaud family, and graft the other on the Baron de Nucingen – a rich banker who pretends to be a Royalist. You understand that during the Empire the sons-in-law did not so much mind having the old Jacobin of '93 under their roof: under Bonaparte what did it signify? But when the Bourbons came back, the old man was a great annoyance to Monsieur de Restaud, and still more so to the banker. The daughters, who for aught I know may have been fond of their father, tried to "run with the hare and hold with the hounds", as we say. They asked Goriot to their houses when they had nobody there; invented, I have no doubt, pretty pretexts: "Oh, do come, papa! It will be so pleasant: we shall have you all to ourselves," and so on. My dear, I always maintain that real feeling is sharp-sighted; if so, poor old '93's heart must have bled. He saw that his daughters were ashamed of him, and that if they loved their husbands he was injuring them. He saw the sacrifice which was required of him, and he made it – made it as only a father can. He sacrificed himself; he banished himself from their homes; and when he saw his daughters happy he was satisfied. Father and daughters were accomplices in this crime against paternity. We see this sort of thing every day. You can well imagine Père Doriot to have been like a spot of cart-grease in his daughters' drawing-rooms. He would have felt it himself, and suffered from it. What happened to him as a father, my dear, happens to the prettiest woman in the world with the man she loves best. If her love wearies him he will go elsewhere, and will treat her like a coward to get away. That is the upshot of all extravagant attachments. The heart is a treasury: empty it all at once, and you will find yourself ruined. We think just as little of those who expend all their love as we do of a man who flings away his last penny. This father gave his all. For twenty years he had lavished his love, his life, on these two girls; his fortune he gave them in one day. The lemon was squeezed, and the daughters flung the rind into the gutter.'

'The world is infamous!' said the viscountess, fringing her ribbon and not looking up, for Madame de Langeais' allusions to herself as she told the story cut her to the quick.

'Infamous? – No,' replied the duchess. 'The world goes on its own way, that is all. I only want to prove to you that I am not its dupe. Yes, I think as you do,' she added, taking the viscountess's hand – 'if the world is a slough, let us stand upon high ground and keep ourselves out of the slime.'

She rose and kissed Madame de Beauséant on the forehead, saying, 'You are lovely at this moment, dear heart; you have the prettiest colour I ever saw,' and she left the room with a slight bow to the student.

'Père Goriot is sublime!' cried Eugène, remembering how he had seen him destroy his pieces of silver in the night-time.

Madame de Beauséant did not hear him; she was thinking deeply. A few moments passed in silence, and our poor youth, in a stupor of shyness, dared neither go nor stay, nor speak to her.

'The world is wicked – it is cruel,' said the viscountess at last. 'When misfortune overtakes us there is never a friend wanting to tell it in our ear; to probe our heart with a dagger and ask us to admire the hilt. Already sarcasm! already the mocking tongues! Ah! I will defend myself!' She lifted her head, like the *grande dame* (the great lady) that she was, and her eyes flashed. 'Ah!' she exclaimed, seeing Eugène, 'you here?'

'Still here,' he answered humbly.

'Monsieur de Rastignac,' she said, 'learn to treat society as it deserves. You wish to succeed in it; I will help you. You will find out how deep is the corruption among women; how wide the range of the contemptible vanity of men. I thought myself well read in the book of the world; I find pages hitherto unknown to me. Now I know all. The more cold-blooded your purpose the surer you will be of success. Strike without pity, and the world will fear you. Treat men and women as post-horses: never mind if you founder them, so long as they get you to the next relay. In the first place, you will make no progress unless you find some woman to take you up and be interested in you. She must be young, rich, and elegant. But if you really care for her, hide your feelings; don't let her suspect them, or you are lost: instead of being the executioner, you will be the victim. If you love, keep your own secret. Never reveal it until you know well the friend to whom you bare your heart. Learn to mistrust the world. Let me tell you, Miguel [she did not notice her mistake], there is something in those Goriot sisters even more shocking than their neglect of their father, whom they wish dead. I mean their rivalry to each other. Restaud is of ancient family; his wife has been adopted by his relatives and presented at court. But her sister, her rich sister, the beautiful Madame Delphine de Nucingen, though the wife of a man made of money, is dying with envy – the victim of jealousy. She is a hundred leagues lower in society than her sister. Her sister is no longer her sister; they renounce each other as they both renounced their father. Madame de Nucingen would lap up all the mud between the Rue Saint-Lazare and the Rue de Grenelle to gain admittance to my *salon*. She thought de Marsay could arrange it for her, and she has been the slave of de Marsay, and bored people with De Marsay. De Marsay cares very little for her. My cousin, here is your opportunity. If you present her to me she will adore you, and lavish everything upon you. You may adore her if you can, but at any rate make use of her. I will let her come here to two or three balls – but only to balls, with the crowd; I will never receive her in the morning. I will bow to her, and that will be quite enough. You have shut her sister's doors against you by pronouncing the name of Père Goriot. Yes, my dear cousin, you may call twenty times at Madame de Restaud's, and twenty times you will be told that she is out. Orders have been given to refuse you admission. Well, make Père Goriot introduce you to her sister; wear the colours of the handsome Madame Delphine de Nucingen; let it be known that you are the man she distinguishes, and other women will go distracted about you. Her rivals, her friends – her dearest friends – will try to win you from her. Some women prefer a man who is the property of another woman – just as women of the middle class think they acquire our manners when they copy our millinery. You will succeed; and in Paris success is everything – it is the key to power. If women think you clever, men will believe you so unless you undeceive them. From this point you may aim at what you will – you have your foot upon the ladder. You will find out that society is a mixture of dupes and cheats. Try to be neither the one nor the other. My cousin, I give you my name, like the clew of Ariadne, to lead you into the heart of the labyrinth. Do not disgrace it,' she added, turning to him with the glance of a queen; 'give it back to me unsullied. Now leave me. Women have their battles to fight as well as men.'

'If you need a man ready to fire a mine for you—' began Eugène.

'What if I should?' she cried.

He laid his hand upon his heart, smiled in answer to her smile, and went out.

It was five o'clock; he was very hungry and half afraid he should not get home in time for dinner. This fear made him appreciate the advantages of whirling along in his glass coach. The fast motion made his mind run on the new thoughts that assailed him. When a youth of his age meets with a rebuff he loses his temper, he grows furious, shakes his fist at society, and vows to be revenged; but at the same time his confidence in himself is shaken. Rastignac was overwhelmed by the words still ringing in his ears – 'You have closed the doors of the countess against you.'

'I will call there again and again,' he cried; 'and if Madame de Beauséant is right, if she has given orders not to admit me – I – Madame de Restaud shall meet me at every house she visits – I will make myself a sure shot; I will kill her Maxime.'

'But how about money?' cried a voice within him. 'Where will you get it? You need money for everything.'

At this thought, the wealth that shone round Madame de Restaud glittered before his eyes. He had seen her lapped in luxury that was doubtless dear to a demoiselle Goriot; gilded and costly ornaments lay strewn about her *salons* with the unmeaning profusion that betrays the taste of a *parvenue* and her passion for squandering money. The fascinations of mere costliness had been effaced by the grandeur of the Hôtel Beauséant. His imagination now whirled him to the summits of Parisian life, and suggested thoughts which seared his heart, while they stimulated his intelligence and widened his perceptions. He saw the world in its true colours. He saw wealth triumphant over morality – triumphant over law and order. He saw in riches the *ultima ratio mundi*. 'Vautrin is right,' he cried, 'luck makes the difference between vice and virtue.'

Having reached the Rue Neuve Sainte-Geneviève, he ran rapidly to his room and returned bringing ten francs for his coachman, and then entered the sickening dining-room where the eighteen guests sat eating their food like animals at a manger. The sight of their collective poverty and the dinginess of the place were horrible to him. The transition from the wealth and grace and beauty he had left was too abrupt, too complete, not to excite beyond all bounds his growing ambition. On the one hand fresh and lovely images of all that was elegant in social life, framed in marvels of art and luxury, and passionate with poetical emotion; on the other, a dark picture of degradation – sinister faces where passions had blighted all but the sinews and the mere mechanism. The advice wrung from Madame de Beauséant in her anguish, and her tempting offers to his ambition came back to his memory, and the misery about him was their commentary. He resolved to open two parallel trenches – law and love; and to win fortune by his profession and as a man of the world. Child that he was!

these lines are geometric aliens, asymptotes that never touch.

'You are solemn, Monsieur le marquis,' said Vautrin, giving him one of those keen glances by which this singular man seemed to catch the hidden thoughts of those around him.

'I am not disposed to permit jokes from people who call me Monsieur le marquis,' Eugène replied. 'To be a marquis in Paris requires an income of a hundred thousand francs, and those who live in the Maison Vauquer are not exactly favourites of fortune.'

Vautrin looked at Rastignac with a patronizing air, which seemed to say contemptuously, 'You young brat! I could gobble you up at a mouthful;' but he answered, 'You are in a bad humour because you have not succeeded with the beautiful countess.'

'She has shut her doors against me for saying that her father dined here with me at this table,' cried Eugène angrily.

All present looked at one another. Père Goriot looked down and turned aside to wipe his eyes.

'You have blown your snuff into my face,' he said to his neighbour.

'Whoever annoys Père Goriot will answer for it to me,' cried Eugène, looking at the man who sat next to the old paste-maker. 'He is better than any of us. I don't include the ladies,' he added, bowing to Mademoiselle Taillefer.

This speech brought the matter to a conclusion, for Eugène had uttered it in a way to silence all the others except Vautrin, who said sarcastically, 'If you are going to take up Père Goriot and make yourself responsible for all he says and does, you will have to learn to use a sword and fire a pistol.'

'I mean to,' said Eugène.

'You declare war then?'

'Perhaps I do,' replied Rastignac; 'but I owe no man an account of my conduct, especially as I don't try to find out what other people are doing in the middle of the night.'

Vautrin shot a side-glance at him.

'My young friend,' said he, 'those who don't want to be deceived at a puppet-show had better go into the booth and not try to peep through holes in the curtain. That's enough for the present,' he added, seeing that Eugène was about to reply; 'we will have a little talk by ourselves whenever you like.'

The rest of the dinner passed in silence. Père Goriot, absorbed by the pang of hearing Eugène's remark about his daughter, was not conscious that a change had taken place concerning him in the opinion of others, and that a young man able to put his persecutors to silence had taken up his defence.

'Can it be possible,' said Madame Vauquer, in a whisper, 'that Père Goriot is really the father of a countess?'

'And of a baroness, too,' said Eugène.

'The *father* is all there is of him,' said Bianchon to Rastignac. 'I have felt his head. It has run to one bump – philoprogenitiveness, the bump of paternity. He is all father – Eternal Father, I should say.'

Eugène was too preoccupied to laugh. He was considering how to profit by Madame de Beauséant's advice, and in what way he could provide himself with money. He was silent and self-absorbed as he saw the rich plains of high society stretching afar as in a vision. The others rose and left him alone when dinner was over.

'You have seen my daughter?' said Goriot in a voice which betrayed emotion.

Startled from his meditation, Eugène took the old man by the hand and said, as he looked at him almost tenderly—

'You are a good and honourable man. We will talk by and by about your daughters,' and without allowing Père Goriot to say more he went to his room and wrote the following letter to his mother—

MY DEAR MOTHER – See if you cannot provide for your grown-up son out of your own breast as you did for him in his infancy. I am in a position which may speedily lead to fortune. I want twelve hundred francs, and I must have them at any price. Do not speak of this to my father. He might object; and if I cannot get this money I shall be in such despair as to be almost ready to blow my brains out. I will tell you all about it when I see you, for I should have to write volumes if I tried to explain to you the situation. I have not gambled, dear mother, and I have no debts; but if you want to preserve the life you gave me, you must manage to find me this money. I have been to visit the Vicomtesse de Beauséant, who takes me under her protection. I have to go into society, and I have not a *sou* to buy gloves to wear. I would willingly eat nothing but bread, and drink nothing but water; I could live on almost nothing if necessary, but I cannot do without my tools to work with – tools which cultivate the vines in this part of the world. I must either make my way or stay in a mud-hole. I know what hopes you have placed on me; and I want as soon as possible to realize them. Dearest mother, sell some of your old jewels; before long I will give them back to you. I know the situation of our family well enough to appreciate such sacrifices, and you may be sure that I would not ask you to make them in vain – if I did I should be a monster. I beseech you to see in this request a cry of imperative necessity. Our future depends on this loan, with which I can open my campaign – for this life of Paris is a ceaseless battle. If to make up the sum there is no other resource than to sell my aunt's old lace, tell her I will hereafter send her some far more beautiful, etc.

He wrote also to his sisters, begging them to send him all their little savings; and as it was necessary that this sacrifice (which he knew they would make gladly for his sake) should not come to the ears of his parents, he enlisted their delicacy by touching those chords of honour which ring so true in the hearts of innocent young girls.

After writing these letters, he was assailed by doubts and fears; he panted and trembled. His ambitious young heart knew the pure nobleness of those tender souls hidden away in the country solitudes; he knew what privations he was bringing on the sisters, yet with what joy they would welcome his request. He could hear them whispering in the distant fields of the 'dear, dear brother'; he saw them counting over their little hoard, inventing girlish devices to send it to him secretly – practising a first deception for his sake. His conscience leapt to the light. 'A sister's heart is like a diamond,' he said to himself; 'a running stream of tenderness, clear and pure.'

He was ashamed of what he had written. How they would pray for him! How they would lift their souls to Heaven for his success! With what passionate delight they would sacrifice themselves for his advantage! How grieved his mother would be if she could not send him the whole sum! And all this goodness, all these sacrifices, were to serve him as a ladder to mount into the favour of Delphine de Nucingen! A few tears – grains of incense flung for the last time on the sacred altar of his home – dropped from his eyes. He walked up and down the room in a state of agitation and despair. Père Goriot seeing him thus, for the door of his room was left ajar, came in and asked –

'Is anything the matter, Monsieur?'

'Ah! my good neighbour,' Eugène replied; 'I am a son and a brother, even as you are a father. You may well tremble for the Countess Anastasie. She is in the power of Monsieur de Trailles, and he will be her ruin.'

Père Goriot drew back to his own room, muttering a few words whose meaning was not intelligible.

The next morning Rastignac went out and posted his letters. He hesitated up to the last moment; but as he flung them into the box he cried, 'I *will* succeed!' So says the gambler; so says the great commander. Superstitious words, that have ruined more men than they have ever saved!

VIII

A few days later Eugène went again to call on Madame de Restaud, and was not received. Three times he tried her door, and three times he found it closed against him, though he chose hours when he knew Monsieur Maxime de Trailles was not there. Madame de Beauséant was right: he was to visit her no more.

Our student now ceased to study. He went to the Law School merely to answer at roll-call; when that was over he decamped. He had persuaded himself, as students often do, that he might as well put off study until it was time to prepare for the examinations. He resolved to take his second and third terms together, and to study law with all his might at the last moment. He could thus count on fifteen months of leisure in which to navigate the ocean of Paris, to try what women's influence might do for him, and find the way to fish for fortune.

During this week he called twice on Madame de Beauséant, taking care not to go till he had seen the carriage of Monsieur d'Adjuda-Pinto driven out of the courtyard. For a little while this distinguished woman, the most poetic figure in the Faubourg Saint-Germain, remained mistress of her field of battle. She broke off for a time the engagement of Monsieur d'Adjuda-Pinto to Mademoiselle de Rochefide; but these last days of intimacy, made feverish by fears that she must finally lose her friend, only served to precipitate the catastrophe. Both the marquis and the Rochefides looked on the estrangement and reconciliation as fortunate circumstances. They hoped that Madame de Beauséant would gradually grow reconciled to the marriage, and by sacrificing the daily visits hitherto so dear to her, permit the marquis to fulfil the destiny that belongs to every man. He himself was playing a part, notwithstanding his protestations to the contrary made daily to Madame de Beauséant. She, meantime, though not deceived, liked his efforts to deceive her. 'Instead of bravely jumping out of the window, she has preferred to roll down stairs step by step,' said her best friend the Duchesse de Langeais. Still, these final moments lasted long enough to let the viscountess launch her young relative, to whom she had taken an almost superstitious fancy, upon the Paris world. He had shown himself full of feeling for her at a time when women find small pity or sympathy from others; if a man utters tender words at such a time, he usually does it on speculation.

For the purpose of knowing his ground before laying siege to Madame de Nucingen, Eugène tried to learn all he could about the early history of Père Goriot; and he gathered certain accurate information, which may briefly be given here.

Jean Joachim Goriot had been, before the Revolution, a journeyman vermicelli-maker; skilful, frugal, and sufficiently successful to buy up the business of his master when the latter was killed by chance in the first insurrection of 1789. His place of business was in the Rue Jussienne, near the Halle aux Blés (Cornmarket); and he had the sound good sense to accept the office of president of the section, and thus secure for his business the protection of the persons who had most influence in those dangerous times. This foresight laid the foundation of his fortune, which began in the time of the great scarcity, real or pretended, in consequence of which flour went up to enormous prices in Paris. People trampled each other to death at the shops of the bakers, while others quietly bought the Italian pastes without difficulty from the grocers. That year Citizen Goriot acquired capital enough to carry on his future business with all the advantages of a man who has plenty of ready money. During the worst days of the Revolution he escaped through a circumstance which he shared with other men of limited capacity – his mediocrity saved him. Moreover, as he was not known to be rich until the danger of being so was at an end, he excited no envy. The flour market seemed to have absorbed all his faculties. In any matter that had to do with wheat, flour or refuse grain – whether it were to sample their various qualities or know where they could best be bought; to keep them in good order or foresee the markets; to prophesy the results of a harvest, bad or bountiful, and buy breadstuffs at the right moment or import them from Sicily or southern Russia – Père Goriot had not his equal. To see him at his desk explaining the laws that regulate the importation of grain, exposing their influence upon trade, and pointing out their deficiencies, he might have been thought fit for a cabinet minister. Patient, active, energetic, always on hand, quick to seize an advantage in business, he had the eye of an eagle in his trade. He foresaw everything, provided for everything, knew everything, and kept his own counsel. Diplomatist in laying his plans, he was a general in executing them. But take him away from his speciality – from his little dark shop, on the threshold of which he spent his leisure moments leaning against the post of its street door – and he fell back into a mere journeyman, rough, stupid, incapable of understanding an argument, insensible to mental enjoyment; a man who would go to sleep at the theatre, and whose only strong point was his dense stupidity.

Men of this type are always much alike; in nearly all of them you will find one deep feeling hidden in their souls. The heart of the old paste-maker held two affections; they absorbed its juices just as the grain-market absorbed his brain. His wife, the only daughter of a rich farmer at Brie, was the object of his fervent admiration; his love for her was unbounded. In her nature, fragile yet firm, sensible and sweet, he found a happy contrast to his own. If there is any sentiment inborn in the heart of man, it is one of pride in protecting a being weaker than himself. Add love to this and the gratitude that simple natures feel towards one who is the fount of all their happiness, and you will comprehend various moral singularities otherwise inexplicable. After seven years of married life without a cloud, Goriot, unhappily for himself, lost his wife. She was beginning to acquire a strong influence over him beyond the simple range of his affections. Had she lived, she might have cultivated his sluggish nature and roused it to some knowledge of life and the world about him. Left to himself, fatherhood became his absorbing passion, and it developed under his lonely circumstances until it passed the bounds of reason. His affections, balked by death, were now concentrated on his daughters, who for a time satisfied to the full his need of love.

Though many prosperous marriages were proposed to him by merchants and farmers who would gladly have given him their daughters, he persisted in remaining a widower. His father-in-law, the only man for whom he had ever felt a liking, declared that Goriot had promised his wife never to be faithless even to her memory. The frequenters of the Halle aux Blés, incapable of understanding so refined a folly, jested roughly on his fidelity. The first who did so in his hearing received a sudden blow on the shoulder from the paste-maker's strong fist, which sent him head foremost on the kerbstone of the Rue Oblin. The blind devotion, the sensitive and nervous affection which Goriot gave to his daughters was so well known, that one day at the Halle a rival in the market, wishing to get him out of the way for a short time, told him that his daughter Delphine had been run over by a cabriolet. Pale as a ghost he left the Halle. On reaching home he found the story false, but was ill for several days from the agitation it had caused him. This time he did not punish with a blow the man who played the trick, but he hunted him from the markets, and forced him at a critical moment into bankruptcy.

The education of his daughters was, naturally, injudicious. As he had sixty thousand francs a year, and spent about twelve hundred francs upon himself, he had enough to satisfy every girlish caprice. The best masters were employed to teach them those accomplishments which are thought to make a good education. They had a *dame de compagnie* who, happily for them, was a woman of sense and spirit. They rode on horseback; they drove in carriages; they lived in luxury. If they expressed a wish, no matter what the cost, their father was eager to grant it; all he asked in return was a caress. He ranked them with the angels, far above himself in every way. Poor man, he loved even the pain they caused him. When they were of age to be married he permitted them to choose their husbands. Each was to have for dowry half her father's fortune. Anastasie, the eldest, had aristocratic tastes, and was courted by the Comte de Restaud for her beauty. She left her father's house to enter an exalted social sphere. Delphine loved money. She married Nucingen, a banker of German origin and a baron of the Holy Empire. Goriot remained a vermicelli-maker. His daughters and sons-in-law were ashamed that he continued this business, although the occupation was life itself to him. After resisting their appeals for five years he consented to retire on the profits of these last years. This capital, as Madame Vauquer ascertained when he first went to live with her, yielded an income of from eight to ten thousand francs. It was despair that drove him to the Maison Vauquer; despair at the discovery that his daughters were forced by their husbands not only to refuse him a home, but even to receive him openly in their houses.

Such was the substance of the information given to Rastignac by a Monsieur Muret, who had purchased the business from Goriot. The account given by the Duchesse de Langeais was thus confirmed, and here ends the introduction to an obscure but terrible Parisian tragedy.

Towards the end of the first week in December Rastignac received letters from his mother and his eldest sister. Their well-known handwriting made his heart beat fast, partly with relief and partly with apprehension. Those slender papers held the sentence of life or death to his ambition. If he dreaded failure as he thought of his parents' poverty, he knew their love for him too well not to tremble lest they might grant his prayer at the cost of their Life's blood. His mother's letter was as follows—

> MY DEAR CHILD – I send you what you ask for. Make good use of this money, for if your life depended on it I could not raise so large a sum again without speaking to your father, and that would cause trouble for our family. To get it we should be obliged to mortgage our property. I cannot judge of the value of plans that I know nothing about; but what can they be if you are afraid to tell them to me? An explanation would not require volumes; we mothers understand our children at a word, and that word would have saved me some sharp pangs of doubt and anxiety. I cannot hide from you the painful impression made upon me by your letter. My dear son, what is it that has led you to make me so uneasy? You must have suffered in writing that letter, for I have suffered so much in reading it. What project have you for the future? Does your life, your happiness – as you say – depend upon appearing what you are not; upon entering a world where you cannot live without spending money which you cannot afford; nor without losing time most precious for your studies?
>
> My own Eugène, believe your mother when she tells you that crooked paths cannot lead to noble ends. Patience and self-sacrifice are the virtues which young

men in your position must cultivate. But I am not reproaching you; I would not mar our offering by a bitter word. I speak as a mother who trusts her son, even though she cautions him. You know your duty, and I know the purity of your heart and the loyalty of your intentions. Therefore I do not fear to say – If all is right, my dearest, follow out your plans. I tremble because I am your mother; but every step you make in life will have my prayers and blessing. You will need to be good and to be wise, for the future of five beings near and dear to you is in your hands. Yes, our prosperity is bound up in your prosperity, as your happiness is our joy. We pray God to be with you in all your undertakings.

Your aunt Marcillac has been unspeakably kind in this affair; she even understood and sympathized with what you said of your gloves. 'But, then,' as she said laughing, 'I have always had a soft spot in my heart for the eldest son.' My Eugène, be grateful to your aunt. I will not tell you what she has done for you until you have succeeded; if I did, the money might scorch your fingers. Ah! you children little know what a pang it is to part with souvenirs; but what would we not do for you! She begs me to say that she sends a kiss, and wishes her kiss could give you strength to prosper. Dear, good woman! she would have written herself but she has gout in her fingers. Your father is well. The grape harvest of 1819 proves better than we expected. Good-by, my dear boy. I say nothing about the sisters, for Laure is writing to you. I leave her the pleasure of telling all the little gossip of the family. Heaven grant you may do well! Ah, prosper, my Eugène! Thou hast made me too anxious – I could not

> bear it a second time. I know at last what it is to be poor, and to long for money that I might give it to my child.
>
> Well! – adieu. Write to us constantly; and take the kiss thy mother sends thee.

When Eugène had read this letter he was in tears. He was thinking of Père Goriot destroying his porringer and selling it to pay his daughter's note of hand. 'My mother has given her jewels,' he cried, turning fiercely on himself. 'My aunt must have wept as she sold her family relics. What right have I to condemn Anastasie? I have done for self what she did for her lover! Which is the worst – she or I?' His whole being was wrung with intolerable remorse. He would relinquish his ambition – he would not touch the money. He was seized by one of those noble secret returns of conscience so little comprehended by men as they judge their fellows; so often, we may believe, taken into the great account when the angels receive the sinners condemned by the justice of the world. Rastignac opened his sister's letter, and its innocent, tender trustfulness fell like balm upon his spirit—

> Your letter came just at the right moment, dear brother. Agathe and I had debated so long what to do with our money, and we had thought of so many ways of spending it, that we could not decide upon anything. You are like the servant of the King of Spain when he threw down all his master's watches – you have made us agree. Really and truly, we were always disputing which of our fancies we should follow; but, dear Eugène, we never thought of this, which exactly suits us both. Agathe jumped for joy. In fact, we were all day in such high spirits 'on sufficient grounds' (aunt's style) that mamma put on her severe manner and said,

'Young ladies, what is the matter with you?' If she had scolded us a little bit, I do believe it would have made us happier still. Surely women must enjoy making sacrifices for those they love. But I was sad in the midst of my joy. I am afraid I shall make a bad wife, I am so extravagant. I had just bought myself two sashes, and a stiletto to punch eyelets in my corsets – mere foolishness! – and so I had less money than that fat Agathe, who is economical and hoards her five-franc pieces like a magpie. She had two hundred francs; while I, O dear Eugène, had only a hundred and fifty! I was well punished for my extravagance. I wanted to fling my sash into the well. I know I shall never have any pleasure in wearing it; I shall feel as if I had stolen it from you. Agathe was so kind: she said, 'Let us send the three hundred and fifty all together.' But I feel as if I must tell you just how it was. Do you want to know how we managed so as not to let any one suspect what we were doing? – as you said we must keep the secret. We took our precious money and went out for a walk. When we got to the high-road we ran as fast as we could to Ruffec. There we gave all the money to Monsieur Grimbert at the Messageries-Royales coach office. We flew home like swallows – so fast because we were so light-hearted, Agathe said. We said lots of things to each other which I should not like to repeat to you, Monsieur le Parisien. They were *all about you*. Oh! dear brother, we love you – there! it is all in those three words.

As for keeping the secret, naughty little girls, as aunt calls us, can do anything – even keep silent! Mamma went to Angouleme mysteriously with aunt the other day, and they would not tell us a word about the high and mighty purposes of the expedition. They have held long private conferences; but we are sent out of the room, and even Monsieur le baron is not admitted. Great affairs occupy all minds in the kingdom of Rastignac. The muslin dress, embroidered in satin-stitch by the infantas for the queen, her majesty, is getting on, though they can only work at it in the utmost secrecy. There are now only two breadths to finish. It has been decided to build no wall toward Verteuil; there is to be a hedge. This will deprive the natives of wall-fruit, but offers a fine view to foreigners. If the heir-presumptive wants any handkerchiefs, he is hereby informed that the dowager-countess de Marcillac, turning over the treasures in her trunks (excavations in Herculaneum and Pompeii), came upon a lovely piece of linen cambric, which she did not know she had. The princesses Laure and Agathe put their thread, needles, and fingers – the latter, alas! a little too red – at his highness's orders. The two young princes, Don Henri and Don Gabriel, keep at their old tricks, gorging themselves with grapes, worrying their sisters, learning nothing, bird's-nesting, making a racket, and cutting, in defiance of the laws of the State, willow twigs for switches. The Pope's nuncio, commonly called Monsieur le curé, threatens to excommunicate them if the sacred canons of grammar are neglected for popguns.

Adieu, dear brother. Never did a letter carry deeper wishes for your happiness, nor so much grateful love. How many things you will have to tell us when you come home! You will tell me all, I know – I am the eldest. Aunt threw out a mysterious hint of success in the great world—

'A lady's name she whispered – but, hush! for all the rest,' a word to the wise, you know – we understand each other!

Tell me, Eugène, would you like shirts instead of handkerchiefs? We can make them for you. Answer this at *once*. If you want some fine shirts, very nicely made, we must set to work immediately. And if there are any new ways of making them in Paris which we do not know here, send us a pattern – particularly for the cuffs. Adieu, adieu. I kiss you over your left eyebrow, for that spot belongs exclusively to me. I leave the other page for Agathe, who has promised not to look at what I have written; but to make sure, I shall stay behind her till she has finished.

Thy sister who loves thee,
LAURE DE RASTIGNAC.

'Oh, yes!' cried Eugène: 'yes! – fortune at any price! No treasures could repay them for their devotion. I will shower upon them every happiness. Fifteen hundred francs!' he added, after a pause. 'Every five-franc piece must do its work. Laure is right; my shirts are all too coarse. A young girl becomes as cunning as a thief when she plans for others. Innocent herself, far-sighted for me! She is like the angels, who forgive the human faults they cannot share.'

The world was all before him! Already a tailor had been called, sounded, and selected. When Eugène first beheld Monsieur de Trailles, he became conscious of the enormous influence tailors exert over the lives of young men. A man's tailor must be either his mortal enemy or his trusted friend. Eugène's choice fell upon a man who took a fatherly position towards his patrons, and considered himself a link between the present and the future of young men who aspired to get on in the world. Rastignac showed his gratitude, and made the man's fortune by one of those clever sayings for which he became celebrated in after years. 'I have known him make two pairs of trousers which made two marriages of forty thousand francs a year,' he said.

IX

Fifteen hundred francs and all the clothes he needed! Our ardent son of the south flung his hesitations to the wind, and went down to breakfast with that indefinable air which a youth puts on when he is conscious of possessing money. The moment that a student jingles coin in his pocket he feels that he is leaning on a pillar of strength. His step becomes assured; his lever has a fulcrum to work on; he looks ahead; he sees his way; his very movements grow alert. Yesterday, timid and despondent, he could hardly resent an injury; to-day he is ready to offer one to the chief of state. A curious transformation is at work within him. He wants all things, feels himself capable of all things; his desires rush forth at random; he is gay, generous and open-hearted – the fledgling has found his wings. As a penniless student he had been content to snatch a scrap of pleasure as a dog steals a bone, cracks it, sucks the marrow furtively, and runs away. But the young man who rattles money in his breeches pocket can afford to linger over his enjoyments; he can suck their juice at leisure; he floats in summer air; for him the harsh word *poverty* no longer has a meaning – all Paris belongs to him. In youth how these things glitter! how they sparkle and flame! Age of glad strength, by which few profit, either men or women; age of debts and anxieties which enhance the joys! He who has never haunted the left bank of the Seine between the Rue Saint-Jacques and the Rue des Saint-Peres knows little of the comedy, or the tragedy, of human life.

'Ah! if the women of Paris did but know!' thought Eugène, as he devoured Madame Vauquer's baked pears at a farthing apiece, 'they would want me to love them.'

At this moment a messenger from the Messageries-Royales came into the dining-room, having rung at the gate-bell. He asked for Monsieur Eugène de Rastignac, for whom he brought two bags of silver coin and the register for signature.

Vautrin threw a glance round Rastignac as keen and sharp as the lash of a whip.

'You will be able to pay for your fencing lessons,' he said, 'and your pistols too.'

'The galleons have come in,' said Madame Vauquer, glancing at the bags.

Mademoiselle Michonneau dared not cast her eyes at them, fearing to show her covetousness.

'You have a good mother,' said Madame Couture.

'Monsieur has a good mother,' repeated Poiret.

'Oh, yes! Mamma has bled herself,' said Vautrin, 'and now you may take your fling if you like; go into the world and fish for *dots*, or dance with countesses and peach-blossoms. But take my advice, young man – stick to the pistol-gallery.'

Vautrin put himself in the attitude of taking aim at an adversary. Rastignac felt in his pocket for a *pour-boire* to the messenger, but found nothing; Vautrin put his hand in his, and flung the man a franc.

'Your credit is good,' he observed, looking at the student.

Rastignac was forced to thank him, although since the sharp words they had exchanged after his first visit to Madame de Beauséant the man had become intolerable to him. For a week Eugène and Vautrin had not spoken, and each had silently watched the other. The student in vain asked himself the reason. There is no doubt that ideas strike with a force proportionate to the vigour of their conception; they hit the mark at which they are aimed by some such mathematical law as that which guides the shell when it leaves the mouth of the cannon. The effects are various. There are tender natures which ideas penetrate and blast to ashes; there are vigorous natures, skulls of iron, from which the thoughts and wills of other men glance off like bullets flattened as they strike a wall; others, again, are soft and cottony, and into them ideas sink dead, like cannon-balls that bury themselves in the earth-works of a fortification.

Rastignac's nature was a powder-flask ready to explode at a touch. He had too much youthful vitality not to be open to this imposition of ideas – this magnetism of mind upon mind, whose capricious phenomena affect us on all sides without our being aware of it. His moral perceptions were as clear as his eyes, keen as those of a lynx. Mentally and physically he had that mysterious power to take and give impressions at which we marvel in men of superior calibre: skilful swordsmen quick to know the weak places in every breastplate. During the past month Eugène's finer qualities had developed in common with his defects.

His defects were nourished by his entrance into the great world, and by some slight accomplishment of his ambitious dreams. Among his finer qualities may be counted that southern vivacity of spirit which compels a man to go straight at a difficulty and master it, and will not suffer him to be baffled by uncertainty. This quality northern people regard as a defect. To their minds, if it was the cause of Murat's rise, it was also the cause of his death: from which we may conclude that when a man unites the trickery of the north to the audacity of the region south of the Loire, he has reached perfection and may aspire to be king of Sweden. Rastignac could not, therefore, long remain passive under Vautrin's fire without making up his mind whether the man was his friend or his enemy. From time to time he was certain that this strange being penetrated his motives, divined his passions, and read his heart; holding guard at the same time over his own secrets with the impassiveness of the sphinx who sees and knows all, and reveals nothing. His pockets being now full of money, Eugène mutinied.

'Do me the favour to wait,' he said to Vautrin, who had risen to leave the room after drinking the last drops of his coffee.

'Why?' asked the latter, putting on his broad-brimmed hat, and picking up his cane. This cane was loaded with iron, and he was fond of twirling it about his head with the air of a man who thought himself a match for half-a-dozen robbers.

'I wish to return your money,' replied Rastignac, unfastening one of his bags and counting out a hundred and forty francs for Madame Vauquer. 'Short accounts make long friends,' he said to the widow. 'Now I have paid up to the last day of December. Can you change me this five-franc piece?'

'Long friends make short accounts,' echoed Poiret, looking at Vautrin.

'Here are your twenty *sous*,' said Rastignac, holding out a franc to the sphinx in a wig.

'One would think you were afraid to owe me anything,' cried Vautrin, plunging his divining glance into the very soul of the young man, and giving him one of those mocking Diogenistic smiles which Eugène had again and again been on the point of resenting.

'Well – yes,' said the student, lifting his bags and preparing to go upstairs.

Vautrin went out of the door that led into the *salon*; the student passed through that leading to the staircase.

'Do you know, Monsieur le Marquis de Rastignacorama, that what you said to me just now was not exactly polite?' said Vautrin, coming through the door leading from the *salon* into the passage, and speaking to the student, who looked at him coolly.

Rastignac shut the dining-room door, and drew Vautrin to the foot of the staircase, in the little square space that separated the dining-room from the kitchen. In this passage there was a glass door opening upon the garden, the glass of which was protected by iron bars. There the student said, before Sylvie, who was coming out of her kitchen—

'*Monsieur* Vautrin, I am not a marquis, and my name is not Rastignacorama.'

'They are going to fight,' said Mademoiselle Michonneau in a tone of indifference.

'Fight a duel,' repeated Poiret.

'Oh, no,' said Madame Vauquer, fingering her pile of five-franc pieces.

'Oh, see! They have gone down under the lindens,' cried Mademoiselle Victorine, getting up and looking into the garden. 'And he was in the right – that poor young man!'

'Let us go to our rooms, my dearest,' said Madame Couture, 'these things do not concern us.'

As Madame Couture and Victorine turned to leave the room they met Sylvie in the doorway, who barred their passage.

'What's the matter?' she cried. 'Monsieur Vautrin said to Monsieur Eugène, "Let us have an explanation," and he took him by the arm, and there they are, trampling down our artichokes.'

At this moment Vautrin re-appeared. 'Madame Vauquer,' he said, smiling, 'don't be afraid; I am going to try my pistols under the trees yonder.'

'Oh! Monsieur,' cried Victorine, clasping her hands, 'why do you wish to kill Monsieur Eugène?'

Vautrin made a step backward and looked at her.

'Oh! ho! – a new story,' he cried, with an amused air which brought a blush to her pale cheek. 'He is very nice, isn't he? A charming young man! You have given me an idea. I'll make you both happy, my little girl.'

Madame Couture had taken her charge by the arm and now drew her away hastily, saying in an undertone, 'Victorine! what has come over you to-day?'

'I beg you will fire no pistols in my garden,' said Madame Vauquer. 'Don't go and frighten the whole neighbourhood, and bring the police upon us.'

'Oh, keep calm, Mamma Vauquer,' replied Vautrin. 'There, there – it's all right. We will go to the pistol-gallery.'

He went back to Rastignac and took him familiarly by the arm: 'If I prove to you that at thirty-six paces I can put a bullet five times through the ace of spades, it won't take away your courage. You look to me like a man who would balk at nothing when his blood was up, and get himself killed as soon as not – like a simpleton.'

'You wish to back out of it,' said Eugène.

'Don't provoke me,' replied Vautrin. 'Come and sit down yonder,' he added, pointing to the benches painted green; 'it is not cold, and nobody can overhear us there. You are a good fellow, to whom I wish no harm. I like you, on the honour of Tromp – thunder! – honour of Vautrin; and I'll tell you why I like you. In the first place, I know you inside and out, just as well as if I had made you; and I will prove it to you. Put your bags down there,' he added, pointing to the round table.

Rastignac put his money on the table and sat down, devoured by curiosity as to this sudden change in a man who having just proposed to kill him, now assumed to be his protector.

'You want to know who I am, what I have done, and what I am doing,' resumed Vautrin. 'You are too inquisitive, young man – stop, stop! be calm! you have more of that to hear. I have had misfortunes. Listen to me first; you can talk afterwards. Here is my past life in three words: Who am I? Vautrin. – What do I do? Just what I please – Pass on. Do you want to know my character? Good to those who are good to me; whose heart answers to mine. From them I'll take anything. They may kick me on the shins if they like, I won't even say, "Take care!" But, *nom d'une pipe*, I'm as wicked as the devil to those who annoy me, or those I don't like. It is as well to let you know at once that I don't mind killing a man any more than – that! [spitting before him.] Only, I endeavour to kill him properly, and when it can't be helped. I am what you may call an artist. I have read the memoirs of Benvenuto Cellini – and read them in Italian too, which may surprise you. I learned from that man – bold, determined fellow that he was! – to imitate the ways of Providence, who kills at random, and to love the beautiful wherever I see it. And, after all, isn't it a fine thing to stand single-handed against the world, with the luck on our side?

'I have reflected deeply on the forces that govern your social order – or disorder. My lad, duels are child's play – absurdities. When in the course of human events one of two living men has to disappear, they must be idiots to leave anything to chance. A duel! heads or tails! – that's what it is. I can put five balls running through the same hole in the ace of spades – and at thirty-six paces, to boot. When any one is gifted with that little talent, he might be supposed to be certain of killing his man. Well, for all that, I've fired at a man at twenty paces, and missed him; and the scoundrel had never pulled a trigger in his life! See,' he continued, opening his shirt and showing a breast as shaggy as a bear's back, with long hair like the mane of a wild animal, which caused a sickening sensation of fear and repulsion; 'that greenhorn scorched me,' he added, catching Rastignac's hand and putting his finger into the scar.

'But in those days I was a youngster; only twenty-one – just your age; and I still believed in something – woman's love, for instance, and a heap of nonsense into which you are just plunging. We might have fought, and you might have killed me, just now. Suppose I was underground, where would you be? Obliged to fly to Switzerland and live on papa's money – only he hasn't got any. Now, I am going to put before you the position in which you stand; and I shall do it with the authority of a man who has looked into things in this lower world, and knows that there are but two paths open to us – blind obedience or revolt. I don't obey – take that for granted. Now, do you know what you need, at the pace you are going? A million of francs, *immediately*. If you don't get them, with your excitable temperament you'll be wandering with your feet in the nets at Saint-Cloud and your head in the air looking for the Supreme Being, before long. I'll give you your million.'

He paused and looked at Eugène.

'Ha, ha! We are getting friendly to Papa Vautrin. When he offers us a million, we are like a young girl to whom the lover says, "To-night," and she begins to prink like a little cat licking her fur when she has lapped her milk. All right! Well, then, between ourselves, this is how it is with you, young man. Down yonder in the country there's papa and mamma, and our great-aunt, and two sisters (seventeen and eighteen years of age), and two little brothers (ten and fifteen). There's the whole ship's company. The aunt teaches the sisters, the curé imparts Latin to the boys. The family eat more boiled chestnuts than wheat bread; papa tries not to wear out his breeches; mamma can hardly buy herself a new gown summer or winter; the sisters get along as they can. I know it all – I've lived in the south of France. Somehow they manage to send you twelve hundred francs a year, though the property only brings in three thousand. We keep a cook and a man-servant for the sake of appearances: papa is a baron, you know. As for ourself, we are ambitious. We have the Beauséants for allies; but we have to go afoot, which does not please us. We want a fortune, and we haven't a *sou*. We eat Mamma Vauquer's messes, but we long for the feasts in the Faubourg Saint-Germain. We sleep on a pallet, but we dream of a mansion. I don't blame you. You are ambitious. It is not every one, my brave boy, who is blessed with ambition. Ask women what sort of men they like best – ambitious men. Their blood has more iron in it, their hearts are warmer.

'I've summed up your wants as a preface to a question. Here it is. We are as hungry as a wolf; our milk-teeth are very sharp; how are we going to fill the pot? Shall we stay our appetite on law? Studying law is dull work; and, besides, it teaches nothing. However, call it the best we can do – for we must do something. So be it, then. Well, we graduate; and by and by we get an appointment as judge in some petty criminal court, and send off poor devils better than ourselves with *T F* branded on their shoulders, that rich men may sleep in peace. Small fun in that! and besides, it is long in coming. In the first place, two years of weary waiting – looking at the sugarplums we long for, but *cannot have*. It is hard to be always craving, never getting what we want. If you were a poor, pale mollusc of a man, there would be nothing to fear; but, no! we have the blood of a lion in our veins, and the capacity for committing twenty follies a day. You will never bear the trial; you will sink under it; it is the worst torture that we have yet heard of in the hell of a good God. But suppose you are irreproachable – that you drink milk and write hymns. After all your privations – enough to drive a dog mad, not to speak of a generous young fellow like you – you will have to begin by taking another man's place in some hole of a town where the Government will pay you a thousand francs a year, just as they fling a bone to the watch-dog. Bark at the robbers, win the cause of the rich, and send to the guillotine men of heart and pluck? – No, thank you! If you have no one to push your fortunes, you will rot in your petty judgeship. When you are thirty you will be promoted to twelve hundred francs per annum – unless by that time you have flung your gown to the nettles. At forty you will marry a miller's daughter, with six thousand francs a year for her portion.

'To all this you say, Never! Well, if you have influence you may possibly at thirty get to be *procureur du roi* [prosecuting attorney], with five thousand francs a year, and marry the mayor's daughter. If you have the luck to do any little meanness for the Government – such as reading the name of Villèle from the register, instead of Manuel – you may at forty become *procureur-général*, and rise to be a deputy. But take notice, my young friend, that by this time we shall have torn some big rents in our conscience; we shall have had twenty years of weary waiting and bitter poverty, and by that time the sisters *auront coiffé Saint-Cathérine* [will have turned into old maids]. I have also the honour to point out to you that there are only twenty *procureurs-généraux* in France; and that twenty thousand young aspirants are standing in line, among whom you will find fellows who would sell their own families to advance a step.

'If this prospect seems unpleasant, let us turn to something else. Would the Baron de Rastignac like to become an *avocat* – a barrister? Delightful! In that case he will earn nothing for ten years, spend a thousand francs a month, need a law-library and an office, kiss the robe of an attorney to get briefs, and lick up the law courts with his tongue. If all this would lead to anything it might be very well. But find me six barristers in Paris who at fifty years of age earn fifty thousand francs a year. Bah! sooner than belittle my soul like that I'd take to piracy. Well, then, how else can we make money? These prospects are certainly not brilliant. There's another resource; and that's a wife's fortune. But if you marry, you tie a stone round your neck for life; and if you marry for money, what becomes of our fine sentiments about *noblesse* and honour? You might as well not put off your revolt against the conventional ideas of humanity. To make such a marriage you would have to wriggle like a snake at some woman's feet, and lick her mother's shoes, and humiliate yourself to things that would disgust a pig – pah! And, after all, you needn't expect happiness. You would wear out like the stones of a drain through continual dropping, if you married a wife in this way. Better fight with men than try your strength against a woman.

Here you are, young man, at the cross-roads of your life. Choose your path. You have chosen? You have been to see our cousin de Beauséant, and you have breathed the atmosphere of luxury. You have been to visit Madame de Restaud, daughter of Père Goriot, and you have scented the *Parisienne*. You came home from those visits with a word written on your forehead. I read it – it was *success*! – success at any price. Bravo! I said, that's the fellow to suit *me*. You wanted money. You cast about to see how you might get it. You bled your sisters: all brothers sponge more or less upon their sisters. And now that you have got your fifteen hundred francs, squeezed – Heaven knows how! – out of a land where chestnuts are more plentiful than five-franc pieces, you will find them disappear like soldiers on a forage.

'What next? Will you set to work again? The sort of work that you call work at present leads in old age to a bed-room in a *pension* like Madame Vauquer's, fit for chaps like Poiret. At this very moment fifty thousand young men, situated just as you are, are revolving in their minds how to make a rapid fortune. You are a unit among fifty thousand. Make your estimate of the chances and the fierceness of the fight before you. The fifty thousand will have to eat each other up, like spiders in a jug; for of course there are not fifty thousand good positions – one apiece all round! Do you know how to win a first place in the struggle? I will tell you. By the highest genius, or the lowest corruption. You must either rend a way for yourself through the crowd like a cannon-ball, or you must creep through it silently like a pestilence. Honesty and uprightness won't help you. People bend beneath the power of genius, but they hate it. Genius is calumniated because it takes what it can get and never shares its takings; but the world bows before its strength. In other words, the world worships on its knees those whom it cannot smother in the mud. Corruption is also strength. Genius is rare. It follows that corruption is the resource of the great commonplace majority; and you will find it everywhere. You will see women whose husbands' pay is six thousand francs at most, spending ten thousand upon their *toilettes*. You will see employees who have a salary of twelve hundred francs acquiring landed property. You will see women prostituting themselves to drive to Longchamps in the carriage of the son of a peer of France which has a right to the middle highway. You have seen that poor fool of a Père Goriot obliged to pay the note endorsed by his daughter, whose husband has sixty thousand francs per annum. I defy you to walk two steps in Paris without stumbling on some infernal perfidy. I'd bet my head to one of those old salad stumps that you will stick your nose into a wasp's-nest the first time you fall in love with any woman, no matter how wealthy, or young or handsome she may be. All women of fashion walk in crooked ways; all are at variance with their husbands. If I were to tell you what things are done for lovers and for frippery, for children and for show, and above all for vanity, I should never have done. Not much that is virtuous you may be sure. An honest man is deemed a common enemy. But where can we find an honest man? In Paris, honour and honesty consist in refusing to go shares, and holding one's tongue. I am not speaking now of those poor Helots who stick to honesty and virtue without expecting any recompense for their labours in this world – the Brotherhood of the Old Shoes of the Good Lord, I call them. Of course they are the flower of virtuous foolishness, but they are always poor. I can imagine the blank faces of that saintly crowd if Heaven were to play us such a joke as to omit the Day of Judgement.

'Now, it follows that if you wish to get on quickly you must either be rich or make believe to be so. To grow rich you must play a strong game – not a trumpery cautious one; no! no! If in the hundred professions a man can choose from he makes a rapid fortune, the world says he must have done it dishonestly. Draw your own conclusions. Such is life. It is no better than a kitchen full of bad smells. If you have fish to fry, you must soil your hands in frying them; only be sure to wash them when you have done your cookery. That is the moral of the times we live in. I own that in speaking to you thus I know myself to have wrongs to avenge upon society. Do you think I blame it for its enmity to me? Not at all; it is natural. Moralists will make no radical changes, depend upon it, in the morality of the great world. Human nature is imperfect. Every man is a hypocrite, and according as he is more or less of one fools will cry out that he is better or worse. I don't say that the rich are any worse than the poor. Man is the same at the top or at the bottom or in the middle of society. You'll find ten bold fellows in every million of such cattle who dare to set things at defiance – including your laws. I am one of them. If you feel yourself to be a man superior to other men, you may walk a straight line possibly and hold your head high. But you will have to struggle with envy, calumny and mediocrity, in short, against the world. Napoleon came near being sent off to the colonies by a minister of war named Aubry. Put yourself to the proof – see if you can get up every morning with more energy than you felt the day before. There's a test.

'Now, in view of all these circumstances, I am going to make you a proposition that I think no man in your position should refuse. Listen! I myself cherish an ideal. My ideal existence is that of a patriarch dwelling upon a vast estate – say a hundred thousand acres – in one of the Southern States of North America. I should like to be a planter, to own slaves, and amass a few millions by selling my cattle, my tobacco and timber. There, living like a king, with every creature round me subject to my will, I should lead a sort of life not conceived of in this country, where people crowd themselves in streets of stucco. I am a poet – only my poems are not made in verse; they have their rise in sentiment, and I turn them into action. I possess at this moment about fifty thousand francs, which would barely buy me forty negroes. I want two hundred thousand francs, because I need two hundred negroes to carry out my dreams of patriarchal existence. You see, negroes are ready-made children; you may do whatever you please with them, without any inquisitive *procureur du roi* pouncing down upon you with questions. With this black capital, in ten years I should make three or four millions. If I succeed, no man will ask "Who are you?" I shall be Monsieur Quatre-Millions, citizen of the United States. I shall be fifty by that time – still in my prime, and eager to amuse myself. In two words – if I get you a *dot* of a million, will you give me two hundred thousand francs? Twenty per cent commission – *hein*? – is that too dear? You will win the affection of your little wife. When you have been married a few weeks you can let her see that you have something on your mind; you can seem disquieted, uneasy. Then, some night, between two kisses, you can own that you are in debt – two hundred thousand francs – in debt, darling! This farce is acted every day, by young men of good family. No young wife will refuse her money to the man she loves. Do you think you will be the poorer? Not at all. You can easily get back your two hundred thousand francs in a good speculation. With your money and your enterprise, you will make as large a fortune as heart could wish. *Ergo*, in six months I shall have made your happiness and that of a sweet little wife. And happiest of all will be Papa Vautrin; to say nothing of your own family, who are now blowing their fingers to keep warm, for lack of fire-wood. You need not be astonished at what I offer, nor at what I ask. Out of sixty good matches made in Paris, forty-seven owe their origin to a similar understanding. The Chambre des Notaires obliged Monsieur—'

'But what is there to be done on my part?' asked Eugène, eagerly interrupting Vautrin.

'Almost nothing,' replied the other, letting a sound escape him like the click of satisfaction given by an angler when he feels the fish at the end of his line. 'Listen. The heart of a young girl used to neglect and poverty is a sponge ready to absorb any affection offered to her – a dry sponge, which begins to swell as soon as a drop of love falls upon it. To make love to a young girl under such circumstances – a poor, lonely, and dispirited girl, a girl who knows nothing of the prospect of great wealth that is in store for her – damn it! it is like holding *quinte* and *quatorze* at piquet; it is like putting into a lottery when you know the numbers; it is like buying into the funds when you've found out the secrets of diplomacy. You are building on a sure foundation. If the young girl inherits millions, she will pour them at your feet as if they were pebble-stones. She will say, "Ah! take them, dearest!" Take them, Alfred, Adolphe, Eugène! – especially if Adolphe, Alfred or Eugène have had the sense to make sacrifices for her. By *sacrifices* I mean such as selling an old coat that he and she may go together to the Cadran-Bleu and eat mushroom toast, or to the Ambigu-Comique – or else pawning your watch to buy her a new shawl. I say nothing about love-scribbling, and all the stuff and nonsense women make so much of – such as sprinkling water on your letter to make it look like tears, when you are parted from her. I fancy you know all that *argot* of the heart well enough already. Paris is like a forest peopled by twenty different tribes of red Indians – Iroquois, Hurons and the like – who all live by hunting the prosperous classes. You are bent on bagging millions. Your trapping will require snares, decoys and bird-lime. There are many ways of going after that kind of game. Some hunt for *dots*; others grow rich by bankruptcy; others angle for consciences, and sell their victims bound hand and foot. He who comes home with a good bag is congratulated, fêted, and received in good society. Let us do justice to the hospitality of Paris; it is the easiest city to get on in in the world. Though the proud aristocracy of every other capital in Europe may decline to countenance a rascally millionaire, Paris will open her arms to him, rush to his parties, eat his dinners, and hob-nob with him and his infamy.'

'But where can I find such a girl?' said Eugène.
'She is here; close at hand.'
'Mademoiselle Victorine?'
'Precisely.'
'But how can that be?'
'She loves you already – your little Baronne de Rastignac.'
'She has not a *sou*!' cried Eugène in amazement.

'Ah! now we are coming to the point. Two words more,' said Vautrin, 'and then you will understand me. Papa Taillefer is an old rascal, who is said to have murdered his best friend during the Revolution. He is one of those fellows I spoke of, who are not tied down by scruples or conventionalities. He is a banker – head of the house of Frédéric Taillefer & Co. He has one son, to whom he intends to leave his whole fortune and disinherit Victorine. I object to such injustice. I am like Don Quixote – I delight in taking the part of the weak against the strong. If it pleased a wise Providence to kill his son, old Taillefer would take back his daughter. He would want some kind of an heir, for that is a folly common to human nature; and he won't have any more children, I know. Victorine is pretty and amiable; she will soon work her way into his favour, and spin him round like a whipping top; her whip will be the liking he will take for her. She will be too grateful to you for loving her when she was poor to throw you over when she is rich, and you will marry her. Well, I take upon myself the duty of a wise Providence – I will play the part of Destiny. I have a friend for whom I have done much, very much – a colonel in the army of the Loire, who has lately come to Paris to enter the Garde Royale. He has taken my advice and become an ultra-royalist: he is not one of those fools who stick to their opinions. I may as well give you another bit of advice, my friend. Don't keep your opinions any more than your promises. When people need them, sell them. When a man boasts that he holds fast to one opinion, he pledges himself to walk a straight line, and is one of those ninnies who believe in infallibility. There are no such things as principles – there are events. Neither are there laws – only circumstances. A wise man grasps circumstances and events, and guides them. If there were essential principles or fundamental laws, the populations could not change them, as they now change them, like a shirt. A man is not bound to be wiser than his generation. The man of all others whose political career has been of least service to France is now an ancient fetich, adored because he was a red republican. He is good for nothing, now, but to be shelved in a Museum and ticketed *La Fayette*; while Talleyrand, at whom everybody casts a stone, and who despises mankind so utterly that he will spit back into the world's face any promises it may require of him, hindered the dismemberment of France at the Congress of Vienna. He ought to be honoured with crowns; but the world flings mud at him. Oh, I know how things work! I have many a man's secret in my keeping. Enough of this. I shall begin to hold fixed opinions on the day when I find any three men agreeing on the practical application of a principle. I expect to wait a good while. You can't find three judges in accord on a question of law. To come back to my man. He would sell his soul – it belongs to me – if I asked him. If Papa Vautrin speaks the word, he will pick a quarrel with that young blackguard who never sends a five-franc piece to his poor sister, and then—'

Here Vautrin rose, put himself on guard, and made a pass as if with a sword – 'To the shades!' he added.

'Monstrous!' cried Eugène; 'you must be joking, Monsieur Vautrin.'

'There, there, keep calm!' replied the other, 'don't be a baby. Still, if it will do you any good, get angry, furious; tell me I am a wretch, a villain, a scoundrel, a robber – anything you like, except cheat or spy. Go on; speak; fire your broadside – I'll forgive you. It is natural at your age; I did the same in my time, even I. But remember *this* – you will do worse than that some day. You will win some pretty woman and accept her money. You have thought of it already,' said Vautrin; 'how else do you expect to succeed if you don't turn her to advantage? Virtue, my dear student, is not a thing you can have by halves. It is – or it is not. We are told to repent of our sins. Another pretty system, that lets a man get rid of his crimes by a mere act of contrition! To plan a woman's infamy that you may mount the social ladder; to put a strain of illegitimacy among the children; to be guilty of cruelties and wrongs for your own pleasure and advantage – are those what you call works of faith, hope and charity? Why should a man of fashion be lightly dealt with for defrauding the rightful heir of half his fortune, while the poor devil who steals a thousand-franc note goes to the galleys? But such is law. Every enactment may be stretched to an absurdity. Between what I propose to you and what you will do some day there is no difference. You believe that there are certain principles as fixed as Fate in this world. Study men, and see how many loop-holes there are through which they set laws and principles at defiance. The secret of a great fortune made without apparent cause is soon forgotten, if the crime is committed in a respectable way.'

'Silence, Monsieur! I will hear no more. You will make me doubt myself – and my only guide is the instinct of my own heart.'

'As you please, *bel enfant*! I thought you stronger than I find you,' said Vautrin. 'I will say no more – yes, a last word.' He looked steadily at the student, 'You have my secret,' he said.

'A young man who declines your offer will know how to forget it.'

'That is well said; I am glad you have said it. Some one, you know, may be less scrupulous. Think over what I have wished to do for you. I will give you two weeks. Take my offer or leave it – as you will.'

'Man of iron!' thought Rastignac, as he watched Vautrin walk leisurely away with his cane under his arm. 'He told me bluntly what Madame de Beauséant said in more ambiguous words. He has torn my heart with his steel claws. Why am I going to Madame de Nucingen's? He guessed my motives – guessed them as soon as I conceived them. This brigand has told me in two words more about virtue than books or men have ever taught me. If there is no compromise with virtue, then I have robbed my sisters,' he cried, pushing the money-bags away from him and sitting down at the table. His thoughts bewildered him. 'To be faithful to virtue,' he said to himself, 'is it to suffer martyrdom? Bah! every one believes in virtue, but who is virtuous? Nations take liberty for their idol, but is there upon earth one nation free? My youth is still unsullied as the blue of heaven. If I resolve to be rich and great, must I bring myself to stooping, lying, grovelling, threatening, flattering, deceiving? Shall I make myself the lacquey of those who lie and crawl and deceive? Before I become their accomplice shall I be forced to do them service? No! I will not! I will toil nobly in the fear of God; I will labour night and day. I will owe my fortune to myself, and myself only. It may be slow in coming, but each night I shall lay my head upon my pillow without a shameful thought. What can be more blessed than to look back upon one's life, and see it pure and stainless as a lily? My life and I are like a bride and her lover – Ah! Vautrin showed me what comes to pass after ten years of marriage. God! My head swims – I will not reason; the heart is my true guide—'

X

Eugène was awakened from his reverie by the voice of Sylvie announcing the arrival of his tailor. He went in to meet him, carrying his bags of money, a trifling circumstance which gave him pleasure. After trying on his evening suit, he put on the morning one which transformed him completely. 'I am quite up to Monsieur de Trailles,' he said to himself complacently. 'At last I look like a gentleman.'

'Monsieur,' said Père Goriot, coming into Eugène's chamber, 'you asked me if I knew to whose house Madame de Nucingen was going.'

'Yes.'

'Well, next Monday she is going to a ball at the Maréchale Carigliano's. If you are there you will tell me how my daughters enjoyed themselves, how they were dressed, and all about them?'

'How did you find it out, my good Père Goriot?' said Eugène, making him sit down by the fire.

'Her maid told me. I know all they do through Thérèse and Constance,' he said gleefully. The old man was like a lover, still boyish enough to be delighted with a stratagem which put him in communication with the object of his adoration without her knowing it.

'And you will be there to see them!' he said in a tone of mixed envy and suffering.

'I don't know yet,' replied Eugène. 'I am going to call on Madame de Beauséant, and I shall ask her to introduce me to the Maréchale.' He was thinking with inward joy of showing himself to the viscountess in his new clothes, and looking as he intended to look for the rest of his days. What moralists call great crises in the human heart are commonly the offspring of deceptive and involuntary movements of self-interest. Sudden changes of purpose hard to understand, unaccountable reversals of a first desire, spring generally from some calculation in favour of self-indulgence. When Rastignac beheld himself well dressed, well gloved, well booted, he forgot his virtuous resolutions. The young dare not look at themselves in the glass of conscience when it reveals them as they should be and not as they would be; older men have the nerve to see themselves reflected undisguised. In this lies the difference between the ages.

For some days past Eugène and Père Goriot had become close friends. Their intimacy had its origin in the same psychological mystery which produced the opposite effect upon the student in his relations with Vautrin. The bold philosopher who seeks to show the influence of mind upon our material being may obtain many a proof by observing the relations between man and animals. What physiognomist is so quick to discern character as a dog is to know whether a stranger likes or dislikes him? *Les atomes crochus* (elective affinities) is an expression which has passed into a proverb, and contains one of those facts permanently embedded in language as a protest against the stupidity of those who make it their business to winnow out of our speech its primitive words.[4] We *feel* ourselves beloved. The feeling stamps itself on everything, and ignores space. A letter holds beneath its seal a human soul. It is so faithful an echo of the voice that speaks too far away for us to hear, that the heart prizes written words

---

[4] Atomes crochus *(hooked atoms) – atoms supposed to be hooked, according to the system of Democritus and Epicurus, so that they catch and hold each other when they meet. –* Littré.

as among the richest treasures in the gift of love. Père Goriot, raised by his instinctive sentiment to the sublimest heights attainable by canine nature, had guessed intuitively the compassion, the friendly admiration and the fresh young sympathy which moved the heart of the student towards him. But this understanding had as yet led to no confidence between them. Though Eugène had expressed a wish to see Madame de Nucingen, it was not because he expected to be introduced to her by her father; he merely hoped that through him something might turn up to aid his plans. Père Goriot had said nothing to him about his daughters, except in connection with what had passed in public on the day of his visit to the countess.

'My dear Monsieur,' the old man had remarked the next morning, 'how could you think that Madame de Restaud was displeased with you for mentioning my name? My daughters both love me dearly. I am a very happy father; only my sons-in-law have not behaved well to me. I did not wish to make my two dear children suffer because of my misunderstandings with their husbands; so I prefer to see them secretly. This mystery gives me many enjoyments, such as fathers never feel who can see their daughters at any moment. I cannot always – you understand. If I do not see them at their homes I go to the Champs-Elysées – after finding out from their maids whether they are going out that day. I wait to see them pass. How my heart beats when I see their carriages! When they come near I admire their *toilettes*, and they give me a pretty laugh as they drive by, which gilds the world around me like a ray of sunshine. Then I stay about till they return. I see them again. The fresh air has done them good; they have a colour in their cheeks. I hear people saying, "There goes a beautiful woman," and my heart leaps for joy. Are they not mine? – my own flesh and blood? I love the very horses in their carriages. I should like to be the lap-dog lying on their knees. I live in their happiness. Everybody has his own way of loving

– mine does no harm to any one. Why should people trouble themselves about me? I am happy after my own fashion. No law forbids my standing in the street to see my daughters when they come out of their houses to go to a ball. Ah! what a disappointment if I get there too late, and the porter says, "Madame is gone." Once I waited till three in the morning to see my Nasie: I had not seen her for two days. Please never speak as if my daughters were not kind to me. They want to give me all manner of presents; but I will not let them. I always say, "Keep your money; what could I do with it? I don't want for anything." Indeed, my dear Monsieur, what am I but an old carcass whose soul is with his daughters all the time? When you have seen Madame de Nucingen you must tell me which of the two you like better,' added the old man after a moment's silence, watching Eugène, who was making ready to go to the Tuileries and lounge away the time until he could call on Madame de Beauséant.

That lounge was fatal to our student. He was so young, so handsome, and so well dressed that several women took notice of him. When he felt himself the object of their admiring glances he forgot the sisters and the aunt whom he had despoiled, and all his virtuous repugnance to crooked paths. Satan, that fallen angel – still angelic to the eye – passed in the air about him floating on prismatic wing; that fatal angel who scatters rubies, wraps women in purple, wings golden arrows at the gates of palaces, and sheds a false radiance upon thrones once in their origin so simple. He gave ear to this demon of vain glory, whose tinsel is the symbol of its power. The words of Vautrin, cynical as they were, had lodged in his heart and seared their way.

After idling about till five o'clock, Eugène presented himself at Madame de Beauséant's, and received one of those sharp checks against which young hearts are defenceless. Up to this time he had always found the viscountess full of the gracious honeyed courtesy which is attainable only through aristocratic training, though it is never in perfection unless it springs from the heart.

When he entered, Madame de Beauséant made a chilling gesture, and said coldly, 'Monsieur de Rastignac, I cannot possibly see you to-day; certainly not at this moment – I am occupied.'

Rastignac had now become a quick observer. The words, gesture, look, the tone of voice, were all signs of the habits and character of her caste. He perceived the iron hand within the velvet glove, the personality and the egoism beneath the manner, the grain of the wood below the polish. He heard the *Moi, le Roi* ('I, the King'), which begins at the throne, but echoes from every well-born gentleman and gentlewoman. Eugène had trusted too implicitly to the generous impulses of women. He had signed in good faith the charming covenant whose first article proclaims the equality of all noble hearts. Kindness given and received aright, and knitting two hearts into one, is a thing of heaven, as rare in this world as a perfect love; both are the overflow of only very rare and beautiful souls.

Rastignac was bent on going to the ball of the Duchesse de Carigliano, and therefore he swallowed his mortification.

'Madame,' he said in a low voice, 'were it not that I had something to ask I would not trouble you. Be so gracious as to let me see you later. I will wait.'

'Well, come and dine,' she said, rather sorry for the harshness with which she had treated him; for at heart she was kind as well as stately.

Though somewhat touched by this sudden relenting, Rastignac said to himself as he left the courtyard, 'Crawl, if you must; bear everything. What can other women be, if in a moment the best among them forgets her promises of friendship and casts me aside like an old shoe? Well, each man for himself! It is true her house is not a shop where I have the right to buy the things I want. I do wrong to have need of her. As Vautrin says, one should be a cannon-ball, and make one's way accordingly.'

Thus, by a sort of fatality, even the trifling events of his life conspired to push him into a career where, as the terrible sphinx of the Maison Vauquer warned him, he must slay to escape being slain, deceive lest he should be deceived, lay down heart and conscience at the threshold, put on a mask, use men for his purposes without pity, and, like the Spartan boy, snatch fortune unperceived, if he wished to wear the crown.

When he went back to dinner at the Hôtel Beauséant he found its mistress full of the gracious kindness she had hitherto shown him. They went together into the dining-room, where Monsieur de Beauséant was awaiting his wife, and where Eugène saw for the first time all that table luxury which, as every one knows, was carried under the Restoration to the highest pitch of perfection. Monsieur de Beauséant, like other men wearied with the pleasures of the world, cared for little now but good eating. His taste in cookery was of the school of Louis XVIII and the Duc d'Escars. His table offered a double luxury to his guests, in the perfection of its service and the perfection of its *menu*. Nothing of the kind had ever come into the experience of Eugène, who was dining for the first time in one of those great houses where domestic splendour is an hereditary tradition. Fashion had done away with the suppers that formerly wound up the balls of the Empire, and as yet Eugène had only been invited to balls. The *aplomb* (social self-possession) for which he subsequently became so distinguished, and which began to show itself even at this early stage of his career, prevented him from betraying his wonder. But the sight of all that glittering silver and the thousand refinements of a sumptuous table, the pleasure enjoyed for the first time of being served noiselessly and without confusion, made it natural for a youth of lively imagination to contrast this elegance with the life of privation he had declared himself willing to embrace only a few hours before. His thoughts went back for a moment to the *pension*; and such horror of it filled his mind that he swore under his breath to leave it on the 1st of January – as much to find himself a better lodging as to escape Vautrin, whose huge hand he seemed always to feel upon his shoulder.

If we remember the thousand shapes that vice takes, disguisedly or undisguisedly, in Paris, a man of sense must wonder what aberration of mind has led the Government to place schools and colleges within the city, and to collect in the very heart of it a vast assemblage of young men. But when we come to discover how seldom crimes, or even misdemeanours, are committed by students, with what respect must we regard these patient sons of Tantalus, who nearly always come off conquerors in their combat with temptation. This struggle of the student against the world of Paris, if it could be painted by the hand of a great master, would be the most dramatic subject for art in our modern civilization.

Madame de Beauséant now looked enquiringly at Eugène, expecting him to explain what he had to ask of her; but Eugène would say nothing before the viscount.

'Shall you take me to-night to the opera?' asked the viscountess of her husband.

'You cannot doubt the pleasure it would give me to be at your disposal,' he replied, with an elaborate gallantry, of which the student was the dupe; 'but I have promised to join some one at the Variétés.'

'His mistress!' she said to herself.

'Is not d'Adjuda coming this evening?' he asked.

'No,' she replied shortly.

'Well, if you are really in need of an escort, here is Monsieur de Rastignac.'

The viscountess looked at Eugène with a smile.

'It may seriously compromise you,' she said.

'"A Frenchman courts danger, if it leads to glory," as Monsieur de Chateaubriand says,' replied Eugène, with a bow.

A few moments later he was driving rapidly with Madame de Beauséant to the fashionable theatre, and felt himself in fairy-land as he entered a box facing the stage, and perceived how many opera-glasses were levelled at himself and the viscountess, whose *toilette* that evening was particularly charming. Our poor student passed from one enchantment to another.

'You had something to say to me?' said Madame de Beauséant. 'Ah! stay – there is Madame de Nucingen, three boxes from ours. Her sister and Monsieur de Trailles are on the other side of the house.'

As she said this, the viscountess was looking at the box where she expected to see Mademoiselle de Rochefide; not finding Monsieur d'Adjuda there, her face brightened exceedingly.

'She is pretty,' said Eugène, after having looked at Madame de Nucingen.

'She has white eyebrows.'

'But what a pretty waist!'

'She has large hands.'

'Fine eyes.'

'Her face is too long.'

'A long face is said to give distinction.'

'That is lucky for her, then. See how she picks up her opera-glass and puts it down! You can see the Goriot in every movement,' said the viscountess, much to the amazement of Eugène.

The truth was, Madame de Beauséant, while apparently looking over all parts of the house and paying no attention to Madame de Nucingen, did not lose a single one of her movements. The audience was remarkably elegant that night, and Delphine de Nucingen was not a little pleased to perceive that she engrossed the attention of Madame de Beauséant's handsome cousin, who seemed to single her out for observation.

'If you continue to look at her you will create a scandal, Monsieur de Rastignac,' said the viscountess. 'You will never succeed if you fling yourself headlong at people in that way.'

'My dear cousin,' said Eugène, 'you have already taken me under your protection. If you would now complete your work, I will only ask you to do me one more favour. It will not hurt you, and it will be of the greatest help to me. Do you know, I have taken a fancy to her.'

'Already?'

'Yes.'

'That woman!'

'Would my devotion be acceptable elsewhere?' he asked, with a keen glance at his cousin. After a pause he resumed—

'Madame la Duchesse de Carigliano is attached to the household of Madame la Duchesse de Berri. You know her, of course. Do me the kindness to introduce me to her, and take me to her ball next Monday. I shall meet Madame de Nucingen there, and make my first essay.'

'Willingly,' she said; 'if you really fancy her, you will get on easily. There is De Marsay in Princess Galathionne's box. Madame de Nucingen can hardly contain herself for spite. There could not be a better moment for making your way with a woman, especially a banker's wife. Those Chaussee d'Antin ladies dearly love revenge.'

'What would you do under similar circumstances?'

'Suffer, and make no sign.'

At that moment the Marquis d'Adjuda came into the box. 'I have dispatched my business very badly that I might be in time to join you,' he said. 'I tell you this, because if it seems a sacrifice in your eyes it is no longer one to me.'

The light that broke over her face taught Eugène the difference between a real affection and the shams of coquetry. He admired his cousin. He grew silent, and yielded his place to Monsieur d'Adjuda with a sigh. 'What a noble creature such a woman is!' he thought; 'and this man gives her up for a wax doll!'

He felt as angry as a boy. He would have liked to fall down at Madame de Beauséant's feet and offer her an unlimited devotion, and he looked at Madame de Nucingen with a revulsion of feeling, as a man looks at an adversary.

The viscountess turned her head and thanked him for his consideration with a little motion of the eyelids. The first act was now over.

'Do you know Madame de Nucingen well enough to introduce to her Monsieur de Rastignac?' she said to the Marquis d'Adjuda.

'She will be charmed to know Monsieur,' said the marquis.

The handsome Portuguese rose, took the student by the arm, and in a moment they were in the box of Madame de Nucingen.

'Madame la baronne,' said the marquis, 'I have the honour to present to you the Chevalier Eugène de Rastignac, a cousin of Madame de Beauséant. You have made so great an impression on him that I am delighted to complete his happiness by bringing him into the presence of his divinity.'

These words were said with a slight tone of irony, which made the speech a little impertinent. But this tone skilfully applied is not altogether displeasing to women. Madame de Nucingen smiled and offered Eugène her husband's seat, the baron having just left the box.

'I dare not propose to you to remain with me, Monsieur,' she said; 'when any one has the happiness to be placed near Madame de Beauséant his first wish is to remain there.'

'But, Madame,' said Eugène, lowering his voice, 'it seems to me that if I wish to please my cousin I shall stay here. Before Monsieur le marquis came into her box we were talking of you,' he said aloud, 'and of your air of distinction.'

Monsieur d'Adjuda retired.

'Are you really going to remain with me, Monsieur?' said the baronne; 'shall we at last make acquaintance with one another? Madame de Restaud has given me a great wish to know you.'

'She is very insincere then. She has shut her doors against me.'

'How is that?'

'Madame, I will tell you plainly the reason; but I must ask your indulgence if I do so. I am the neighbour of Monsieur, your father – our rooms adjoin. I did not know that Madame de Restaud was his daughter. I had the want of tact to speak of him, most innocently but in a way that offended Madame de Restaud and her husband. You cannot imagine how much Madame la Duchesse de Langeais and my cousin condemn the want of filial feeling on the part of your sister. I told them the story, and they laughed at my blunder. It was then that, comparing you with your sister, Madame de Beauséant spoke most warmly of you, and told me how kind you are to my neighbour Monsieur Goriot. How indeed could you help loving him? He adores you so passionately that I feel jealous already. We were talking of you two hours this morning. This evening, as my mind dwelt on what he had told me, I said to my cousin with whom I was dining, that I did not believe you could be as beautiful in person as you were amiable in heart. Willing no doubt to favour my admiration, Madame de Beauséant brought me with her this evening, telling me, in her gracious way, that I should certainly see you here.'

'Ah! Monsieur, do I owe you gratitude already?' said the banker's wife; 'a little more and we shall be old friends.'

'Friendship must be a noble sentiment when inspired by you,' said Rastignac; 'but I shall never ask for your friendship.'

Such stereotyped nonsense in the mouths of *débutants* seem to please women, and are only absurd when written down in cold blood. The gesture, the tone, and the glance of a young man lends to such speeches a certain charm. Madame de Nucingen was delighted with Eugène. Then, as she could say nothing in reply to such sentiments, she responded to another part of his speech–

'Yes, my sister does herself harm by the way she neglects our poor father, who has been a perfect Providence to both of us.

Monsieur de Nucingen was obliged to give me peremptory orders not to receive my father among my other guests before I would yield the point to him. It has made me very miserable; I have wept over it. His violence on this subject, joined to other conjugal unkindness, has greatly troubled my domestic happiness. I may be a fortunate woman in the eyes of Paris, but I consider myself one of the most pitiable. You will think me mad to speak to you in this way. But since you know my father I cannot feel to you as a stranger.'

'Indeed, you could meet no one,' cried Eugène, 'more desirous of doing you service. What are all women striving for? Is it not happiness? And if happiness for a woman is,' he added, in a low voice, 'to be loved, adored; to possess a friend in whom she may unhesitatingly confide her desires, her fancies, her griefs, her joys – before whom she can lay bare her heart with all its excellences and all its weaknesses, and know that her confidence will never be betrayed – then, believe me, such a friend can only be found in a young man full of illusions, who knows nothing of the world, nor ever will know, because you will be all the world to him. You will laugh at my *naiveté* when I tell you that I have just come up from the country, that I am new to the world, that I have never known any one who was not good and true. I thought I should live without love here in Paris; but I have been thrown with my cousin, who has deeply touched my feelings; she has let me see into her heart, and I have guessed at treasures of affection. Like Chérubin, I am the lover of all women until I may devote myself to one. When I saw you to-night for the first time, I felt as if I were floated towards you by the force of a current. I had been thinking of you so much! But in my dreams you were not as beautiful as you are in reality. Madame de Beauséant ordered me not to fix my eyes upon you. She could not understand the attraction of your sweet lips, your lovely colour, your soft eyes. I, too, am talking madly, but suffer me to say these things to you.'

Nothing pleases some women more than to hear such honeyed words. The strictest among them will listen, even though she does not respond. Having thus begun, Rastignac ran on with more of the same kind, telling his beads of coquetry in a low and vibrant voice; while Madame de Nucingen encouraged him by her smiles, all the while keeping an eye upon De Marsay, who was still in the box of the Princess Galathionne.

Rastignac stayed with Madame de Nucingen till her husband came to take her home.

'Madame,' said Eugène, 'I shall have the honour of calling upon you before the ball of the Duchesse de Carigliano.'

'If Matame bresents you there,' said the baron, a fat Alsatian, whose round face showed signs of dangerous cunning, 'so vill you be vell receifed.'

'I am getting on apace,' thought Eugène. 'She was not the least angry when I said, "Could you love me?" I have bridled my mare; now let me ride her.' So thinking, he went to Madame de Beauséant's box to make his bow. She was leaving with Monsieur d'Adjuda. Our inexperienced student little knew that Madame de Nucingen had not listened to half that he said to her. Her mind was occupied by a letter she was expecting from De Marsay, that would decide her fate. Charmed, however, with his imaginary success, Eugène accompanied the viscountess to the vestibule, where all were waiting for their carriages.

'Your cousin does not seem like himself,' said the Portuguese, laughing, when Eugène had quitted them. 'He has the air of a fellow who means to break the bank. He is as supple as an eel, and I think he will get on. It was clever of you to pick out for him a woman in need of consolation.'

'Ah!' said Madame de Beauséant; 'but all depends, you know, on whether she loves the man who is forsaking her.'

Eugène walked back from the theatre to the Rue Neuve Sainte-Geneviéve with his head brimful of visions. He had noticed the attention with which Madame de Restaud observed him when in the box of the viscountess, and also in that of Madame de Nucingen; and he argued that her doors would not long be closed against him. Already he had made four important acquisitions in the great world of Paris; for he took it for granted that he should win the good graces of the Maréchale. Without precisely settling how to carry out his plans, he was intuitively conscious that in the game he had to play among so many complicated interests, he would do well to attach himself to some one chariot that would whirl him onward, conscious that he was strong enough, when his end was gained, to put on the brakes.

'If Madame de Nucingen is interested in me,' he thought, 'I will teach her to manage her husband. The baron makes money hand over hand: he might help me to some stroke of fortune.'

He did not say this bluntly; the notion was but a light cloud floating above the verge of his horizon; he was not as yet sufficiently advanced to sum up possibilities and make his calculations – but his ideas, though they had not the crude ugliness of Vautrin's, would scarcely, if tested in the crucible of conscience, have shown much that was pure. It is by a course of mental compromises of this kind that men reach the stage of relaxed morality which characterizes our epoch – an epoch when it is rare, rarer than in any other age of the world's history, to find men of high principle, men with a sturdy sense of right and wrong, firm wills that never bow the knee to evil, natures to whom the smallest deviation from the straight path seems a sin. Such interpretation of virtue has given to the world two masterpieces – one, the Alceste of Molière; the other, Jeannie Deans and her father, by Sir Walter Scott. Perhaps the same subject seen from its other side – a picture of the shifts and windings of a man of the world; an ambitious man, with no fixed conscience, who seeks to pick his way along the edge of wickedness, and yet save appearances while he gains his end – may be neither less useful, less moral, nor less dramatic.

By the time Rastignac reached his own door he had worked himself into a sham passion for Madame de Nucingen. He thought her graceful as a swallow; he admired the enchanting softness of her eyes, the delicate and silky texture of her skin tinged with the blood that flowed beneath it, the music of her voice, and her abundant fair hair – he remembered every particular; and perhaps his walk, which had quickened his pulses, added to the fascination. He knocked sharply at Père Goriot's door.

'My neighbour,' he said, 'I have seen Madame Delphine.'

'Where?'

'At the opera.'

'Did she enjoy herself? Come in,' said the old man, who got out of bed in his shirt and opened his door, and then went back to bed again. 'Tell me all about her,' he said.

Eugène, who found himself for the first time in Père Goriot's chamber, could not repress a start of amazement at the wretchedness in which the father lived – comparing it with what he knew of the luxury of his daughters.

The window had no curtain; the paper had peeled in strips from the damp wall, showing the plaster yellow with smoke and age. The old man lay upon a wretched bed, with one thin blanket and a wadded quilt made out of scraps of Madame Vauquer's old gowns. The tiles of the floor were damp, and their crevices were filled with dust and dirt. Against the wall, opposite to the window, stood an old bureau with a swelled front and brass handles representing grape-shoots intertwined with leaves and flowers, and a wooden stand on which was a water-jug in its basin, and a number of shaving utensils. In one corner of the room a heap of shoes; at the bed's head a dilapidated night-stand without a door. Beside the fireplace, where there were no traces of fire, stood the square walnut table which had enabled Père Goriot to destroy his porringer. A miserable writing-desk with the old man's hat upon it, an armchair stuffed with straw, and two smaller chairs made up the wretched furniture. The pole of the bedstead, fastened by a rag to a hook in the ceiling, upheld a coarse curtain of red checked gingham. The poorest errand-boy in a garret was surely not so miserably lodged as Père Goriot at Madame Vauquer's. The aspect of the room chilled and wrung the heart; it was desolate as the condemned cell of a prison.

Fortunately, Père Goriot could not see the expression on Eugène's face as he put his candlestick on the table at the head of the bed. The old man turned towards him, and lay covered up to the chin.

'Well, which do you like better?' he asked, 'Madame de Restaud or Madame de Nucingen?'

'I prefer Madame Delphine,' replied the student, 'because she loves you best.'

As Eugène said these words warmly, Père Goriot put his arm out of bed and pressed his hand.

'Thank you, thank you!' he cried eagerly. 'What did she say about me?'

The student repeated the words of the baronne, adding some affectionate touches of his own, the old man listening as if to a voice from heaven.

'Dear child!' he said. 'Yes, yes, she loves me dearly. But you must not believe what she told you of Anastasie. The sisters are a little jealous of each other. It is another proof of their affection. Madame de Restaud loves me dearly too; I know it. A father is to his daughters what the good God is to all. He sees into their hearts, he knows their springs of action. Both are affectionate. Oh! if I had had good sons-in-law I should have been a happy man! I suppose there is no perfect happiness on earth. If I had been able to live with them, to hear their voices, to know them near me, to see them as they went out and came in, as I did before they married, my heart might not have borne such joy. Were they well-dressed?'

'Yes,' said Eugène. 'But, Monsieur Goriot, how is it that with daughters so wealthy as yours, you live in this wretched lodging?'

'Oh!' said the old man carelessly, 'what better do I want? I cannot explain everything to you; I never could put words together. It is all here!' he added, striking his breast. 'My life is bound up in my daughters. If they enjoy themselves, if they are well-dressed, and have carpets under their feet, what matters it what kind of coat I wear, or what sort of a place I sleep in? I am not cold if they are warm; I am not dull if I know they laugh; I have no sorrows but theirs. When you have children you will say, as you watch the little creatures prattling round you, "They are part of myself, of my flesh and my blood, the flower of my own being." Yes, I live anew in their bodies; I move with their limbs; I hear their voices answering to mine. One look of theirs, if they are sad, chills my blood. Some day you will know that it is better to be happy in our children's happiness than in our own. I cannot explain it. There are wells of inward joy that nourish life. I live three lives – my own and theirs. Shall I tell you a strange thing? When I became a father I comprehended God. He is present in all things, because all Nature has proceeded from him. Monsieur, I am so with my daughters; only I sometimes think our world, such as it is, cannot seem so beautiful to God as my girls are to me. My heart has such strange connection with all concerning them that I know what is happening to them. I knew that you would see them this evening. Ah, me! if any one would make my little Delphine happy, I would black his boots and do his errands. How could she have brought herself to marry that dull log of an Alsatian? They ought to have had noble young husbands, manly and amiable and good – but they chose for themselves!'

Père Goriot was stirred out of himself. Never till now had Eugène seen him thus lighted up by the passion of paternity. We may here remark on the infiltrating, transforming power of an over-mastering emotion. However coarse the fibre of the individual, let him be held by a strong and genuine affection, and he exhales, as it were, an essence which illuminates his features, inspires his gestures, and gives cadence to his voice. It happens sometimes that the dullest soul under the lash of passion attains to such eloquence of thought, if not of language, that it seems to move in luminous air. As the old man spoke, his voice and manner had the magnetic power of noble acting. Are not our loftiest emotions the poetry of the human will?

'I am to see Madame Delphine to-morrow,' said Eugène, 'and I am to meet her at the ball of the Duchesse de Carigliano on Monday.'

'Ah! how I should love you, my young friend, if you could shed a ray of brightness on her life! You are good yourself, and kind. But I forget – this room is too cold for you. *Mon Dieu*, you heard her voice! What message did she give you for me?'

'None at all,' thought Eugène; but he said aloud, 'She told me to tell you that she sent you a daughter's kiss.'

'Adieu, my friend. Sleep sound; dream pleasant dreams; mine will be perfect with that kiss to think of. You have been to me to-night like a blessed angel. The fragrance of my daughter hangs about you still.'

'Poor man!' sighed Eugène as he went to bed. 'What he says would touch a heart of stone. His daughter no more thought of him than she did of the Grand Turk.'

After this conversation, Père Goriot and his young neighbour became intimate friends. Between them existed the sole link that could have bound the old man to a human being. Strong passions never miscalculate. Père Goriot saw in Rastignac a means of communication with his daughters and the possibility of drawing nearer to them if the student became intimate with the baronne. Eugène was, to use his own expression, the most engaging young fellow he had ever seen; and the old man admitted him to his friendship and encouraged an intercourse which alone has made it possible for us to relate circumstantially the development of this tale.

XI

The next morning at breakfast the interest with which Père Goriot looked at Eugène as he took his place beside him at the breakfast table, the few words that were exchanged between them, and the great change in the old man's face, usually as dull as a lump of plaster, surprised the other guests. Vautrin, who saw the student for the first time since their conference, tried to read his soul. During the night-watches Eugène, far too restless to sleep, had surveyed the fields before him, and having naturally thought of Mademoiselle Taillefer and her *dot*, now looked at her as the most virtuous young man in the world looks at a rich heiress. It happened that their eyes met. The poor girl thought Eugène charming in his new clothes. The glance they exchanged was significant enough to show him that he was the object of those confused desires which come into the hearts of all young girls and attach themselves to the first comer who proves attractive. A voice within him cried, 'Eight hundred thousand francs!' Then, with a look at Vautrin, he went back to recollections of the opera, and fancied that his sham passion for Madame de Nucingen would be the antidote to involuntary thoughts of evil.

'They gave us Rossini's "Barber of Seville" last night,' he said. 'I never heard such delicious music. Dear me! how delightful it must be to have a box at the opera!'

Père Goriot snatched at this speech like a dog snapping at a morsel flung from his master's hand.

'Ah! you men live in clover,' cried Madame Vauquer; 'you can have anything you wish for.'

'How did you get home?' asked Vautrin.

'On foot,' said Eugène.

'For my part,' said the tempter, 'I don't like half pleasures. I should prefer to drive to the opera in my own carriage, sit in my own box, and come home comfortably. All or nothing – that's my motto.'

'And a very good one,' said Madame Vauquer.

'Perhaps you will see Madame de Nucingen to-day,' said Eugène in a low voice to Père Goriot. 'She will receive you with open arms; she will like to hear some particulars about me. I have heard that she wishes to be invited to my cousin's, Madame de Beauséant. Don't forget to tell her how much I admire her, and that I hope to have the pleasure of procuring her the invitation.'

Then Rastignac rose and went off to his lecture, not caring to spend a moment more than he could help in that odious *pension*. He loitered about the streets nearly all day with the fever of youth and its first hopes coursing through his veins. He was pondering the conditions of social life as revealed by Vautrin's chain of reasoning when he met Bianchon in the gardens of the Luxembourg.

'What makes you so grave, old fellow?' said the medical student, taking his arm as they walked along the front of the palace.

'I am tormented by evil thoughts.'

'What sort of evil thoughts? Tell me; thoughts can be cured.'

'How?'

'By giving in to them.'

'You don't know what you are laughing at. Did you ever read Rousseau?'

'Yes.'

'Do you remember where he asks the reader what he would do if he could make himself rich by killing an old mandarin in China by simply willing it in Paris?'

'Yes.'

'Well, I want your opinion. What would you do?'

'Pooh! I've got to my thirty-third mandarin.'

'Don't joke; be serious. Suppose it was proved to you that such a thing was possible, and that it only needed just a nod from you – would you do it?'

'Is the mandarin very old? – But, bah! young or old, well or paralysed – Heavens and earth! – the deuce! Well, then – No!'

'You are a good fellow, Bianchon. But suppose you loved a woman well enough to turn your soul wrong-side out for her; and if she wanted money, lots of money, for her *toilette*, her carriage, her whims—'

'You bewilder my faculties, and then you want me to reason!'

'Well, see here! Bianchon, I am mad. I want you to cure me. I have two sisters who are angels of beauty and goodness, and I want them to be happy. How can I, between now and five years hence, get two hundred thousand francs for their *dot*? There are circumstances you know in which one must play high and not waste one's luck in winning pennies.'

'But that's the very question that stands upon the threshold of every man's life; and you want to cut the Gordian knot with the sword! To do this, my dear fellow, one must be Alexander – or else we commit some crime and are sent to the galleys. For my part, I am quite content with the life which I expect to lead in the provinces, where I shall succeed my father in a commonplace way. After all, a man's affections can be as fully satisfied in a little round as in a vast circumference. Napoleon could not eat two dinners a day. A man's happiness lies between the soles of his feet and the crown of his head. Whether that happiness costs a million of francs a year, or a hundred *louis*, our intrinsic perception of it is the same. So I go in for letting the mandarin alone.'

'Thank you, you have done me good, Bianchon. Let us always be friends.'

'Look here!' resumed the medical student, as they left the

Cours de Cuvier in the Jardin des Plantes, 'I have just seen old Michonneau and Poiret on a bench talking with a man whom I saw during the troubles of last year in the neighbourhood of the Chamber of Deputies. He looks to me like a police spy disguised as a respectable *bourgeois* living on his income. Let us watch that couple. I will tell you why later. Adieu, I must be off to the four o'clock call.'

When Eugène returned to Madame Vauquer's, he found Père Goriot waiting for him.

'See,' said the old man, 'here is a note from her. *Hein!* what pretty writing!'

Eugène broke the seal and read—

> MONSIEUR – My father tells me that you are fond of Italian music. I should be happy if you would do me the pleasure to accept a seat in my box on Saturday next. We shall have Fodor and Pellegrini; I am sure therefore that you will not refuse my invitation. Monsieur de Nucingen joins me in begging you to dine with us on that day without ceremony. If you accept, you will render him grateful to be released from his conjugal duty of escorting me to the opera. Do not reply, but come. Accept my compliments.
> D. de N.

'Let me look at it,' said Père Goriot to Eugène when he had read the letter. 'You will certainly go, won't you?' he added, putting his cheek to the paper. 'How good it smells! Her fingers have touched it!'

'A woman does not fling herself at a man without some motive,' said the student to himself. 'She must want to make use of me to get De Marsay back again. Nothing but spite could account for her sending me such a letter.'

'Well,' said Père Goriot, 'what are you thinking of?'

Eugène knew nothing of a social delirium that possessed the women of the Chaussee d'Antin at that period. He was not aware that the wife of a banker in that quarter would do almost anything that might open her way into the *salons* of the Faubourg Saint-Germain. At that period fashion was just beginning to exalt above all other women those who composed the society of the old nobility, known by the name of *Les Dames du petit Château*. Among them Madame de Beauséant, her friend the Duchesse de Langeais, and the Duchesse de Maufrigneuse held the first rank. Rastignac was the only man with an *entrée* to these houses who was not aware of the eagerness of the Chaussée d'Antin ladies to enter that superior sphere and shine among its constellations. But his mistrustfulness befriended him on this occasion. It made him receive the invitation very coldly, and gave him the poor power of doing a favour instead of accepting one.

'Yes, I will go,' he said.

Thus the chief motive that took him to Madame de Nucingen's was curiosity; had she shown indifference, he might have been influenced by passion. Nevertheless, he looked forward to the meeting with some impatience, and enjoyed, as he dressed for dinner, all those little satisfactions which young people are ashamed to speak of for fear of ridicule, but which pleasantly stimulate their self-love. He thought as he arranged his hair how the eyes of a pretty woman would linger among the black curls; he played the little tricks and vanities of a young girl dressing for her first ball, and smiled at the reflection of his slim figure as he smoothed out the folds of his new coat, and turned himself about before the glass.

'One thing is very certain,' he said complacently; 'it is not every man who is well-made.'

He went downstairs at the moment when the household were sitting down to dinner, and laughed as he received a broadside of nonsensical remarks on his elegant appearance. The excitement produced by any attention to the toilet is a trait of manners peculiar to *pensions bourgeoises*, where every one has a word to say on the unaccustomed appearance of a new dress or a new coat.

'Kt, kt, kt, kt!' cried Bianchon, clicking his tongue as if exciting a horse.

'Duke and peer of France!' said Madame Vauquer.

'Monsieur is arrayed for conquest,' observed Mademoiselle Michonneau.

'Cock-a-doodle-doo!' crowed the painter.

'My compliments to your wife,' said the employee at the museum.

'Has Monsieur a wife?' asked Poiret.

'A wife in compartments – that will go in the water – warranted fast colours – at all prices from twenty five to forty – the most fashionable patterns in plaids – sure to wash – very pretty wear – half thread, half cotton, half wool – cures the toothache and all other maladies under the patronage of the Academy of Medicine – excellent for children – better still for head-ache, plethora, and other affections of the stomach, ears, and eyes!' cried Vautrin, with the intonation and volubility of an auctioneer. 'How much do you bid for this wonder, gentlemen? Two *sous*! What did you say? Nothing? It is the last article made for the Great Mogul, which all the Reigning Sovereigns of Europe, including the Gr-r-r-r-r-rand Duke of Baden, have been on the look-out for. Walk in; keep straight before you; pass into the inner office. Strike up the music! Brooum, la, la, trinn! la, la, boum, boum! Monsieur the clarinet, you are out of tune,' he went on in a hoarse voice; 'I'll rap you over the knuckles!'

'*Mon Dieu*! how agreeable that man can make himself!' said Madame Vauquer to Madame Couture, 'I should never have a moment's *ennui* if I lived with him.'

In the midst of the laughter and the jokes led off by this

absurdity, Eugène intercepted a furtive glance of admiration from Mademoiselle Taillefer, who whispered a few words in her aunt's ear.

'The cabriolet is here,' announced Sylvie.

'Where does he dine?' asked Bianchon.

'With Madame la Baronne de Nucingen.'

'Père Goriot's daughter,' added the student.

At these words everybody looked at the old man, who was gazing at Eugène with envy in his eyes.

Rastignac found the house in the Rue Saint-Lazare one of those flimsy buildings, with slim pillars and fanciful porticos, which in Paris are classed as *pretty*; a banker's house, in short – overloaded with costly ornament and stucco, the halls and staircase-landings inlaid with marbles. Madame de Nucingen received him in a small room filled with Italian pictures and decorated in the style of a restaurant. She seemed to be in trouble, and the efforts which she made to conceal her feelings affected Eugène all the more because they were evidently genuine. He came expecting to charm her by his presence; he found her the image of despair, and the disappointment piqued his self-love.

'I have little claim to your confidence, Madame,' he said, after bantering her slightly on her preoccupation, 'and if I am in your way I count upon your kindness to tell me so frankly.'

'No, stay,' she said; 'I should be alone if you left me. Nucingen dines out to-day, and I do not wish to be alone. I need something to interest me.'

'What troubles you?'

'You are the last person I could tell it to,' she cried.

'But you must tell me. Have I anything to do with it?'

'Perhaps – But, no!' she resumed, 'it is one of those family quarrels that ought to be hidden from other eyes. Did I not tell you the other evening that I am far from happy? A chain of gold is the heaviest to bear.'

When a woman tells a young man that she is not happy, and when the young man is clever, handsome, well-dressed, and has fifteen hundred francs worth of leisure in his pocket, he will probably think all that Rastignac now thought, and speak as he did – like a coxcomb.

'What can you lack?' he said. 'You are young, beautiful, wealthy, and – beloved!'

'Do not let us talk of myself,' she cried, arresting him with a gesture. 'We will dine together *tête-à-tête*, and then go and hear some delicious music. Do you like me in this dress?' she continued, rising and displaying a robe of white cashmere embroidered with Persian designs, very elegant and costly.

'I would you were altogether mine!' cried Eugène. 'You are lovely!'

'You would have a melancholy possession,' she said with a bitter smile. 'Nothing about me indicates unhappiness, and yet in spite of appearances I am wretched. I cannot sleep for thinking of my troubles. I am growing ugly—'

'Oh, that can never be!' cried the student. 'Tell me, what troubles have you that my devotion cannot cure?'

'Ah! if I told you, you would turn and leave me,' she said; 'your love for me is only the conventional gallantry that men affect towards women. If you really loved me, and I were to tell you my troubles you would fall into despair. So you see I must not tell you. For pity's sake,' she added, 'let us talk of other things. Come and see my apartments.'

'No, let us stay here,' said Eugène, seating himself on a low couch near the fire beside Madame de Nucingen, and taking her hand with assurance. She allowed him to do so, and even pressed his fingers with the nervous grasp that betrays strong emotion.

'Listen!' said Rastignac, 'if you have griefs, confide them to me. Let me prove how much I love you. Either speak, and tell me these troubles and let me help you – I am capable of killing six men for your sake – or I will leave this house never to return.'

'Well, then!' she exclaimed, moved by an impulse which made her strike her forehead with her hand, 'I will put you to the proof at once. Yes,' she added, 'there is no other way.'

She rang the bell.

'Is Monsieur's carriage waiting?' she said to the servant.

'Yes, Madame.'

'I will take it. You can give him mine and my horses. You need not serve dinner till seven o'clock.'

'Now, come,' she said to Eugène, who found himself as in a dream sitting beside her in Monsieur de Nucingen's coupé.

'To the Palais-Royal,' she said to the coachman, 'and stop near the Théatre Français.'

As they drove on she seemed greatly agitated, and would not answer Eugène, who knew not what to think of the mute obtuse resistance she opposed to his enquiries.

'In another moment she may escape me,' he said to himself.

When the carriage stopped, she looked at him with an expression which silenced the foolish speeches he was beginning to utter.

'Do you love me then so very much?' she asked.

'Yes,' he replied, concealing his uneasiness.

'You will think no evil of me whatever I ask of you?'

'No.'

'Will you obey me?'

'Blindly.'

'Did you ever go to a gambling-house?' and her voice trembled.

'Never.'

'Ah! then I breathe. You will have luck. Here is my purse. Take it,' she said, 'yes, take it. There are one hundred francs in it – all the money owned by this wealthy and fortunate woman!

Go into some gambling-room. I do not know where they are, but I know there are many in the Palais-Royal. Stake these hundred francs at a game they call *roulette*, and either lose them all or bring me back six thousand francs. I will tell you my troubles when you return.'

'The devil take me if I understand what you wish me to do, but I am ready to obey you,' he said, reflecting with satisfaction that she was thus putting herself in his power.

He took the pretty purse and hastened to Number Nine, after obtaining from a neighbouring shopkeeper the direction of the nearest gambling-house. He went upstairs, permitted an attendant to take his hat, and entered the room, where he asked to be shown the *roulette*. All present looked astonished as the man in attendance took him to a long table. Eugène, who was followed by the whole company, asked, without the least embarrassment, where he was to place his money.

'If you put one *louis* on any of these thirty-six numbers and it comes up, you will win thirty-six *louis*,' said a respectable-looking old man with white hair.

Eugène placed the whole hundred francs on the number of his own age – twenty-one. A cry of astonishment broke from every one before he knew himself what had happened. He had won.

'Take up your money,' said the old gentleman; 'people do not win twice in that way.'

Eugène took a rake which the speaker handed to him, and drew in three thousand six hundred francs. Once more, knowing nothing of the game, he placed his money on the red. The bystanders looked at him with envy, seeing that he played on. The wheel turned – he won again; and the croupier threw him another three thousand six hundred francs.

'You have won seven thousand two hundred francs,' whispered the old gentleman. 'Take my advice and go away. The red has come up eight times. If you are kind-hearted, you will acknowledge my good advice and have pity on the poverty of an old prefect of Napoleon, who is penniless.'

Rastignac, bewildered, suffered the old man with the snow-white hair to help himself to ten *louis*, and then went downstairs with his seven thousand francs, understanding nothing of the game, and stupefied by his good fortune.

'*Ah, çà!* where will you take me now?' he said, showing the seven thousand francs to Madame de Nucingen as soon as the carriage door was shut.

Delphine threw her arms about him and kissed him effusively, but without passion.

'You have saved me!' she cried. Tears flowed down her cheeks. 'I will tell you all, my friend – for you are my friend, are you not? You see me rich and prosperous. I want for nothing – so it seems to you? Well, then, I must tell you that Monsieur de Nucingen does not give me a single penny to spend as I choose. He pays for everything – for the household, for my carriages, even my opera-box. He allows me a sum insufficient for my *toilette*; he has reduced me to secret poverty. I am too proud to beg for money. Do you ask why, when I brought him seven hundred thousand francs, I have suffered myself to be thus despoiled? Through pride, through indignation! A girl is so young, so easily deceived, when she is first married. To have asked my husband for money then would have scorched my mouth; I dared not. I lived on what I had saved, and on what I could get from my poor father. Then I ran in debt. My marriage from first to last has been a horrible deception; I cannot speak of it. We live apart; I would rather fling myself from a window than be reconciled to him. When I was forced to tell him of my debts, for jewellery and various whims and trifles (my poor father had accustomed us to every indulgence), I suffered martyrdom. At last I took courage and made my confession – had I not brought him a fortune? Nucingen was furious. He said

I should ruin him – Oh! he said such horrible things! I wished myself a hundred feet under ground. He paid my bills on that occasion because he had possession of my *dot*; but he stipulated that in future I should take a fixed annual allowance for my personal expenses. I agreed, for the sake of peace. Since then I have been anxious to do credit to one whom you know of,' she continued. 'He has not been true to me, but I must not cease to do justice to the nobleness of his character. He has cruelly forsaken me. – Oh! no one should forsake a woman, especially when they have flung her a pile of money in the day of her distress – oh! they *ought* to love her always. You, with the nobility of youth, pure and fresh, you may well ask me how a woman could take gold from a man in that relation! But is it not natural to have all things in common with those to whom we owe our happiness? Money has no importance in itself – none, until love grows cold. Do we not fancy that love will last a lifetime? Who calculates on separation? Shall those who have vowed to be true eternally set up divided interests? I can never tell what I suffered to-day when Nucingen refused to give me six thousand francs – less than he gives each month to his mistress, a *danseuse* at the opera! I longed to kill myself: I envied my own waiting-maid. Ask my father for money? – it would be madness. Anastasie and I have ruined him. My poor father would sell himself for either of us, if anyone would pay six thousand francs for him. I should drive him to despair in vain. You have saved me from shame, from death! I was frantic in my wretchedness. Ah! Monsieur, I owe you this explanation. I have been beside myself this evening – let that be my excuse. When you left me, when I lost sight of you, I had an impulse to jump from the carriage and flee away on foot, I knew not whither. Such is the life led by half the women of Paris – luxury without, and bitter cares within. I know poor creatures more wretched than I am. There are women who get their creditors to send in false accounts, and rob their husbands. Some men believe that cashmeres worth two thousand francs are sold for five hundred; others that a shawl worth five hundred francs costs a thousand. There are women who even starve their children; women who will commit any meanness to get enough to buy a gown. I am pure at least from such deceptions. Ah! to-night Monsieur De Marsay will no longer have the right to think of me as a woman he has paid!' She dropped her face between her hands that Eugène might not see her tears; but he drew them away and looked at her.

'To mix up money with love! – is it not horrible?' she said. 'You can never think well of me!'

This union of good feelings and acquired faults – faults forced upon her by the corrupt society in which she lived – overcame Eugène, who said soft words of consolation as he gazed at the beautiful creature so naively imprudent in the excitement of her grief.

'You will not turn this confession against me? Promise me that you never will,' she said.

'Ah, Madame, I am incapable of doing so.'

She took his hand and placed it on her heart, with a gesture full of grace and gratitude. 'Thanks to you I am free and happy. I was pressed to earth by an iron hand. I am free; I will live simply from this moment; I will spend little. You will like me as I am, will you not? – as I am, my friend. Keep this,' she added, retaining six notes of a thousand francs, and offering Rastignac the seventh. 'In strict justice I owe you half, for I consider that we are partners.'

Eugène protested with a sense of shame, till Madame de Nucingen exclaimed, 'I shall regard you as my enemy if you refuse to be my accomplice.'

'Then I will hold it in reserve in case of future ill-luck,' he said, as he took the note.

'Ah! that is what I feared,' she said, turning pale. 'If you wish me to be your friend, promise me – swear to me – that you will never return to the gambling table. Alas, alas! think of my corrupting you! I ought to perish sooner!'

Thus they reached the house in the Rue Saint-Lazare. The contrast of its opulence with the poverty of its mistress stunned the student, in whose ears the words of Vautrin re-echoed as with fatal truth.

'Sit there,' said Madame de Nucingen, pointing to a sofa near the fire, when they entered her room. 'I have to write a trying letter. Give me your advice.'

'Do not write at all,' said Eugène. 'Put the notes in an envelope, address it merely, and send the letter by your waiting-maid.'

'Oh! you are too delightful!' she cried. 'See, Monsieur, what it is to have been brought up in the traditions of good breeding. *Ceci est du Beauséant tout pur,*' she added, smiling.

'She is charming,' thought Eugène, pleased with the flattery. He looked round the room, which was arranged with a meretricious taste better suited, he thought, to the *quartier* Bréda.

'Do you like it?' asked Madame de Nucingen, ringing for her maid. 'Thérèse, take this letter to Monsieur De Marsay. Give it into his own hand. If you do not find him, bring it back.'

As Thérèse left the room she threw an inquisitive glance at Eugène. Dinner was now served, and Rastignac gave his arm to Madame de Nucingen, who led him into a gorgeous dining-room where he again found all the table luxury he had admired at his cousin's.

'On the nights of the Italian opera you must always dine with me,' she said, 'and escort me to the theatre.'

'I could soon accustom myself to so delightful a life if it would only last,' he answered; 'but I am a poor student, with my fortune to make.'

'It will make itself,' she said laughing; 'you see how things come to pass. I little expected to be so happy.'

It is the nature of women to argue the impossible from the possible, and to destroy facts by building on presentiments.

When Madame de Nucingen and Rastignac entered their box at the opera she was so beautiful in her recovered peace of mind that people began to whisper those trifling calumnies against which women are defenceless, however false may be the premises on which they are based. Those who know Paris well are careful to believe nothing that they hear, and also to tell nothing that they know. Eugène took the hand of his companion, and they silently communicated to each other by pressure the sensations with which the music flooded their souls. The evening was full of enchantment, and when they left the Opera House Madame de Nucingen insisted on taking Eugène as far as the Pont-Neuf, disputing with him on the way another of those kisses which she had given him of her own accord in the Palais-Royal. Eugène reproached her for the inconsistency.

'No – *then,*' she said, 'it was gratitude for an unexpected deliverance; now it would be a pledge—'

'And you will not grant me that pledge,' he said, half angrily. She made a gesture of impatience and gave him her hand to kiss, which he took with an ill grace that completely charmed her.

'Monday – at the ball,' she said as they parted.

Eugène walked home in the brilliant moonlight with his mind full of serious reflections. He was pleased and yet dissatisfied: pleased at an adventure which threw him into the closest intimacy with one of the prettiest and most fashionable women of Paris; dissatisfied at seeing his projects for the future overthrown – for he now perceived how much he had really built upon the vague visions of the day before. Want of success increases rather than diminishes the strength of our wishes. The more Eugène tasted the pleasures of Parisian life, the less he liked the prospect of toil and poverty. He fingered the bank-note in his pocket, and thought of a hundred reasons to justify him in keeping it. As he reached the Rue Neuve Sainte-Geneviève and ran upstairs, he saw a light on the landing. Père Goriot had left his door ajar and his rush-light burning, that the student might not forget to come in and *relate to him his daughter*, as he expressed it. Eugène told him everything.

'What!' cried Père Goriot, in a transport of jealous despair, 'do they think me ruined? I have still an income of thirteen hundred francs. *Mon Dieu!* my poor darling, why did she not come to me? I could have sold out my stocks. I could have given her what she wanted from the capital, and bought an annuity with the rest. Why did you not come and tell me, my good neighbour? How could you have had the heart to risk her poor little hundred francs? It breaks my heart – This is what it is to have sons-in-law! And she wept – you say she wept? – my Delphine, who never wept before when she was my own little one! By her marriage contract she is entitled to her money. I shall see Derville the lawyer, to-morrow. I shall insist on the separate investment of her fortune. I know the law. I am an old wolf – yes! and I shall get the use of my teeth again!'

'See, *père*, here are a thousand francs which she insisted on giving me out of our winnings. Keep them for her.'

Goriot looked at Eugène and grasped his hand, on which the old man dropped a tear.

'You will succeed in life,' he said. 'God is just, you know. I know what honesty is, and I tell you few men would have done as you have done. My son, go now; go – and sleep. You *can* sleep, for you are not yet a father – Oh, she wept! While I was quietly eating my dinner, dull fool that I am, she was suffering! I – who would sell my soul to save them from unhappiness!'

'On my honour,' said Eugène, as he laid his head on his pillow,

'I will be an honest man as long as I live. There is great happiness in following the inspirations of one's conscience.'

Perhaps none but those who believe in a good God can do good in secret. Eugène was a believer still.

On the evening of the ball Rastignac went to Madame de Beauséant's, who took him with her and presented him to the Duchesse de Carigliano. He had a gracious reception from the Maréchale, and found Madame de Nucingen already there. Delphine, who had dressed with the intention of pleasing others that she might the better please Eugène, waited impatiently to catch his eye, though carefully concealing her impatience. For one who can read a woman's heart such a moment is full of charm. What man does not delight in making a woman wait eagerly for his judgement, disguising his own pleasure that he may win this signal of her preference, enjoying her uneasiness as he plays upon the fears he can set at rest by a smile?

As the evening advanced, Rastignac began to perceive the full bearings of his position, and to understand that he held rank among those around him as the acknowledged cousin of Madame de Beauséant. The conquest of Madame de Nucingen, with which he was credited, placed him at once under observation; young men looked at him with envy, and as he caught their glances he tasted the first sweets of gratified social vanity. Passing from room to room and from group to group, he heard his own praises; ladies predicted his success; and Delphine, afraid of losing him, promised not to refuse the kiss she had denied him the day before. He received several invitations during the evening, and was presented by his cousin to a number of ladies noted for their elegance, whose houses ranked among the most agreeable in the Faubourg. Thus he found himself admitted into the inner circle of the great world of Paris. This evening was for him a brilliant *début*, remembered to the last hour of his life, as a young girl remembers the ball where she won her first triumphs.

The next morning, at the breakfast-table, when he began to relate his successes to Père Goriot in presence of the other guests, Vautrin listened with diabolical amusement to the tale.

'Now, do you really think,' exclaimed that fierce logician, 'that a young man of fashion can continue to live in the Rue Neuve Sainte-Geneviève, in the Maison Vauquer? – a *pension* infinitely respectable in every way, no doubt, but which assuredly is not fashionable. It is comfortable, it is cosy, delightful in its abundance, proud of being temporarily the abode of a de Rastignac; but after all it is in the Rue Neuve Sainte-Geneviève, and it boasts no luxury – being above all things *patriarchalorama*. My young friend,' continued Vautrin, with paternal irony, 'if you hope to make a figure in Paris, you must have three horses and a tilbury for the morning, and a coupé for the evening: nine thousand francs for the equipages alone. You will fall shamefully below the requirements of your destiny if you spend less than three thousand with your tailor, six hundred with your perfumer, and six hundred more between your bootmaker and your hatter. As for your washerwoman, she will cost you a thousand francs. Young men of fashion are above all things bound to be irreproachable in the matter of washing. Love and the Church alike demand fine linen. Now, we have got up to fourteen thousand. I don't count all that cards and bets and presents will cost you – you certainly can't do with less than two thousand francs a year for pocket-money. I have led that life myself, and I know how it goes. Now, add to these things – which are indispensable, mind you – three hundred *louis* for subsistence, and a thousand francs for rent. That brings us up, my boy, to the pretty little sum of twenty-five thousand francs a year, which we must have in hand, or over we go into the mud, with people laughing at us, and our future lost – including all our youthful dreams of fortune and women! Ah! I forgot the groom and the valet. Could Christophe carry your *billets-doux*? Shall you write them upon law-paper? My dear boy, you would cut your throat. Take the advice of an old man full of experience,' he concluded; 'either transport yourself into a virtuous garret and wed toil, or – choose some other way to reach your end.'

Here Vautrin glanced at Mademoiselle Taillefer, with an eye that recalled and emphasized the seductive arguments he had already dropped into the student's heart to breed corruption.

XII

Several days passed, and Rastignac led a dissipated life. He dined constantly with Madame de Nucingen, and accompanied her into the great world, getting home at three or four o'clock in the morning. He usually rose at midday and made his toilet; after which, if it were fine, he drove to the Bois with Delphine – idling away his days without thought of their value, and assimilating the lessons and seductions of luxury with the eagerness of the female date-tree as it absorbs the fecundating pollen from the atmosphere. He played high, lost and won heavily, and soon accustomed himself to the extravagant habits of the young men around him. Out of the first money which he won he sent fifteen hundred francs to his mother and sisters, accompanying the restitution with some pretty presents. Although he had given out his intention to quit the Maison Vauquer, he was still there in the last week of January, and did not well see how he could get away. Young men are governed by a law that seems at first sight inexplicable, but which springs from their youth and from the species of madness with which they fling themselves into the enjoyments of life. Be they rich or be they poor, they never have money enough for the necessities of living, though they always find the wherewithal to spend on their caprices. Lavish when they can buy on credit, stingy as to all that they must pay for in hard cash, they seem to indemnify themselves for the lack of what they crave by squandering what they have. Thus – by way of illustration – a student takes more care of his hat than he does of his coat. The enormous profit of the tailor makes it reasonable that he should wait for his money; but the small gains of a hatter render him impervious to the question of credit. Though the young man sitting in the *balcon* of a theatre may display to the opera-glasses of pretty women the most magnificent of waistcoats, no one can be certain that his socks would bear inspection: the hosier is one of those who must be paid in ready money. Rastignac had reached this point in his career. His purse, always empty for Madame Vauquer, always full for the needs of vanity, had its ups and downs, its ebbs and flows, which by no means agreed with the natural demands upon it. Before quitting that abject and evil-smelling abode, where his new pretensions were daily humiliated, must he not pay a month's lodging to his landlady, and buy furniture fit for a man of fashion before he could install himself in a new apartment? This remained steadfastly the thing impossible. To get money for the gambling-table, Rastignac had readily found out how to buy watches and chains from his jeweller at enormous prices, to be paid for out of his winnings, and to be pawned as soon as bought with that solemn and discreet friend of youth, the Mont-de-Piété; but his ingenuity had failed to discover any device whereby to pay Madame Vauquer, or to buy the tools necessary to keep up his life of elegance and fashion. Vulgar present necessity, or the debts contracted for past pleasures, gave him no inspiration. Like most of those who lead this life of chance, he put off as long as possible paying his current debts (which are the most sacred in the eyes of plain people), after the example of Mirabeau, who never paid his baker's bill till it took the compelling form of a promissory note. At this special time – the last of January – Rastignac had been losing heavily, and was in debt. He was beginning to see that he could not continue to lead this kind of life without fixed resources. But sighing over the difficulties of his precarious position did not bring him to resign the pleasures of the great world; on the contrary, he felt incapable of the sacrifice, and resolute to push on at any price. The chances on which at first he had built his hopes of fortune he now saw to be chimerical, while his real difficulties grew greater every day. As he became familiar with the domestic secrets of Monsieur and Madame de Nucingen, he saw that to convert love into an instrument of fortune it was necessary to drink the cup of shame to the very dregs, and renounce forever all those noble ideas which are the absolution of youthful errors. To this life, outwardly splendid, inwardly gnawed by the *tœnias* of remorse, and whose fugitive pleasures were dearly paid for by persistent anguish, he was now wedded. Like La Bruyère's absent-minded man, he had made his bed in the slime of the ditch; but, like him again, he had as yet only soiled his clothes.

'Well! have we killed the mandarin?' said Bianchon one day as they rose from table.

'Not yet,' he answered, 'but he is at his death-rattle.'

The medical student took this for a joke, but he was mistaken. Eugène, who had dined that day at the *pension* after a long absence, seemed thoughtful and preoccupied. Instead of leaving after the dessert, he remained in the dining-room sitting near Mademoiselle Taillefer, on whom from time to time he threw reflecting glances. Some of the guests still lingered at table eating nuts; others were walking up and down continuing their conversation. They left the room, as they did every evening, each as he pleased, according to the interest he took in the conversation or the amount of rest required by his digestion. In winter the dining-room was seldom empty before eight o'clock; after which hour the four women remained alone and made up for the silence imposed upon them by the masculine majority. Struck by Eugène's preoccupation, Vautrin, who at first had seemed in a hurry to get away, stayed after the others had departed, and placed himself cautiously just within the door of the *salon*, so that Eugène could not see him, and might therefore believe him gone. He read the mind of the student, and saw that a crisis was at hand.

Rastignac was in fact in a difficult though perhaps not uncommon position. Whether Madame de Nucingen loved him or was trifling with him, she had made him pass through the fluctuations of a real passion, and had used against him all the resources at the command of Parisian feminine diplomacy. Having compromised herself in the eyes of the world to secure the devotion of a cousin of Madame de Beauséant, she now repelled his advances and would go no further. For a month she had coquetted with his feelings, and had ended by gaining some power over his heart. If in the first hours of their intimacy the student had been master of the situation, Madame de Nucingen was now the stronger of the two. She had contrived by skilful management to excite in Rastignac the varied feelings, good and bad, of the two or three men who exist in a young Parisian. Was this from calculation? No, women are always true even in the midst of their utmost falsity; they are true, because they are influenced by native feeling. Perhaps Delphine, alarmed at the power she had at first allowed Eugène to assume over her, and at the unguarded confidence she had shown him, was prompted by a feeling of dignity to assume reserve. She may have hesitated before her fall, and have sought to test the character of the man to whom she was about to commit her future, having already had good reason to distrust the faith of lovers. Perhaps she had noticed in Eugène's manner – for his rapid success had greatly increased his self-conceit – a certain disrespect caused by the singularities of their situation. Be this as it may, whatever were her reasons, Eugène had made no progress with her since the first days of their intercourse. He grew irritable, his self-love was deeply wounded; he was like a sportsman jealous for the honour of Saint-Hubert if a partridge is not killed on the first day of the sport. His angry self-conceit, his futile hopes, were they false or real, and his daily anxieties bound him more and more to this woman. Yet sometimes when he found himself penniless and without prospects, his mind turned, in defiance of his conscience, to the chance Vautrin had held out to him through a marriage with Mademoiselle Taillefer. There were days when his poverty was so importunate that he yielded almost involuntarily to the snare of the terrible sphinx whose glance dominated him with a dangerous fascination.

When Poiret and Mademoiselle Michonneau had gone up to their rooms, Rastignac, believing himself alone between Madame Vauquer and Madame Couture, the latter of whom was knitting herself a pair of muffêtees and dosing by the stove, turned to Mademoiselle Taillefer with a glance sufficiently tender to make her eyes droop.

'Is anything troubling you, Monsieur Eugène?' she said, after a slight pause.

'Who is without trouble?' he replied. 'Yet perhaps if we young men were sure of being truly loved, with a devotion that would compensate us for the sacrifices we are ready to make, we should have no troubles.'

Mademoiselle Taillefer for all answer gave him a look whose meaning was unmistakable.

'Even you, Mademoiselle, who are so sure of your heart to-day, can you be sure that you will never change?'

A smile played about the lips of the poor girl; a ray of sunshine from her heart lighted up her face with so bright a glow that Eugène was frightened at having called forth such a manifestation of feeling.

'What! if to-morrow you were rich and happy, if immense wealth came to you from the skies, would you still love a poor young man who had pleased you in the days of your own distress?'

She made a pretty motion of her head.

'A very poor unhappy man?'

Another sign.

'What nonsense are you talking?' cried Madame Vauquer.

'Never mind,' said Eugène; 'we understand each other.'

'Ah! an understanding! – a promise of marriage between the Chevalier Eugène de Rastignac and Mademoiselle Victorine Taillefer!' said Vautrin in his bluff voice, as he stood on the threshold of the dining-room.

'How you frightened me!' cried Madame Vauquer and Madame Couture together.

'I might make a far worse choice,' said Eugène, laughing.

The voice of Vautrin at that moment caused him the most painful emotion he had ever yet known.

'No jests on that subject, if you please, gentlemen,' said Madame Couture. 'My dear, let us go upstairs.'

Madame Vauquer followed the two ladies, that she might economize fire and lights by spending the evening in their room. Eugène found himself alone and face to face with Vautrin.

'I knew you would come to it,' said the latter, with his imperturbable *sang-froid*. 'But, stay! I can be delicate and considerate as well as others. Don't make up your mind at this moment; you are not altogether yourself; you are in trouble, in debt. I don't wish it to be passion or despair but plain common-sense which brings you to me. Perhaps you want a few thousand? Here, will you have them?'

The tempter took a purse from his pocket and drew out three bank-notes of a thousand francs each, which he fluttered before the eyes of the student. Eugène's situation at this time was very harassing. He owed the Marquis d'Adjuda and the Comte de Trailles a hundred *louis* lost at cards. He had no money to pay the debt, and dared not go that evening to Madame de Restaud's where he was expected. It was one of those informal parties where people drink tea and eat little cakes, but lose their thousands at whist.

'Monsieur,' said Eugène, striving to hide a convulsive shiver, 'after what you have confided to me, you ought to know that I cannot put myself under obligations to you.'

'Well,' said Vautrin, 'I should be sorry to have you say otherwise. You are a handsome young fellow, and sensitive; proud as a lion and gentle as a little girl. You would be a fine morsel for the Devil: I like the strain. A little more study of men and morals, and you will see the world in its true light. A man of your stamp generally relieves his conscience by playing a few scenes of virtuous indignation and self-sacrifice, highly applauded by the fools in the pit. In a few days you will be one of us. Ah! if you become my pupil, I will make you anything you please. You could not form a wish but it should be gratified – were it for honour, fortune or the love of women. All civilization should be turned into ambrosia for you. You should be our spoiled child, our Benjamin; we would lay down our lives for you with pleasure. Every obstacle in your path should be swept away! If you are still scrupulous, I suppose you take me for a scoundrel? Let me tell you that a man who was quite as high-minded as you can pretend to be, Monsieur de Turenne, had his little arrangements with the brigands of his day without thinking himself at all compromised by it. You don't want to be under obligations to me, *hein*? That need not hinder,' he said with a smile; 'take the notes, and write across this,' he added, pulling out a stamped paper, '*Accepted for the sum of three thousand, five hundred francs, payable in twelve months*; sign it, and add the date. The five hundred francs interest is enough to relieve you of all scruples. You may call me a Jew if you like, and consider yourself entirely released from gratitude. I have no objection to your despising me now, for I am certain you will come to me in the end. You will find in me the unfathomable depths and the vast concentrated emotions which ninnies call vices; but you will never find me false or ungrateful. I'm not a pawn, nor a knight – I'm a castle, a tower of strength, my boy!'

'Who are you?' cried Eugène. 'Were you created to torment me?'

'No, no; I am a kind man, willing to get splashed that you may be kept out of the mud for the rest of your life. I have startled you a little with the chimes of your Social Order, and by letting you see, perhaps too soon, how the peal is rung. But the first fright will pass, like that of a recruit on the battlefield. You will get accustomed to the idea of men as well as of soldiers dying to promote the good of others who have crowned themselves kings and emperors. How times have changed! Formerly we could say to a *bravo*, "Here are a hundred crowns; go kill me So-and-so," and eat our suppers tranquilly after sending a man to the shades by a *yes* or a *no*. To-day I propose to give you a handsome fortune; and yet you hesitate, when all you have to do is to nod your head – a thing which cannot compromise you in any way. The age is rotten!'

Eugène signed the paper, and exchanged it for the bank-notes.

'Come, let us talk sense,' resumed Vautrin. 'I want to start for America in a few months and plant my tobacco. I will send you the cigars of friendship. If I get rich I will help you. If I have no children (and that is probable, for I am not anxious to propagate myself), I will leave you all my fortune. Don't you call that being a friend? But I have a passion for devoting myself to others – I have sacrificed myself before now in my life. I live in a sphere above that of other men; I look on actions as means to ends, and I make straight for those ends. What is the life of a man to me? – not that!' he added, clicking his thumb-nail against a tooth. 'A man is all, or nothing. Less than nothing when he is Poiret: one may crush such a man as that like a bed-bug – he is flat and empty, and he stinks. But a man gifted as you are is a god; he is not a machine in human skin, but a theatre where noble sentiments are enacted. I live in sentiments! A noble sentiment, what is it? – the whole of life in a thought. Look at Père Goriot: his two daughters are his universe – they are the threads of fate that guide him through created things. I say again, I have dug deep into life, and I know there is but one enduring sentiment – man's friendship for man. Pierre et Jaffier – I know "Venice Preserved" by heart. Have you seen many men virile enough when a comrade said, "Come, help me bury a corpse," to follow without asking a question or preaching a moral? I have done that! But you, you are superior to others; to you I can speak out – you will comprehend me. You'll not paddle long in the marsh with the dwarfs and the toads! – Well, it is settled: you will marry her. Let us each carry our point. Mine is steel, and will never yield! Ha! ha!—'

Vautrin walked away without listening to the negative reply of Rastignac. He seemed to know the secret of those feeble efforts at resistance, those ineffectual struggles with which men try to cheat themselves, and which serve to excuse their evil actions to their own minds.

'Let him do what he likes; I will never marry Mademoiselle Taillefer,' said Eugène.

The thought of a compact between himself and a man he held in abhorrence, yet who was fast assuming great proportions in his eyes by the cynicism of his ideas and the boldness with which he clinched society, threw Rastignac into an inward fever, from which, however, he rallied in time to dress and go to Madame de Restaud's. For some time past the countess had shown him much attention, as a young man whose every step led him more and more into the heart of the great world, and whose influence might eventually become formidable. He paid his debts to Messieurs d'Adjuda and de Trailles, played whist far into the night, and regained all he had lost. Being superstitious, as most men are whose future lies before them to make or mar, and who are all more or less fatalists, he chose to see the favour of Heaven in his run of luck – a recompense granted for his persistence in the path of duty. The next morning he hastened to ask Vautrin for the note of hand, and repaid the three thousand francs with very natural satisfaction.

'All goes well,' said Vautrin.

'But I am not your accomplice,' said Eugène.

'I know, I know,' replied the other, interrupting him; 'you are still hampered with some childish nonsense. Once across the threshold, and you'll be all right.'

Two days later Poiret and Mademoiselle Michonneau were sitting on a bench in the sun, in a quiet alley of the Jardin des Plantes, talking with the gentleman who had rightly enough been an object of suspicion to Bianchon.

'Mademoiselle,' said Monsieur Gondureau, 'I cannot see why you should have any scruples. His Excellency Monseigneur the Minister of Police of this kingdom—'

'Ah! His Excellency Monseigneur the Minister of Police of this kingdom,' repeated Poiret.

'Yes; His Excellency is personally interested in this affair,' said Gondureau.

It seems at first sight improbable that Poiret, an old government employee, who had presumably the virtues of the *bourgeois* class though destitute of brains, should have continued to listen to this man after he had plainly acknowledged himself to be a police spy, an agent of the Rue de Jerusalem disguised as an honest citizen. Yet the thing was really natural enough. The reader will better understand the place that Poiret held in the great family of fools after hearing some remarks made not long since by certain keen observers of society, but which have never yet appeared in print. There is a nation of quill-drivers placed in the budget between the Arctic zone of official life inhabited by clerks who receive twelve hundred francs annually – the Greenland of our public offices – and the temperate regions where salaries rise from three to six thousand francs, nay, even blossom in spite of the difficulties of cultivation. One of the characteristic traits of the tribe inhabiting the middle region – a narrow, down-trodden class – is its involuntary, mechanical, instinctive respect for that Grand Llama of office, known personally to the petty employee only by an illegible signature, and spoken of with reverence as His Excellency Monseigneur the Minister; five words equivalent to '*Il Bondo Cani*' of the Caliph of Baghdad – words which to this humble class represent a power sacred and beyond appeal. What the Pope is among Christians, Monseigneur is to the employee. Regarded as infallible in his administrative capacity, the light that emanates from this luminary is reflected in his acts and words, and in all that he does by proxy. It covers with a mantle and legalizes every act that he may ordain. His very title of *Excellency* seems to attest the purity of his motives and the sanctity of his intentions, and is a cloak to ideas that would not otherwise be tolerated. Things that these poor officials would never do to serve themselves, they do willingly in the great name of His Excellency. Public offices have their duty of passive obedience as well as the army; they are controlled by a system which stifles conscience, annihilates manliness, and ends by making the human being a mere screw, or nut, in the government machinery. Thus Monsieur Gondureau, who appeared to have a knowledge of men, soon discovered in Poiret the bureaucratic ninny, and trotted out his *Deus ex machinâ*, the talismanic words 'His Excellency', at the moment when, unmasking his batteries, it was desirable to dazzle the old fellow – whom he regarded as a male Michonneau, just as the Michonneau appeared to him a female Poiret.

'Since His Excellency himself, His Excellency Monseigneur – ah! that alters the case,' said Poiret.

'You hear what Monsieur says – a gentleman in whose judgement you appear to place confidence,' said the pretended *bourgeois*, addressing Mademoiselle Michonneau. 'Well, His Excellency has now obtained the most complete certainty that a man calling himself Vautrin, who lives in the Maison Vauquer, is an escaped *forçat* [convict] from the Torlon galleys, where he was known by the name of Trompe-la-Mort—'

'Ah! Trompe-la-Mort – one who cheats Death!' interrupted Poiret. 'He is lucky if he has earned his name.'

'Yes,' said the agent, 'the nickname is due to the luck he has had in never losing his life in any of the extremely audacious enterprises he has engaged in. The man is dangerous; he has qualities that make him very remarkable. His condemnation itself was a thing that did him infinite honour among his comrades.'

'Is he a man of honour?' asked Poiret.

'After his own fashion – yes. He consented to plead guilty to the crime of another – a forgery, committed by a handsome young man to whom he was much attached; an Italian and a gambler, who afterwards went into the army, where he has conducted himself with perfect propriety ever since.'

'But if His Excellency the Minister of Police is certain that Monsieur Vautrin is Trompe-la-Mort, what does he want of me?' asked Mademoiselle Michonneau.

'Ah! yes,' echoed Poiret; 'if the Minister really, as you do us the honour to say, has the certainty—'

'Certainty is not the word. The fact is strongly suspected. Allow me to explain. Jacques Collin, alias Trompe-la-Mort, has the entire confidence of the prisoners of the three Bagnes [galleys]. They have appointed him their agent and banker. He makes money by taking care of their affairs – an office which necessarily requires a man of mark.'

'Ha! ha! do you see the pun, Mademoiselle?' cried Poiret. 'Monsieur calls him a "man of mark" because he has been branded!'

'This Vautrin,' continued the agent, 'receives the money of the convicts at the galleys, invests it, takes care of it and holds it until claimed by those who escape, or by their families if disposed of by will, or by their mistresses when drawn upon for their benefit.'

'Their mistresses! you mean their wives?' said Poiret.

'No, Monsieur, the convict seldom has any but an illegitimate wife. We call them concubines.'

'What! do they live in concubinage?'

'That follows of course.'

'Well,' said Poiret, 'these are horrors that Monsigneur if he hears of them will never tolerate. Since you have the honour of communicating with His Excellency, you, who seem to me to have philanthropic views, should enlighten him on the bad example set to society by the immoral conduct of these men.'

'But, Monsieur, Government does not send them to the galleys to offer a model of all the virtues.'

'True enough; but still, Monsieur, allow—'

'Let Monsieur go on with what he was saying, my dear,' said Mademoiselle Michonneau.

'You can understand, Mademoiselle,' resumed Gondureau, 'that Government might be very glad to put its hand on this illicit capital, which is said to amount to a very large sum. Trompe-la-Mort has a great deal of property in his possession from the moneys turned over to him by the convicts; and also from what is placed in his hands by the Society of the Ten Thousand—'

'Ten thousand thieves!' ejaculated Poiret, aghast.

'No. The Society of the Ten Thousand is an association of robbers of the first class; men who work on a large scale, and engage in no enterprise unless sure of making at least ten thousand francs by it. This Society is made up of the most distinguished men among those who go through the criminal courts. They know the law, and never risk their lives by doing anything that could condemn them to the guillotine. Collin is their trusted agent, their counsellor. By the aid of his immense resources he has managed to get up a force of private detectives, and has connections widely extended which he wraps in a mystery really impenetrable. For a year we have surrounded him with spies, but we have not yet been able to fathom his game. His money and his ability are meantime promoting vice, making a capital for crime, and supporting a perfect army of bad men who are perpetually making war upon society. To arrest Trompe-la-Mort and seize his funds would pull the evil up by the roots. The matter has thus become an affair of State and of public policy, capable of doing honour to all who engage in it. You, Monsieur, might perhaps be reemployed by the Government – as secretary, possibly, of a police commissioner, which would not hinder you from drawing your pension as a retired functionary.'

'But,' said Mademoiselle Michonneau, 'why does not Trompe-la-Mort run off with the money?'

'Oh!' said Gondureau, 'wherever he went he would be followed by a man with orders to kill him if he stole from the Bagne. Money cannot be carried off as quietly as a man can run away with a pretty girl. Moreover, Collin is a fellow incapable of such an act. He would feel himself dishonoured.'

'Monsieur,' said Poiret, 'you are right; he would be altogether dishonoured.'

'All this does not explain why you do not simply arrest him at once,' said Mademoiselle Michonneau.

'Well, Mademoiselle, I will tell you. But,' he whispered in her ear, 'keep your gentleman from interrupting me, or we shall never have done. He ought to be very rich to get any one to sit and listen to him. – Trompe-la-Mort when he came here put on the skin of an honest man. He gave himself out as a plain citizen, and took lodgings in a commonplace *pension*. Oh! he is very cunning, I can tell you. He is not a fish to be caught without a worm! So Monsieur Vautrin is a man of consideration, who carries on important business of some kind.'

'Naturally,' said Poiret to himself.

'The minister, if any mistake should be made, and if we were to arrest a real Vautrin, would bring down upon himself all the tradespeople of Paris, and have to face public opinion. Monsieur the prefect of police is not very sure of his place; he has enemies; and if we were to make a mistake, those who want to step into his shoes would profit by the yelpings and outcries of the liberals to get rid of him. We must act now as we did in that affair of Coignard, the false Comte de Sainte-Hélène; if he had been the real count we should have been in the wrong box. So we are careful to verify.'

'Yes, but for that you want a pretty woman,' said Mademoiselle Michonneau quickly.

'Trompe-la-Mort will never put himself in the power of any woman,' said the detective. 'He will have nothing to do with them.'

'Then I don't see how I could help you to the verification, even supposing I were willing to undertake it for two thousand francs.'

'Nothing easier. I will give you a phial containing one dose of liquid which will produce a rush of blood to the head – not in the least dangerous, but with all the symptoms of apoplexy. The drug may be put either into his wine or his coffee. As soon as it has had its effect, carry your man to his bed, undress him – to see if he is dying, or any other pretext – contrive to be alone with him, and give him a smart slap on the shoulder, paf! and you will see the letters reappear.'

'That's not much to do,' said Poiret.

'Well, do you agree?' said Gondureau to the old maid.

'But, my dear Monsieur,' said Mademoiselle Michonneau, 'suppose there are no letters. Shall I have the two thousand francs?'

'No.'

'What will you pay me in that case?'

'Five hundred francs.'

'It is very little for doing such a thing as that. Either way it is equally hard upon my conscience. I have my conscience to quiet, Monsieur.'

'I assure you,' said Poiret, 'that Mademoiselle has a great deal of conscience; and, besides, she is a most amiable person and well informed.'

'Well,' said Mademoiselle Michonneau, 'give me three thousand francs if it is Trompe-la-Mort, and nothing at all if he proves to be an honest man.'

'Done!' said Gondureau, 'but on condition that you do it to-morrow.'

'Not so fast, my dear Monsieur. I must consult my confessor.'

'You are a sly one!' said the detective, rising. 'Well, I'll see you to-morrow then; and if you want me before then, come to the Petite Rue Sainte-Anne, at the farther end of the Court of the Sainte-Chapelle. There is only one door under the arch. Ask for Monsieur Gondureau.'

Bianchon, who was coming from the Cours de Cuvier, caught the singular name of Trompe-la-Mort, and heard the 'Done!' of the celebrated chief of the detective police.

'Why did not you settle it at once?' said Poiret to Mademoiselle Michonneau. 'It would give you three hundred francs annuity.'

'Why?' said she. 'Well, because I want to think it over. If Monsieur Vautrin is really Trompe-la-Mort perhaps it would be better to make a bargain with him. Still, if I broached the subject I should give him warning, and he is just the man to decamp *gratis*. It would be an abominable cheat.'

'Even if he did get away,' said Poiret, 'Monsieur told us he was watched by the police. But you – you will lose everything.'

'There is this to be said,' thought Mademoiselle Michonneau, 'I don't like him. He is always saying disagreeable things to me.'

'Besides,' said Poiret, returning to the charge, 'you will be acting for the Government. According to what that gentleman told us (he seemed to me a very nice man, and very well dressed too), it is an act of obedience to the laws; it rids the world of a criminal, however virtuous he may be. He who has drunk will drink. Suppose he took a fancy to murder us in our beds – devil take me! – we should be guilty of his homicides; and be ourselves the first victims.'

The preoccupation of Mademoiselle Michonneau prevented her from giving ear to these sentences, which dropped one by one from the lips of Poiret like water trickling through a spigot carelessly closed. When once the old man was set going, and Mademoiselle Michonneau did not stop him, he ticked on like a mechanism wound up to go till it runs down. Having broached a subject, he was usually led by his parentheses through a variety of irrelevant topics without ever coming to a conclusion. By the time they reached the Maison Vauquer he had maundered through a quantity of examples and quotations which led him finally to relate his own deposition in the affair of the Sieur Ragoulleau and the Dame Morin, in which he had figured as a witness for the defence. On entering the house his companion observed that Eugène de Rastignac was engaged in close conversation with Mademoiselle Taillefer, and that their interest in each other was so absorbing that they paid no heed to the pair who passed them in crossing the dining-room.

'I knew it would come to that,' said Mademoiselle Michonneau to Poiret, 'they have been making eyes at each other for the last week.'

'Yes,' he replied, 'but after all, she was pronounced guilty.'

'Who?'

'Madame Morin.'

'I was talking of Mademoiselle Victorine,' said Michonneau, following Poiret into his chamber without noticing where she was going, 'and you answer me by Madame Morin. Who is that woman?'

'What has Mademoiselle Victorine been guilty of?' asked Poiret.

'She is guilty of being in love with Monsieur Eugène de Rastignac, and running headlong without knowing what she is coming to, poor innocent!'

XIII

Eugène had that morning been driven to despair by Madame de Nucingen. In his inmost soul he now yielded himself up to Vautrin, not choosing to fathom either the motives of that strange man in befriending him, or the future of the alliance that would be riveted between them. Nothing but a miracle could save him now from the abyss, on the verge of which he stood as he exchanged with Mademoiselle Taillefer the sweetest of all promises. Victorine listened as to the voice of angels; the heavens opened for her, the Maison Vauquer shone with tints that artists lavish upon palaces; she loved, and she was loved – alas, she thought she was! And what young girl would not have thought so, as she looked at Rastignac and listened to him for that one sweet hour stolen from the argus eyes that watched her! While he fought his conscience, knowing that he was doing evil and choosing to do evil, saying to himself that he would atone for this sin by giving lifelong happiness to his wife, the fires of the hell within him burned from the inner to the outer, and the anguish of his soul heightened the beauty of his face. Mercifully for him the miracle took place.

Vautrin entered gaily, reading at a glance the souls of the young pair whom he had married by the machinations of his infernal genius, and whose joy he killed as he trolled forth in his strong mocking voice—

> 'My Fanny is charming
> In her simplicity.'

Victorine fled away, carrying with her more of joy than she had yet known of sorrow. Poor child, a pressure of the hands, the sweep of her lover's curls upon her cheek, a word whispered in her ear so close that she felt the warm touch of his lips, an arm folded trembling about her, a kiss taken from her white throat – these were the troth-plights of her passion, which the near presence of Sylvie, threatening to enter that radiant dining-room, only rendered more ardent, more real, more tender than the noblest pledges of devotion related in the love-tales of the knights of old. These *menus suffrages* – to borrow the pretty expression of our ancestors – seemed almost crimes to the pure heart that confessed itself weekly. In this short hour she had lavished treasures of her soul more precious far than hereafter, rich and happy, she could bestow with the gift of her whole being.

'The affair is arranged,' said Vautrin to Eugène. 'All passed very properly. Difference of opinion. Our pigeon insulted my falcon. It is for to-morrow – in the redoubt at Clignancourt. By half-past eight o'clock Mademoiselle Taillefer will be heiress of all the love and all the money of her father, while she is quietly dipping her bits of toast into her coffee! Droll, isn't it? It seems young Taillefer is a good swordsman, and he feels as sure of having the best of it as if he held all the trumps in his hand. But he'll be bled by a trick of mine; a pass I invented – raising the sword and giving a quick thrust through the forehead. I'll show it to you some day, for it is immensely useful.'

Rastignac looked at him and listened in a stupid manner, but said nothing. At this moment Père Goriot came in with Bianchon and some of the other guests.

'You are taking it just as I hoped,' said Vautrin. 'You know what you are about. All right, my young eaglet – you will govern men. You are strong, firm, virile. I respect you.'

He offered his hand, but Rastignac drew back quickly and

dropped into a chair, turning very pale; a sea of blood rolled at his feet.

'Well, well! we still have a rag of our swaddling-clothes spotted with virtue,' said Vautrin in a whisper. 'The papa has three million. I know his fortune. The *dot* will make you white as the bridal gown – in your own eyes, too; never fear.'

Rastignac hesitated no longer. He determined to go that evening and warn the Taillefers, father and son. At this moment, Vautrin having left him, Père Goriot said in his ear—

'You seem out of spirits, my dear boy; but I can make you merry. Come!'

The old man lit his rush-light at one of the lamps, and went upstairs. Eugène followed him in silence.

'Let us go to your room,' he said. 'You thought this morning that she did not care for you, *hein*? She sent you away peremptorily; and you went off angry. Oh, you simpleton! She was expecting *me*. We were going together – yes, *together* – to arrange a little jewel of an *appartement* where you are to live three days from now. Don't tell her that I told you. It was to be a surprise; but I can't keep the secret any longer. It is in the Rue d'Artois, two steps from the Rue Saint-Lazare. You will be lodged like a prince. We have been getting furniture fit for a bride. We have been very busy together for the last month, but I would not tell you anything about it. My lawyer has taken the field. Delphine will have her thirty thousand francs a year, the interest of her *dot*; and I shall insist on her eight hundred thousand francs being invested in good securities – securities in open day-light, you know.'

Eugène was silent. He walked up and down the miserable, untidy room with folded arms. Père Goriot seized a moment when his back was turned to put upon the chimney-piece a red morocco case, on which the arms of Rastignac were stamped in gold.

'My dear boy!' said the poor old man, 'I have gone into this thing up to my chin. To tell you the truth, there is some selfishness in it. I have my own interests to serve in your change of quarters. I have something to ask of you.'

'What is it?'

'There is a little room attached to the *appartement* that will just suit me. I shall live there, shall I not? I am getting old – I live so far from my daughters. I shall not be in your way; but you will come and tell me about them constantly – every evening? That will not trouble you, will it? When you come in, and I am in my bed, I shall hear you, and say to myself, "He has seen my little Delphine; he has taken her to a ball; she is happy with him." If I were ill, it would be balm to my heart to hear you go out and come in. It would bring me nearer to my daughters: you belong to their world, but you are my friend. It will be but a step to the Champs Elysées, where they drive every afternoon; I could see them daily, whereas now I often get there too late. Sometimes my little Delphine would come there, and then I should see her, in her pretty wadded pelisse, trotting about as daintily as a little cat. She has been so bright and merry for a month past – just what she was as a girl at home, with me. She said to me just now as we walked together, "Papa, I am so happy!" When they say ceremoniously, "My father," they freeze me; but when they call me "Papa," I seem to see my little ones again; the past comes back to me; they are mine once more.'

The old man wiped the tears from his eyes. 'I had not heard her say "Papa" for so long! She had not taken my arm for years: yes! it is ten years since I have walked beside either of my daughters. Oh! it was good to hear the flutter of her dress, to keep step with her, to feel her so warm and soft beside me! This morning I went everywhere with Delphine; she took me into the shops; I escorted her home. Ah! you and I will live together. If you have any want I shall know it – I shall be at hand. If that rough log of an Alsatian would only die! if his gout would fly to his stomach! then you could make my poor girl a happy woman.

She may have done wrong, but she has been so wretched in her marriage that I excuse all. Surely the Father in Heaven is not less kind than an earthly father! – She was praising you to me,' he went on after a pause. 'She talked of you as we walked: "Is he not handsome, Papa? Is he not kind and good? Does he ever speak of me?" From the Rue d'Artois to the Passage des Panoramas she talked of you. All this happy morning I was no longer old – I was light as a feather. I told her how you gave me the thousand-franc note. Oh! the darling! she shed tears – Why! what is that you have on your chimney-piece?' he said, impatient at Rastignac's immobility.

Eugène, stunned and silent, looked at his neighbour with a bewildered air. The duel, with all its consequences, announced by Vautrin for the morrow, presented such a frightful contrast to this fulfilment of his pleasant dreams that his mind struggled as it were with a nightmare. He turned to the fireplace and saw the little case, opened it, and found inside a scrap of paper, beneath which lay a Bréguet watch. On the paper were written these words—

'I wish you to think of me every hour, *because*—
'DELPHINE.'

The last word no doubt alluded to something that had passed between them. Eugène was much affected. His arms were inlaid in gold inside the case. This *bijou* – a pretty thing he had long coveted – the chain, the key, the case, the chasing, were all exactly what he liked. Père Goriot was delighted. He had doubtless promised to carry to his daughter an account of how Eugène received her unexpected gift; for he was a third in their youthful pleasures, and not the least happy of the three.

'You will go and see her this evening?' he said. 'She expects you. That log of an Alsatian sups with his *danseuse*. You will take me with you, will you not?'

'Yes, my good Père Goriot. You know that I love you—'

'Ah! you are not ashamed of me – not you! Let me kiss you;' and he strained the student in his arms. 'To-night! – we will go and see her to-night.'

'Yes; but first I must go out on business which it is impossible to postpone.'

'Can I help you?'

'Why, yes, you can. While I go to Madame de Nucingen's, you might go to the house of Monsieur Taillefer, the father, and beg him to give me an hour this evening, to speak to him on a subject of the utmost importance.'

'Can it be possible, young man,' cried Père Goriot, whose whole aspect changed – 'can it be true that you are paying court to his daughter, as those fools say downstairs? Heavens and earth! You don't know what it is to get a tap from Goriot. If you are playing false, one blow of my fist – But it is not possible!'

'I swear to you, I love but one woman in the world,' cried the student; 'and I did not know it till a moment ago. But young Taillefer is to fight a duel, and he is certain to be killed.'

'What is that to you?' asked Goriot.

'I *must* tell the father to save his son!' cried Eugène.

His words were interrupted by the voice of Vautrin standing on the threshold of his chamber, singing—

"'O Richard, ô mon roi!
L'univers t' abandonne —"
'Broum! broum! broum! broum! broum!
"Long have I wandered here and there,
And wherever by chance –
Tra, la, la, la, la—"

'Gentlemen,' said Christophe, 'the soup is waiting; everybody is at table.'

'Here, Christophe,' said Vautrin. 'Come in and get a bottle of my claret.'

'Is the watch pretty?' whispered Père Goriot. 'Is it in good taste – *hein*?'

Vautrin, Père Goriot and Rastignac went down to dinner, and by reason of their being late were placed together at the table. Eugène showed marked coldness to Vautrin, though the man had never displayed greater gifts of intellect; he sparkled with wit, and even roused something of it in the other guests. His *sang froid* and assurance struck Eugène with consternation.

'What herb have you trodden on to-day?' said Madame Vauquer to Vautrin; 'you are as gay as a lark.'

'I am always gay when I have done a good stroke of business.'

'Business!' said Eugène.

'Well, yes. I have delivered over some goods to-day which will bring me in a handsome commission. Mademoiselle Michonneau,' he continued, perceiving that the old maid was looking at him attentively, 'is there anything in my face which is not agreeable to you, that you stare at me like an American? If so, pray mention it, and it shall be changed to please you. Ha! Poiret, we won't quarrel about that, will we?' he added, winking at the employee.

'*Sac-à-papier!* You ought to sit for the Joking Hercules,' said the young painter to Vautrin.

'Faith! I'm willing, if Mademoiselle Michonneau will pose as the Venus of Père-la-Chaise,' replied Vautrin.

'And Poiret?' said Bianchon.

'Oh, Poiret shall sit – as Poiret, god of gardens!' cried Vautrin. 'He derives from *poire* [pear].'

'All that is nonsense,' said Madame Vauquer. 'You had better give us some of your claret, Monsieur Vautrin; I see the neck of a bottle. It will keep up our spirits, and it is good for the stomach.'

'Gentlemen,' said Vautrin, 'Madame la présidente calls us to order. Madame Couture and Mademoiselle Victorine have not yet declared themselves shocked by your jocular discourse, but please respect the innocence of Père Goriot. I propose to offer you a little *bottleorama* of claret, which the name of Lafitte renders doubly illustrious: this remark, you will understand, bears no allusion to politics. Come on, Chinaman!' he added, looking at Christophe, who did not stir. 'Here, Christophe! don't you know your name? Chinese! bring forth the liquid!'

'Here it is, Monsieur,' said Christophe, giving him the bottle.

After filling Eugène's glass and that of Père Goriot, he poured out a few drops for himself and tasted them slowly, while the other two drank theirs off. Suddenly he made a grimace.

'The devil!' he cried; 'this wine is corked. Here, Christophe, you may have the rest of it; and go and get some more. You know where it is – right hand side. Stay! we are sixteen; bring down eight bottles.'

'Regardless of cost,' said the painter. 'I'll pay for a hundred chestnuts.'

'Ah! ah!'

'Bra-vo! Oh!'

'Hur-rah! – rah!'

Every one uttered an exclamation, popping, as usual, like fireworks.

'Come, Madame Vauquer, give us two bottles of champagne,' cried Vautrin.

'Listen to that! You might as well ask for the house itself! Two bottles of champagne! Why, they cost twelve francs! I don't make that in a week. But if Monsieur Eugène will pay for the champagne, I'll give some currant wine.'

'Pah! That stuff of hers is as bad as a black dose,' said the medical student in a whisper.

'*Will* you hold your tongue, Bianchon!' said Rastignac; 'the very name of a black dose makes me sick at – Yes, bring on your champagne! I'll pay for it,' he added.

'Sylvie,' said Madame Vauquer, 'give us the biscuits and some little cakes.'

'Your little cakes are too old,' said Vautrin; 'they have grown a beard. As for the biscuits, produce them!'

In a few moments the claret circulated, the company grew lively, the gayety redoubled. Above the din of laughter rose a variety of cat-calls and imitations of the noises of animals. The employee of the museum reproduced a street-cry popularly supposed at that time to resemble the amorous maulings of the roof-cats; whereupon eight voices joined chorus in well-known Paris cries—

'Knives to grind – grind!'

'Chick – weed for your little birds!'

'*Plaisir!* ladies – *Plaisir!* taste my sweet *Plaisir!*'

'China! China to mend!'

'To the barge! To the barge!'

'Beat your wives – your coats! Beat your coats!'

'Old clo'es, gold lace, old hats to sell!'

'Cherries! cherries! ripe cherries!'

But the palm fell to Bianchon, as he miauled through his nose, 'Umbrellas! – Umbrellas to mend!'

The racket was ear-splitting, the talk sheer nonsense, a veritable medley, which Vautrin conducted like the leader of an orchestra, keeping an eye meanwhile on Eugène and Père Goriot, who both had the appearance of being drunk already. Leaning back in their chairs, they gazed stolidly at the extraordinary scene around them, and drank little. Both were thinking of what they had to do that evening, but neither felt able to rise from his chair. Vautrin, who watched every change in their faces out of the corner of his eye, seized the moment when their heads were beginning to droop, to lean over Rastignac, and whisper in his ear—

'My lad, we are not clever enough to get the better of Papa Vautrin. He loves you a great deal too well to let you commit a folly. When I have made up my mind, nothing but the hand of Providence can stop me. Ha! ha! my little school-boy; we thought we would go and tell Father Taillefer, did we? Bah! the oven is hot, the dough is light, the bread is in the pan – to-morrow we will eat it and brush off the crumbs. So you thought you could keep it out of the oven! No! no! it is bound to bake. If any little bits of remorse stick in our gullet, they will pass off with the digestion. While we are sleeping our sound little sleep, Colonel Count Franchessini will open us a way to the money-bags of Michel Taillefer with the point of his sword. Victorine as her brother's heiress will have fifteen thousand francs a year at once. I have made the proper enquiries; the mother left more than three hundred thousand.'

Eugène heard, but he had no power to answer. His tongue clove to the roof of his mouth; he was overcome with an unconquerable drowsiness. He saw the table and the faces of the people through a luminous haze. Presently the noise diminished, the guests were leaving one by one. When Madame Vauquer, Madame Couture, Victorine, Vautrin and Père Goriot alone were left, Rastignac saw, as in a dream, Madame Vauquer going round the table collecting the bottles and emptying their contents together to make full bottles.

'Are they not foolish; are they not young?' she said. Those were the last words Eugène understood.

'There is nobody like Monsieur Vautrin for playing such tricks,' said Sylvie. 'Just listen to Christophe snoring like a top!'

'Good-by, Mamma,' said Vautrin. 'I am off to the boulevard to admire Monsieur Marty in *Le Mont Sauvage*, a new play taken from "Le Solitaire". If you like, I will take you and these two ladies.'

'I thank you, no,' said Madame Couture.

'Oh! my dear lady!' said Madame Vauquer, 'how can you refuse to see a play taken from "Le Solitaire" – a work by Atala de Chateaubriand, that we all read and wept over under the *lieuilles* last summer; a perfectly moral tale, which might edify your young lady?'

'We are forbidden to go to theatres,' said Victorine.

'There! those two are off,' said Vautrin, looking at Rastignac and Père Goriot in a comical way, and placing the student's head back in his chair so that he might rest more comfortably; singing as he did so—

'Sleep! sleep! for thy sweet sake,
I watch, I wake.'

'I am afraid he is ill,' said Victorine.

'Then stay and nurse him,' replied Vautrin. 'It is,' he whispered in her ear, 'a part of your submissive duty as a woman. He adores you, that young man; and you will be his little wife. Remember, I predict it. *And then,*' he added aloud, '*they were much esteemed throughout the neighbourhood, and had a large family, and lived happily ever after.* That's the ending of all love-stories. Come, Mamma,' he continued, turning to Madame Vauquer, and putting his arm round her. 'Put on your bonnet and the beautiful dress with the flowers all over it, and the countess's scarf, and let us be off. I'll call a coach myself,' and he departed, singing—

'"Sun, Sun! divinest Sun!
That ripenest the lemons thou shinest on."'

'*Mon Dieu!* Madame Couture, I could live happy in a garret with that man!' said Madame Vauquer. 'Look at Père Goriot! that old miser never offered to take me nowhere. He'll be on the floor presently. Heavens! it isn't decent for a man of his age to lose his senses in that way. I suppose you'll say he never had any. Sylvie, get him upstairs.'

Sylvie took the old man under the arms and made him walk up to his room, where she threw him, dressed as he was, across the bed.

'Poor young man!' said Madame Couture, putting back Eugène's hair which had fallen over his forehead; 'he is like a young girl; he did not know the wine would be too much for him.'

'I can tell you,' said Madame Vauquer, 'that though I have kept this *pension* forty years, and many young men have passed in that time through my hands, I never knew one as well behaved and gentlemanly as Monsieur Eugène. Isn't he handsome as he lies asleep? Let him rest his head upon your shoulder, Madame Couture. Ah! he has turned it towards Mademoiselle Victorine. Well, there's a Providence for children; a little more, and he would have cracked his skull against the back of the chair. Are not they a pretty couple?'

'Please be silent,' cried Madame Couture, 'you are saying things which—'

'Bah!' said Madame Vauquer, 'he can't hear anything. Come, Sylvie, and dress me. I am going to put on my best corset.'

'Madame! your best corset after dinner!' cried Sylvie. 'No, get somebody else to lace it. I won't be the death of you. You risk your life, I tell you that!'

'I don't care; I am going to do honour to Monsieur Vautrin.'

'You must be very fond of your heirs!'

'Come, Sylvie, no talking,' said the widow, leaving the room.

'At her age!' said Sylvie, pointing at her mistress and looking at Victorine.

Madame Couture and her ward remained alone in the dining-room, the head of Eugène resting against Victorine's shoulder. Christophe's loud snoring echoed through the house and made a contrast to the peaceful slumbers of the student, who was sleeping as quietly as an infant. Happy in allowing herself one of those tender acts of charity so dear to womanhood, and in feeling, without reproach, the heart of the young man beating against her own, Victorine's sweet face took on a look of maternal pride and protection. Across the thousand thoughts that stirred her heart there came a tumultuous sense of her new joy, filling her young veins with pure and sacred warmth.

'Poor darling!' said Madame Couture, pressing her hand.

The old lady gazed into the fair sad face, round which for the first time shone the halo of human happiness. Victorine resembled one of those quaint pictures of the Middle Ages, where the accessories are meagre or left to the imagination, while the artist spends the magic of his calm and noble art upon the face of his Madonna, yellow perhaps in tone, but reflecting from the heaven above its golden tints of glory.

'He only drank two glasses, Mamma,' she said, passing her fingers over his hair.

'If he were a dissipated man, my dear, he could have taken his wine like all the rest; the fact that it overcame him proves the contrary.'

The sound of carriage wheels was heard.

'Mamma,' said the young girl hastily, 'here comes Monsieur Vautrin; take my place by Monsieur Eugène. I would rather not be seen thus by that man. He says things that sully the soul, and his look abases me.'

'No, no,' said Madame Couture, 'you do him injustice. Monsieur Vautrin is a worthy man – somewhat in the style of the late Monsieur Couture, brusque but kindly; a benevolent bear.'

At this moment Vautrin came softly in and looked at the young couple, on whom the light of a lamp fell caressingly.

'Well, well!' he said, folding his arms, 'there's a scene that might have inspired some of the finest pages of that good

Bernardin de Saint-Pierre, author of "Paul and Virginia". Youth is very beautiful, Madame Couture. Sleep, my poor boy,' he added, looking down on Eugène; 'our blessings come to us sleeping. Madame,' he said presently, 'what attaches me to this young man, and moves my heart as I gaze upon him, is that I know the beauty of his soul to be in harmony with the beauty of his face. See! is it not the head of a cherubim resting on the shoulder of an angel? He is worthy of a woman's love. If I were a woman I would be willing to die – no! not such a fool – to live for him. As I gaze upon those two, Madame,' he whispered, bending till he almost touched her ear, 'I cannot help thinking that God has created them for one another. The ways of Providence are full of mystery; they try the reins and the heart. Seeing you together, my children,' he added aloud, 'united by an equal purity, and by every emotion of the human heart, I feel it is impossible that anything should part you in the future. God is just. But,' he continued, addressing the young girl, 'I think I have noticed on your hand the lines of prosperity. I know something of palmistry. I often tell fortunes. Let me take your hand, Mademoiselle Victorine – don't be afraid. Oh! what do I see? On the word of an honest man, it will not be long before you are one of the richest heiresses in Paris! You will make the man who loves you supremely happy. Your father will call you to him. You will marry a man of title, young, handsome, and who adores you.'

At this moment the heavy steps of the coquettish widow interrupted Vautrin's prophecies.

'Here is Mamma Vauquer-r-re, as fair as a star-r-r, and decked out like a carrot. Are we not just a little bit uncomfortable?' he added, putting his hand on the top of her busk. 'It strikes me we are squeezed a shade too tight, Mamma. If the play should make us cry, there would be an explosion: but I will pick up the pieces with the care of an antiquary.'

'He knows the language of French gallantry, doesn't he?' whispered the widow in the ear of Madame Couture.

'Farewell, my children!' said Vautrin, turning towards Victorine and Eugène. 'I bless you,' he added, laying his hands upon their heads. 'Believe me, Mademoiselle, there is value in the blessing of an honest man; it will bring you joy, for God hears it.'

'Good-by, my dear friend,' said Madame Vauquer to Madame Couture. 'Do you think,' she added in a whisper, 'that Monsieur Vautrin has intentions towards me?'

'Ah! my dear mother,' said Victorine, looking at her hands with a sigh after the others had departed, 'suppose that good Monsieur Vautrin spoke the truth?'

'One thing could make it true,' replied the old lady; 'your monster of a brother need only be thrown from his horse—'

'Oh, Mamma!'

'*Mon Dieu*, perhaps it is a sin to wish harm to one's enemy. Well, I will do penance for it. But, truly, I should not be sorry to lay flowers on his grave. He has a hard heart. He never defended his mother; he took all her fortune, and cheated you out of your share of it. My cousin had a great deal of money. Unfortunately for you there was no mention of her *dot* in her marriage contract.'

'My prosperity would be hard to bear if it cost any one his life,' said Victorine; 'and if to make me happy my brother had to die, I would rather be as I am now.'

'Well, well! As that good Monsieur Vautrin says, who, you see, is full of religious feeling,' said Madame Couture – 'I am glad to think he is not an unbeliever, like so many others, who talk of God with less respect than they do of the Devil – well, as he says, who knows by what ways it will please Providence to guide us?'

Aided by Sylvie, the two women took Eugène to his chamber and placed him on his bed, Sylvie unfastening his clothes to make him more comfortable. Before leaving him, and when Madame

Couture had turned to go, Victorine laid a little kiss upon his forehead, with a rapture of happiness naturally to be expected from so criminal an act! She looked round the chamber, gathered up, as it were, in one thought memory that she treasured long, and fell asleep the happiest creature in all Paris.

The gay frolic under cover of which Vautrin had drugged the wine of Eugène and Père Goriot decided his own fate. Bianchon, half tipsy, forgot to question Mademoiselle Michonneau concerning Trompe-la-Mort. If he had uttered that name he would have put Vautrin on his guard – or rather, to give him his true name, Jacques Collin, one of the celebrities of the galleys. Moreover, the nickname of Venus of Père-la-Chaise decided Mademoiselle Michonneau to give him up at the very moment when, confident of his liberality, she had calculated that it was better policy to warn him and let him escape during the night. Accompanied by Poiret, she went in search of the famous chief of detectives in the Petite Rue Sainte-Anne, under the impression that she was dealing with an upper-class employee named Gondureau. The director of the secret police received her graciously. Then, after a conversation in which the preliminaries were settled, Mademoiselle Michonneau asked for the dose by the help of which she was to do her work. The gesture of satisfaction made by the great man as he searched for the phial in the drawer of his writing-table, gave her a sudden conviction that there was more in this capture than the mere arrest of an escaped convict. By dint of beating her brains and putting two and two together, she came to the conclusion that the police hoped, through revelations made by convicts won over at the galleys, to lay their hands upon a large amount of money. When she expressed this conjecture to the fox with whom she was dealing, he smiled and tried to turn aside her suspicions.

'You are mistaken,' he said. 'Collin is the most dangerous *sorbonne* ever known among our robbers. That's the whole of it. The rascals know this. He is their shield, their banner – their Bonaparte, in short. They all love him. That scoundrel will never leave his *tronche* on the Place de Grève.'

Mademoiselle Michonneau did not understand him; but Gondureau explained to her the slang expressions he had made use of. *Sorbonne* and *tronche* are two energetic words of the thieves' vocabulary, invented because these gentry were the first to feel the need of considering the human head from two standpoints. *Sorbonne* is the head of the living man – his intellect and wisdom. *Tronche* is a word of contempt, expressing the worthlessness of the head after it is cut off.

'Collin baffles us,' resumed the chief. 'When we have to do with men of his stamp, of steel and iron, the law allows us to kill them on the spot if, when arrested, they make the slightest resistance. We expect a struggle which will authorize us to shoot Collin to-morrow morning. We thus avoid a trial and the costs of imprisonment and subsistence, and society is quit of him. The lawyers and the witnesses, their pay and expenses, the execution, and all the rest that is required to rid us legally of such villains cost more than the three thousand francs we are to pay you. Besides, it saves time. The thrust of a bayonet into Trompe-la-Mort's paunch will prevent a hundred crimes, and spare us the consequences of the corruption of fifty ill-disposed scoundrels, who are always hovering on the verge of mischief. That's the true function of the police – prevention of crime. Philanthropists will tell you so.'

'It is serving one's country,' cried Poiret.

'Yes,' replied the chief; 'certainly we are serving our country: you are talking some sense this morning. People are very unjust to us in this respect. We render society great services, and society overlooks them. It takes superior men to endure prejudice; only a Christian can accept the reproach that doing good incurs when it is not done exactly in the line of received traditions. Paris is Paris, you know. That saying explains my life. I have the honour to salute you, Mademoiselle. I shall be with my men in the Jardin du Roi to-morrow morning. Send Christophe to the Rue de Buffon and ask for Monsieur Gondureau at the house where I was staying. Monsieur, your servant. If anybody ever robs you, let me know, and I will recover what is lost for you. I am at your service.'

'Well,' said Poiret to Mademoiselle. Michonneau, 'there are fools in the world who are all upset by the word "detective". That gentleman is very amiable; and what he asks of you is as easy as saying "How do you do?"'

XIV

The next day was one long remembered in the annals of the Maison Vauquer. Hitherto the most remarkable event in its history had been the meteoric apparition of the fraudulent countess. But all was to pale before the catastrophes of this great day, which for the rest of her life supplied Madame Vauquer with topics of conversation. In the first place, Père Goriot and Eugène slept till eleven o'clock. Madame Vauquer, who did not get home from the theatre till very late, stayed in bed till half-past ten. Christophe, who had finished the bottle of wine made over to him by Vautrin, slept so late that everything was behindhand in the household. Poiret and Mademoiselle Michonneau made no complaint about breakfast being late. As for Victorine and Madame Couture, they also slept far into the morning. Vautrin went out before eight o'clock, and got home just as breakfast was on the table. No one, therefore, offered any remonstrance when, at a quarter past eleven, Sylvie and Christophe knocked at all the doors and said that breakfast was served. While they were out of the dining-room, Mademoiselle Michonneau, who was the first person down that morning, poured her liquid into the silver goblet belonging to Vautrin, in which the cream for his coffee was heating in the *bain-marie*, together with the portions of the other guests. The old maid had counted on this custom of the house to accomplish her purpose.

It was not without difficulty that the family were finally got together. At the moment when Rastignac, still stretching himself, came last of all into the dining-room, a messenger gave him a note from Madame de Nucingen, which ran as follows—

'I will not show false pride, nor will I be angry with you, my friend. I waited, expecting you, till two in the morning. To wait for one we love! – He who has known such pain would not impose it on another. It proves to me that you have never loved till now. What has happened? I am very anxious. If I did not fear to betray the secrets of my heart I should have gone to find out whether joy or sorrow had befallen you. I feel the disadvantage of being only a woman. Reassure me; explain to me why you did not come after what my father told you. I may be angry, but I shall forgive you. Are you ill? Why do you live so far away from me? One word for pity's sake! You will be here soon, will you not? Say merely, "I am coming," or "I am ill." But if you were ill, my father would have been here to tell me. What has happened?'

'Yes, what has happened?' cried Eugène, hurriedly entering the dining-room, and crumpling up his note without reading the rest of it. 'What o'clock is it?'

'Half-past eleven,' said Vautrin, putting sugar in his coffee.

The escaped convict gave Eugène that glance of cold compelling fascination which very magnetic people have the power of giving – a glance which is said to subdue the maniacs in a mad-house. Eugène trembled in every limb. The roll of a carriage was heard in the still street, and a servant in the Taillefer livery, which Madame Couture recognized at once, came hurriedly into the dining-room, with an excited air.

'Mademoiselle,' he cried, 'Monsieur your father has sent for you. A great misfortune has befallen him. Monsieur Frédéric has fought a duel. He received a sword-thrust in the forehead. The doctors have no hope of saving him. You will hardly be in time to see him breathe his last. He is unconscious already.'

'Poor young man!' exclaimed Vautrin, 'how can people quarrel when they have thirty thousand francs a year! Most assuredly young men do not tread the paths of wisdom—'

'Monsieur!' interrupted Eugène.

'Well! – and what of it, you big baby?' said Vautrin, quietly finishing his cup of coffee, an operation which Mademoiselle Michonneau watched so intently that she paid no heed to the extraordinary event that stupefied the people around her. 'Are there not duels every day in Paris?'

'I shall go with you, Victorine,' said Madame Couture.

The two women flew off without hats or shawls. Victorine, with tears in her eyes, gave Eugène a parting glance, which said, 'I did not think our happiness would so soon have turned to grief!'

'Why, you are quite a prophet, Monsieur Vautrin,' said Madame Vauquer.

'I am all things,' replied Jacques Collin.

'It is most singular,' said Madame Vauquer, breaking forth into a string of commonplaces. 'Death takes us without warning. Young people are often called before the aged. It is lucky for us women that we are not expected to fight duels. But we have maladies of our own unknown to men – child-bed especially. What unexpected luck for Victorine! Her father will be forced to acknowledge her.'

'Just think,' said Vautrin, looking at Eugène, 'yesterday she had not a *sou*; this morning she has a fortune of millions.'

'Ah! Monsieur Eugène,' cried Madame Vauquer, 'you put your hand in the bag at the right moment.'

As Madame Vauquer said this, Père Goriot looked at Eugène and saw the crumpled letter in his hand.

'You have not read it,' he said. 'What does that mean? Are you like all the rest?'

'Madame, I shall never marry Mademoiselle Victorine,' said Eugène, addressing Madame Vauquer with an expression of mingled horror and disgust which astonished the others at the table.

Père Goriot seized the student's hand and pressed it; he would fain have kissed it.

'Oh! oh!' said Vautrin, 'they have an excellent saying in Italy – *col tempo.*'

'I was to wait for an answer,' said the messenger to Rastignac.

'Say I am coming.'

The man went away. Eugène's agitation was so great that he could not be prudent.

'What can be done?' he said aloud, though speaking to himself, 'I have no proofs.'

Vautrin smiled. At this moment the potion absorbed by the stomach began to take effect. Nevertheless the convict was so vigorous that he rose, looked at Rastignac, and said in a hollow voice, 'Young man, our blessings come to us while we sleep.'

As he said the words he fell down, to all appearance dead.

'The justice of God!' cried Eugène.

'Why, what's the matter with him, poor dear Monsieur Vautrin,' exclaimed Madame Vauquer.

'It is apoplexy,' cried Mademoiselle Michonneau.

'Sylvie! run, my girl, go for the doctor,' said the widow. 'Ah, Monsieur Rastignac, go, please, and get Monsieur Bianchon; perhaps Sylvie will not find our own doctor, Monsieur Grimpel.'

Rastignac, glad of the excuse to escape from that horrible den, rushed away at full speed.

'Christophe! here – go as fast as you can to the apothecary's, and ask him to give you something for apoplexy. Père Goriot, help us to carry him up to his own room.'

Vautrin was seized; dragged with difficulty up the staircase, and laid upon his bed.

'I can be of no further use; I am going to see my daughter,' said Monsieur Goriot.

'Selfish old thing!' cried Madame Vauquer. 'Go! I only wish you may die like a dog yourself.'

'See if you have any ether, Madame Vauquer,' said Mademoiselle

Michonneau, who with the aid of Poiret had unfastened Vautrin's clothes.

Madame Vauquer went to her own room and left Mademoiselle Michonneau mistress of the field.

'Come, quick! – take off his shirt and turn him over. Be good for something – so far, at least, as to save my modesty,' she said to Poiret; 'you stand there like a fool.'

Vautrin being turned over, Mademoiselle Michonneau gave him a smart tap on the shoulder, and the two fatal letters appeared in the midst of the red circle.

'Well, you have not had much trouble in earning your three thousand francs,' cried Poiret, holding Vautrin up while Mademoiselle Michonneau was putting on his shirt again. 'Ouf! but he is heavy,' he said, laying him down.

'Hold your tongue! I wonder if there is a strong-box – or a safe?' said the old maid with avidity, her eyes almost looking through the walls as she glanced eagerly at every bit of furniture in the room. 'If one could only open this writing-desk on some pretext,' she said.

'Perhaps that wouldn't be right,' remarked Poiret.

'Where's the harm? Stolen money belongs to no one – it is anybody's. But we have not time, I hear the Vauquer.'

'Here is the ether,' said the widow. 'Well, I declare, this is a day of adventures – but, look! that man cannot be so very ill; he is as white as a chicken.'

'As a chicken,' repeated Poiret.

'His heart beats regularly,' said Madame Vauquer, placing her hand upon it.

'Regularly? – does it though?' said Poiret, surprised.

'He is all right.'

'Do you think so?' asked Poiret.

'Why, yes! he looks as if he were sleeping. Sylvie has gone for the doctor. Look, Mademoiselle Michonneau, he is sniffing the ether. Bah! it was only a kind of spasm; his pulse is good. He is as strong as a Turk. Just see, Mademoiselle, what a fur tippet he has got on his breast! He will live to be a hundred, he will! His wig hasn't tumbled off – goodness! why, it is glued on. He has got some hair of his own – and it's red! They say men with red hair are either very good or very bad: he is one of the good ones.'

'Good enough to hang,' interrupted Poiret.

'Round a pretty woman's neck, you mean,' cried Mademoiselle Michonneau quickly. 'Go downstairs, Monsieur Poiret. It is our place to take care of you men when you are ill. You had better go out and take a walk – for all the good you do,' she added. 'Madame Vauquer and I will sit here and watch this dear Monsieur Vautrin.'

Thus admonished, Poiret slunk off without a murmur, like a hound that has got a kick from its master.

Rastignac had gone to walk, to breathe fresh air, for he was stifled. What had happened? The crime had been committed at the hour fixed; he had wanted to put a stop to it the evening before – what had hindered? What must he do now? He trembled lest in some way he was an accomplice. Vautrin's cool assurance horrified him still.

'Suppose he dies without speaking?' he asked himself.

He was walking breathlessly along the alleys of the Luxembourg, as if pursued by a pack of hounds: he seemed to hear them yelping on his traces.

'Here!' cried the voice of Bianchon, 'have you seen the *Pilote*?'

The *Pilote* was a radical paper edited by Monsieur Tissot, which made up a country edition a few hours after the appearance of the morning papers, and often contained items of later news.

'There's a great affair in it,' said Bianchon; 'young Taillefer has fought a duel with Comte de Franchessini of the Old Guard, who ran two inches of his sword into his forehead. So now the little Victorine is one of the best matches in Paris. *Hein*! if one had only known it! What a game of chance life is – and death, too. Is it true that Victorine looks upon you with an eye of favour, my boy?'

'Hush, Bianchon! I will never marry her. I love a charming woman – a woman who loves me. I—'

'Well, you say it in a tone as if you were goading yourself not to give up your charming woman. Show me the lady worth the sacrifice of the wealth of the house of Taillefer.'

'Are all the devils on my track?' cried Rastignac.

'Why, what are you about? Have you gone mad? Give me your wrist,' said Bianchon, 'I want to feel your pulse. You have got a fever.'

'Go at once to Mother Vauquer's,' said Eugène: 'that scoundrel Vautrin has just dropped dead.'

'Ah-h!' cried Bianchon, dropping Rastignac's hand, 'that confirms my suspicions; I will make sure about them.'

During his long walk Eugène passed through a solemn crisis. He made, as it were, the circuit of his conscience. If he struggled with his own soul, if he hankered and hesitated, it must be owned that his probity came out of that bitter and terrible discussion like a bar of iron, proof against every test. He remembered the secret Père Goriot had let drop the day before. He thought of the *appartement* chosen for him by Delphine in the Rue d'Artois. He took out her letter, and re-read it, and kissed it.

'Her love is my sheet anchor,' he said. 'The poor old man, too – he has had much to suffer! He says nothing of his griefs, but who cannot guess what they have been to him? 'Well, I will take care of him as if he were my father; I will give him the joys he longs for. If she loves me she will sometimes come and pass the day with him. – That grand Comtesse de Restaud is a vile woman; she shuts her doors against her father. Dear Delphine! she is kinder to the poor old man – yes! she is worth loving.' He drew out his watch and admired it. 'Everything will go well with me,' he said. 'When people love each other, what harm is there in accepting mutual gifts? I may keep it. Besides, I shall succeed, and repay her a hundredfold. In this *liaison* there is no crime – nothing to make the strictest virtue frown. We deceive no one: it is falsehood that makes us vile. How many honourable people contract just such unions! Her quarrel with her husband is irremediable. – Suppose I were to ask him, that big Alsatian, to give up to me a woman he can never render happy?'

The struggle of his mind lasted long. Though the victory remained with the virtues of youth, and he repulsed the temptation to make himself the accomplice of a deed of blood, he was nevertheless drawn back at dusk to the Maison Vauquer by an irresistible impulse of curiosity. He swore to himself that he would quit the place forever, but he must know if Vautrin was dead.

Bianchon after administering an emetic had taken the matters vomited by Vautrin to his hospital for chemical analysis. When he saw Mademoiselle Michonneau's anxiety to have them thrown away his suspicions increased; but Vautrin got over the attack so quickly that he soon dropped the idea of a plot against the life of that jovial merry-maker.

When Rastignac came in, Vautrin was standing by the stove in the dining-room. The guests had come together earlier than usual, anxious to learn the particulars of the duel and to know what influence it would have on the future of Victorine. As Eugène entered, he caught the eye of the imperturbable sphinx. The look the latter gave him pierced deep into his heart, and touched some chords of evil with so powerful a spell that he shivered.

'Well, my dear fellow,' said the escaped convict, 'Death will have a fierce struggle to get hold of me. These ladies tell me I have recovered from a rush of blood to the head that would have killed an ox.'

'Indeed, you might say a bull,' said Madame Vauquer.

'Are you sorry to see me alive?' said Vautrin to Eugène in a whisper, divining his thought. 'You will find, on the contrary, that I am devilishly strong.'

'Ah, by the by!' exclaimed Bianchon, 'the day before yesterday Mademoiselle Michonneau was speaking of a man named Trompe-la-Mort. That name would suit you, Monsieur Vautrin.'

The words were a thunderbolt to Vautrin. He turned pale and staggered. His magnetic glance fell on Mademoiselle Michonneau, who sank beneath the power of his eye. She fell back on a chair, her knees giving way under her. Poiret stepped nimbly between the two, understanding instinctively that she was in danger, so ferocious was the expression of the convict as he threw off the mask of good humour under which he had so long concealed his real nature. Without the least comprehending what was taking place before their eyes, the others saw that something was wrong, and stood by bewildered. At that moment footsteps were heard and the rattle of muskets in the street, as a squad of soldiers brought their pieces to the pavement. While Collin cast a quick glance at the windows and the walls, instinctively looking for the means of escape, four men showed themselves at the door of the dining-room. The foremost was the chief of the detective police, and the three others were members of his force.

'In the name of the law and the King!' said one of the latter, his words being drowned by a murmur of amazement; but in a moment silence reigned in the room as the guests stood aside to give passage to these men, each of whom had his right hand in a side-pocket where he held a loaded pistol. Two *gendarmes*, who stepped in after the detectives, stood by the doorway leading to the *salon*, while two more appeared at that which opened towards the staircase. The tread and the guns of a squad of soldiers outside sounded on the pebble-paved space along the side of the building. Every chance of flight was thus cut off from Trompe-la-Mort, on whom all eyes now turned in his extremity. The chief went straight to him, and gave him a blow so vigorously applied that it tore the wig from its place, and showed the head of Collin in all its horrible integrity. The hair, red and close-cropped, gave to his face a look of mingled strength and cunning; and the harmony of the face and head with the stalwart chest revealed the whole being of the man as by a flash from the fires of hell. All present comprehended Vautrin – his past, his present, the future before him, his implacable dogmas, the religion of his own good pleasure, the dominion he had exercised by the cynicism of his ideas and his acts, and by the force of his extraordinary organism. The blood rushed to his face, and his eyes glittered like those of a wildcat. He made one bound of savage energy; he uttered one roar, so ferocious that the people near him shrank back in fear. At this movement, like that of a lion at bay, and assuming to be justified by the terror of the bystanders, the detectives drew their pistols. Collin no sooner heard the cocking of the triggers than he understood his danger, and gave instant proof of the highest of human powers – horrible, yet majestic spectacle! His whole being passed through a phenomenal change which can only be compared to that which takes place in a boiler full of the steam that can blast mountains in its might, and yet at the touch of a drop of cold water sinks into instant dissolution. The drop of water which in a moment calmed his rage was a reflection that flashed, quick as lightning, through his brain. He smiled quietly, and glanced at his wig.

'This is not one of your polite days,' he said to the chief of police, stretching out his hands to the *gendarmes* with a motion of his head. 'Messieurs, put on the handcuffs. I take all present to witness that I make no resistance.'

A murmur of admiration, called forth by the promptitude with which this wondrous man mastered the fire and molten lava of the volcano in his breast, ran through the room.

'That puts an end to your kind intentions,' he said, looking full at the celebrated director of the detective police.

'Come, undress!' said the chief, in a tone of contempt.

'What for?' asked Collin. 'There are ladies present. I deny nothing, and I surrender.'

He paused, and looked on all around him with the air of an orator about to hold the attention of his audience.

'Write down, Papa Lachapelle,' he said, addressing a little old man with white hair, who placed himself at the end of the table, taking from a portfolio a form for the official report of the arrest, 'that I acknowledge myself to be Jacques Collin, condemned to twenty years' imprisonment; and I have just given proof that I did not steal my nickname. If I had so much as lifted a hand,' he said, turning to his late companions, 'those fellows would have spilled my claret on the domestic hearthstone of Mamma Vauquer. These rogues delight in setting snares for their victims.'

Madame Vauquer turned pale on hearing these words. '*Mon Dieu!*' she cried, 'it is enough to bring on an illness! To think of my having been at the theatre with him only last evening!' she said to Sylvie.

'Show more philosophy, Mamma,' said Collin. 'Was it really a misfortune to amuse yourself in my box at the Gaîté last night? Are you better than we? We have less infamy branded on our shoulders than you have in your hearts – you flabby members of a gangrened society! Even the best among you could not hold out against me.' His eyes turned to Rastignac, to whom he gave a kindly smile in strange contrast to the harsh expression of his features. 'Our little bargain holds good, my lad,' he said; 'that is, in case of acceptance. You know—' and he sang—

"'My Fanny is charming
In her simplicity.'"

'Don't be uneasy,' he resumed. 'I shall be all right again before long. They fear me too much to play me false.'

The *bagne*, with its manners and vocabulary, its abrupt transitions from the jocose to the horrible, its fiendish grandeur, its familiarity, its degradation, were all exhibited to the eye in the person of this man – no longer a man, but the type of a degenerate race; of a savage people, lawless yet logical, brutal but pliant. On a sudden Collin had become an infernal poem, an exposition of all human emotions save one – repentance. His glance was that of the fallen angel, prepared to carry on a losing war. Rastignac bent his head, accepting the comradeship thus forced upon him, in expiation of the evil thoughts which had brought him near to crime.

'Who betrayed me?' said Collin, casting his glance around the circle. It stopped at Mademoiselle Michonneau. 'Ah! it was *you*, sleuth-hound! – you gave me a sham apoplexy, you prying devil! If I said two words, your head would be mown off in a week. But I forgive you. I'm a Christian. Besides, it was not you who sold me. But who, then? – Ha, ha! you are rummaging up there,' he cried, hearing the detectives overhead, who were opening his closets and taking possession of his effects. 'The birds are flown, the nest is empty. You can find nothing there. My ledgers are here,' he added, tapping his forehead. 'Now I know who sold me. It can be no other than that dirty blackguard, Fil de Soie. Isn't it so, Father Catch'em?' he said to the chief of police. 'I guess it from the way you are looking for the bank-notes upstairs. None there, my little spies! As for Fil de Soie – he'll be under the sod in a fortnight, even if you try to guard him with the whole force of your *gendarmerie*. How much did you pay that old Michonnette?' he asked, turning to the police agents. 'Only a thousand crowns? Why, I was worth more than that, you decayed Ninon – Pompadour in tatters – Venus of the cemetery! If you had given me warning, I'd have paid you double. Ha! you did think of it? – Haggler in human flesh! Yes, I would have given you six thousand francs to spare myself a journey which I don't like – and which puts me out of pocket,' he added, as they were screwing on the handcuffs. 'These people will take pleasure in letting things drag along, just to keep me idle. If they would only send me off to the galleys at once, I should soon get back to my work, in spite of those simpletons at the prefecture of police. *Là bas* [down there] they would turn their souls inside out to set their general at liberty – their trusty Trompe-la-Mort. Is there any one of you who can boast of having, as I have, ten thousand brothers ready to do everything for you?' he asked proudly. 'There is virtue here,' striking his breast. 'I have never betrayed any one. Ha! old adder!' he continued, addressing the old maid. 'Look at these people. They fear me, but they loathe you. Pick up your gains and begone!'

He made a pause, and looked round upon the other guests.

'What fools you are!' he said. 'Did you never see a convict? A convict of the stamp of Collin, here present, is a man who is less base than other men, and who protests against the glaring deceptions of the social contract, as Jean Jacques called it – whose pupil I am proud to be. For myself, I stand alone against the Government, with all its courts of law, its budgets and *gendarmes* – and I get the better of it.'

'The devil!' exclaimed the painter. 'I should like to sketch him now.'

'Tell me,' he continued, turning to the chief of police – 'tell me, equerry to Monseigneur the executioner, governor of the Widow [*La Veuve* – appalling name, full of terrible poesy, given by the convicts to the guillotine]; come, be a good fellow and say, was it Fil de Soie who sold me? I should be sorry if he died for another; it would not be just.'

At this moment the detectives, who had opened everything and taken an inventory of all that was in his apartment, came down and said something in a low voice to the chief of police. The *procès-verbal* (written official report of all the circumstances of the arrest) was now completed.

'Gentlemen,' said Collin, turning to his late companions, 'they are about to take me from you. You have all been very amiable to me during my residence among you, and I shall think of you with gratitude. Receive my adieux. You will permit me to send you figs from Provence.'

He went a few steps, and then turned and looked at Rastignac.

'Adieu, Eugène,' he said, in a gentle, sad voice, strangely in contrast with the rough tone he had used hitherto. 'If you are ever in trouble, remember – I leave you a devoted friend.' Notwithstanding his handcuffs, he put himself on guard, gave the word like a fencing-master – one, two – and made a pass as if with the sword. 'In case of misfortune, go *there*. Man or money – all are at your disposal.'

This strange being put so much buffoonery into these last words that no one present understood their meaning except Rastignac.

When the house was vacated by the *gendarmes*, the soldiers, and the agents of the police, Sylvie, who was bathing her mistress's forehead with vinegar, looked round upon the assembled household and said—

'Well – all the same, he was a good man.'

These words broke the spell which the rush of events and the diversity of emotions had exercised over the spectators of this strange scene. They glanced at each other, and then by a common impulse all turned to Mademoiselle Michonneau, who crouched near the stove, cold, bloodless, withered as a mummy – her eyes cast down as though she felt the protection of the green shade insufficient to conceal their expression. The cause of the aversion they had long felt for her was suddenly made clear to their minds. A murmur of disgust, which by its unanimity expressed the common feeling of all present, sounded through the room.

Mademoiselle Michonneau heard it, but she did not change her attitude. Bianchon was the first to speak. He turned to the man next him and said, in a low voice—

'I shall decamp if she is to eat her dinner here.'

Instantly every one, except Poiret, accepted the suggestion; and the medical student, sustained by public opinion, walked up to the old man.

'You who enjoy a special intimacy with Mademoiselle Michonneau,' he said, 'had better speak to her. Make her understand that she must leave this house without delay.'

'Without delay?' repeated Poiret, astonished.

Then he went up to the old maid and said something in a whisper.

'But I have paid a month in advance; I have a right to stay here while I pay my money like everybody else,' she said, darting a viperous glance at the company.

'That need not hinder,' said Rastignac, 'we will all subscribe and return you the money.'

'Monsieur stands up for Collin?' she replied, casting a venomous and searching look at Rastignac. 'It is easy to guess why. We all heard his last words.'

Eugène sprang forward as though he would have seized and strangled her.

'Let her alone!' cried the others.

Rastignac folded his arms and stood mute.

'We must get rid of Mademoiselle Judas,' said the painter, turning to Madame Vauquer. 'Madame, if you do not turn out *la* Michonneau we shall all leave you; and we shall report everywhere that your *pension* is frequented by spies and convicts. If you do as we demand, we will be silent about what has happened – which, indeed, is liable to take place in the best establishments, until galley-slaves are branded on the forehead and prevented from disguising themselves as honest citizens and playing the buffoon as they please.'

Hearing this, Madame Vauquer miraculously recovered her senses, sat upright, folded her arms, and opened her cold light eyes, which showed no trace of tears.

'But, my dear Monsieur,' she said, 'do you mean to ruin my house? There is Monsieur Vautrin – oh! *Mon Dieu,*' she cried, interrupting herself, 'I cannot help giving him his honest name! – he leaves me a whole suite of rooms vacant; and now you ask me to consent to have two more rooms unoccupied at a season when everybody is settled!'

'Come, gentlemen, get your hats. We will go and dine in the Place Sorbonne at Flicoteaux's,' said Bianchon.

Madame Vauquer made a rapid mental calculation as to which side her interest lay, and then waddled up to Mademoiselle Michonneau.

'Come, my dear good lady,' she said, 'you don't want to be the death of my establishment, I am sure. You see to what an extremity I am reduced by the behaviour of these gentlemen. Go up to your room for this evening.'

'That won't do! That will not do at all!' cried all the others. 'We insist upon her leaving the house at once.'

'But she has not dined,' said Poiret piteously.

'She can get her dinner somewhere else,' cried several voices.

'Begone, spy!'

'Down with the spies – with both of them!'

'Gentlemen,' said Poiret, suddenly exhibiting the courage of an old ram defending his favourite ewe, 'respect her sex.'

'Spies are not of any sex.'

'Famous sex-orama!'

'*À la porte-orama!*'

'Gentlemen, this is indecent. When people are dismissed from a house there are certain formalities to be observed. We have paid our board in advance, and we shall stay,' said Poiret, putting on his amorphous old hat, and taking a chair beside Mademoiselle

Michonneau, to whom Madame Vauquer was appealing in a low voice.

'Ah! you bad boy!' cried the painter; '*petit méchant, va!*'

'Come on, then,' said Bianchon, 'if they are not going, we are.'

At this summons all the guests moved in a body to the door of the *salon*.

'Mademoiselle! what shall I do? I shall be ruined!' cried Madame Vauquer. 'You cannot stay – they will proceed to violence.'

Mademoiselle Michonneau rose.

'She is going!'

'She won't go!'

'Yes, she will!'

'No, she won't!'

These alternating exclamations and the increasing hostility of all around her decided the old maid, and she prepared to leave, after a few whispered stipulations with her landlady.

'I am going to Madame Buneaud's,' she said with a menacing air.

'Go where you choose, Mademoiselle,' cried Madame Vauquer. to whom this choice of the rival establishment added insult to injury. 'Go, if you like, to Madame Buneaud's. She will give you wine fit to make the goats caper with stomach-ache, and stews made of cold pieces from the eating-houses.'

The guests stood in a double row in profound silence. Poiret looked so tenderly at Mademoiselle Michonneau, and yet was so naively undecided whether he ought to go or stay, that the victorious party, put in good humour by the departure of the old maid, began to laugh at him.

'Xi, xi, xi, Poiret!' cried the painter, as if setting on a dog; 'hi, old fellow!'

The Museum employee began to sing, with comic gestures, a well-known ballad—

'Partant pour la Syrie
Le jeune et beau Dunois.'

'You had better go, Poiret; you are dying to follow her,' cried Bianchon – '*trahit sua quemque voluptas.*'

'Like follows like – translation more liberal than literal from Virgil,' said a tutor who was one of the guests.

Mademoiselle Michonneau looked hard at Poiret, and made a movement as if to take his arm. He was unable to resist the appeal, and came forward to support her. There was a burst of applause and peals of laughter.

'Bravo, Poiret!'

'Good for old Poiret!'

'Poiret-Apollo!'

'Poiret-Mars!'

'Plucky Poiret!'

At this moment a messenger came in with a note for Madame Vauquer. She read it, and sank down upon a chair.

'Now there is nothing left but to be struck by lightning,' she said, 'and burn the house down! Young Taillefer died at three o'clock. I am rightly punished for having wished those ladies good luck at the expense of that poor young man. Madame Couture and Victorine have sent for their things, and are going to live with the father. Monsieur Taillefer allows his daughter to keep the widow Couture as her companion. Four *appartement* vacant! Five lodgers gone!' she said, with tears in her voice. 'Misfortune has visited my house!'

The roll of a carriage echoed up the quiet street and stopped before the door.

'Here's some lucky windfall,' cried Sylvie.

Goriot came in, radiant with happiness; his face shone; he seemed transfigured.

'Goriot in a hackney-coach!' cried the others; 'the end of the world has come!'

The old fellow went straight to Rastignac, who was standing apart dumb-founded, and took him by the arm. 'Come!' he cried eagerly.

'Do you know what has happened?' said Eugène; 'Vautrin was a convict escaped from the galleys; they have just arrested him. And young Taillefer is dead.'

'Well – what is that to us?' replied Père Goriot; 'I am to dine with my daughter to-day at your rooms; you understand? She is waiting for us. Come!'

He pulled Rastignac violently by the arm, and carried him off as if he were a lover and Rastignac a woman.

'Let us sit down to dinner,' said the painter, and each took his place at table.

'I declare,' said Sylvie, 'things do go wrong to-day! My haricot of mutton has got stuck. Well! you will have to eat it burned, whether or no!'

Madame Vauquer had no heart to say a word when she saw ten persons instead of eighteen sitting down to table; but they all made a good-natured effort to console her and cheer her up; and though at first they could think of nothing but Vautrin and the startling events of the day, the serpentine current of their talk soon led them to duels, the galleys, law-courts, prisons, and the reform of the criminal code, from whence they wandered far away from Jacques Collin and Victorine and her brother. Although there were but ten of them, they made noise enough for twenty, and gave the impression of being more in number than usual – which was the only apparent difference between the dinner of to-day and the dinners of other days. The habitual *insouciance* of that devil-may-care world of Paris, which each day gluts its maw with the events of the last twenty-four hours, resumed its sway, and even Madame Vauquer permitted herself to listen to the voice of hope – that divinity being represented by the fat Sylvie.

XV

This day was destined to be, from morning till night, a phantasmagoria to Eugène, who in spite of his self-command and his strength of mind could not collect his scattered senses when he found himself in the coach beside Père Goriot, whose babble flowed joyously as from a fount of unexampled happiness, sounding in Eugène's ears, after so many emotions, like the words of a dream—

'We finished our work this morning. We are all three to dine together – together, do you understand? It is four years since I last dined with Delphine – my own little Delphine! I shall be there all the evening. We have been at your rooms since the morning. I have been working like a day-labourer, coat off. I helped to bring in the furniture. – Ah! ah! you don't know how charming she can be at the head of a table. She will look after me. She will say, "Come, Papa, eat some of this – it is good!" and then I shall not be able to swallow a mouthful. Oh! it is so long since I have spent an evening with her; but the happy time is coming!'

'Ah!' cried Eugène, 'the world seems upside down.'

'Upside down!' exclaimed Père Goriot. 'Why, it never seemed to me so right-side-up before. I see none but happy faces in the streets; everybody seems to be shaking hands; some people are hugging each other; men look as gay as if they were all going to dine with their daughters, and *gobble down* the good dinner I heard her order from the chef at the Café Anglais. But, bah! what matter? Sitting beside her, aloes would taste as sweet as honey.'

'Am I coming to life again?' said Eugène.

'Get on faster, coachman,' cried Père Goriot, letting down the front glass of the carriage. 'Drive faster! I will give you five francs drink-money if you get me there in ten minutes.'

On hearing this promise, the man dashed across Paris at breakneck speed.

'The fellow crawls,' cried Goriot.

'But where are you taking me?' asked Rastignac.

'To your own rooms,' said Père Goriot.

The carriage stopped in the Rue d'Artois. The old man got out first, and flung ten francs to the coachman with the prodigality of a widower in the first flush of his release.

'Come! let us go upstairs,' he said to Rastignac, marshalling him across the courtyard and taking him to an *appartement* on the third floor, in the rear of a new and handsome building. Père Goriot had no need to ring the bell. Thérèse, Madame de Nucingen's waiting-woman, opened the door, and Eugène found himself in a charming bachelor establishment, consisting of an ante-chamber, a little *salon*, a bed-room, and a dressing-room looking out upon a garden. In the little *salon*, whose furniture and decorations would have borne comparison with everything beautiful and graceful of its kind, be saw Delphine by the soft light of wax-candles, who rose from a couch by the fire and, laying the hand-screen she had been using on the chimney-piece, said in a voice full of tenderness, 'So you had to be sent for – Monsieur, who is so dull of comprehension!'

Thérèse left the room. Eugène took Delphine in his arms, and as he pressed her to his heart tears came into his eyes. The contrast between what he saw and what he had so lately seen overwhelmed him, and the emotions of this strange day, when so much had wearied his spirit and confused his brain, brought on a rush of nervous agitation.

'I knew all along how he felt,' whispered Père Goriot to his daughter, while Eugène lay back upon a sofa unable to say a word, or to explain why this last wave of the magic wand had so powerfully affected him.

'Come and see your rooms,' said Madame de Nucingen, after a pause, taking his hand and leading him through the pretty *appartement*, where the carpets, the furniture, and all the lesser decorations were of the same style, in miniature, as those of Delphine's own rooms.

'We will keep our happiness a secret from all except ourselves,' she whispered, smiling.

'Yes, but I must have my share in it,' said Père Goriot.

'You know you are included: *ourselves* means you, too.'

'Ah! that is what I wanted you to say. You will not think me in the way, will you? I shall come and go like some good spirit, always at hand, though he does not make himself known. – Well, my Delphinette, Ninette, Dedel! was I not right to tell you of this pretty little *appartement*, and to say, "Let us furnish it for him"? At first you did not like the idea. It is I who planned all this pleasure. Fathers should give their children everything, just as they gave them life. Give all, give ever – that is a father's motto.'

'Have we guessed what you like best?' said Delphine to Eugène as they came back into the *salon*.

'Yes,' he said, 'only too well. Alas! the luxury of these rooms is complete; my every dream is realized. The poetry of such a life, so fresh, so elegant – I feel it all! But I cannot accept it from you, and I am too poor as yet—'

'Ah! would you dare to cross me already?' she asked, with a mock air of authority, making one of those pretty grimaces by which women try to laugh away a scruple. But Eugène had that day too solemnly interrogated his conscience – the arrest of Vautrin, revealing the horrible abyss into which he had so nearly plunged – had too powerfully forced his mind back to thoughts of duty and delicacy, to let him now yield to her caressing assault upon his scruples. A profound sadness came over him.

'Is it possible,' cried Madame de Nucingen, 'that you refuse me? Do you know all that such a refusal means? It means that you doubt the future, that you doubt me or that you fear to be false yourself to my affection. If you love me and if I love you, why do you draw back and refuse such trifling obligations? If you knew the pleasure I have had in preparing these rooms for you, you would not hesitate; you would beg my pardon for the very thought of refusing me. Besides, you must remember that I have money of yours: I have laid it out to the best advantage – that is all. You fancy that your refusal is a proof of high-mindedness: it is the contrary. Oh, Papa! give him good reasons why he should not refuse us,' she exclaimed after a pause, turning to her father. 'Does he think I would be less fastidious than himself on a point of honour?'

Père Goriot listened to this dispute with the absorbed smile of an Oriental snake-charmer.

'Child that you are, reflect!' continued Madame de Nucingen, taking Eugène's hand. 'You stand on the threshold of life; between you and success there lies a barrier insurmountable for most young men – the barrier of poverty, of obscurity; the hand of a woman removes it, and you draw back! You will succeed; you will make a brilliant future; I read success upon your brow. When this comes to pass, can you not pay back to me what I lend you now? In olden times ladies gave to their knights armour and swords and helmets, coats of mail and horses, that they might fight at tournaments and win them honour. Eugène, the things I offer you are the arms of the nineteenth century; tools essential to the man who wishes to rise above his fellows. Ah!' she added, 'the garret where you live must be sumptuous, if it is anything like Papa's! Do you wish to make me miserable? Answer!' she said, slightly shaking his hand. '*Mon Dieu*, Papa! make him accept, or I will go away and never let him see me again.'

'I can settle it,' said Père Goriot, coming out of his trance. 'My dear Monsieur Eugène, you would be glad no doubt to borrow money from the Jews, wouldn't you?'

'I must,' he replied.

'Very good; now, then, I have you,' said the old man, drawing out a shabby leather pocket-book. 'I am your Jew. I have paid all the bills, and here they are. Not a *sou* is owing for anything in this *appartement*. The furniture did not cost a great deal – at most five thousand francs. I lend you that sum. You won't refuse me; I am not a woman. You can write me an acknowledgement upon a scrap of paper, and repay me some of these days.'

Delphine and Eugène looked at each other in astonishment, and tears filled their eyes. The student took the hand of the old man and pressed it warmly.

'Why, you need not think so much of it; are you not both my children?' said Goriot.

'But, my poor Father, how did you manage it?' said Madame de Nucingen.

'Ah! now you want me to tell you all,' he answered. 'Well, after I had persuaded you to let him live here, and I saw you buying things fit for a bride, I said, "She will find herself in trouble about the money." My lawyer tells me the suit against your husband cannot be settled for six months. It can wait. I have sold out my securities, that brought me in thirteen hundred and fifty francs a year. With fifteen thousand francs of the capital I have bought an annuity of twelve hundred francs, and I have paid these bills with the remainder, my children. I have a bed-room here which will cost only a hundred and fifty francs a year, and I can live like a prince on forty *sous* a day and have something left over. I hardly ever wear out my clothes, and I shall never need any new ones. For a fortnight past I have been laughing in my sleeve, saying to myself, "How happy we shall be!" Was I not right? – are you not happy?'

'Oh, Papa, Papa!' cried Madame de Nucingen, springing into the arms of her father, who placed her tenderly on his knee. She covered him with kisses; her blonde hair touched his cheeks as she shed tears upon the aged face all glowing now with happiness. 'Dear Father – you are indeed a father. No! there is not another father in the world like you. Eugène! you loved him before, but you will love him better now.'

'Why, my children,' said Père Goriot, who for six years had not felt a daughter's heart against his bosom; 'my Delphinette, do you want to kill me with joy? My poor heart cannot bear it. Ah! Eugène, the debt is repaid already!'

And the old man pressed his daughter to his heart with an embrace so frantic that she cried out, 'Oh! you hurt me.'

'Hurt you!' he said, turning pale. He looked at her with an expression of anguish. 'No, no! I could not hurt you,' gently kissing the waist his arm had pressed too roughly. 'It was you who hurt me by that cry of pain. – The furniture cost more than I told him,' he whispered in her ear; 'but we must deceive him a little, or we shall not be able to manage him.'

Eugène, amazed at the inexhaustible self-devotion of Père Goriot, gazed at him with a naive admiration which in the young expresses implicit faith.

'I will make myself worthy of such goodness!' he exclaimed.

'Oh, my Eugène, those words are noble!' and Madame de Nucingen kissed him on the forehead.

'For thy sake he refused Mademoiselle Taillefer and her millions,' said Père Goriot. 'Yes, the little girl was fond of him; her brother is dead, and she is as rich as Croesus.'

'Do not say that!' cried Rastignac.

'Eugène,' whispered Madame de Nucingen. 'I have now a regret to mar my happiness; but I will love you the better for it – and forever.'

'This is the happiest day of my life since your marriages,'

cried Père Goriot. 'I am willing to suffer all that it may please God to send me, so long as it does not come through my children. As long as I live I shall say to myself, "In February, 1820, there was a day when I was happier than other men are in a lifetime!" Look at me, Fifine,' he said to his daughter. 'Ah! is she not lovely? Tell me, where can you find another little woman with such a skin, and such pretty dimples? She is mine – I made her, the little darling! Ah! my friend, be good to her, make her happy, and I will reward you. If there were but one chance to go to heaven and I had got it, I would give it to you. But, come! let us dine – let us dine,' he said, as if beside himself. 'All is ours.'

'Poor Father!'

'Ah! my child,' he added, taking her head between his hands, and kissing her hair; 'you make my heaven here. Come and see me often; my room is close by; you have not far to go. Come often; promise me – say that you promise it.'

'Yes, dear Father.'

'Say it again.'

'Yes, my good Father.'

'Hush, now! for I should make you say it a hundred times if I thought of myself only. Let us dine.'

The evening was spent in tender child's play such as this – Père Goriot not the least childish of the three. He sat at his daughter's feet and kissed them; he gazed into her eyes; he laid his head upon her dress. He was guilty of a thousand follies, like a lover with his first love.

'You see now,' whispered Delphine to Eugène, 'that when my father is here he exacts all my attention. It will often be very troublesome.'

Eugène, who had already felt some twinges of jealousy, could not exactly blame this speech, although it breathed the quintessence of ingratitude.

'When will the *appartement* be finished?' he asked, looking round him. 'Must we leave it to-night?'

'Yes; but to-morrow you dine with me: it is the opera night, you remember.'

'I shall go and sit in the pit,' said Père Goriot.

It was now midnight; Madame de Nucingen's carriage was waiting. Père Goriot and Eugène walked back to the Maison Vauquer, talking of Delphine on the way with an enthusiasm that revealed a curious contrast of expression in the two individual passions. Eugène could not conceal from himself that the father's love, stained by no selfish interest, crushed his out of sight by its vehemence and grandeur. To the father the idol was all purity and goodness, and his adoration was nourished as much by recollections of the past as by his visions of the future.

They found Madame Vauquer sitting over the stove with Christophe and Sylvie on either side of her, like Marius among the ruins of Carthage. She was waiting for the two who were to-night her sole lodgers, and bemoaning herself to Sylvie. Though Lord Byron puts very beautiful lamentations into the mouth of Tasso, they have not the ring of truth which vibrated in those now proceeding from the lips of the unfortunate landlady.

'Only three cups of coffee to make to-morrow, Sylvie! Is not my empty house enough to break my heart? Alas! what will life be to me without my lodgers? Nothing. My house is desolate, deserted by its men. They were its furniture. What is life without furniture? What have I done that Heaven should send me these misfortunes? We laid in potatoes and beans – yes, beans enough for twenty people. The police in my house! – Must we eat nothing but potatoes? I shall send Christophe away.'

The Savoyard, who was asleep, woke up on hearing his name and said, 'Madame?'

'Poor fellow! he is as faithful as a dog,' said Sylvie.

'A lost season! People are housed. Can lodgers drop from heaven? I shall lose my senses. And that witch of a Michonneau, to have carried off Poiret! How did she get such a grip on the man? He follows her about like a puppy-dog.'

'Bah!' said Sylvie, shaking her head. 'Those old maids! they know the tricks of things.'

'That poor Monsieur Vautrin, whom they turned into a convict!' resumed the widow. 'Well, Sylvie, it is too much for me; I can't believe it yet. A man as gay as he, who drank his *gloria* at fifteen francs a month, and paid on the nail!'

'And who was generous, too,' remarked Christophe.

'There's some mistake,' said Sylvie.

'No, there can't be. He owned it himself,' said Madame Vauquer. 'And to think that all these things happened here in this neighbourhood, where even the cats don't come! I must be dreaming, it can't be possible! We saw Louis XVI meet with his accident; we saw the fall of the Emperor; we saw him come back and fall again – all that belonged to the order of possible things. But there are no such hap-hazards about *pensions*. People can get along without a king, but they must have breakfast and dinner; and when an honest woman, *née* de Conflans, gives dinners, with all sorts of good things, unless the very end of the world should come – but that's what it is; it is the end of the world!'

'And to think that that Michonneau, who has done all the mischief, is to receive, they say, three thousand francs a year!' cried Sylvie.

'Don't mention her to me! she is a wicked woman,' cried Madame Vauquer; 'and she has gone off to Buneaud's: she is capable of anything. She must have done horrible things in her lifetime – robbed, murdered, no doubt. She ought to have gone to the galleys, instead of that poor, dear man—'

At this moment Eugène and Père Goriot rang the bell.

'Ah! there are my two faithful ones,' said the widow, with a sigh.

The faithful pair, who at that moment had but slight remembrance of the disasters of the *pension*, unceremoniously announced to their landlady that they were to leave her on the following day and take up their quarters in the Chaussée d'Antin.

'Sylvie!' cried the widow. 'My last trump is gone! Gentlemen, you have given me my death-blow. It has pierced to my vitals – I feel it there. This day has laid the weight of years upon my head. I shall go mad – upon my word, I shall! What can be done with the beans? I am left desolate. You shall go to-morrow, Christophe. Good night, gentlemen – good night.'

'What is the matter with her?' said Eugène to Sylvie.

'Oh, Lord! everybody has left the house because of what happened this morning. It has upset her head. There! I hear her crying; it will do her good to blubber a bit. This is the first time I've known her to wet her eyes since I have lived with her.'

The next morning Madame Vauquer *s'était raisonnée*, as she expressed it – that is, she had come to her senses; and though afflicted as a woman might well be who had lost all her lodgers, and whose life was suddenly turned topsy-turvy, she had her wits about her, and displayed no more than a reasonable grief caused by such sudden disasters. The glances that a lover casts upon the sacred places of a lost mistress were not less moving than those with which she now looked round her deserted table. Eugène tried to comfort her with the idea that Bianchon, whose term at the hospital was to end in a few days, might step into his vacant room; and told her that the employee at the Museum had frequently been heard to wish for the *appartement* of Madame Couture; and that no doubt in a few days the house would be full again.

'Heaven grant it, my dear Monsieur Eugène! But misfortune has come to my roof: before ten days are gone, death will be here. You will see,' she added, casting a lugubrious glance around the dining-room. 'Which of us will he summon?'

'If that is the case, we had better be off,' whispered Eugène to Père Goriot.

'Madame!' cried Sylvie, bursting in excitedly. 'I have not seen Mistigris for three days!'

'Ah! if my cat is dead; if he too has left me, I—'

The poor woman could not finish her sentence. She clasped her hands and threw herself back in her armchair, overwhelmed by this ominous loss.

Toward noon, the time of day when postmen make their rounds in the neighbourhood of the Pantheon, Eugène received a letter in an elegant envelope, sealed with the arms of Beauséant. It enclosed an invitation addressed to Monsieur and Madame de Nucingen, for a ball about to be given by the viscountess, which had been announced for some weeks. A little note to Eugène accompanied the invitation—

> I think, Monsieur, that you will undertake with pleasure to interpret my sentiments to Madame de Nucingen. I send you the invitation you asked of me, and shall be delighted to make the acquaintance of the sister of Madame de Restaud. Come to my ball, and bring that charming lady with you; but do not let her absorb all your affection. You owe me a little, in return for that which I feel for you.
> VICOMTESSE DE BEAUSÉANT.

'Well,' said Eugène, reading this note for the second time, 'Madame de Beauséant tells me plainly that she does not wish to see the Baron de Nucingen.'

He went at once to Delphine's, delighted that he had it in his power to bestow a pleasure of which no doubt he would reap the reward. Madame de Nucingen was in her bath; and Rastignac waited for her with the eager impatience of his years, and in the grasp of emotions which are given but once to the lives of young people. The first woman to whom a man attaches himself, if she appears to him in all the splendours of Parisian life, need fear no rival. Love in Paris is not the love of other regions. Neither men nor women are there duped by the time-worn ideas which all display like banners, for the sake of decency, over affections calling themselves disinterested. In Paris, a woman seeks to be loved not only for her charms, but for all the satisfactions she can give to the social ambitions of her lover; she knows that she must gratify the thousand vanities which make up life in the great world. In that world, Love is braggart, spendthrift, gayly deceitful, and ostentatious. If the women of the court of Louis XIV envied Mademoiselle de la Valliere the ardour which caused that mighty prince to forget the fabulous cost of the ruffles which he tore in facilitating the entrance of the Duc de Vermandois into the world, what can be expected of a lesser humanity? Be young and rich and titled, ye Parisian lovers! Be something better, if you can. The more incense you burn before your idol, if idol you have, the more that deity will bend a favourable ear. Love is here an idolatry – his rites more costly by far than those of any other worship; he flits and vanishes like an imp, delighting to leave his path marked out by havoc. True passion is the poetry of garrets; without it, could the vestal flame of love be kept alive? Exceptions to the laws of this Draconian code of Paris maybe found in oases of that wilderness – in hearts not led astray by social theories, that dwell retired near some fount of purity, some ever-bubbling spring of living waters, where, faithful to these quiet shades, they listen to the teachings of the Infinite written for their learning on all things, even their own hearts, patiently waiting to rise on wings of angels, and compassionating the earth-bound tendencies of the world about them.

Rastignac, like other young men who begin life among the traditions of rank, expected to enter the lists fully equipped. He had caught the fever of the world and thought himself able to master it, without in truth understanding the means or the ends of his ambition. When the heart finds no pure and sacred love to fill its cup of life, a draught of mere success may have its value; nay, the thirst for power is glorious when, stripped of personal ambition, it takes the form of patriotism. But Rastignac had by no means reached the heights whence men may contemplate the course of life and form a judgement on it. As yet he had not wholly shaken off those fresh sweet theories and dreams which enfold young people brought up in country solitudes, as the green calyx does the bud. Up to this time he had hesitated to cross the Parisian rubicon. In spite of his ardent curiosity, he clung to the traditions of the noble life led by men of breeding in their ancient manors. Nevertheless, his last scruples vanished the night before, as he stood in his new rooms in the Rue d'Artois. There, coming into possession of the material advantages of wealth, in addition to his natural advantages of rank and family, he stripped off the skin of a country gentleman and slid with ease into the new circumstances which his ambition told him would lead to fortune. As he waited for Delphine, luxuriously seated in her pretty boudoir, he seemed so far removed from the Rastignac of the year before, that as he looked at himself with the moral optics of his own mind he wondered if he were indeed the same.

'Madame will see you,' said Thérèse, whose voice startled him.

He found Delphine on a couch beside the fire, fresh and restful. As she lay back in her muslin draperies, it was impossible not to compare her to one of those Oriental plants whose fruit comes with the flower.

'At last we are together,' she said with some emotion.

'Guess what I bring you,' said Eugène, sitting down beside her and lifting her arm that he might kiss her hand.

Madame de Nucingen made a gesture of delight as she read the invitation; and turning to Eugène with tears in her eyes, she threw her arms around his neck and drew him down to her in a delirium of gratified vanity.

'And it is you to whom I owe this happiness!' she said. 'Obtained by you, it is more than a triumph of self-love. No one has ever been willing till now to introduce me into that charmed circle. Perhaps you think me at this moment as frivolous and light-minded as any other Parisian; but remember, my friend, I am yours, and if I wish more than ever to enter the society of the Faubourg Saint-Germain it is because that society is yours.'

'Do you not think,' said Eugène, 'that Madame de Beauséant intimates pretty plainly that she does not wish to see Monsieur de Nucingen at her ball?'

'Yes, I do,' said Delphine, returning the note to Eugène: 'those great ladies have a genius for impertinence. But no matter; I shall go. My sister is to be there. I know she has ordered a bewitching dress for the occasion. Eugène,' she resumed, in a low voice, 'she wants to appear at that ball in all her glory, that she may give the lie to dreadful rumours. You don't know what things are said about her. Nucingen told me this morning that they talked of her at the club, and handled her without mercy. Ah, *mon Dieu!* upon how slight a thread hangs the honour of a woman! – and her family as well, for I feel myself involved in these attacks upon my poor sister. They say that Monsieur de Trailles has given notes to the amount of a hundred thousand francs; that these have gone to protest, and that he has even been in danger of arrest. In this extremity, so they say, my sister has sold her diamonds to a Jew – those beautiful diamonds which you have seen her wear, heirlooms belonging to the Restaud family. I am told that for two days nothing else has been talked of. I understand now why Anastasie has ordered a dress of gold tissue: she means to attract all eyes at Madame de Beauséant's by appearing in a superb *toilette*, and wearing the diamonds. But she shall not outshine me! She has always tried to crush me; she was never kind to me, though I have done much for her – I have even lent her money when she was in trouble. But do not let us talk about her now. To-day I wish to think of nothing but happiness.'

Rastignac did not leave Madame de Nucingen till an hour after midnight. As she bade him farewell she said, with a tone and expression of melancholy, 'I am timid, superstitious! Call my presentiments foolish if you will, but I feel as if some terrible catastrophe were hanging over me.'

'Child!' said Eugène.

'Ah! it is I who am the child to-night,' she answered laughing.

Rastignac returned to the Maison Vauquer, as he believed, for the last time; certain of quitting it forever the next day. As he walked along he surrendered himself to happy dreams, as young men will who taste upon their lips the draught of joy.

'Well?' said Père Goriot, as Rastignac passed his door.

'Good night,' answered Eugène; 'I will tell you all to-morrow.'

'Ah, to-morrow!' cried the old man. 'Go to bed now, and good night. To-morrow our happy life begins!'

XVI

The next morning Goriot and Rastignac were waiting for the porters to remove their effects to the Rue d'Artois, when, about noon, the noise of an equipage stopping before the Maison Vauquer echoed up the Rue Neuve Sainte-Geneviève. Madame de Nucingen got out of the carriage, and learning from Sylvie that her father was still there, ran lightly up to his room. Eugène was in his own chamber, but his neighbour did not know he was there. At breakfast he had asked Père Goriot to attend to the removal of his luggage, promising to rejoin him at four o'clock in the Rue d'Artois. But while the old man was out of the house searching for porters, Eugène, after answering to his name at the law-school, returned to settle his account with Madame Vauquer, not wishing to leave the bill with Goriot, lest the old man in his enthusiasm might insist on paying it for him. The landlady was out, and Eugène ran upstairs to make sure that nothing had been left behind; congratulating himself for his precaution when he found in a table-drawer the acceptance given to Vautrin, which he had carelessly flung aside at the time when he paid the debt. Not having any fire, he was about to tear it into little pieces, when his hand was arrested in the act by hearing the voice of Delphine in Père Goriot's chamber. He stopped short to listen to what she was saying, confident that she could have no secrets from him. Then, after her first words, he found the conversation between father and daughter too deeply interesting to resist the temptation of hearing more.

'Ah, my Father,' Delphine cried, 'would to heaven you had interfered about my fortune in time to save me from ruin! Can I speak freely?'

'Yes, the house is empty,' said Père Goriot in a strange tone.

'What is the matter with you, Father?' she asked; 'are you ill?'

'I feel as if you had struck me with an axe upon my head. God forgive you, darling! you do not understand how much I love you, or you would not tell me bluntly such terrible things – especially if the case is not desperate. What has happened? Why are you here now, when in half an hour we should have been in the Rue d'Artois?'

'Ah, Father, how could I think of that when a great catastrophe has befallen me? I am out of my senses. Your lawyer has brought things to light which we must have known sooner or later. Your great experience in business is now my only hope, and I have rushed to you as a poor drowning creature catches at a branch. When Monsieur Derville found that Monsieur de Nucingen was opposing him with all sorts of evasions he threatened him with a law-suit, saying that an order from the Court for such a proceeding could easily be obtained. Nucingen came to my room this morning and asked me if I was bent on his ruin and mine. I answered that I knew nothing about all that; that I had my own fortune; that I ought to be allowed to spend the income of it as I pleased; that all business in connection with the matter was in the hands of my lawyer; and, finally, that I was totally ignorant on such matters, and did not wish to discuss them. That was exactly what you advised me to say, was it not?'

'Yes, that was right,' said Père Goriot.

'Well,' continued Delphine, 'then he told me plainly about his affairs. He has embarked all his own money and mine in speculations that have not yet matured, in furtherance of which he has sent great sums of money to other countries. If I force him to account for my fortune now, I shall oblige him to show his books and file his schedule; whereas if I will wait one year, he promises on his honour to double my fortune and invest the whole – his and mine – in landed property which shall be settled on me. My dear Father, he meant what he said; he frightened me. He asked my pardon for his past conduct. He gave me back my liberty; he promised not to interfere with my life in any way provided I would agree to let him manage our affairs in my name. He promised, as a proof of his good faith, that I should call in Monsieur Derville at any time to examine the legality of the papers by which the property was to be made mine. In short, he put himself into my power, tied hand and foot. He wishes for the next two years to keep the expenditure of the household under his control, and he besought me to spend no more than my allowance during that period. He proved to me that he is doing all he can to save appearances. He has sent away his *danseuse*, and is going to practise the most rigid though quiet economy, so that he may come safely out of his speculations without impairing his credit. I answered him as unkindly as I could. I appeared to doubt him, so that by pushing him to extremities I might force him to tell me everything. He showed me his books; and at last he burst into tears. I have never seen a man in such a state. He lost his head; he talked of killing himself; he was out of his mind. I felt for him.'

'And you believed him?' cried Père Goriot. 'He was playing a part. They were lies. I know what Germans are in business. They seem honest and open enough; but under that air of frankness they are shrewd and cunning, and worse to deal with than any others. Your husband is imposing on you. He finds himself close-pressed, and feigns death. He wants to be more completely master of your fortune under your name than he could be under his own. He will make use of you to save himself in the event of business losses. He is as cunning as he is false. He is a bad fellow. No, no! I will not go to my grave leaving my daughters stripped of everything. I know a little about business still. He says he has embarked all his capital in speculations. Well, then, his interest in these speculations must be represented by stocks or some kind of securities. Let him produce them, and allow you to take your share. We will choose the safest, and run our chance. We will have all the papers registered under the name of *Delphine Goriot, wife, separated as to property from the Baron de Nucingen*. Does he take us for fools? Does he suppose I would patiently permit him, were it only for a day, to leave you without fortune? Never! not for a day, nor a night – no, not for two hours! If such a thing should come to pass I could not survive it. What! have I worked for forty years; have I carried sacks of flour on my back and toiled in the sweat of my brow; have I pinched and denied myself all the days of my life for you, my angels – who repaid my toil and lightened my burden – that to-day my fortune and my life should pass away in smoke? I should die raving mad! By all that is sacred in heaven and earth we will drag this matter to the light; we will examine into his books, his coffers, his speculations. I will not sleep; I will not lie down upon my bed; I will not eat, until I find out if your fortune is all there. Thank God! you are at least separated as to property. You shall have Monsieur Derville for your lawyer; he is an honest man. Heavens and earth! you shall have your poor little million to yourself – you shall have your fifty thousand francs income to spend as you please to the end of your days – or I will make such a stir in Paris – Ha! ha! I will appeal to the Chamber of Deputies, if the law courts will not right us. If I can see you happy and at ease about money I shall forget my own sorrows. Our money is our life; money does everything. What does that big log of an Alsatian mean? Delphine, don't yield a farthing to that brute, who has held you in bondage and made you miserable. If he needs your help, he shall not have it unless we can tie him tight and make him march a straight line. *Mon Dieu!* my whole head is on fire; there are flames in my skull. Think of my Delphine being brought to want! Oh, my Fifine, if that should happen to thee! – *Sapristi*! where is my hat? Come, I must go directly. I shall insist on looking into everything – his books, his business, his correspondence. We will go this moment. I cannot be calm until it is proved that your fortune is secure beyond all risks, and I have seen it with my own eyes!'

'My dear Father, you must set about it cautiously. If you put the slightest desire for vengeance into this affair, if you even show hostile feeling to my husband, you will ruin me. He knows you; he thinks it natural that influenced by you I should be anxious about my fortune; but I swear to you, he has it in his power, and he means to keep it there. He is capable of running away with it, and leaving me without a *sou*. He knows I would not dishonour the name I bear by bringing him to justice. His position is both strong and weak. Indeed, I have examined into it all. If you push him to extremities, I am lost.'

'Is he dishonest? Is he a rogue?'

'Yes, Father, he is,' she cried, throwing herself into a chair and bursting into tears. 'I did not mean to acknowledge it. I wished to spare you the pain of knowing that you had married me to such a man. Vices and conscience, body and soul – all are in keeping. It is terrible. I hate him, and yet I despise him. A man capable of flinging himself into such transactions as he has confessed to me, without shame or remorse, fills me with disgust. My fears spring from what I know of him. He offered me – he, my husband! – my full liberty (and you know what he meant), if I would play into his hands; if I would lend my name to dishonourable transactions, under cover of which he can escape if he meets with losses.'

'But there are laws! There is the guillotine for such men,' exclaimed Père Goriot.

'No, Father, there are no laws that can reach him. Listen to what he told me. This is the substance of it, stripped of his circumlocutions: "Either all will be lost, and you will not have a farthing – you will be ruined; for I can take no one into partnership but yourself – or you must let me carry out my speculations as they now stand, to the end." Is that plain speaking? He still trusts me. He knows that I shall not touch his fortune, and shall be satisfied with my own. It has come to this – either I must enter into a repulsive and dishonest partnership, or I am ruined. He buys my complicity in his crimes by giving me the liberty to live as I please. He says, "I will take no notice of your faults, if you will not prevent my plotting the ruin of poor people." Is that clear? Do you know what he means by "speculations"? He buys unimproved land in his own name, and puts forward men of straw to build houses on the land. These men contract with builders on an agreement for long credits; and afterwards, for a nominal sum, they make over the buildings to my husband. They then go into sham bankruptcy, and the contractors lose everything. The name of Nucingen & Co. serves as a decoy. I understand now how it is that to prove the payment of money, should enquiry be aroused, he has sent away enormous sums to Amsterdam, London, Naples and Vienna. How could we get hold of those sums?'

Eugène heard the dull sound of Père Goriot's knees falling on the tiled floor of his chamber.

'Good God! What have I done?' he cried. 'I have delivered my daughter over to this man! He will strip her of everything! Oh, forgive me, my poor girl!'

'True. If I am now in the depths of trouble, it is partly your fault, Father,' said Delphine. 'A girl has so little sense up to the time she is married. What do we know of the world, or of men or manners? It is the duty of our fathers to see to these things. Dear Father, I don't mean to blame you – forgive me for saying so. In this case the fault was all mine. No – don't cry, Papa,' she said, kissing his forehead.

'Don't you cry, either, my little Delphine. Stoop lower, that I may kiss away your tears. Ah! I will find my wits again. I will unravel the tangle thy husband has made of thy affairs.'

'No, let me manage him. I think I can get him to put some of my money at once into land. Perhaps I can make him buy back Nucingen in Alsace in my name. I know he wants it. But come to-morrow, Papa, and look into his books and his affairs. Monsieur Derville knows nothing whatever about business. Stay! don't come to-morrow – it will agitate me; Madame de Beauséant's ball is the day after, and I want to take care of myself and be as beautiful as possible, to do honour to my dear Eugène. Let us go and look into his chamber.'

At this moment another carriage drew up in the Rue Neuve Sainte-Geneviève, and Madame de Restaud's voice was heard speaking to Sylvie.

'Is my father in?'

This circumstance saved Eugène, who was on the point of throwing himself upon the bed and pretending to be asleep.

'Ah, Papa, have you heard about Anastasie?' said Delphine, recognizing her sister's voice. 'It seems that very strange things have been going on in her household.'

'What things?' cried Père Goriot. 'Is this to be my end? My poor head cannot bear another blow!'

'Papa,' said the countess, entering. 'Ah, you here, Delphine?'

Madame de Restaud seemed embarrassed at the sight of her sister.

'Good morning, Nasie,' said Madame de Nucingen. 'Do you think my being here so extraordinary? I see my father every day.'

'Since when?'

'If you came here, you would know.'

'Don't aggravate me, Delphine,' said the countess, in a

lamentable voice. 'I am very unhappy. I am ruined, my poor Father – utterly ruined, at last!'

'What is it, Nasie?' cried Père Goriot. 'Tell me all, my child. Oh, she is fainting! – Delphine, come, help her; be kind to her, and I will love you better than ever – if I can.'

'My poor Nasie,' said Madame de Nucingen, making her sister sit down, 'speak; we are the only ones in the world who love you enough to forgive everything. You see, family affections are the safest, after all.'

Père Goriot shivered. 'I shall die of this,' he said, in a low voice. 'Come,' he continued, stirring the miserable fire; 'come to the hearth, both of you; I am cold. What is it, Nasie? Speak – you are killing me.'

'Father!' said the poor woman. 'My husband knows all. You remember, some time ago, that note of Maxime's which you paid for me at Gobseck's? Well, it was not the first. I had paid many before. About the beginning of January he was greatly out of spirits; he would tell me nothing. But it is so easy to read the heart of those we love – a trifle tells everything; besides, there are presentiments. He was more loving and tender than I had ever known him. Poor Maxime! In his heart he was bidding me goodby; he was thinking of blowing out his brains. At last I besought him so earnestly that he told me – but not until I had been two hours on my knees – that he owed a hundred thousand francs. Oh, Papa! – a hundred thousand francs! I was beside myself. I knew you had not got them; I had eaten up your all—'

'No,' said Père Goriot, 'I have not got them. I cannot give them to you – unless I stole them. Yes! I could have gone out to steal them. Nasie, I will go—'

At these words, forced out like the death-rattle of the dying – the groan of paternal love reduced to impotence – the sisters paused: what selfish souls could listen coldly to this cry of anguish that like a pebble flung into an abyss revealed its depths?

'I obtained them, my Father,' said the countess, bursting into tears. 'I sold that which did not belong to me.'

Delphine, too, seemed moved, and laid her head upon her sister's shoulder.

'Then it was all true?' she said.

Anastasie bowed her head. Madame de Nucingen took her in her arms and kissed her tenderly.

'You will always be loved, not judged, by me,' she said.

'My angels!' said their father in a feeble voice; 'alas! that your union should come only through misfortune.'

'To save Maxime's life, to save my own happiness,' resumed the countess, comforted by these proofs of loving kindness, 'I carried to that money-lender whom you know of – that man born in hell, whom nothing moves to pity; that Monsieur Gobseck – the family diamonds, heir-looms treasured by Monsieur de Restaud: his, my own, all, everything. I sold them. Sold them, do you understand? I saved Maxime; but I killed myself. Restaud knows all.'

'Who told him? Who? that I may strangle them!' cried the old man passionately.

'Yesterday my husband sent for me to his chamber. I went. "Anastasie," he said to me, in such a voice – oh, his voice was enough! I knew what was coming – "Where are your diamonds?" "In my room," I answered. "No," he said, looking full at me, "they are there, on my bureau." He showed me the case, which he had covered with his handkerchief. "You know where they have come from," he said. I fell at his feet; I wept; I asked him what death he wished me to die—'

'Did you say that?' cried Père Goriot. 'By all that is sacred, any one who blames or harms my children, while I live, may be sure – that I—'

The words died in his throat, and he was silent.

'And then, dear Father, he asked me to do something harder

than to die. Heaven preserve other women from hearing what he said to me!'

'I shall kill him,' said Père Goriot, slowly. 'He has but one life, yet he owes me two. What followed?'

'He looked at me,' she continued, after a pause, 'and said, "Anastasie, I will bury all in silence. I will not separate from you – there are children to be considered. I will not fight with Monsieur de Trailles – I might miss him. Human justice gives me the right to kill him in your arms; but I will not dishonour the children. I spare you and your children, but I impose two conditions. Answer me. Are any of these children mine?" I said, "Yes." "Which?" "Ernest, our eldest." "It is well," he said. "Next, swear to obey me in future on one point." I swore. "You will sign over to me your property when I demand it?"'

'Sign it not!' cried Pore Goriot. 'Never sign it! Nasie, Nasie, he cares for his heir, his eldest. I will seize the child. Thunder of heaven! he is mine as well as his; he is my grandson. I will put him in my village where I was born. I will care for him – oh, yes, be sure of that! I will make your husband yield. I will say to him, if you want your son, give me back my daughter; restore her property; leave her in peace—'

'Father!'

'Yes, thy father. I am thy true father. Let this great lord beware how he maltreats my daughter! A fire is running through my veins; I have the blood of a tiger in me! Oh, my children, my children! is this your life? – it is my death. What will become of you when I am gone? Why cannot a father live out the life of his child? Oh, my God, thy world is wrong! – and yet thou art a father. Oh, Father in heaven! why are we condemned to suffer through our children? Ah, my angels, it is only your griefs that make you come to me – only your tears that you share with me! Yes, yes, but that is love; I know you love me. Come, both of you, come, pour your troubles into my heart: it is strong, it is large, it can hold them all. Yes, though you rend it into fragments, each fragment is a living heart – a father's heart. Could they but take your griefs and bear them for you! Ah! when you were my little ones I made you happy.'

'We have never been happy since,' said Delphine. 'Where are those days when we slid down the sacks in the great granary!'

'Father, I have not told you all,' whispered Anastasie to the old man, who started convulsively. 'The diamonds did not bring a hundred thousand francs. They are still pursuing Maxime. We have twelve thousand francs more to pay. He has promised me to reform; to give up gambling. All I have in the world is his affection; and, oh, I have paid too terrible a price for it! – I cannot lose him now! I have sacrificed honour, fortune, children, peace of mind for him. Oh, do something for me, that he may not be imprisoned, not driven from society! I know he will yet make himself a position in the world. I have nothing left to give him now. But we have children; they must be provided for. All will be lost if they put him in Sainte-Pélagie – a debtors' prison!'

'I have nothing – nothing left, Nasie – nothing! The world is at an end; I feel it quaking, crumbling. Fly, fly! save yourselves! Stay! I have still my silver buckles, and six forks and spoons, the first I ever owned. But I have no money, only my annuity—'

'What have you done with your money in the funds?'

'I sold it out, keeping a trifle for my wants. I wanted the rest, twelve thousand francs, to furnish some rooms for Fifine.'

'For you, Delphine?' cried Madame de Restaud.

'Never mind, never mind,' said Père Goriot, 'the twelve thousand francs are gone.'

'I guess where,' said the countess, 'to help Monsieur de Rastignac. Ah, my poor Delphine, pause! see what I have come to.'

'My dear, Monsieur de Rastignac is a man incapable of ruining the woman who loves him.'

'Thank you, Delphine. In the terrible position I am in, you might have spared me that. But you never loved me.'

'Ah, but she does love you, Nasie; she was saying so just now. We were speaking of you, and she said you were beautiful, but she was only pretty—'

'Pretty!' cried the countess; 'her heart is stone-cold.'

'And if it were!' exclaimed Delphine, colouring, 'how have you behaved to me? You have disclaimed me; you have shut against me the doors of houses where I longed to go; you have never let slip an opportunity to give me pain. A cold heart! Did I come like you, and squeeze out of our poor father, little by little, a thousand francs here, a thousand francs there – all he possessed? Did I reduce him to the state he is now in? This is your doing, my sister. I saw my father as often as I could. I never turned him out of doors, and then came and licked his hands when I had need of him. I did not even know that he was spending those twelve thousand francs for me. I at least have some decency – and you know it. Papa may sometimes have made me presents, but I never begged for them—'

'You were better off than I. Monsieur De Marsay was rich, as you had good cause to know. You have always been despicable as to money. Adieu, I have no sister, no—'

'Hush, Nasie!' cried Père Goriot.

'No one but a sister – a sister like you – would insinuate what the world itself does not believe. It is monstrous!' cried Delphine.

'My children! my children! hush, or you will kill me before your eyes—'

'I forgive you, Nasie,' continued Madame de Nucingen, 'for you are unhappy; but I am better than you – think of your saying that, just as I was making up my mind to do everything that I could for you. Well, it is worthy of all that you have done to me for the last nine years!'

'My children! oh, my children! Kiss each other, be friends,' said the father. 'You are two angels.'

'No, let me alone!' cried the countess, whom Père Goriot had taken by the arm; 'she has less pity for me than my husband. An example of all the virtues, indeed!'

'I had rather be supposed to owe money to Monsieur De Marsay than to own that Monsieur de Trailles had cost me two hundred thousand francs,' replied Madame de Nucingen.

'Delphine!' cried the countess, making a step towards her.

'I say the truth; but what you say of me is false,' replied the other, coldly.

'Delphine, you are a—'

Père Goriot sprang forward and prevented the countess from saying more by putting his hand over her mouth.

'Good heavens, Papa! what have you been touching?' cried Anastasie.

'Ah, yes, yes! I ought not to have touched you,' said the poor father, wiping his hand upon his trousers, 'I did not know you were coming. I am moving to-day.'

He was glad to be able to draw upon himself a reproach that diverted the current of his daughter's anger.

'Ah!' he sighed, sitting down, 'you break my heart. I am dying, children; my head burns as if my skull were full of fire. Be kind to each other; love one another. – You will kill me. Delphine! Nasie! you were both right, you were both wrong. Come, Dedel,' he resumed, turning to Madame de Nucingen with his eyes full of tears, 'she needs twelve thousand francs; let us see how we can get them for her. Oh, my daughters, do not look at each other like that!' He fell down on his knees before Delphine: 'Ask her pardon for my sake,' he whispered; 'she is more unhappy than you are.'

'My poor Nasie,' said Delphine, frightened by the wild and maddened expression on her father's face, 'I was wrong. Kiss me.'

'Ah, that is balm to my heart!' cried the old man. 'But the twelve thousand francs – how can we get them? I might offer myself for a substitute in the army—'

'Oh, Father!' cried the daughters, flinging their arms about him. 'No!'

'God will bless you for that thought,' cried Delphine. 'We are not worthy of it – are we, Nasie?'

'And besides, my poor Father, it would be but a drop in the bucket,' observed the countess.

'Will flesh and blood bring nothing?' cried the old man wildly. 'I would give myself away to whoever would save thee, Nasie; I would commit crimes for him; I would go to the galleys, like Vautrin; I—' he stopped as if struck by a thunderbolt, and grasped his head. 'Nothing more! – all gone!—' he said. 'No, I could steal – if I knew where: it is hard to know where. Oh, there is nothing I can do – but die! Let me die! I am good for nothing else. I am no longer a father: she appeals to me; she needs my help, and I have none to give her! Ah, wretch! why did I buy that annuity? – I! who have children! Did I not love them? Die, die! like a dog, as I am. Yet the beasts love their young – Oh, my head, my head! it bursts!'

He sobbed convulsively. Eugène, horror-stricken, took up the note he had once signed for Vautrin, the stamp of which was for a much larger sum than that named on the face of it; he altered the figures, making it a note for twelve thousand francs payable to the order of Goriot, and went into the old man's chamber.

'Here is the sum you want, Madame,' he said, giving Madame de Restaud the paper. 'I was asleep in my room, and was wakened by what you were saying. I learned for the first time what I owe to Monsieur Goriot. Here is a paper on which you will be able to raise the money. When it matures, I promise faithfully that it shall be paid.'

The countess stood motionless, holding the paper. 'Delphine,' she said, pale, and trembling with anger, rage and fury, 'I take God to witness that I forgave you all – oh! but *this!* What! Monsieur has been there, and you knew it? You have had the meanness to feed your spite by letting him hear my secrets – mine, my children's – my shame, my dishonour! Go, you are a sister no longer! I hate you! I will harm you, if I can. I—'

Anger cut short her words; her throat was parched and dry.

'My child! he is one of us; he is my son, your brother, our deliverer,' cried Père Goriot. 'Kiss him, thank him, Nasie. See, I embrace him,' he went on, clasping Eugène to his breast with a sort of fury. 'Oh, my son!' he cried, 'I will be more than a father to thee. Nasie, Nasie! bless him and thank him.'

'Don't speak to her, Father, she is out of her senses,' said Delphine.

'Out of my senses! And you? – what are you?' cried Madame de Restaud.

'Oh, my children! I die if you continue,' cried the old man, falling across his bed as if struck by a shot. 'They are killing me,' he said.

The countess turned to Eugène, who stood motionless, struck dumb by the violence of the scene before him.

'Monsieur?' she said, and her gesture, tone and look were interrogative. She paid no attention to her father, whose waistcoat was being loosened by Delphine.

'Madame, I shall pay and keep silence,' he said, answering her question before she asked it.

'You have killed our father, Nasie,' cried Delphine, pointing to the old man now senseless on the bed.

Madame de Restaud left the room.

'I forgive her,' he said, opening his eyes; 'her position is dreadful, and would turn a wiser head. Console her, Delphine. Be good to her – promise your poor father, who is dying,' he went on, pressing her hand.

'But what ails you?' she said, much frightened.

'Nothing, nothing,' her father answered. 'It will go off presently. I have a weight upon my forehead; a headache. Poor Nasie, what will become of her?'

At this moment Madame de Restaud returned and threw herself down beside her father. 'Oh, forgive me!' she cried.

'Come, come,' said Père Goriot, 'that hurts me more than anything.'

'Monsieur,' said the countess, turning to Rastignac with tears in her eyes, 'my troubles have made me unjust. You will be a brother to me?' she added, holding out her hand.

'Nasie,' said Delphine, 'my little Nasie, let us forget everything.'

'No,' she said, 'I shall remember.'

'My angels,' said Père Goriot, 'you lift the curtain that was falling before my eyes. Your voices call me back to life. Let me see you kiss each other once more. Tell me, Nasie, will this note save you?'

'I hope so. But, Papa, will you endorse it?'

'Why, what a fool I was to forget that! – but I was ill. Nasie, don't be vexed with me. Let me know when you are out of your troubles. But, stay, I will go to you – No, I will not go. I dare not see your husband. As to his doing what he pleases with your fortune, remember, I am here. Adieu, my child.'

Eugène stood stupefied.

'Poor Anastasie! she was always violent,' said Madame de Nucingen; 'but she has a kind heart.'

'She came back for the endorsement,' whispered Eugène in her ear.

'Do you think so?'

'I wish I did not think it. Do not trust her,' he added, lifting up his eyes, as if to confide a thought not to be put into words.

'Yes, she was always acting a part; and my poor father was completely taken in by her.'

'How are you now, dear Père Goriot?' asked Rastignac, bending over the old man.

'I feel like going to sleep,' he answered. Eugène helped him to go to bed; and after he had fallen asleep holding his daughter's hand, Delphine quietly left him.

'To-night, at the opera,' she said to Eugène, 'you will bring me word how he is. To-morrow you will change your quarters, Monsieur. Let me peep into your room – oh, what a horrid place! it is worse than my father's. Eugène, you behaved beautifully! I would love you more than ever for it – if I could. But, my child, if you mean to get on in the world you must give up throwing twelve thousand franc-notes about in that way. Monsieur de Trailles is a gambler, though my sister will not admit it. He could have picked up that twelve thousand francs in the place where he has lost and won a mint of money.'

A groan brought them hastily back to Père Goriot. He was to all appearances asleep, but as they approached they heard him say, 'Not happy; they are not happy!' Whether he were asleep or awake, the tone in which he uttered the words struck so painfully to his daughter's heart that she leaned over the wretched bed on which her father lay and kissed him on his forehead. He opened his eyes and murmured, 'Delphine!'

'How are you now?' she said.

'Better. Do not worry about me. I shall get up presently. Go away, my children, and be happy.'

Eugène took Delphine home; but not liking the condition in which they had left Père Goriot, he refused to dine with her, and went back to the Maison Vauquer. He found him better, and just sitting down to dinner. Bianchon had placed himself so that he could watch the old man unobserved. When he saw him take up his bread and smell it to judge the quality of the flour, the medical student, observing a total absence of all consciousness of the act, made a significant gesture.

'Come and sit by me, graduate of the Cochin Hospital,' said Eugène.

Bianchon did as he was asked, all the more readily because it placed him nearer to the old man.

'What is the matter with him?' whispered Rastignac.

'If I am not mistaken, he's done for. Something out of the common must have excited him. He is threatened with apoplexy. The lower part of his face is calm enough, but the upper part is drawn and unnatural. The eyes have the peculiar expression which denotes pressure on the brain; don't you notice that they are covered with a light film? To-morrow morning I shall be able to judge better.'

'Is there any cure for it?'

'None. Possibly we might retard his death if we could set up a reaction in the extremities; but if the present symptoms continue, it will be all up with the poor old fellow before to-morrow night. Do you know what brought on his illness? He must have had some great shock that his mind has sunk under.'

'Yes, he has,' said Rastignac, remembering how the daughters had struck alternate blows at their father's heart. 'But, at least,' he said to himself, 'Delphine loves her old father.'

XVII

That night, at the opera, Eugène took some precautions not to alarm Madame de Nucingen.

'Oh, you need not be so anxious about him,' she said, as soon as he began to tell her of the illness. 'My father is very strong; this morning we shook him a little, that is all. Our fortunes are in peril: do you realize the extent of that misfortune? I could not survive it, if it were not that your affection makes me indifferent to what I should otherwise consider the greatest sorrow in the world. I have but one fear now – to lose the love which makes it happiness to live. All outside of that I have ceased to care for; you are all in all to me. If I desire to keep my wealth, it is that I may better please you. I know that I can be more to a lover than to a father; it is my nature. My father gave me a heart, but you have made it beat. The world may blame me – I do not care; you will acquit me of sins into which I am drawn by an irresistible attachment. You think me an unnatural daughter? No, I am not: who would not love a father kind as ours has been? But how could I prevent his knowing the inevitable results of our deplorable marriages? Why did he not prevent them? Was it not his duty to think and judge for us? I know that he suffers now as much as we do; but how can I help that? Ought we to make light of our troubles? That would do no good. Our silence would have distressed him far more than our reproaches and complaints have injured him. There are some situations in life where every alternative is bitter.'

Eugène was silent, touched by this simple expression of native feeling. The clear judgement a woman shows in judging natural affections when a privileged affection separates and holds her at a distance from them, struck him forcibly. Madame de Nucingen was troubled by his silence.

'What are you thinking of?' she said.

'Of what you have just said to me. Until now, I thought that I loved you more than you love me.'

She smiled, but checked the expression of her feelings, that she might keep the conversation within the conventional limits of propriety.

'Eugène,' she said, changing the conversation, 'do you know what is going on in the world? All Paris will be at Madame de Beauséant's to-morrow evening. The Rochefides and the Marquis d'Adjuda have agreed to keep the matter secret; but it is certain that the king signs the marriage contract to-morrow morning, and that your poor cousin as yet knows nothing of it. She cannot put off her ball, and the marquis will not be there. All the world is talking of it.'

'Then the world is amusing itself with what is infamous,' cried Eugène, 'and makes itself an accomplice. Don't you know that it will kill Madame de Beauséant?'

'Oh, no, it will not,' said Delphine, smiling; 'you don't understand that sort of woman. But all Paris will be at her ball – and I too, I shall be there! I owe this happiness to you.'

'Perhaps,' said Rastignac, 'it is only one of those unfounded rumours which are always flying about Paris.'

'We shall know to-morrow.'

Eugène did not go back to the Maison Vauquer. The pleasure of occupying his new rooms in the Rue d'Artois was a temptation too great to withstand. The next morning he slept late; and towards midday Madame de Nucingen came to breakfast with him. Young people are so eager for these pretty enjoyments that he had well-nigh forgotten Père Goriot. It was like a delightful festival to make use of each elegant trifle that was now his own; and the presence of Madame de Nucingen lent to them all an added charm. Nevertheless, about four o'clock they remembered the old man, and as they recalled the happiness he had shown at the thought of living there, Eugène remarked that they ought to get him there at once – especially if he were likely to be ill; and he left Delphine to fetch him from the Maison Vauquer.

Neither Goriot nor Bianchon were at the dinner table.

'Well,' said the painter, 'so Père Goriot has broken down at last! Bianchon is upstairs with him. The old fellow saw one of his daughters this morning – that Countess de Restau-rama. After that he went out, and made himself worse. Society is about to be deprived of one of its brightest ornaments.'

Eugène rushed to the staircase.

'Here, Monsieur Eugène!'

'Monsieur Eugène! Madame is calling you,' cried Sylvie.

'Monsieur,' said the widow, 'you and Père Goriot were to have left on the 15th of February; it is three days past that time – this is the 18th. I shall expect both of you to pay me a month's lodging; but if you choose to be responsible for Père Goriot, your word will be satisfactory.'

'Why so? Cannot you trust him?'

'Trust him! If he were to go out of his mind or die, his daughters would not pay me a farthing; and all he will leave is not worth ten francs. He carried off the last of his forks and spoons this morning. I don't know why. He had dressed himself up like a young man. Heaven forgive me, but I do think he had put rouge on his cheeks. He looked quite young again.'

'I will be responsible,' cried Eugène, with a shudder, foreseeing a catastrophe.

He ran up to Père Goriot's chamber. The old man was lying on his bed, with Bianchon beside him.

'Good evening, Father,' said Eugène.

Père Goriot smiled gently and said, turning his glassy eyes upon the student, 'How is she?'

'Quite well; and you?'

'Not very ill.'

'Don't tire him,' said Bianchon, drawing Eugène apart into a corner of the room.

'Well?' asked Rastignac.

'Nothing can save him but a miracle. The congestion I expected has taken place. I've put on mustard plasters, and luckily they are drawing: he feels them.'

'Can he be moved?'

'Not possibly. You must leave him where he is, and he must be kept perfectly quiet, and free from emotion.'

'Dear Bianchon,' said Eugène, 'we will take care of him together.'

'I called in the surgeon-in-chief of my hospital.'

'What did he say?'

'He will give no opinion till to-morrow evening. He has promised to come in after he gets through his work for the day. It is quite certain that the old fellow has been up to some imprudence; but he won't tell me what. He is as obstinate as a mule. When I speak to him he either makes believe he does not hear, or that he has gone to sleep; or if his eyes are open, he begins to groan. He went out this morning and walked all over Paris, nobody knows where. He carried off everything he owned of any value; he has been making some infernal sale of his things, and exhausting his strength. One of his daughters was here.'

'Ah!' said Rastignac, 'the countess; a tall, dark woman, with fine eyes, a pretty foot, and graceful figure?'

'Yes.'

'Leave me a moment alone with him,' said Eugène. 'I can get him to tell me everything.'

'Well, then, I'll go and get my dinner. Be careful not to agitate him. There is still some hope.'

'I'll be careful.'

'They will enjoy themselves to-morrow,' said Père Goriot to Eugène as soon as they were alone. 'They are going to a great ball.'

'What did you do this morning, Papa, to knock yourself up and have to go to bed?'

'Nothing.'

'Was Anastasie here?'

'Yes,' replied Père Goriot.

'Well, then, don't keep any secrets from me. What did she ask you for this time?'

'Ah!' he replied, rallying his strength to speak. 'Poor child! she was in great trouble. Nasie has not a *sou* of her own since the affair of the diamonds. She had ordered for this ball a beautiful dress of gold tissue, which would set her off like a jewel. The dressmaker – infamous creature! – refused to trust her, and her maid paid a thousand francs on account – poor Nasie! that she should come to that! it breaks my heart; – but the maid, finding that Restaud had withdrawn all confidence from Nasie, was afraid of losing her money, so she arranged with the dressmaker not to deliver the dress till the thousand francs were paid. The ball is to-morrow; the dress is ready; Nasie is in despair. She wanted to borrow my forks and spoons and pawn them. Her husband insists that she shall go to the ball in order to show all Paris the diamonds she was said to have sold. Could she say to him, "I owe a thousand francs; pay them for me"? No: I felt that myself. Her sister Delphine is to be there in a beautiful dress; Anastasie ought not to be less brilliant than her younger sister – certainly not. Besides, she was drowned in tears, my poor little daughter! I was so mortified that I had not those twelve thousand francs yesterday! I would have given the rest of my miserable life to make amends.

You see, I have borne up till now against everything; but this last want of money has broken my heart. – Well, well, I made no bones about it; I patched myself up; I tried to make myself look spruce, and I sold my forks and spoons and the buckles for six hundred francs. Then I made over my annuity for one year to old Gobseck for four hundred more. – Bah! I can live on dry bread: I did when I was young. – So my Nasie will appear to-morrow evening. I have got the thousand francs under my pillow. It warms me up to feel them there under my head, and to know that they are going to give comfort to my poor child. She is to come for them at ten o'clock to-morrow morning. I shall be quite well by that time. I don't want them to think me ill; they might not like to go to the ball – they would wish to stay and nurse me. Nasie will kiss me to-morrow as if I were a baby. After all, I might have spent that money on the apothecary; I'd rather give it to my Cure-all – my Nasie. I can still comfort her in her troubles: that makes up in part for having sunk my money in an annuity. She is down in the very depths, and I have no strength to pull her up again! – I am going back into business; I shall go to Odessa and buy wheat: wheat is worth three times as much with us as it costs there. The importation of cereals as raw material is forbidden; but the good people who make the laws never thought of prohibiting manufactured articles of flour. Ha! ha! the idea came into my head this morning. I shall make millions out of my pastes.'

'He is losing his mind,' thought Eugène, looking down upon the old man. 'Come, now, lie still, and don't talk,' he said.

Rastignac went to dinner when Bianchon came up. Both passed the night taking turns beside the sick bed. One occupied himself in reading medical books, the other in writing to his mother and sisters. The next morning Bianchon thought the symptoms somewhat more favourable, but the patient needed the intelligent personal care which the two students alone could give him. Leeches were put on the emaciated body of the poor old man, and poultices; mustard foot-baths were administered, and a number of medical devices resorted to which required all the strength of the two young men. Madame de Restaud did not come, but sent a messenger for the money.

'I thought she would have come herself; but perhaps it is best so – she might have been anxious,' said her father, trying to make the best of his disappointment.

At seven o'clock in the evening Thérèse appeared, bringing a letter for Eugène—

> 'What can you be doing, dear friend? Am I neglected as soon as loved? You have shown me, in the outpourings of heart to heart, a soul so beautiful that I trust you as one of those forever faithful through many phases and shades of feeling. Do you remember what you said as we were listening to the prayer of Moses in Egypt? "To some it seems but a single note; to others the infinite of music." Do not forget that I expect you this evening to go with me to Madame de Beauséant's. Monsieur d'Adjuda's marriage contract was signed by the king this morning, and the poor viscountess did not know of it till two o'clock. All Paris will be at her house to-night; just as a crowd flocks to the Place de Grève to see an execution. Is it not horrible that people should go there to see if she can hide her grief – if she knows how to die? I certainly would not go if I had been to her house before. But she will probably never receive again, and then all the efforts I have made to go there would be thrown away. My situation is different from that of others. And besides, I shall be there for your sake. If you do not come to me within two hours, I am not sure that I shall pardon you for the crime.'

Eugène seized a pen and replied thus—

> 'I am waiting for a doctor, who will say how long your father has to live. He is dying. I will come and tell you what the medical opinion is. I fear it can only be that he will not recover. You will judge whether you can go to the ball. Tender remembrances.'

The doctor came at half-past eight, and though he could hold out no hopes of improvement he thought death was not imminent. He said there would be changes to better or worse, and on these would hang the life and reason of the patient.

'Far better that he should die,' were his last words.

Eugène consigned Père Goriot to the care of Bianchon, and went to Madame de Nucingen with the sad news, which to his mind, still imbued as it was with tender memories of his home, precluded all possibility of amusement for a daughter.

'Tell her to go to the ball and enjoy herself all the same,' said Père Goriot, who they hoped was dozing, but who started up in bed when he saw that Rastignac was going.

The young man entered Delphine's presence with his heart full of grief and pity. He found her with her *toilette* made, her hair dressed, and nothing more to be done than to put on her ball-dress. But like an artist's final work upon his canvas, the finishing touches took more time than the picture itself.

'What! are you not dressed?' she said.

'But, Madame, your father is—'

'Why do you harp upon my father?' she cried, interrupting him. 'You need not teach me my duty to my father. I have known my father for a long time. Not another word, Eugène; I will not listen to you till you have made your *toilette*. Thérèse has laid out everything in your room. My carriage is at the door; take it, and come back as soon as possible. We can talk about my father as we are driving to the ball. I wish to start early, for if we are caught in the line of carriages it may be midnight before we get there.'

'Madame!—'

'Go, go! not another word,' she cried, running into her boudoir for a necklace.

'Go, Monsieur Eugène – go!' said Thérèse, 'or you will make Madame very angry.'

So saying, she pushed the young man, who stood dismayed and silenced by this elegant parricide. He went away and dressed himself, filled with melancholy and disheartening reflections. The world seemed to him like an ocean of slime, in which a man sank up to his throat if he so much as put his foot into it.

'Its wickednesses are mean – are paltry,' he cried. 'Vautrin's crimes at least were great.'

He had now seen, by experience, the three great phases of society – Obedience, Struggle and Revolt: Family-life, the World and Vautrin. He dared not make his choice among them. Obedience had become to him stagnation; revolt was impossible; struggle false and uncertain. He thought of his home; he remembered the pure emotions of that peaceful life; his mind went back to the years passed among the dear ones who fondly loved him. He said to himself that those who conformed in all things to the natural laws of family life were fully, perfectly, permanently happy.

But though he owned these things, he had not the courage to assert them to Delphine. Could he confess the faith of purity to her? Could he talk to her of virtue in the guise of love? His worldly training was already bearing fruit; his love was selfishness. His instinct enabled him to sound the inner nature of Delphine: he believed her capable of going to this ball over the dead body of her father; but he had neither the strength to oppose her by argument, nor the courage to displease her, nor the virtue to give her up. 'She would never forgive me for being right where she was bent on doing wrong,' was his reflection. Then he recalled the doctor's words. He persuaded himself that Père Goriot was not so dangerously ill as he had thought; he multiplied heartless arguments that he might justify Delphine: she could not know her father's true condition; the poor old man himself would send her to the ball if she went to see him. He reflected also that the laws of social life are absolute, and make no allowances for differences of character, or interests, or situations. He tried to deceive himself, and find reasons to sacrifice his conscience to his mistress. For two days past everything within him and about him had changed. Woman had turned the current of his whole existence; home and its ties had paled before her influence; she had confiscated all things to her profit.

'Tell me now, how is my father?' said Madame de Nucingen, when he came back dressed for the ball.

'Very ill,' he said. 'If you would give me a proof of your affection, you would let me take you to him at once.'

'Well – yes;' she said; 'but it must be after the ball. Eugène, be good; don't preach to me. Come!'

They drove away. Eugène sat silent for a part of the way.

'What are you thinking of?' she asked.

'I am listening to the rattle in your father's throat,' he answered in a tone of anger; and he began to relate, with the fiery eloquence of youth, the cruelty to which Madame de Restaud's vanity had pushed her, the last supreme act of their father's self-devotion, and the mortal cost of that golden robe in which Anastasie was now about to appear. Delphine wept.

'But it will make me ugly,' she thought – and her tears dried at once. 'I will go and nurse my father. I will stay beside his pillow,' she said aloud.

'Ah! now, indeed, thou art all that I would have thee!' cried Eugène.

The lamps of five hundred carriages lighted the approach to the Hôtel de Beauséant, and on either side of the illuminated gateway was a mounted *gendarme*. The great world flocked thither in such crowds, eager to gaze on this great lady at the moment of her downfall, that the ball-rooms on the ground-floor of the Hôtel were filled when Madame de Nucingen and Rastignac entered them. Since the famous occasion when a whole Court rushed to see *la grande Mademoiselle*, after Louis XIV had torn her lover from her arms, no disaster of the heart had excited such intense interest as this of Madame de Beauséant. On this occasion the daughter of the semi-royal house of Burgundy rose superior to her woe, and swayed to her latest moment that world whose homage she had valued only as incense to be offered on the altar of her friend. The loveliest women in Paris adorned the rooms with their dresses and their smiles. The most distinguished men of the Court – ambassadors, ministers, heroes illustrious in a hundred ways, and covered with crosses, medals, and ribbons of all orders – pressed around their hostess. The great world had arrayed itself as if to make a last obeisance to its sovereign. The music of the orchestra floated in tender harmonies along the gilded ceilings of the palace now desolate for its queen. Madame de Beauséant stood within the doorway of the first *salon*, receiving those who called themselves her friends. Dressed in white, without an ornament, and with simply braided hair, she appeared calm, and exhibited neither grief nor pride, nor any pretence of joy. No one saw into her heart. She seemed a marble Niobe. The smiles she gave to her intimate friends had occasional gleams of irony; but to all present she appeared unchanged, and bore herself so truly the same as when happiness shed its halo round her that the most unfeeling person in that crowd admired her, as the Roman youths admired the gladiators who smiled as they died.

'I feared you might not come,' said Madame de Beauséant to Rastignac.

Taking her words for a reproach, he answered with emotion, 'Madame, I have come to be the last to leave you.'

'That is well,' she said, taking his hand. 'You are perhaps the only person present whom I can trust. My friend, when you love, let it be a woman whom you can love forever. Never forsake a woman!'

She took Rastignac's arm, and led him to a sofa in the card-room.

'Go for me,' she said, 'to the Marquis d'Adjuda. Jacques, my footman, will tell you where he is to be found, and will give you a note for him. It asks for my letters. He will give them up to you – I trust he will. If you obtain them, go up to my rooms on your return; they will tell me when you are there.'

She rose and went forward to greet the Duchesse de Langeais, who was entering the *salon*. Rastignac did as he was told. He asked for the Marquis d'Adjuda at the Hôtel Rochefide, where he was to pass the evening, and found him. The Marquis took him to his own house, and gave him a casket, saying, 'They are all there.' He seemed to wish to say more; perhaps to question Eugène about the viscountess, possibly to own himself already in despair about his marriage (as, in fact, he became soon after); but a ray of pride shone in his eyes, and he had the melancholy courage to triumph over his better feelings. 'Tell her nothing about me, my dear Eugène,' he said. He pressed Rastignac's hand with a grasp of affection and regret, and made a sign that he should leave him.

Eugène returned to the Hôtel de Beauséant, and was shown up to his cousin's chamber, which was strewn with preparations for a journey. He sat down near the fire holding the cedar casket, and fell into a state of the deepest melancholy. For him, Madame de Beauséant took on the proportions of a goddess of the *Iliad*.

'Ah! my friend,' she said, coming in and laying her hand upon his shoulder.

He turned and saw her in tears. Her eyes were raised, the hand upon his shoulder trembled, the other was lifted up. Suddenly she took the casket, put it on the fire, and watched it burn.

'They are dancing – they came early – Death may keep me waiting long. Hush, dear friend,' she said, laying her hand upon the lips of Rastignac as he was about to answer. 'To-night I take my leave of Paris and the world. At five o'clock to-morrow morning I go to bury myself in the solitude of Normandy. Since three o'clock to-day I have made my preparations, signed papers, transacted business. I had no one I could send to—' She paused. 'It was certain he would be at—' She stopped again, overcome with emotion. At such times it is pain to speak; certain words it is impossible to utter. 'You see,' she resumed, 'that I counted upon you for this last service. I should like to give you a remembrance – something to make you think of me. I shall often think of you; you have seemed to me kind and noble, fresh and true, in this world where these qualities are rare. See,' she said, casting a glance about the room, 'here is the box in which I have always kept my gloves. Every time that I took them from it – for a ball, an opera – I felt myself beautiful, for I was happy. I never opened it that I did not leave within it some smiling thought. Much of myself is in that box – much of a Madame de Beauséant, who is gone forever. Accept it. I will take care that it is carried to your rooms in the Rue d'Artois. – Madame de Nucingen looks well to-night. Treat her tenderly. If we never meet again, dear friend, be sure that I shall pray for you, who have been very good to me. Let us go down now; I would not have them think that I have wept. I have an eternity before me, where I shall be alone – where no one will ask whether I smile or weep. Let me give a last look round my chamber.'

She stopped, hid her eyes for a moment with her hand, then bathed them with cold water, and took the student's arm. 'Let us go,' she said.

Rastignac had never in his life been so much moved as he now was by the grief thus nobly kept under control. When they reached the ball-rooms, Madame de Beauséant made the circuit of her guests leaning on her cousin's arm – a last and thoughtful act of kindness bestowed by this gracious woman. He soon saw the two sisters, Madame de Restaud and Madame de Nucingen. The former was blazing in diamonds – which no doubt burned her as they blazed, conscious, as she was, that she was wearing them for the last time. Though she bore herself proudly and was exquisitely dressed, she seemed unable to meet the eye of her husband. This sight did not make Rastignac less bitter at heart. If Vautrin had appeared to him in the Italian colonel, he now saw through the glittering diamonds of the two sisters the neglected deathbed of Père Goriot.

His depression was noticed by Madame de Beauséant, who attributed it to another cause, and released his arm.

'Go now,' she said; 'I would not deprive you of a pleasure.'

Eugène was soon claimed by Delphine, charmed with the sensation she had created, and anxious to lay at his feet the homage she was receiving from the great world, in which she now might hope for adoption.

'What do you think of Nasie?' she asked him.

'She has discounted even her father's death,' he answered.

About four in the morning the crowd began to thin, and presently the music ceased. The Duchesse de Langeais and Rastignac at last stood alone in the great ball-room. The viscountess, expecting to find only Rastignac, came in after taking leave of Monsieur de Beauséant, who had gone to bed, saying—

'Indeed you are wrong, my dear, to shut yourself up – at your age! Why not remain among us?'

On seeing the duchess, Madame de Beauséant started and gave a little cry.

'I guess what you are about to do, Clara,' said Madame de

Langeais. 'You are going to leave us, and you will never return. But you shall not go without hearing what I have to say. We must not part misunderstanding each other.'

She took her friend by the arm and led her into a smaller *salon*. There, looking at her with tears in her eyes, she pressed her in her arms and kissed her cheeks.

'We must not part coldly, dear,' she said; 'it would make me too unhappy. You may rely on me as you would upon yourself. You have been noble this evening: I feel that I am not unworthy of you, and I wish to prove it. I have not always treated you as I should have done: forgive me, dear. I take back every word that may have pained you – would that I could unsay them altogether! We are passing through the same sorrow; I know not which of us is the most unhappy. Monsieur de Montriveau was not here to-night: you know what that means. All who saw you at this ball, Clara, will never forget you. For myself – I shall make a last effort: if it fails, I shall go into a convent. And you? Where are you going?'

'To Normandy – to Courcelles: to love, to pray, till it shall please God to take me from the world.' Then, with a break in her voice, Madame de Beauséant called to Eugène, remembering that he was waiting for her in the great *salon*.

He knelt beside her, and took her hand and kissed it.

'Antoinette, adieu,' she said; 'be happy. Monsieur de Rastignac, you are happy – for you are young, and can still have faith. Here, where I renounce the world, I have beside me – as some rare death-beds have had – two hearts that feel for me with sacred and sincere affection.'

Rastignac left the house about five o'clock, having put Madame de Beauséant into her travelling-carriage and received her last farewells mingled with tears. He walked home to the Maison Vauquer in the damp dawn of a cold morning. He was making progress in his education.

'We can't save poor old Goriot,' said Bianchon, when Rastignac entered the room of his sick neighbour.

'Bianchon,' said Rastignac, looking down upon the old man, who lay asleep, 'keep to the humble destiny to which you limit your ambition. For me – I am in hell, and I must stay there. Whatever evil they may tell you of the world, believe it. No Juvenal that ever lived could reveal the infamies concealed under its gold and jewels.'

Later in the day Rastignac was awakened by Bianchon, who being obliged to go out, requested him to take charge of Père Goriot, who had grown much worse during the morning.

'Poor old fellow! He can't live two days – perhaps not more than six hours,' said the medical student; 'though of course we must do all we can for him. We shall have to try certain remedies that cost money. You and I can take care of him – but how are we to pay for the things? I haven't a *sou*, myself. I have turned out his pockets and searched his cupboards – nothing! absolutely zero! I asked him in a lucid moment, and he told me he had not a farthing. How much have you?'

'I have only twenty francs,' said Rastignac; 'but I will go and play them, and win more.'

'Suppose you lose?'

'Then I will ask money from his sons-in-law and his daughters.'

'And suppose they won't give it to you?' said Bianchon. 'However, the important thing now is not to get the money, but to wrap the poor fellow in hot mustard, from his feet up to the middle of his thighs. If he cries out, so much the better: it will show there's a chance for him. You know how to manage it, and Christophe will help you. I will stop at the apothecary's and make myself responsible for the things we may want. What a pity he could not have been taken to the hospital! He would have been much better off there. Come on, and let me give you the directions; and don't leave him till I get back.'

The two young men went into the room where the old man lay. Eugène was shocked by the great change that a few hours had made in the weak, blanched and distorted features.

'Well, Papa!' he said, leaning over the bed.

Père Goriot raised his dim eyes and looked attentively at him, but did not recognize him. The student could not bear the sight, and turned away weeping.

'Bianchon,' he said, ought there not to be curtains to his window?'

'Oh, no; atmospheric conditions can't affect him now. It would be a good sign if he felt either heat or cold. Still, we must keep up a little fire, to heat the mustard and prepare his drinks. I'll send you some fagots, which will do till we can buy wood. Last night and yesterday I burned up yours, and the poor old fellow's bark as well. It was so damp, and the walls were dripping with moisture. I could hardly keep the floor dry. Christophe swept it up, but it is as bad as a stable. I have been burning juniper, the room smelt so infernally.'

'Good God!' said Rastignac. 'Think of his daughters!'

'Now, if he wants anything to drink, give him this,' said the medical student, showing a large white pitcher. 'If he complains of his stomach being hot and hard, call Christophe, and he will help you to give him – you know. If he should get excited and insist on talking, or be a little out of his head, don't check him. It is not a bad symptom. But send Christophe at once to the hospital; and either the surgeon or my comrade and I will come and apply the actual cautery. This morning, while you were asleep, we had a great consultation here, between a pupil of Dr. Gall the phrenologist, the head-surgeon of the Hôtel Dieu, and our own chief from the Cochin Hospital. They thought there were some curious symptoms in the case; and we are going to make notes on its progress, in hopes of throwing light on some important scientific points. One of the doctors thinks that if the pressure of the serum should be more upon one organ than upon any other, we may see some singular developments. So in case he should begin to talk, listen to what he says, and note what kind of ideas his mind runs on – whether memory is all he has left, or whether he still has his reasoning powers; whether he is thinking of material things, or only of feelings; whether he is calculating as to the future, or only reverting to the past. In short, give us an exact report. It is possible that the invasion of the brain may be complete – all over it; in that case, he will die imbecile, as he is at this moment. The course of an illness like this is often very singular. If the rush were here,' continued Bianchon, putting his finger upon the occiput, 'the case might show some very remarkable phenomena. The brain might then recover some of its faculties, and death would be slow in coming. The matter that presses on the brain might then be absorbed through channels which we could only discover in the *post-mortem*. There is an old man now in the Hospital for Incurables, with whom the matter in question is slowly passing away down the spinal column. He suffers horribly – but he lives.'

'Did they enjoy themselves?' said Père Goriot, who now recognized Eugène.

'He thinks of nothing but his daughters,' said Bianchon. 'He said to me over and over again during the night, "they are dancing", "she has got her gown". He called them by their names. He made me cry – the devil take me! – by his piteous way of saying "Delphine! my little Delphine! Nasie!" Upon my word of honour,' said the medical student, 'it was enough to make any fellow shed tears.'

'Delphine?' said the old man. 'Is she there? Did you say so?' And his eyes glanced wildly at the walls and doorway.

'I'll go and tell Sylvie to get the mustard,' said Bianchon. 'It is a good time now.'

XVIII

Rastingnac remained alone with the old man, sitting at the foot of the bed, with his eyes fixed on the aged head now coming with sorrow to the grave.

'Madame de Beauséant has fled,' he said to himself, 'Père Goriot dies: natures that have deep affections cannot abide long in this evil world. How should noble minds live, allied to a society that is mean, petty, and superficial?'

Scenes of that splendid ball rose up in awful contrast to this bed of death. Bianchon reappeared.

'Look here, Eugène!' he said. 'I have just seen our surgeon-in-chief, and I have run back to tell you. If he should recover his reason, if he should talk, wrap him in mustard, from his neck half-way down his loins, and send somebody at once for me.'

'Dear Bianchon!' said Eugène.

'Oh, it's a case of great scientific interest!' exclaimed the medical student, with the fervour of a neophyte.

'Alas!' cried Eugène; 'am I the only one to care for the poor old man out of affection?'

'You would not say that, if you had seen me this morning,' said Bianchon, not offended. 'The other doctors thought of him only as a case; but I thought also of the poor patient, my dear fellow.'

He went away, leaving his friend alone with the old man. Eugène dreaded a crisis, which was not long in coming.

'Ah! is that you, my dear boy?' asked Père Goriot, recognizing Eugène.

'Are you better?' said the student, taking his hand.

'Yes; my head was in a vice – but it is free now. Did you see my daughters? Will they be here soon? They will come as soon as they know that I am ill. I wish my room were clean. There was a young man here last night who burned up all my fuel.'

'I hear Christophe bringing up some wood which that young man has sent you.'

'Good – but who is to pay for the wood? I have no money. I have given it all away – all! I must come on charity. – Was the dress of gold tissue very handsome? – Ah, how I suffer! Thank you, Christophe, my good man. God will reward you; I have nothing now.'

'I will pay you and Sylvie handsomely for all you do,' whispered Eugène to the Savoyard.

'My daughters said they would be here, did they not, Christophe? Go to them again; I will give you a five-franc piece. Tell them that I am not very well; that I should like to see them – to kiss them before I die. But don't alarm them.'

Christophe went off on a sign from Rastignac.

'They will come,' resumed the old man. 'I know them. Dear, kind Delphine – if I die, what sorrow I shall cause her; and Nasie too. I don't want to die. To die, my good Eugène, is – not to see them. There, where I am going, how lonely I shall be! Hell, to a father, is to be without his children. I have served my apprenticeship in it ever since they married. My heaven was in our home – Rue Jussienne. Tell me, if I go to heaven, can I come back in spirit and hover near them? I have heard of such things; are they true? – I see them now, as they were in the Rue Jussienne. "Good morning, Papa," they used to say. I took them on my knee and played with them – a thousand little tricks: they caressed me so prettily. We used to breakfast together, to dine together. Ah, I was a father then! I was happy in my children. They never reasoned then; they knew nothing of the world – they only loved me. Oh, my God! why could I not have kept my little ones? – I suffer – my head! my head! Forgive me, my children, but I am in such pain – no, this must be anguish; for you have hardened me to pain. – If I could but hold them in my arms, I should not suffer so. Are they coming? Will they come? Christophe is so stupid. I ought to have gone myself. – You saw them at the ball. They did not know that I was ill, did they? they would not have danced, poor darlings. Oh! I must not be ill – they need me: their fortunes are in danger. Ah! to what husbands they are bound! Save me! cure me! – Oh, I suffer, suffer! – I must be cured, for they need money, and I know where to make it. I am going to Odessa; I shall make my pastes there. I'm shrewd: I shall make millions. – Oh, I suffer too much! – too much!'

He was silent a few moments, and seemed to be rallying all his strength to bear the pain.

'If they were here I would not complain,' he said. 'Why should I complain if they were here?'

He dozed off lightly. The sleep lasted some time. Christophe returned, and Rastignac, who thought Père Goriot had fallen back into a stupor, let him give an account of his mission.

'Monsieur,' he said, 'first of all, I went to find Madame la comtesse; but I was told I could not speak with her because she was settling some business with her husband. I said that I must see somebody; so Monsieur de Restaud came himself, and he talked just this way. He said: "Well, if Monsieur Goriot is dying, it is the best thing he can do. I want Madame de Restaud to settle some very important business, and she can't go till it is finished." He looked very angry, he did. I was just going away when Madame came through a side door into the antechamber and said to me, "Christophe, tell my father that I am arranging important matters with my husband, and that I cannot leave at present; but as soon as I can I will go to him." As for Madame la baronne, that was another matter. I couldn't see her, and I couldn't get word to her.

Her maid said, "Madame did not get home from a ball till half-past four, and she's asleep. If I wake her she will scold me. I will tell her that her father is worse when she rings her bell. It is always soon enough to tell bad news." I begged her and begged her; but it was no use. Then I asked to see Monsieur de Nucingen, but he was out.'

'So neither of his daughters will come to him!' cried Rastignac. 'I will write to both of them.'

'Neither!' cried the old man, rising in his bed. 'They are busy; they sleep; they will not come. I knew it. We must die, to know what our children are. Friend, never marry; never have children. You give them life – they will give you death. You bring them into the world – they drive you out of it. No! they will not come. I have known it these ten years. I have said it to myself, but I dared not believe it.'

Tears welled up to the red rims of his poor eyes, but they did not fall.

'Ah, if I were rich; if I had kept my fortune; if I had not given them all, all – they would be here, they would lick my cheeks with kisses. I should live in a mansion; I should have a fine chamber, servants, a fire. They would be all in tears, husbands and children. All would be mine. – But now, nothing; I have nothing. Money gives all things, even children. – Oh, my money! where is it? If I had treasures to bequeath, they would nurse me, they would watch me. I should hear them; I should see them. Ah, my son! my only child! I would rather be as I am, forsaken and destitute: if a poor creature is loved, he knows that love is true. – But, no, no! if I were rich I should see them. My God! who knows? They have hearts of stone – both, both! I loved them too well; they gave me no love in return. A father should always be rich; he should curb his children like vicious horses. But I – I was on my knees to them! – Ah, cruel hearts! they fitly crown their conduct to me for ten years past. If you knew the tender care they took of me the first year of their marriage! – oh, I suffer a martyrdom of pain! – I had just given eight hundred thousand francs to each, and neither they nor their husbands could be rude to me. They welcomed me. It was "My good Papa," "My dear Papa." My place was laid at their table; I dined with their husbands; I was treated with respect. Why? Because I had said nothing of my affairs; because a man who gives away a million and a half of francs must have something left to leave: he is a man to be thought of. And so they paid me attentions – but it was for my money. The world is not noble: I saw it all. They took me to the theatre in their carriages; I went if I pleased to their parties. They called themselves my daughters; they acknowledged me to be their father. Ah, I have my sight; I saw through it all – nothing escaped me; it struck home and pierced my heart: I knew that all was a pretence. – But the evil was without remedy. I was less at my ease dining with them than at the table downstairs. I was dull; I could say nothing. These fashionable people whispered to my sons-in-law, "Who is that, Monsieur?" "The papa with the money-bags." "Ah, the devil!" they cried, and looked at me with the respect due to wealth. – My head, my head! I suffer, Eugène! I suffer! It is my death-struggle.'

He paused a moment, and then continued: 'But it is nothing, nothing compared to the first look Anastasie gave me, to make me feel I had said an ignorant thing which mortified her. That look! it bled me from every vein. I was ignorant; yes, but one thing I knew too well – there was no place for me among the living. The next day I went to Delphine to console me; and there I did an awkward thing which made her angry. I went nearly out of my mind; for eight days I was beside myself, not knowing what to do: I was afraid to go and see them, lest they should speak their mind to me. And so it came to pass that I was turned from their doors. – My God! thou who hast known the sufferings and the misery I have endured! who hast counted the stabs that

I have received throughout the years which have changed and whitened and withered me! why dost thou let me suffer so horribly to-day? Have I not expiated the crime of loving them too well? – they have punished it themselves; they have tortured me with hot irons! – Ah, fathers are fools! I loved them so well that I went back like a gambler to his play. My daughters were my vice – my mistresses. They wanted this and that – laces, jewels – their waiting-women told me; and I gave that I might buy a welcome. But all the same they tutored me about my behaviour in their world: they let me see they were ashamed of me.'

His voice sank, then rose again: 'Oh, I suffer! The doctors! where are they? If they would split my head open with an axe, I should suffer less. – Send for them, send for my daughters – Anastasie, Delphine! I must see them! Send the *gendarmes*; use force! Justice is on my side; all is on my side – nature, laws! The nation will perish if fathers are trodden underfoot; society, the world – all rest upon fatherhood: they will crumble to nothing if children do not love their fathers. Oh, to see them! to hear them! no matter what they say to me; their voices would calm me – my Delphine especially. But when they come, tell them not to look at me so coldly. Ah, my friend, my good Eugène! do you know what it is to see the golden glance of love change to leaden grey? Since that day, when their eyes no longer lightened up for me, my life has been an arctic winter; grief has been my portion and I have eaten my fill of it. I have lived only to be insulted and humiliated. Yet I loved them so much that I swallowed the affronts each shameful pleasure cost me. A father hiding himself! waiting in the streets to see his child! – I have given them all my life: they will not give me one hour to-day. I thirst, I burn! they will not come to ease my death – for I am dying; I feel it. Do they know what it is to trample on the corpse of a father? There is a God in heaven; he will avenge us, whether we will or no. – Oh, they will come! Come, my darlings! a kiss, a last kiss! – the viaticum of your father. I go to God, and I will tell him you have been good to me; I will plead for you – for you are innocent; yes, Eugène, they are innocent. The fault was mine. I taught them to tread me underfoot. Divine justice sees the truth and will not condemn them. I abdicated my rights; I neglected my duty; I abased myself in their eyes. The noblest natures would be corrupted by such weakness. I am justly punished: my children were good, and I have spoiled them; on my head be their sins. I alone am guilty; but guilty through love. – Their voices would still my heart. – I hear them: they come! They will come; the law requires them to see their father die – the law is on my side. Write to them that I have millions to bequeath. It is true, upon my honour. I am going to Odessa to make Italian pastes. I know what I am about. It is a great project – millions to make, and no one has yet thought of it. Transportation does not injure pastes as it does wheat and flour. Yes, millions! you may say millions – avarice will bring them. – Well, even so, I shall see them! – I want my daughters; I made them; they are mine!' he cried wildly, rising in his bed, his dishevelled white hair giving to his head a look of unutterable menace.

'Dear Père Goriot, lie down again,' said Eugène. 'As soon as Bianchon comes back I will go myself and fetch them, if they do not come—'

'If they do not come!' sobbed the old man; 'but I shall be dead! dead, in a rush of madness – madness! I feel it coming. At this moment I see my life. I am a dupe. They do not love me – they never loved me. If they have not come, it means that they will not come. The longer they delay, the less they will resolve to give me this last joy. I know them. They have never divined my sorrows, nor my wants, nor my pains: why should they divine my death? They have never even entered into the secret of my tenderness for them. – Yes, I see it all. I have so long plucked out my entrails for their sakes that my sacrifices have ceased to be of value. Had they asked me to tear out my eyes, I should have answered, "Take them!" I have been a fool. They thought all fathers were like me. – But their own children will avenge me. Tell them it is for their interest to come here; tell them to think of their own death-beds. Go, go! tell them to come: not to come is parricide! – they have committed that already; they have given me a death in life. – Call out! call out, as I do, "Here, Nasie! Here, Delphine! Come to your father who has been so good to you, and who is dying!" – Are they coming? No? Am I to die like a dog? – This is my reward – abandoned, forsaken! – They are wicked, they are criminal. I hate them! I curse them! I will rise from my coffin to curse them again! – Friends, am I wrong? They do wrong – Oh, what am I saying? – Is Delphine there? Delphine is good; but Nasie is so unhappy! And their money! – Oh, my God! let me die! I suffer so! My head! my head! Cut it off, but leave me my heart!'

'Christophe! go for Bianchon,' cried Eugène, horror-stricken; 'and bring me a cabriolet. I am going to fetch your daughters, dear Père Goriot. I will bring them to you.'

'Yes, by force, by force! Get the *gendarmes*, the troops,' he cried. 'Tell the Government, the public prosecutor, to send them. I will have them!'

'But you cursed them.'

'Who says I did?' answered the old man with amazement. 'You know I love them: I adore them. I shall recover if I see them. Yes, go for them, my good friend, my dear son. You have been very kind to me. I wish I could thank you; but I have nothing to give except the blessing of a dying man. You love your father and mother – I know you do,' he continued, pressing the student's hand in his failing grasp. 'You feel what it is to die as I am dying – without my children. To be thirsty, and never to drink – that is how I have lived ten years. My sons-in-law have killed my daughters. I lost them when they married. Fathers! petition the

Chambers for a law against marriage. No more marriages! – they take our children from us, and we die desolate. Make a law for the death of fathers! – Oh, this is horrible, horrible! – Vengeance! it is my sons-in-law who keep them away from me! They assassinate me! Death, or my daughters! – Ah, it is finished! I die without them! Fifine! Nasie! Fifine! come!—'

'My good Père Goriot! be calm, be still, don't think.'

'Not to see them! – it is the agony of death.'

'You shall see them.'

'Shall I?' cried the old man, wandering. 'See them? I am to see them, to hear their voices? I shall die happy. – Well, yes, I don't ask to live; I don't wish it; my troubles are too heavy. But, oh, to see them! to touch their pretty dresses! – it isn't much – to smell the fragrance – ah! put my hands upon their hair, will—'

He fell back heavily on his pillow, felled like an ox. His fingers wandered over the coverlet as if searching for his daughters' hair. 'I bless them,' he said, making an effort. 'I bless—'

He sank unconscious. At this moment Bianchon came in.

'I met Christophe,' he said. 'He is bringing you a carriage.' Then he looked at the sick man and lifted his eye-lids. Both saw that the power of sight had gone.

'He won't come out of this; that is, I think not,' said Bianchon. He felt the pulse, and laid his hand upon the old man's heart. 'The machine is still running, more's the pity. He had better die.'

'Yes,' said Rastignac.

'What's the matter with you? You are as pale as death.'

'Bianchon! I have been listening to such cries, such anguish! There is a God. Oh, yes, there is a God! and he has prepared for us a better world, or this earth would be foolishness. If it were not so tragic I could weep; my whole being is wrenched.'

'Dear fellow! – We shall want several things; where can we get the money?'

Rastignac drew out his watch. 'Here, pawn this at once. I can't wait a moment. I hear Christophe. I have not a farthing; and shall have to pay the coachman when I get back.'

XIX

Rastingnac ran downstairs and started for the Rue du Helder to find Madame de Restaud. As he drove through the streets, his imagination, excited by the horrors he had witnessed, increased his indignation. When he reached the antechamber and asked for Madame de Restaud, the servants told him she could see no one.

'But,' he said to the footman, 'I come from her father, who is dying.'

'Monsieur, we have the strictest orders from Monsieur le comte—'

'If Monsieur de Restaud is at home, tell him the condition of his father-in-law, and say that I beg to see him immediately.'

Eugène waited a long time. 'He may be dying at this moment,' he thought.

The footman came back and showed him into the outer *salon*, where Monsieur de Restaud received him standing, without asking him to sit down, and with his back to a fire-place where there was no fire.

'Monsieur le comte,' said Rastignac, 'your father-in-law is dying at this moment in a wretched lodging, without a farthing even to buy fuel. He is about to draw his last breath, and is asking for his daughter.'

'Monsieur,' replied the Comte de Restaud, coldly, 'you are doubtless aware that I have very little affection for Monsieur Goriot. He has compromised himself by unseemly transactions with Madame de Restaud; he is the author of the chief misfortunes of my life; in him I see the enemy of my domestic happiness. I cannot care whether he lives or dies; to me it is perfectly indifferent. Such are my feelings concerning him. The world may blame me – I despise its opinion; I have matters of far more importance to think of than the opinion of fools or third parties. As for Madame de Restaud, she is in no condition to leave her own house; nor do I wish her to leave it. You may tell her father that as soon as she has fulfilled the duty she owes to me and to my child, she may go to him. If she loves her father, she can be free to go in a few moments.'

'Monsieur le comte, it is not for me to pass judgement on your conduct; you have the right to deal with your wife as you think best: but I am sure that I can rely upon your word. Will you promise to tell her that her father cannot live another day, and that he has already cursed her because she has not come to him?'

'Tell her yourself,' said Monsieur de Restaud, struck by the tone of indignation with which Rastignac uttered these words.

Eugène followed the count into the inner room where Madame de Restaud usually sat. They found her bathed in tears, lying back in her chair like a woman who longed to die. Eugène pitied her. Before noticing him, she turned a timid look upon her husband – a look which showed how completely she was prostrated, mentally and physically, by the power he now wielded over her. The count made a sign with his head, which she took as a permission to speak.

'Monsieur, I have heard all,' she said. 'Tell my father that if he knew my situation he would forgive me. I did not expect this additional misery: it is more than I have strength to bear. But I will resist to the last,' she continued, turning to her husband: 'I am a mother. Tell my father I am not to blame, in spite of appearances,' she added, with an accent of despair.

Rastignac bowed to husband and wife. He could guess through what a trial the woman was passing, and he went away silenced. From Monsieur de Restaud's tone, he saw that remonstrances were useless; and he judged that Anastasie herself would not dare to make them.

He hastened to Madame de Nucingen.

'I am quite unwell, my poor friend,' she said, as he entered. 'I took cold coming away from the ball, and I am afraid it may settle on my lungs. I am expecting the doctor—'

'If death were on your lips,' said Eugène, interrupting her, 'you should drag yourself to your father's bedside. He is dying – and he calls for you. If you heard but the least of his cries, you would not fancy yourself ill.'

'Eugène, perhaps my father is not as ill as you think. But I should be in despair if you thought me to blame. I will try to please you. He, I know, would be filled with grief if my illness were made serious by the imprudence of going out to-day. But I will go, after I have seen the doctor. – Ah! what have you done with your watch?' she cried, observing that he did not wear the chain.

Eugène hesitated.

'Eugène! Eugène! if you have sold it, or lost it – oh! it would be very—'

Rastignac leaned over her and said, in a low voice, 'Do you wish me to tell you? Well, know it, then! Your father has not money to buy the winding-sheet in which they will wrap him this evening. Your watch is in pawn: I had nothing else.'

Delphine sprang up and ran to her writing-table, from which she took her purse and gave it to Rastignac. She rang her bell and cried, 'I am coming, I am coming, Eugène! Let me get dressed. Oh, I should be a monster not to go! Go back; I will be there before you. Thérèse,' she said, turning to her waiting-maid, 'ask Monsieur de Nucingen to come up at once and speak to me.'

Eugène, glad to comfort the dying man with the news that one of his daughters was coming, reached the Rue Neuve Sainte-Geneviève almost in good spirits.

When he paid his coachman, he discovered that the purse of this wealthy, elegant and envied woman contained sixty-six francs! Père Goriot, supported by Bianchon, was being operated upon by the hospital surgeon, under the superintendence of the chief physician. They were applying the actual cautery – a last resource of science, but in this case wholly ineffectual.

'Can you feel it?' asked the physician.

Père Goriot, seeing the student enter the room, cried out, 'Are they coming?'

'He may pull through,' said the surgeon. 'He can speak.'

'Yes,' replied Eugène; 'Delphine is on her way.'

'It won't do,' said Bianchon; 'he is only talking of his daughters. He cries after them as a man impaled cries, they say, for water.'

'We may as well give it up,' said the physician to the surgeon. 'There is nothing more to be done; we cannot save him.'

Bianchon and the surgeon replaced the dying man upon his wretched bed.

'You had better change the linen,' said the physician. 'There is no hope; but something is always due to human nature. I will come back, Bianchon,' he said to his pupil. 'If he seems to suffer, put laudanum on the diaphragm.'

The surgeon and physician went away.

'Come, Eugène, courage, my lad!' said Bianchon when they were left alone. 'We must put on a clean shirt, and change the bed. Go down and ask Sylvie to bring up some sheets and stop and help us.'

Eugène went down and found Madame Vauquer helping Sylvie to set the dinner-table. At his first words the widow came up to him with the sour civility of a shopkeeper doubtful about the payment, yet unwilling to lose a customer.

'My dear Monsieur Eugène,' she said, 'you know as well as I do that Père Goriot has not a *sou*. To furnish sheets to a man just giving up the ghost is throwing them away – one of them at least must be sacrificed for the winding-sheet. Besides this, you owe me one hundred and forty-four francs; add forty francs for the sheets and some other little things, including the candles – which Sylvie will give you – and it mounts up to not less than two hundred francs; a sum which a poor widow like me cannot afford to lose. Come! do me justice, Monsieur Eugène. I have lost enough the last few days since ill-luck got hold of me. I would have given five *louis* if the old man had gone away when he gave notice. My lodgers don't like this sort of thing. It would not take much to make me even now send him off to the hospital. Put yourself in my place. My establishment is the chief thing to me, of course. It is my support, my all.'

Eugène ran up swiftly to Père Goriot's chamber.

'The money for the watch, Bianchon, where is it?'

'On the table. You will find three hundred and sixty-odd francs left. I have paid all we owe. The pawn ticket is under the money.'

'Here Madame,' said Rastignac, rushing headlong down the staircase, 'let us settle our accounts. Monsieur Goriot will not long be with you, and I—'

'Yes, he will go out feet foremost, poor old man,' she said, counting up her two hundred francs with an air of complacent melancholy.

'Let us make an end of this,' cried Rastignac.

'Sylvie, give out the sheets, and go and help the gentlemen upstairs. You will not forget Sylvie,' whispered Madame Vauquer to Eugène. 'She has sat up two nights, you know.'

As soon as Eugène's back was turned, the old woman ran after her cook. 'Take the sheets that have been turned, Sylvie – No. 7. Good enough for a corpse,' she whispered.

Eugène being already halfway up the stairs did not hear his landlady's words.

'Now, then,' said Bianchon, 'we will change his shirt. Hold him up.'

Eugène went to the head of the bed and supported Père Goriot, while Bianchon drew off his shirt. The old man made a gesture as if to grasp something on his breast, uttering plaintive inarticulate cries, like an animal in pain.

'Oh! oh!' said Bianchon, 'he wants a little hair-chain and locket which we took off when we applied the fire. Poor old man! Put it around his neck again; it is on the chimney-piece.'

Eugène took up the little chain, made of a tress of chestnut hair, which was doubtless Madame Goriot's. Attached to it was a locket, with the names 'Anastasie' on one side and 'Delphine' on the other; fit emblem of his constant heart, it lay upon that heart continually. The curls in the locket were so fine that they must have been cut off when the little girls were infants. As Eugène replaced the trinket on his breast the old man gave a long-drawn sigh of relief, heart-breaking to hear. It was well-nigh the final echo of his living emotions, as they drew in to the unknown centre from which spring and to which return our human sympathies. His face, much distorted, wore an unnatural expression of joy. The two young men, deeply moved by this sudden explosion of a feeling which had outlived the power of thought, let fall hot tears, which touched the face of the dying man. He uttered a piercing cry of pleasure.

'Nasie! Fifine!' he exclaimed.

'He is still living,' said Bianchon.

'What's the use of that?' said Sylvie.

'To suffer,' replied Rastignac.

Making Eugène a sign to do as he did, Bianchon knelt down beside the bed to pass his arms beneath the sick man's knees, while Rastignac on the other side did the same, supporting the shoulders. Sylvie stood by to draw the sheet as the weight was raised, and slip through one of those she had brought up with her. Misled no doubt by the tears that he had felt upon his face, Père Goriot used his last strength to stretch out his hands on either side of the bed and grasped the hair of the two students, muttering feebly, 'Ah, my angels!' – two words sighed forth by the spirit as it took its flight.

'Poor, dear man!' said Sylvie, much affected by this exclamation – the utterance of the ever-dominant passion drawn forth by an involuntary deception. The last conscious sigh of the unhappy father was a sigh of joy. It expressed his whole life – delusion; deluded even in death! They laid him gently back upon the wretched pallet, and from that moment his face showed only fluctuations between life and death – the movements of the machinery no longer guided by the brain, in which alone resides the consciousness of human joy and misery.

'He will lie as he is for some hours, and die so quietly that no one will perceive when the end comes. There will be no rattle in his throat. His brain has ceased to act,' said Bianchon.

At this moment they heard the rapid footsteps of a young woman.

'It is Delphine,' said Rastignac; 'she comes too late.'

It was not Delphine, but Thérèse, her waiting-woman.

'Monsieur Eugène,' she said, 'there has been an angry scene between Monsieur and Madame, about some money Madame asked for, for her father. She fainted away; the doctor came and bled her. She kept saying, "Papa is dying, I must go to him!" Her cries were enough to break one's heart.'

'That will do, Thérèse. Her coming would be superfluous now. Monsieur Goriot has lost consciousness.'

'Poor, dear Monsieur! is he so bad as that?' said Thérèse.

'You don't want me any more; I must go and see after my dinner. It is half-past five now,' said Sylvie, who as she went downstairs nearly fell over Madame de Restaud.

The countess glided into the death-chamber like an apparition. She gazed at the bed by the light of the one poor candle, and shed tears as she looked down upon the face of her dying father, where the last flickerings of life still quivered. Bianchon left the room, out of respect for her feelings.

'I could not escape soon enough,' she said to Rastignac.

The student sadly shook his head to imply that this was time. Madame de Restaud took her father's hand and kissed it.

'Forgive me, oh, my Father!' she exclaimed. 'You used to say that my voice would call you from the tomb. Come back to life one moment to bless your repentant daughter! Oh, hear me! – This is dreadful! Your blessing is the only one I can hope for here below. All hate me; you alone in this wide world can love me. My children will abhor me. Oh, take me with you! I will love you; I will wait upon you – He does not hear me. I am mad—'

She fell upon her knees, gazing at the wreck before her.

'My cup of misery is full,' she cried, looking up at Eugène. 'Monsieur de Trailles has gone, leaving enormous debts behind him – and I now know that he deceived me all along. My husband can never forgive me; I have made over to him the disposal of my fortune; my children are destitute. Alas! for what, for whom, have I betrayed the only faithful heart that loved me? I did not understand him; I cast him off; I did so many cruel things to him – Oh, wicked woman that I am!'

'He knew it,' said Rastignac.

At that moment Père Goriot opened his eyes; but the movement was only convulsive and involuntary. The gesture by which his daughter showed her hope of recognition was not less terrible to witness than his dull, dying eyes.

'Can he not hear me?' she cried. 'Ah, no!' she added after a pause, sitting down beside the bed.

As she expressed the wish to watch him, Eugène went downstairs to take some food. The guests were all assembled in the *salon*.

'Well,' said the painter, 'so we are to have a little *death-orama* upstairs?'

'Charles,' said Eugène, 'choose some less melancholy subject to joke upon.'

'Dear me! is it forbidden to laugh under this roof? What does it matter? Bianchon says the old fellow has lost his senses.'

'If that is so,' said the employee, 'he will die as he lived.'

'My father is dead!' shrieked Madame de Restaud.

Rastignac and Bianchon ran upstairs, where they found her fainting on the floor. After bringing her back to consciousness, Eugène took her down to the hackney coach in which she had come, and consigned her to Thérèse, with orders to take her to Madame de Nucingen.

'Yes, he is quite dead,' said Bianchon, coming down again.

'Come, gentlemen, sit down to table,' said Madame Vauquer. 'The soup is getting cold.'

The two students took their places by each other.

'What is to be done next?' said Eugène to Bianchon.

'I have closed his eyes, and composed him properly. When the doctor from the Mayor's office has certified to the death, which we will report at once, he will be sewn up in a sheet and buried. Where do you mean to put him?'

'He will never sniff his bread any more, like this,' said one of the guests, mimicking the trick of the poor old man.

'The devil! gentlemen,' cried the tutor, 'do leave Père Goriot alone. We don't want any more of him. You have served him up with every kind of sauce for the last hour. One of the privileges of this good city of Paris is that you can come into the world, live in it and go out of it, and nobody will pay any attention to you. Avail yourselves of the advantages of civilization. According to statistics, sixty persons have died in Paris this very day. Are we called upon to weep over Parisian hecatombs? If Père Goriot is dead, so much the better for him. If you were all so fond of him, you can go and keep watch beside him; but leave the rest of us to eat our dinners in peace.'

'Oh, yes,' said the widow. 'It is much better for him that he is dead. It seems the poor man has had plenty of troubles all his life long.'

This was the only funeral oration pronounced over a being who in the eyes of Rastignac was the incarnation of Fatherhood.

The fifteen guests began to talk about other things. When Eugène and Bianchon had finished eating, the clatter of knives and forks, the laughter, the jests, the various expressions on the callous, greedy faces round the table struck them with horror. They went in search of a priest to watch and pray during the night beside the dead. It was necessary to calculate the last duties they could render to their poor old friend by the slender sum they had to spend. About nine o'clock in the evening the body was placed on a bier between two tallow candles, in the centre of the wretched chamber; and a priest came to watch beside it. Before going to bed, Rastignac, who had obtained information from the ecclesiastic as to burial fees and the cost of funeral rites, wrote to the Baron de Nucingen and the Comte de Restaud, asking them to send their men of business with orders to provide for a suitable interment. He sent Christophe with these notes, and then went to his own bed and slept, worn out with fatigue.

The next morning Bianchon and Rastignac were forced to go themselves and declare the death, which was certified to officially by midday. Two hours passed; neither of the sons-in-law sent money, nor did any one appear who was authorized to act in their names. Rastignac had already been obliged to pay the priest, and Sylvie having demanded ten francs for sewing the corpse in its winding-sheet, Rastignac and Bianchon came to the conclusion that as the relatives would do nothing, they had barely enough money to provide the cheapest funeral. The medical student undertook to place the body himself in a pauper's coffin, which he sent from the hospital, where he could buy it for less cost than elsewhere.

'Play a trick upon those people – they deserve it,' he said to Rastignac. 'Buy a grave for five years in Père-La-Chaise, and order a third-class funeral service at the Church, and from the Pompes-Funèbres, and send the bills to the family. If the sons-in-law and the daughters don't choose to pay it, we will have engraved upon his tombstone, "Here lies Monsieur Goriot, father of the Comtesse de Restaud and the Baronne de Nucingen. Buried at the expense of two students."'

Eugène did not take his friend's advice until he had been, but in vain, to Monsieur and Madame de Nucingen's house and to Monsieur and Madame de Restaud's. He could not gain admittance. Both porters had strict orders.

'Monsieur and Madame,' they said, 'receive no one: they are in deep affliction, owing to the death of their father.'

Eugène had had enough experience of Parisian life to know that it was useless to persist further. He was greatly wounded when he found that he could not see Delphine. 'Sell a necklace,' he wrote in the porter's lodge, 'that your father may be decently consigned to his last resting-place.'

He sealed the note, and begged the porter to give it to Thérèse for her mistress; but the man gave it to the Baron de Nucingen, who put it in the fire.

Having made all his arrangements, Eugène came back a little after three o'clock to the Maison Vauquer, and could not help shedding tears when he saw the bier at the iron gate, scantily covered with black cloth and placed upon two chairs in the lonely street. An old holy-water sprinkler, which no hand had yet touched, lay beside it in a plated copper vessel full of holy water. The gateway was not even hung with black. It was a pauper funeral – no pomp, no attendants, no friends, no relatives. Bianchon, whose duties kept him at the Hospital, had left a note for Rastignac to let him know what arrangements he had made for the Church services. He told him that a Mass could not be had for the sum they were able to pay; that they must put up with a less costly service at vespers; and that he had sent Christophe to notify the Pompes-Funèbres.

As Rastignac finished reading Bianchon's scrawl, he saw in Madame Vauquer's hands the gold locket which had lain upon the old man's heart.

'How dared you take that?' he said to her.

'Bless me!' cried Sylvie, 'did you mean to bury him with that? Why, it's gold.'

'Yes,' answered Eugène indignantly. 'Let him at least take with him to the grave the only thing that represents his daughters.'

When the hearse came, Eugène ordered the coffin to be taken back into the house, where he unscrewed the nails, and reverently placed upon the old man's heart that relic of the days when Delphine and Anastasie had been young and pure, and 'did not reason', as he had said in his dying moments.

Rastignac and Christophe and two of the undertaker's men were all who accompanied the hearse which carried the poor man to the nearest church, Saint-Étienne du Mont, not far from the Rue Neuve Sainte-Geneviève. There the corpse was placed in a little chapel, low and dark, round which the student looked in vain for the daughters of Père Goriot or their husbands. He was alone with Christophe, who thought himself under an obligation to pay the last duties to a man who had been the means of procuring for him many large *pour-boires*. While waiting for the two officiating priests, the choir-boy and the beadle, Rastignac pressed Christophe's hand, but could not speak.

'Yes, Monsieur Eugène,' said Christophe, 'he was a good and honest man; he never said an angry word; he never tried to injure anyone; he never did an unkind thing.'

The two priests, the acolyte and the beadle came and gave all that could be had for seventy francs in an epoch when religion is too poor to pray for nothing. The clergy sang a psalm, the *Libera* and the *De profundis*. The service lasted twenty minutes. There was only one mourning-coach, intended for the priest and the choir-boy; but they allowed Rastignac and Christophe to go with them.

'As there is no procession,' said the priest, 'we can go fast, so as not to be late. It is half-past five now.'

However, just as the coffin was replaced in the hearse two carriages with armorial bearings, but empty (those of the Comte de Restaud and the Baron de Nucingen), made their appearance and followed the funeral to Père-La-Chaise. At six o'clock the body of Père Goriot was lowered into its grave, round which stood the footmen of his daughters, who disappeared with the clergy as soon as a short prayer – all that could be given for the students' money – was over. When the two grave-diggers had thrown a few shovelful of earth upon the coffin they came out of the grave, and turning to Rastignac asked him for their drink-money. Eugène felt in his pockets, but nothing was there. He had to borrow a franc from Christophe. This circumstance, trivial in itself, produced in his mind a horrible depression. Day was departing; a damp mist irritated his nerves. He looked down into the grave and buried there the last tear of his young manhood – a last tear springing from the sacred emotions of a pure heart, which from the earth on which it fell exhaled to heaven. He folded his arms and stood gazing upward at the clouds. Seeing him thus, Christophe went away.

Left alone, Rastignac walked a few steps until he reached the highest part of the cemetery, and saw Paris as it lies along the winding shores of the Seine.

Lights were beginning to glitter in the gathering darkness. His eyes turned eagerly to the space between the column of the Place Vendôme and the dome of the Invalides. There lived that world of fashion which it had been his dream to enter. He gave the humming hive a look that seemed to suck it of its honey, and then he cried aloud, 'War! war between us, henceforth!'

And as a first act of hostility to Society, Rastignac went to dine with Madame de Nucingen.